Praise for Lois Richer and her novels

"Lois Richer's *His Answered Prayer* is another winner and will please readers who love traditional story lines with new twists and terrific characters."
—*RT Book Reviews*

"*Mother's Day Miracle* by Lois Richer is quite possibly her finest book!"
—*RT Book Reviews*

"Small town flavor and three meddling grannies add spice to the fun in this heartwarming love story."
—*RT Book Reviews* on *Faithfully Yours*

"Lois Richer's sensitive *Healing Tides* is a wonderful story."
—*RT Book Reviews*

LOIS RICHER
This Child of Mine

&

His Answered Prayer

Love Inspired

Recycling programs for this product may not exist in your area.

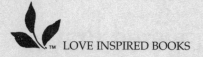 LOVE INSPIRED BOOKS

ISBN-13: 978-0-373-65145-0

THIS CHILD OF MINE AND HIS ANSWERED PRAYER

THIS CHILD OF MINE
Copyright © 1999 by Lois M. Richer

HIS ANSWERED PRAYER
Copyright © 2000 by Lois M. Richer

www.LoveInspiredBooks.com

Printed in U.S.A.

CONTENTS

Books by Lois Richer

Love Inspired

Love Inspired Suspense

LOIS RICHER

likes variety. From her time in human resources management to entrepreneurship, life has held plenty of surprises. She says, "Having given up on fairy tales, I was happily involved in building a restaurant when a handsome prince walked into my life and upset all my career plans with a wedding ring. Motherhood quickly followed. I guess the seeds of my storytelling took root because of two small boys who kept demanding, 'Then what, Mom?'" The miracle of God's love for His children, the blessing of true love, the joy of sharing Him with others—that is a story that can be told a thousand ways and yet still be brand-new. Lois Richer intends to go right on telling it.

THIS CHILD OF MINE

I am with you and will watch over you wherever
you go, and I will bring you back to this land.
I will not leave you until I have done
what I have promised you.
—*Genesis* 28:15

To Darcy,
who constantly teaches me about
tenacity and following my own path.

Chapter One

Darcy Simms stared in disbelief at the pink slip attached to her meager paycheck.

Laid off! How could she be laid off? She needed that job and the money it provided if she was going to survive. Where was the justice in laying her off now, of all times? How would she manage?

Darcy ignored the sound of the ringing telephone reverberating down the hall of the old, rundown apartment building. The thing was always ringing. But the calls were never for her. How could they be? She'd made very sure that her new life didn't involve anyone from her past, and her friends at work didn't know where or how she lived. They thought she was just like them— young and carefree.

What a joke!

The sudden pounding on her door sent her heart shifting into overdrive. That awful man down the hall had been watching her coming and going for the past week. His beady little eyes took in everything about her. She wondered if he was even now outside her door, waiting. Her gaze flew to the dead-bolt locks, to be sure they were fastened securely, even though she knew one good kick would easily splinter the tired old wood.

"Yes?" She called out finally when the banging resumed. She glanced just once toward the curtained bedroom. "What is it?"

"Darcy Simms?" The voice was low and hesitant, as if the owner weren't sure he had the right place.

"Y-yes." Darcy stood behind the door, waiting. Why would a man be outside her door? "What do you want?"

"I have something for you, Miss Simms. Would you please open the door?" The voice was firmer now, determined. The only good thing was that he didn't sound like her neighbor.

"Who are you? What do you want?" When there was no immediate answer, she panicked and backed away. "Go away or I'll call the police!" He couldn't know that she didn't have a telephone, could he?

"My name is Luke Lassiter, Miss Simms. Please. Just hear me out. I'm from Colorado. You might say your parents sent me."

"Then you're just a bit late." She laughed harshly. "And so are they. About five years too late, I'd say. Now go away."

"I can't. I promised that I'd do this and I intend to keep my word. I'll wait out here if you insist, but I *am* going to speak to you."

He waited a long time. As hard as she listened, Darcy could hear no impatient shuffling beyond the door. There was no sound of footsteps moving down the hall. It seemed that Mr. Luke Lassiter would not give up easily on this mission of his.

If that's who he really was. Images of yesterday's bloody fistfight in the corridor flew through her mind and Darcy cast another protective glance at the bedroom. But since everything was quiet for now, she decided to risk speaking to this man. Whomever he was.

"I'm going to undo the door just enough to talk to you—but the chain stays on."

"In this neighborhood, I don't blame you." The reply was agreeable. There was silence then and Darcy undid the top and bottom bolts loudly and noisily, pausing a moment before she finally opened the door.

Darcy peered through the crack in the door. Luke Lassiter was tall and lean and weathered looking. Dressed from head to foot in clean but worn denim, he wore a thick sheepskin-lined jacket to keep out the brisk November chill. Darcy doubted that the black Stetson on his head did much to keep his ears warm.

"Hello, ma'am," he drawled, tipping his hat. "I'm Luke Lassiter. I live just outside of Raven's Rest. I've been asked to give you this." He pulled a plain white envelope out of his pocket and handed it through the crack in the door. "It's from Reverend Anderson. He's the pastor out our way these days."

Something glowed out of his dark brown eyes. What was it? Pity? Darcy immediately tore her gaze away from his and slit the letter open.

"I can't imagine what your Reverend Anderson would have to—oh, no!" Darcy stared in horror at the words scrawled across the page in big black letters.

I regret to inform you that your parents, Martha and Lester Simms, were killed six weeks ago in a terrible car accident. We have spent some time searching for you in the hope that you might return home as your parents last requested. I trust this will be possible for you and urge you to have every confidence in my friend Luke Lassiter, who will be happy to accompany you on your return journey.

Yours,
Reverend David Anderson

Never—not once in the past five years since she'd shaken the dust of her hometown off her feet—had Darcy even considered not seeing her parents again. She'd wished a lot of things on those stern, unforgiving people. But not this. Never this!

"Would you please let me in now?" Darcy barely heard Luke's low-voiced request, and automatically moved to unsnap the chains that would allow him entry to her home. "Are you all right? Can I get you anything?" His voice slid over her like a warm, soothing blanket, numbing the pain that threatened to spill out and destroy her thin veneer of calm.

"No." She sank onto the ratty old sofa that sat on one leg and three coffee cans, and stared at the paper. "No, nothing. Thanks."

"I'm sorry that it took us so long to find you, Miss Simms." The tall cowboy folded himself until he was hunkered beside her. "There was no forwarding address, you see. Not much to go on."

"That was the point," she murmured dazedly, wondering now why it had mattered so much that she hide away in New York.

"I had no idea you were this far away until a friend of mine got a tip from the IRS about your tax records. I followed you home from the factory." He smiled grimly at her start of fear and surprise. "Well, we had to find you somehow." His smile was sympathetic. "There's the ranch and everything."

"Yeah, the ranch." She grimaced at the very thought of it. "Thank you for coming all this way and telling me, Mr. Lassiter. I appreciate the time and effort. But there's nothing for me in Raven's Rest anymore. And I have no intention of going back."

She fluttered the papers attached to Reverend Anderson's letter. "According to this they've been gone some time. I'm sure there's already been a funeral and my parents are buried in the local cemetery. There's nothing left for me to do."

"Not even to mourn?" His voice accused her of something, and Darcy couldn't help but let her hackles rise at the old pattern from the past repeating itself. *Ungrateful daughter.*

"I did mourn, Mr. Lassiter. Five years ago, when I left good old Raven's Rest and its narrow-minded citizens. On that day I vowed I'd never return. I see no reason to go back and dig up the past. I have to move on."

"What about the ranch?"

"What about it? It's not my home. It never was. It was merely a place I stayed until I could get away." She stood and marched over to the sink, intent on drying the three plastic dishes she'd used for supper, if only to get away from the knowing look in Mr. Lassiter's piercing dark eyes.

"So what's stopping you from coming back—just one

last time? To hear the will and dispose of what's left."
She figured that he'd noticed the jerk of her shoulders
at the word "will" and pressed on that one weak spot.
"It's their final word on the only earthly goods they had
to leave you, Darcy. It's your heritage—"

"Mommy, mommy!"

Darcy whirled, eyes wide with surprise as four-and-a-
half-year-old Jamie raced across the room and grabbed
her around the knees.

"I had a bad dream," he cried, staring at Luke Lassiter
with that immediate intensity that all children possess.
"There was a bad man." His eyes were huge pools of
violet as he stared at their guest.

"Hi, little guy," Luke said, bending down slightly
to meet the boy's gaze. "I'm not a bad man. I'm one
of the good guys. Come to take you and your mommy
for a ride to a ranch that's far, far away. Would you like
that?"

To Darcy's surprise, her shy, introverted son left her
embrace to walk over and stand in front of their guest.

"Yes, I would," he said clearly, arms folded across
his chest. "Are there horses?"

"A ranch always has horses." Luke watched as the
little boy stared wide-eyed at his scuffed cowboy boots.
"Maybe I could even take you for a ride. If it's okay with
your mom." He twisted his head to study her. "Is it okay,
Mom?"

"I don't know. I'll have to see." She gave him her most
furious look, hoping he understood how difficult he was
making it for her. "You have no right," she whispered
angrily as Jamie moved away.

"*He* does," Luke asserted gravely. "He has a right to see the heritage that you're so intent on giving up."

"I'm not giving it up. It was never mine." She let the bitter smile curve her lips. "Perhaps you didn't get the whole picture, Mr. Lassiter. My parents didn't know what to do with me. I wasn't exactly what they expected."

"How do you know that?" He sank down into the rickety armchair with an ease that Darcy envied.

"Believe me, I learned early on that a scruffy tomboy was the last thing Martha and Lester expected. They should have gotten a boy, or at least a dainty, little girl who would have accepted all their rules and settled down with a nice local boy."

"And that wasn't you?" He looked genuinely interested, Darcy decided. That in itself was unusual. Her life was something less than interesting.

"Hardly." She grimaced. "I'm five feet nine inches, Mr. Lassiter, and no one has ever called me dainty. Besides, I never could learn to sit still for hours on end while some man stood in the pulpit, berating people for being human."

"Are you sure that's what he was doing?"

Darcy stared at him. "Maybe you had to be there." She shrugged. "It was doom and gloom. All the time. Feel guilty, you sinner. Ask forgiveness. Repent. Evil, wrong, no good. That's all I ever heard."

"Sounds pretty bad," Luke Lassiter agreed, smiling. "Can't say it's my idea of a good service either."

Darcy stared. "You think it's funny? Believe me, there was no joy there."

"No, I don't imagine there was," he murmured gently.

"But then a lot of people feel that way about God. They haven't found the real meaning of love, I guess."

"And what, pray tell, is the *real* meaning of love?"

"I don't think it's something you can explain. It's something you have to feel as it heals you."

"Love doesn't heal. It just hurts people, makes them obligated to someone else when they should be free to live their own lives." Darcy couldn't disguise the acid edge to her voice.

"Yeah, sometimes love hurts. Nobody said life was without pain. But it can also heal and renew and rejuvenate. Love isn't ever wasted."

The very idea was a whole new concept in Darcy's young life, especially since she'd wasted twenty-three long years loving people who couldn't possibly love her back.

"Can you be ready to leave tomorrow morning? I don't like to be away too long," he asked, interrupting her thoughts.

"From the farm?" Darcy remembered well that a rancher's dedication to his cattle was par for the course in Raven's Rest. Sometimes, she remembered bitterly, it even exceeded a father's duty to his own family.

"Well, there's that." Luke grinned at Jamie as he piled up blocks on the floor and then swatted them down. "But actually, I was thinking of my Aunt Clarice. She's all alone and I worry about her."

"Clarice?" Darcy frowned. "I don't remember any Clarice at Raven's Rest."

"Ah, but you've been gone five years, haven't you," he reminded her with a smile. "Things change. Even at Raven's Rest."

"Nothing about that one-horse, narrow-minded, little town could change enough to make me want to live there again." Darcy laughed angrily. "I'm sorry, Mr. Lassiter, but I have no intention of going back."

"Why?" He glanced around the room, assessing its ugliness. His inquisitive eyes fell on the pink slip she'd laid on the table before answering the door. "There's nothing here holding you back, is there?" His gaze was steady, daring her to deny what he'd already surmised.

"Don't worry, I'll get another job," she told him defiantly. "I've managed this long."

"But there's no need. Why not take a break? Just for a while. You could relax on the ranch until the will has been sorted out. New York's not going anywhere."

His tone was smooth and cajoling and Darcy ached to give in. She was tired, desperately tired of just barely managing. It would be nice to release that tight control over things, even if only for a little while. Nice not to have to be on guard every moment of the day. She glanced at her son and smiled, thinking of the freedom of running in a yard of grass instead of the asphalt playground he was confined to at the day care.

And then the memories resurfaced from a time she'd tried so hard to forget. In five years that awful feeling of loss hadn't lessened one whit. "I can't," she muttered finally. "I just can't."

"Sure you can." He was so sure of himself, his eyes calm but serious. "You just take it one day at a time and trust that somehow God will work it all out."

"Like He's done so far, you mean?" Her eyes mocked the ugliness of the dingy room and its threadbare furnishings. "You'll understand if I find that a little difficult to do."

Luke Lassiter covered her hand with his. "I didn't say it would be easy." He smiled. "I just said you could do it."

Darcy didn't understand any of this. She didn't want to. What good would be served by rehashing the agony of the past?

She glared at him, gathering Jamie in her arms. "Why are you so interested? I don't mean anything to you."

"Of course you do. You're the daughter of some friends of mine and you're alone. Right now I think you could use a break." A funny look drifted across Mr. Lassiter's eyes as Jamie leaned his head against her legs and yawned noisily.

"I think Jamie needs some special time with his mom and maybe a place where he can run and yell to his heart's content. Raven's Rest certainly has enough room."

He hadn't said a word about the pathetic little apartment or the perpetual odor of boiled cabbage that seemed to hang in the air, but Darcy knew Luke Lassiter hadn't missed a single detail of the ugliness of her life.

"I have to put him back to bed." She said the words softly, as Jamie's eyes began to close. "Have a seat if you want." She padded across the floor and slipped behind the curtain to lay Jamie in the cot next to hers. He smiled in his sleep, shifting a little under the coarse woolen blanket.

"At least I did one thing right," she muttered to herself as tears of tiredness welled in her eyes.

"He's a wonderful little boy." The voice came from

behind her left shoulder. "They look so innocent when they're sleeping, don't they?"

"Do you have children?" she asked, frowning.

"I did." The words were so soft that she barely caught them. The look on his face spoke of immense sadness, and Darcy couldn't deal with that. Not now.

"You didn't have to follow me in here," she whispered. "I'm not going anywhere. Not tonight at least." Urging him out of the room, she pulled the curtain into place. "And I don't think I'll be going anywhere tomorrow. Raven's Rest just isn't the place for me anymore."

"It doesn't have to be permanent. It's just while the will is settled and the estate disposed of. People will understand why you're there and that you need some time and space." His voice dropped. "Can't you do even that for your parents?"

"Why should I?" Darcy glared at him bitterly. "What difference could it possibly make now?"

Luke Lassiter's face was all shadows and inscrutability. But she could see the understanding in his eyes as he met her glance squarely. "Why not? What would it hurt you? They're dead now, Darcy. Your parents are gone. They can't hurt you anymore."

"They don't have to. They did a pretty good job while they were alive."

"But they're dead now."

The starkness of those words drilled a hole straight through to her heart. She'd wanted to come back to her hometown triumphant, successful. She'd wanted to show her parents that she had survived—prospered even—without them. And now, suddenly, everything she'd done, striven for for so long, was futile. She was never going to hear the words she'd waited for. What did it matter whether she kept her pride and stayed holed up in this dump or relaxed on the old homestead for a few days. No one could force her to do anything anymore. She'd left all that behind five years ago.

"Come back, Darcy. Rest for a while. Stay with Aunt Clarice and me. Let her coddle you and that little boy for a bit. Get a new start, a new perspective on things. I guarantee you won't be sorry."

His eyes held hers steadily as his voice cajoled her. His hand on her arm added strength to his words, and all at once Darcy knew she had to give in. To just let go and forget about pretending to be strong. It would be so wonderful to lean on someone else. Maybe she really was going to get a second chance.

God's got something in mind for you, Darcy. Was it only yesterday that her friend Mona had told her that? "I don't know what it is. I just know that He wants you to let Him be your father." Could dear, sweet Mona have known something about the future? Was this some sort of heavenly sign? The timing of the layoff was rather convenient, wasn't it?

Darcy snorted at her own silliness. This wasn't any spiritual mission. This was just a simple matter of cleaning up loose ends. Tending to business while she dealt the old hometown a few facts. Nothing more.

"All right." Darcy tamped down the doubts and agreed at last. "I'll go." She sighed heavily. "I'm sure not promising to stick around for more than a couple of days. But I'll go back long enough to hear the will and give the old place one last glance. Satisfied?"

"More than satisfied." He grinned boyishly, and the

smile wiped years off his face, making him seem like one of her cohorts from the old days. "I'll be by in the morning to pick you up. What time will you be ready?"

Darcy stared at him in surprise. "In the morning? But I have to give notice on this place and all sorts of things!" She saw his eyes narrow and knew what he was thinking. "I'm not backing down. I just need a little time." She handed him his Stetson.

"All right." He scratched his chin thoughtfully. "But I can't wait long. I'll pay whatever notice needs to be covered." He held up a hand at her protest. "The tickets aren't open-ended so I'll have to call the airline and see what's available after lunch. Will you have a lot of luggage?"

"There's nothing much worth taking, as you can very well see." She stood stiffly by the door. "But I don't intend to leave behind a mess for someone else to clean up. I'll throw out what I don't take. Most of it's junk anyway. After lunch will be fine." She opened the door and stood waiting.

"Great! I'll see you at one." He was almost through when he stopped in front of her. "I forgot. My aunt sent a few things with me. I left them in my hotel room. I'll bring them along."

"Things?" She frowned, wondering what kind of woman this Aunt Clarice would turn out to be. "I don't even know her."

His laughter was a deep burst of pleasure that resounded down the long, dark hallway. "That wouldn't stop her." He chuckled. "If Aunt Clarice feels the Lord tells her to do something, she does it. No questions asked."

Inwardly, Darcy groaned. A busybody, she decided. And probably a bossy one. Just what she needed to make her return to Raven's Rest complete.

"Actually, I think there are some dresses and stuff. She wasn't too specific." He stood looking down at her for a long time. Darcy shifted uncomfortably, hating being scrutinized so closely. She lifted a nervous hand to the tangle of curls that covered her head. "See you tomorrow," he said at last.

"Good night." Darcy closed the door behind him and bolted it carefully. She waited, listening for the tapping sounds of his booted heels as he walked away.

I've done it now, she told herself later as she lay in her sagging narrow bed. She stared up at the water-stained ceiling, fear and trepidation battling for supremacy in her mind.

Trust God, Luke had said. Darcy wanted to laugh but the fear inside went too deep. She'd long since given up depending on God to help her, but Luke wasn't to understand about all that. No, she was on her own and she would manage. Somehow.

Still, it would be a break. She wouldn't have to look for a new job right away or stretch her money for day care. Best of all, Jamie could have some time away from the grit and grime of the city in winter. She wanted that more than anything. Maybe they would even celebrate Christmas this year.

Not that I'm taking anything back, she whispered, eyes squeezed closed. *I still think You abandoned me when I needed You the most. And I'm not going to forget that.*

The noises of the night closed around her as car horns honked and someone upstairs stamped on the floor. Scuffling footsteps and grunts of pain sounded from outside her door.

At least I've been lucky so far, she told herself. It's probably a good time to get out.

She giggled nervously at the silly thought, her fingers closing around the prickly, abrasive fabric of her surplus-store blanket.

Lucky? Who was she kidding? She was the unluckiest person alive. And going back to Raven's Rest was an undertaking only a fool would attempt.

Chapter Two

With a tentative hand, Luke flipped through the rack of dresses, disgusted by the skimpy fabrics and suggestive necklines. Aunt Clarice would have his hide if he got anything like this for Martha's daughter. He walked out of the department store and headed for a women's store across the way. But he had to get something. He'd promised Clarice that he would buy a few things.

"Just in case she feels like she doesn't want to come back here looking poorer than when she left." Clarice had insisted, stuffing a wad of money into his palm. "I have a feeling she needs help, Lucas. Lord knows, she can't have had an easy time of it. You get her a few really nice things."

"Aunt Clarice, I don't know anything about women's clothes! I won't have a clue what to buy."

"You'll do fine, son. I'll ask the Lord for a little heavenly guidance." Aunt Clarice was a great believer in the Lord imparting heavenly guidance to his children. Luke just hoped heaven had heard her orders.

"Sir? May I help you?" a friendly looking saleswoman asked.

"My aunt sent me to buy some things for a friend." He explained what he wanted—some nice but sturdy clothes that would withstand life on a ranch. "And maybe some things she could wear to church or a social," he added at the last minute.

The saleswoman nodded and began her search. "What size is your friend?"

"Size?" Luke frowned. "I don't know. She's tall and slim."

"Hmm. That's not much to go on. Come with me for a moment." He followed the woman to the front of the store and stood behind her as she gazed out at the passing crowds. "That woman in the short skirt. Is she about that size?"

"Nope, smaller." Luke searched again. "There, that one with the dog. See her? Blond hair all piled up. Darcy's that size, I think." He studied the woman again. "Yeah, she looks about right. Darcy's got shorter dark hair though. And blue eyes. Sad blue eyes." He stopped then, suddenly aware of the curious look the woman gave him.

"A size seven, I'd say." The woman nodded. She began pulling out warm fuzzy shirts, denim skirts and thick bright sweaters. "These are the latest fall colors, and with that dark hair, she'll look beautiful in them." Soon a vast array of outfits lay spread out across the counter.

"If you mix and match them, you can get quite a bit of mileage out of these things," the woman assured him, holding up a pure white angora sweater and matching skirt. "And we've got a sale on. Of course, jeans would go with any of these."

"Fine, I'll take them all." Luke watched as she folded each garment. "Be sure the tags are off, will you? And maybe you could give me a box instead of those bags. I don't want her to know I just bought them."

"Of course." The woman looked as if this was a perfectly normal request. "Just let me check." She disappeared for a moment and then returned. "I'm sorry, I haven't a box the right size. But Gina's across the way stocks suitcases. Maybe that would be more appropriate. That way, it would look like you brought them with you from—where? Texas?"

Luke grinned. "Colorado. I'll be right back." He started down the aisle, but stopped when the woman called out.

"I know it's presumptuous," she told him, winking. "But I'm going to suggest it anyway. Gina has a lovely leather handbag that would tie in so perfectly with the leather bits on this vest and skirt. You might want to have a look at it."

And so it happened that Luke arrived at Darcy's with his own small overnight bag and a much larger one that he presented to her. "This is from Aunt Clarice. The plane doesn't leave until four so if you want to repack things, we have time. Hi, chum!" He lifted the grinning little boy into his arms and swung him up high. "Are you ready to go for a ride?"

"Yes, a plane ride. Mommy tol' me. We go up in the clouds." He pushed to get down, and Luke set him on the floor. "Mommy? Mommy, you're crying."

"No, sweetie. I just got a bit of dust in my eye." She dashed away the tears and looked up at Luke. "I can't possibly take these," she told him. "They're worth a fortune."

"Well, I'm not wearing 'em!" He frowned down at her, frustrated that he'd picked out clothes she obviously hated. "You'd better take it up with Aunt Clarice. Although—" he pretended to study the array of bright colors "—I don't think there's much here that's her style. She mostly wears jeans." He picked up the royal blue anorak he'd chosen especially to go with her eyes. He fingered its cozy fleece lining before holding it out.

"I'd put this on, though. It'll be mighty cold when we get off that plane. I'm sorry if they're not what you'd wear. Aunt Clarice probably has different ideas about women's clothes than you do."

"Are you kidding? They're wonderful!"

Luke watched as she slid one small hand over the silky soft material. He could see the look of longing before her eyes moved to the dowdy brown tweed hanging behind the door.

"I'll pay her back," she whispered, slipping her arms into the sleeves as he held it out. "However long it takes."

"Please, don't." He noted the spark of life in her tired eyes and how those pale cheeks seemed to glow now. "Clarice would be hurt. If you don't want all of them, that's all right. Maybe we can return them or something." He fingered the envelope with the tags stuffed inside his coat pocket.

"But she'd be really hurt if you tried to pay her for them. I know—why don't you just do something nice for her sometime." He didn't miss the way her fingers lingered on the soft cashmere. Luke had already noticed that Jamie's clothes were far newer than her own and in very good repair.

"But why would she do this? I don't mean anything to her. We don't even know each other." Darcy stared at him, face perplexed. "What does she want from me?" She pulled out the knitted gloves that he'd stuffed in the pocket.

Luke could see the puzzlement in her eyes and prayed for guidance as he tried to explain. "Aunt Clarice doesn't want anything *from* you, Darcy. She's trying to make you feel welcome. It's just the kind of thing she does." That wasn't very clear. He tried again.

"Clarice thinks God means for her to touch as many people's lives as she can, and so she tries to do that the best way she can. I guess this time she decided buying you those clothes would be right. She'd tell you He told her to do it."

There was a long drawn-out silence, and Luke waited for her decision, hoping God would forgive him for phrasing it in just that way.

"All right. I'll accept them. For now." Darcy looked dubious but she quickly tore open the paper bags at her feet and with several swift movements had tucked the contents inside. They were mostly Jamie's clothes, Luke noticed, with only a couple of shirts and a pair of jeans for herself.

"I don't have many clothes," she told him defensively. "We always wore uniforms."

"Really cuts down on what you need, doesn't it?" Since when did factory workers wear uniforms? he wondered? Luke motioned down toward his own case. "I figured that out when I left the navy. One little duffel bag was all I had." He pulled a package out of his pocket. "This truck is for Jamie. Should I wait until we're on the plane?"

She nodded. "Maybe you should keep it till then. He could play with it while we travel. He's already pretty excited." She cast one more glance around the ugly room and then picked up her purse. "I'm ready to go."

"The furniture?"

"Comes with the place. Such as it is. Do you want to call a cab?"

"There's one waiting." He watched silently as she gathered her son's hand firmly into her own. "If you open the doors, I'll manage the bags."

A big burly man stopped them at the bottom of the stairs. "Leaving, Sleeping Beauty?" he muttered, his words slurred.

"Yes, I'm moving. Here's the key, Mr. Munson. You can keep my damage deposit in lieu of notice." She met his gaze head-on, but Luke saw the ripple of fear that shook her and the panic that flew into her blue eyes.

"That's too bad, honey. You ain't seen much of anything but that room of yours." The man reached out as if to touch Jamie's hair, and the little boy pushed behind Luke, who quickly stepped forward and set down the cases.

"I think she's seen more than enough." He said it quietly but clearly enough to ensure his meaning. "Please move back. We have a cab waiting."

The beady black eyes seemed to assess Luke's height and lean physique. "Yeah, sure," he muttered, stepping backward.

"Thanks." Luke ushered the woman and child through

the door and down the steps to the waiting car. While the cabbie hoisted their bags into the trunk, Luke helped Darcy in and set Jamie in beside her. As the car drove away, he could clearly hear her sigh. Of relief? "Has he bothered you before?"

"No," she said softly. "But I don't think it would have been much longer. This isn't a place for single women." Her fingers unclenched from around the handles of her bag and she glanced up at him with the beginning of a smile at the corner of her wide, expressive lips. "Thanks."

Luke tipped his hat. "My pleasure," he grinned, only looking away after she did. The city flashed by him in a kaleidoscope of sights and sounds. Jamie scrambled onto his knees to get a better look as they rode for a while in silence.

"Mommy, I'm hungry." The little boy tapped his stomach. "My food box is empty."

Luke burst out laughing. "So's mine, kiddo. Bone dry." He guessed from the fleeting look in Darcy's eyes that she wasn't averse to eating either. "How about if we have a little snack when we get to the airport?"

"But won't they serve food on the plane?" She frowned, her eyes clouded. Probably figuring the cost, Luke decided.

"Airline food?" He shook his head, making a face. "Not for *this* boy. I need good wholesome nourishing grub that sticks with you. Not six packets of peanuts and a few pretzels with some fancy water in a bottle!"

Darcy laughed at his indignant look, the sound tinkling in the car interior. "Pardon me! And airport food is any better?"

"We're not eating just any airport food," he told her, winking. "We're going to sample the finest of the fine— as children's menus go." Luke felt suddenly young again as he cajoled these two solemn souls into a bit of fun. "What do you like to eat, Jamie?"

"Noodle soup!" Jamie grinned happily. "With lots of crackers. And chocolate milk."

"Done. And you, madame?" He glanced across at Darcy, only to find his face enclosed by a pair of tiny cold hands. He turned back to Jamie. "What is it, son?"

"I don't know what to call you." The simple little request reminded Luke of another child who'd sat on his lap just three years ago. Younger than this, but filled with as many questions.

"Luke," he said around the lump in his throat. "Or Lucas. That's what Aunt Clarice calls me."

"Mister Luke is a nice name. Isn't it, Mommy?" The little boy beamed happily, peering up at his mother for confirmation.

"Very nice," she murmured, her eyes meeting Luke's. "And I like soup, too."

Because it's cheap, Luke guessed, but didn't say the words. Instead he teased her. "Oh, no. Soup is for the kids only. The adults have to have something awful like roast beef and mashed potatoes or deep-fried chicken. I'll give you some time to choose."

She waited until Jamie was busy playing with a button on his coat before asking the question that lurked in the back of her eyes. "Why are you being so nice to us? We don't mean anything to you."

"Sure you do." He countered her quietly. "You're

Martha and Lester's daughter. And I owe them a huge debt of gratitude."

"Why?" She frowned as if she couldn't believe that her parents could have done anything good.

"Because once, not that long ago, they dragged me out of my stupor and back into reality. If it hadn't been for your parents and Aunt Clarice treating me like a son, I don't know where I'd have been. I want to do something to feel like I've at least paid a little of the debt I owe them."

"You don't owe me anything, Luke," she whispered, her eyes once more reflecting that stark pain he'd glimpsed earlier. "And especially because of them. If they could make you a part of the cold little world they inhabited, then I'm glad. Because they never did it for me."

Luke studied the slim, hunched form with the haunted eyes, as a thousand thoughts raged through his brain.

Help me, Lord, he said silently. *There's so much hurt there. Shine Your healing love into her life.*

The cabbie pulled up just in time to prevent further discussion. Darcy clung to Jamie's hand as Luke carried the bags into the airport terminal, motioning her toward the nearest desk. Once they'd checked the luggage and received their boarding passes, they were free for over an hour.

"We don't have to be at the gate for a while. Let's find someplace to eat." Jamie begged to eat at the first fast-food place they came to, and Luke readily agreed, wanting to give the boy a treat. He could well imagine that little Jamie had not eaten out often.

"What are they called again, Mister Luke?" Jamie

asked the same question for the fifth time, his fat little hand clutching the chicken tightly.

"Nuggets. Chicken nuggets. Do you like them?"

"Yes! Better than soup. I like these, too." The boy popped several fries into his grinning mouth and munched happily.

"And how about you, Darcy? Are you enjoying your meal?" He watched as the startled blue eyes lifted from her silent contemplation of the towering triple-burger on the plate in front of her.

"It's, uh, very nice," she murmured. "But how do you ever get a bite out of that without getting it all over?"

"That's half the fun." He chuckled, lifting up his own. "And that's one advantage of eating at a mostly kids' place. Nobody notices the mess!" He wiped the sauce off his chin as if to emphasize his point.

Darcy, shrugged, slipped out of her new blue coat and set it carefully behind her. Tucking a napkin onto her lap, she carefully lifted the concoction with both hands and took a dainty nip from the edge.

"Not like that!" Luke laughed as she dabbed at her lips. "You've got to get your mouth around it or all the good stuff will fall out the other side." He took a gigantic bite just to show her.

Darcy shook her head. "Too messy," she said, and proceeded to separate the layers and make two burgers out of the one. Then she lifted a piece to her mouth, grinning up at him as she bit into it. "Now *this* is a burger," she told him smugly.

Luke crunched away on the extra dill pickles he'd ordered, content to watch her face light up. "Do you want some of these?" He offered the plate. "Pickles are my favorite food. They form their own separate food group, you know."

"I've heard an argument very similar to that from Jamie," she giggled, taking one. "Only it had to do with chocolate bars." She raised her eyebrows. "He didn't win."

"Ah, well. But now he's got me on his side. We're a formidable force." Luke smiled, sipping his coffee.

"Isn't this the greatest coffee?" She blew across the mug and then delicately sipped the steaming brew. "I love freshly brewed coffee with a dollop of real cream."

"That isn't real cream. That's some junk they imported and reconstituted. On the ranch we have real cream. But I like it on pumpkin pie the best." He leaned back, enjoying the sight of two hungry people cleaning their plates. "The beef's fresher, too," he told her.

"In fact, everything's better in Colorado, right?" She laughed out loud at his frown of dismay. "I've heard it before. My dad thought that anybody who lived outside of the state had truly missed out on the best part of life." She said it automatically, without thinking. It was only after the words were spoken that she realized what she'd said. "He never wanted to see or hear about anything else," she whispered, her face pale.

"Well, it is a good thing to be content with your lot in life." Luke murmured it diplomatically, glancing down at Jamie, who was studying his mother's sad face. "But I think it's a good thing to broaden your horizons, too."

Darcy pushed away the remains of her burger, and leaned back in her chair. He could see the defiance in the tilt of her head and winced at the flash of those intensely blue eyes.

"Did you get along with my father?"

It wasn't what he'd expected, but Luke answered her. "Yes, pretty much. He was getting tired of doing it all himself, and by the time I came along, Lester had some problems that made the heavy work almost impossible for him."

She frowned. "I didn't know. But then why would I?" She shrugged almost carelessly, but Luke knew it was to hide the pain that he could see in her eyes.

"Lester talked about you all the time," he told her, hoping this was the right tack to take.

"He did? Why would he talk about me?"

"Well, it started when I asked him to sell a couple of the horses he had. He didn't ride anymore, and I figured it was costing too much money to keep feeding them all winter long." Luke tilted back on his chair, staring across the crowded restaurant. "He wouldn't hear of it. They were *your* horses, he said. Left in his care. When you came back, he wanted to be sure they were there, waiting for you. He spent hours currying them."

Luke saw the quick rise of tears in her clear blue eyes and the downward tilt of her head as she tried to hide the evidence.

"I didn't know."

"Of course you didn't. It was his dream, anyway. Not yours." Luke wiped Jamie's hands and face and gave him a dollar to buy an ice cream at the nearby counter. "He'll be fine," he murmured when Darcy shifted, ready to follow. "We can see from here." They watched as the boy proudly presented his money and waited for the treat. "Your mother would have adored him."

"He looks a bit like her," Darcy said, then pursed her lips. "There's no point," she told him fiercely as she straightened her shoulders. "So you can just stop it. I'm not going to forget the past that easily, no matter how wonderful you make it sound. It was never a rose garden."

"Life seldom is," he agreed quietly. *Somehow, someway, Lord,* he prayed. *Break through that shell of pain and let her see the love of Your light. Let her know that You are there. Waiting.*

Chapter Three

Nothing had changed, Darcy reflected as she peered through the windshield of the half-ton and watched the familiar landmarks pass by. Lookout Point, Pike's Pond, Willow Woods—it all sat there, waiting to bring back memories she'd stifled for so long.

"The house looks different," she said to Luke once they reached the old two-story. "It seems bigger."

"It is. Lester and I built a sunroom on the west side and he put a hot tub in the new master bedroom on the main floor."

"A hot tub?" Darcy frowned. Her father had hated excess. He'd scrimped and saved for as long as she could remember. Sometimes he'd overdone it and they'd gone without when they could have afforded some small luxuries. "Why a hot tub?"

"Your mother's arthritis got very bad." Although he said the words quietly enough, Darcy shifted uneasily. Was he blaming her? "Her hands particularly, although her knees and feet pained her a lot. When your dad saw how much the hot water at the nursing home helped her, he decided to get one out here so she wouldn't have to go into town for the treatments. She loved it."

"She used to say that she could tell the weather by the joints in her fingers," Darcy told him. She roused herself from the saddening thoughts. "It looks like there's something new on the other end, too."

"Yes. We added a couple more bedrooms. When Clarice and I came, we were prepared to stay somewhere else, but your parents wanted us on the premises." He stopped abruptly. "I hope you don't mind. We've kept to the same arrangements. There's Aunt Clarice."

Darcy stared at him, wondering at the odd tone in his voice. "Of course not. I imagine you need to be close to keep things running. I'm sure that's what my parents would have wanted."

She peered through the gloom at a thin, tall woman who stood in the doorway, illuminated from behind by a blaze of house lights. When Luke pulled up in front of the building, she caught a glimpse of gray hair combed back from a face with piercing eyes, high cheekbones, a long straight nose and thin lips. Strangely enough, it was the warmth of her smile that held Darcy's attention.

"I'm Clarice Campion." Luke's aunt introduced herself as Darcy got out of the car. "It's an old French name—-means mushroom or something like that. Come in, come in, my dear. Oh, a little boy!" Clarice peered down into Jamie's sleepy face. "What a handsome fellow. The spitting image of Martha. You carry him, Luke," she ordered brusquely, sliding her fingers under Darcy's arm. "He's too heavy for her. Come on, girl."

"Yes, ma'am." Luke grinned at them both and scooped the little boy up. "Okay, champ. We're home."

The air was frosty, and Darcy was glad to hurry up the steps and scoot inside. Until she looked around. It was the same. Exactly the same. Yes, a room or two had been added, but basically this was the same cold, hateful house she'd grown up in. She shrugged away the memories and closed the door behind Luke while reminding herself that the past was the past. This was supposed to be a new beginning.

"Lit a fire an hour ago," Clarice informed them, lifting the jacket from Darcy's shoulder. "Lovely color, this. On you," she added at the last moment.

"All due to you and I need to say thank-you," Darcy murmured, staring up into the hawk-like features. "The clothes you sent are lovely and I really appreciate them. But you spent far too much."

"Nonsense! What in the world is money for if not to spend?" Clarice nodded her head sternly. "No good socking it away in some moldy old bank. Doesn't do a body a bit of good there. Why not use it to give some joy? Hope you like them." The words came out clipped and sharp, but there was a twinkle in the black button eyes that warmed Darcy's heart just a bit.

"Did you ever tell my father your views?" Darcy wondered aloud, grinning at the heresy of waste that Lester Simms had preached against all during her childhood.

"Certainly! Told him many times. Came to see I was right, too. Just had to break through that shell of his. Wonderful giving man underneath. Sorry about your loss." Clarice patted Darcy's hand firmly. "No point in fussing, though. They're in heaven and the good Lord is treating them just fine." Clarice motioned her into the living room. "Warmer here. Sit down. Tea coming."

Seconds later she whisked from the room and into the kitchen.

"Mommy?" Jamie, finally awake, pressed himself down from Luke's arms and looked around worriedly. "Is this Mister Luke's ranch?"

"This is where we're going to stay for a little while, honey," she told him softly, removing his jacket and brushing down his wayward strands of hair. "I used to live here when I was a little girl."

"I hope it doesn't bring back too many unpleasant memories." Luke watched as she hugged the little boy close. "Coming home, I mean."

"The past can't hurt me anymore," she told him bitterly. "I've put it all behind me. I had to. Anyway, it *is* the past."

Clarice came in then, bearing a loaded tray with sandwiches, a dish of pickles and beverages, so Darcy didn't hear exactly what he muttered. It sounded remarkably like "I wonder."

She studied him with a frown, just now noting the few strands of gray above his ears and the faint red seam of a scar along his neck. She knew nothing about him, she realized, despite the three-hour plane trip and one-and-a-half-hour drive from the airport.

Luke Lassiter didn't wear a ring and there had been no mention of anyone but Aunt Clarice, so she doubted that he was married, even though he had spoken of a child. And although he talked about a number of the town's inhabitants, Luke hadn't mentioned any other family or special friends.

Jamie's happy giggles drew her from her introspection and she saw that he was seated by the coffee table, happily peeling his sandwich apart.

"Wait a minute, Jamie. I think we should go to the kitchen just in case something accidentally gets spilled." She eyed the glass of milk nervously, knowing how easily her son tipped them.

"Hogwash! Houses are for living in. If something spills, we'll clean it up. Sit down and eat up, you two. Both look like a pair of skinned beanpoles!"

"I don't think you should be talking." Luke chuckled as he plopped down onto the sofa beside his aunt. "You aren't exactly flabby yourself." He winked at Darcy. "You have to dish out as good as you get or she runs all over you," he told her, grinning. "Clarice's biggest complaint is that God took my uncle Herbert home before she was finished bossing him."

To Darcy, the comment seemed almost sacrilegious, but Clarice smiled benignly. "Man needed bossing around," she said firmly. "Couldn't find his left foot without me there to direct him. Got his money's worth when he married me, he did."

Darcy couldn't help smiling at the smug look of satisfaction on Clarice's bony face.

"You're not going to side with her, are you?" Luke complained, grabbing the dish of pickles and unloading most of it onto his plate. "It's not fair to gang up on a man like that." He turned to Jamie. "We're going to have to stick together, James, old man. You and me against the ladies."

While her son giggled his agreement, Darcy felt a jolt of shock run through her system. She dropped the half-eaten ham sandwich onto her plate, and shifted it to the table before surging to her feet.

"Why did you call him that?" She searched his dark eyes. "Have you been prying into my personal life or something?"

"I—I'm sorry," Luke stuttered, staring at her. He shook his head. "I just assumed Jamie was a nickname. It usually stands for James." He set down his plate and stood suddenly, reaching out his hand toward her shoulder. "What's wrong, Darcy?"

"Nothing." She felt stupid for her outburst. He couldn't know, could he? Nobody knew. They hadn't wanted to know back then and she sure wasn't going to bring it all up now. "I'm sorry. I guess I'm a little bit tired."

"Natural enough reaction, girl. Humanity wasn't made for streaking across the sky." Clarice poured out the tea. "Sip this. Then bed."

"I'd better go see to the chores," Luke murmured. Darcy noticed that he'd left most of the pickles and half of his sandwich on the plate. "I guess I'll see you in the morning. Good night, Jamie. Have a good sleep." He brushed his hand over the glossy dark curls and leaned down to accept the hug that the little boy offered.

Darcy met his dark apologetic glance when he straightened, and forced a smile to her lips. "Thank you for getting us here," she said solemnly. "I'm sorry if I barked at you. I guess it's just having everything come at me at once." She held out a hand. "I apologize."

Luke enfolded her hand in both of his and hung on for a long time, staring deeply into her eyes as if asking a question and searching for the answer.

"Welcome home, Darcy Simms. I hope you can

remember the good times that you had here and not dwell on the bad moments. Good night." He let her hand go finally, but by that time, tiny shivers of awareness had trickled up her arm to her brain.

He was a tall, strong man who had marched into her life and confronted her with a past that she was desperately trying to avoid. But in all her twenty-three years, Darcy had never met anyone like him. The intense look in his eyes was reflected in his face as she pulled her hand away and hid it behind her back in an effort to avoid the unwanted sensations.

She *couldn't* be attracted to him. She wouldn't allow herself to be! That road only led to heartache. The men she knew only ever wanted one thing from her. And hadn't she learned the hard way that there was only pain and suffering when you followed your emotions?

"I need to get Jamie to bed," she said firmly, loudly enough for Clarice to hear. "Is there someplace where you'd prefer I put him?"

"Your old room might be best." Clarice carried the small paper bag of toys Darcy had packed up the stairs, leading the way. She put the light on in the bathroom and then bid Jamie good-night before going back downstairs.

"Come on, Love Bug," Darcy said, "this one time we'll skip brushing your teeth. You look like you're going to fall asleep in your clothes." She slid him into his pajamas without a protest, hugged him fiercely, and then waited until his dark lashes drooped closed. "I love you, Jamie." The words came out in a fierce whisper as Darcy watched him sleeping cozily in the single bed.

And then, turning her back, she went back downstairs

to clean up the kitchen, steeling herself against the flood of memories that returned, stronger than ever. How many times had she washed dishes in this sink? How often had she scrubbed this floor on hands and knees in penance for some misdeed. It hurt to remember the silent meals she'd endured at the table.

She straightened her back defiantly. She was strong and competent. She would get past this guilty feeling.

Darcy Simms had not come home. She had only returned to a place where she used to live. And sooner or later the rotten reality of the past would creep up from behind and threaten to overwhelm her. She had to be strong. She had to face it. She had to beat it.

The next morning, Darcy left the cushy comfort of the renovated master suite and headed toward the kitchen with reluctance. It was the only room in the house that didn't hold memories for her and she'd been able to relax and sleep more deeply than she could ever remember. But the sun had risen long ago, streaming through the bank of east-facing windows, and she knew that it was way past time to get up.

"'Morning." Clarice's low voice came from under the sink. "Gonna snow tonight. I've got to get those everlastings in and hanging upside down in the barn if I want to save 'em for Thanksgiving. Twine's gone."

Darcy couldn't think of a thing to say to this. So instead she asked, "Where's Jamie? I checked his room but he was gone."

"Lucas took him. Likely in the barn looking at the animals." She stood, triumphantly bearing a ball of string. "Coffee's on if you want some. If you eat it, you can get your own breakfast. Don't partake myself. Makes me logy. I'll be out back."

Darcy would have said "thanks," but Clarice disappeared out the back door in a rush, a gust of icy cold wind signaling her departure. Darcy helped herself to one of the freshly baked cinnamon rolls on the counter and poured a big mug full of coffee. There was cream in the fridge and, remembering Luke's comments from the day before, she poured some in and sipped her coffee with a grin. Colorado cream really was better!

The kitchen table was the same weathered old slab that had sat here for as long as she could remember. There were two initials carved into one of the legs. Her mother had once explained that they belonged to her grandfather, who had placed them there long ago.

"If Clarice is the one who's keeping house, she hasn't changed much of Mom's setup." Darcy glanced around the spacious area after finishing her small breakfast. She rinsed off her hands and moved quickly through the old familiar rooms of the house, noting the changes that had been made, before finally returning to the kitchen. "Evidently dusting is not Clarice's forte," Darcy said half under her breath as she trailed one finger over the top of her mother's china cabinet.

"Despise dusting." Clarice's voice crackled behind her, startling Darcy. "Be much obliged if you'd take that over. Don't like cooking much either." Clarice held a huge bunch of straw flowers in her arms and tilted her head toward the china cabinet. "Never did understand why folks need special dishes they only eat off of once or twice a year. Seems to me, less is more. That's what I always say."

"She does," Luke said with a chuckle as he entered the room. "About twenty times a day. Good morning, Darcy. Did you sleep well?" His eyes took in the bright red sweater that she'd chosen from among Clarice's gifts. "That's a good choice for today. It's pretty and warm."

Darcy tried not to appreciate just how handsome Luke Lassiter looked this morning.

"Where's Jamie?"

"In the barn with Ernie, our ranch hand. I never saw a child take to animals so well." Luke poured himself a cup of coffee and grabbed a roll. "He's born to ranch." As if he'd just realized what he said, his eyes opened wide and he stared at Darcy. "Sorry."

"It's all right." She shifted uncomfortably. "Are you sure he'll be okay there? He's not used to horses."

"The horses are in the pasture. Besides, Ernie will stay with him while he checks out the other animals. He'll be fine." He drank deeply from the cup, savoring the flavor. Red spots of color stood out on his cheekbones, and the ends of his fingers were white with cold. "What are you planning to do today?"

Darcy took a deep breath. "Since I'm here to settle the estate, I guess I'd better go into town and see the lawyer." She forced herself not to fidget. "That should be a lot of fun."

"Nobody going into town today," Clarice muttered, bundling yet another group of flowers together, her fingers nimbly tying them tightly while leaving a length of cord at the end. "Why not get used to the place again? After all, it is your home."

"But I'm not going to stay," Darcy explained carefully,

wondering if the older woman was quite all there. "I'm just here to settle the estate. Then it's back to the city for me."

"Wonderful place, was it, this city?" The black eyes bore straight into Darcy's. "Everything hunky-dory there?"

"N-no." Darcy swallowed, opening her eyes wide at the strange expression on Clarice's face. She glanced at Luke for direction, but he looked away. "Actually it was pretty awful. When Luke came along I was glad to leave."

"And you need to rush back because...?" Clarice stood straight and tall, waiting for an answer.

"I don't have to rush back. I just wanted to get things started. Find out how things stand. You know?"

"No, I don't. But I expect you want to run away again. Don't know why. No learning when you run away all the time."

She'd never had someone coax out her private thoughts this way, Darcy decided. It was very intimidating. But she had to set the record straight.

"Look. I don't know what my parents told you, but I have never been afraid to come back here. Not really," she added at Clarice's knowing stare. "It's just—" she drew in a breath of air "—it's painful for me here. I don't want to dig it all up again."

"It'll come up. Whether you want it to or not. That's life." Clarice set the last bundle into the box and carried it to the door. "Face your ghosts and move on, girl. That's the best way. You cooking lunch?" She grabbed a thick black coat from the peg and tossed it over her shoulders.

"Uh, yes. All right." It was difficult to change the subject so quickly. Darcy glanced stupidly from Clarice to Luke. "What would you like?"

"We'll eat just about anything as long as we don't have to cook it." Luke smiled, a glint of admiration in his eyes. "We've got two freezers full of beef and chickens and a whole lot of vegetables. Think you can come up with something from that?"

"Of course. I'm quite a good cook actually. I've just never had much opportunity." She checked the clock. "But I don't have a lot of time to defrost anything. Are there any eggs? I could scramble them."

"Eggs are good, healthy food. I can eat them," Clarice declared, stomping out the door and down the stairs.

"She's a bit abrupt sometimes," Luke explained from his position behind her. "I hope she didn't hurt your feelings."

"Of course not. It's just rather difficult to follow her at times, that's all." She turned to face him. "How do you work things around here?"

"I've been managing the place for a while now," he told her quietly, sinking into a chair. "Your parents trusted me to do the best I could, and the lawyers have continued that."

"There are an awful lot of horses out there." Her eyes studied the paddock across the road. "Are they all ours?"

"Not all. I started breeding some to sell. We—that is, your parents—needed the cash. It took off. Now, we've got more horses than we actually need, but I hired a man to help out a few months ago and things are working out very well. They're actually quite a profitable business."

He reached across and swiped another cinnamon roll. "These are delicious."

"I thought Clarice said she didn't cook." Darcy frowned.

"She doesn't. One of the women from the church brought these. Maybe you remember her. Jalise Penner?"

"Jalise? She married Billy Penner? Oh, brother!" Darcy giggled to herself as she checked the cupboards for a tin of mushrooms. "She trailed around him from first grade on, right through high school. At least somebody around here got their dream." She laughed out loud at the thought of the tall, slim girl with the rather plain face, and the handsome boy who'd had his pick of women.

"He died two years ago," Luke murmured. "Accident."

Darcy sat down abruptly. "How awful!"

"I guess you expected that everything would stay the same, didn't you?" His voice was filled with compassion. "I'm sorry to be the bearer of bad news." His hand covered hers on the table, and, strangely, Darcy didn't mind. His touch communicated empathy and caring, comfort that she was starving for.

"Billy was the same age as me." She tried to absorb it. "He was always laughing and teasing everyone, trying to make jokes." The thought of that wide-toothed grin forever gone made her shiver.

"Are you all right?"

"Yes. It's just the shock." She pulled out the eggs, onions, ham and cheese and began cracking the shells for an omelette. "Why did Clarice say I couldn't go to town?" she asked suddenly. "Surely you don't intend to keep me out here?"

"Of course not! You're not a prisoner any more than I am." He looked horrified at the thought. "It's just that a storm is on the way and I'd rather you not go. I wouldn't like to have to haul you out of a snowdrift. Can you wait?"

"Believe me, if it means that I'll be able to avoid all the nasty looks and whispered words from those busybodies, I can wait." Darcy rolled her eyes. "I suppose I just wanted to get this will thing started."

She pulled out her mother's favorite frying pan and set it on the stove. But the questions rolling around in her brain wouldn't go away. Everything was the same, and yet it was so different. Darcy turned around, hands tightening on the counter behind her. "Luke, did my parents leave a lot of money?"

His eyes narrowed. "I don't know. Why?"

"I'm not here because of the money." Darcy hurried to reassure him, noting the skeptical look on his face. "I know that there are things that need to be settled. But the place looks far better than I remember. This stove and the fridge are new. The barn looks like it was re-sided not long ago, and the machinery I saw out in the yard is not the same stuff we had five years ago." She took a breath and continued.

"My dad was as tight as they come. He wouldn't buy a thing until he absolutely had to, and then he went for the cheapest. This stove is self-cleaning, and the fridge has an ice-maker. There's an air conditioner outside and everything's been freshly painted. Why?"

"Perhaps he changed." Luke frowned at her. "People do change, you know. Even you."

"Lester Simms could never have changed that much!" She shook her head in utter disbelief. "It would take a miracle."

"Then I suppose there was a miracle because I assure you, Lester bought everything himself. He loved getting a glass of water from that fridge. He giggled like a kid when the ice cubes plopped into the glass." Luke watched as she diced the onions and ham. "The air conditioner has been a real bonus these past two summers. They were scorchers. Your mom loved to invite folks out here so they could relax in the cool. The youth group came quite often."

"The youth group?" Darcy squeaked in amazement. "But she hated all that noise. I always had to have my birthday parties outside because she said we made such a mess." Darcy laid the knife down and turned to study his placid features. "It sounds as if we're talking about different people," she whispered.

"Yeah, it does, doesn't it?" He snatched a few bits of ham and popped them into his mouth. "Maybe you didn't know them as well as you thought you did. Or maybe you just remember things differently."

That made Darcy mad. She angrily slapped his hand away from the food, then stood before him, hands on her hips, and gave him the lowdown on life in the Simms's household.

"I lived here for eighteen long, unhappy years. And during that time, I cut the potato peels as thin as possible, made do with shoes that pinched my toes because new ones were too expensive, and wore more hand-me-

downs than Cinderella. Don't talk to me about the wonderful good old days." She flounced across the kitchen
and pointed to a big hook.

"A flyswatter used to hang there. I can remember
it even though I was only about three at the time. My
parents used it on my hands when I spilled some milk on
my grandmother's lace tablecloth. I never did it on purpose. But they acted as if I'd deliberately made a mess."
She swallowed the pain and glared at him. "Every single
thing I did was wrong. And I can never forget that!"

"I'm sorry." Luke's apology was quiet. "I'm really
sorry, Darcy. I wasn't trying to make you sad or remind
you of things you'd rather forget. I just thought maybe
you'd—"

"You thought I'd forget all about the past, didn't you?
Pretend that nothing happened, that I imagined it all."
She was crying furiously now, but didn't care. "Well,
I didn't imagine any of it. They were mean-spirited,
unhappy people who tried to take it out on me. Maybe
they liked you—I don't know. They always said a son
would have been able to carry on the ranch."

"Darcy, I think I should tell you something." Luke's
voice was low and ominous.

"I don't want you to tell me anything. If you liked
my parents and they treated you well, I'm glad. Too bad
they couldn't do the same for me." She dashed away the
tears and sniffed inelegantly. "They left me with one
thing," she whispered. "Just one. The assurance that
I will never, never, treat my son the way they treated
me."

"Darcy, I know they regretted how harsh they'd been.
I think that after you left they realized that they'd been

too strict with you, and since you were gone and they couldn't make amends, they tried to make it up with other people."

"They were *sorry*. They *regretted* things. Isn't that just wonderful?" Darcy sneered bitterly. "And then they repented of that sin, discussed it with Pastor Pringle, and all was well again in their narrow little world. Well, it wasn't all right for me! I'm the one who paid." The tears flowed unstopped as she leaned against the counter.

"I paid, and I paid and I paid. Because of them. And not once did they bother to find me and tell *me* that they were sorry." The pain yawned inside her brain, big and black and terrifying because this time she wasn't sure if she could stop it from enveloping her. She could hear herself sobbing and could do nothing to hold it back.

Luke's arms wrapped around her. He pulled her against his shirt, and Darcy let him. No, it was more like she couldn't stop him. She had no strength, no will-power. Nothing but an ache in her heart that wouldn't quit.

"Why did they have to go, without saying anything, without contacting me? Without even seeing Jamie. Why, Luke?" She scrunched his shirt up under her fingers and squeezed, willing the hurt away. "The youth group, you, Clarice. They gave to everyone but me. And I was their daughter, Luke. Their own *daughter*." She felt his hand move soothingly up her back as his other brushed over her hair.

"It's all right. Let it out. You've carried this for far too long." He murmured soothing phrases as the slide show in her head continued flashing images from the past.

"Why couldn't they have said, just once, that they loved me? That they liked me just because I was me? Why did they have to always keep trying to make me into someone else?"

"I don't know. I don't know." His chin rested on her head, and she relaxed against him weakly.

"I tried to do what they wanted. I tried to be who they needed. But I'm me, Luke. Me, *Darcy*. I was neither the little china-doll daughter nor the in-control son that they wanted. But I wasn't all bad! I *wasn't*, Luke."

"I know. The three of you just got off the track somewhere and couldn't get back on. If only you'd come back home, Darcy. Maybe then you and your parents could have straightened things out."

Darcy yanked herself out of his arms, red-hot fury chasing away all the other emotions that clawed at her. "Come back?" she gasped. "To what? Being told how much of a disappointment I was because I'd had a child out of wedlock? Come back to the sad, commiserating glances between my parents and their friends that the local bad girl had taken that final step to perdition?" She laughed harshly.

"Yeah, that would have been a barrel of laughs, Luke. And Jamie would have grown up feeling like he was a mistake, a problem, something to be avoided." She shook her head vehemently. "No, thank you very much!"

"Darcy, they wouldn't have thought that! They would have loved him."

"They couldn't love me," she told him bitterly. "And I was their own flesh and blood."

"But you don't know the whole story." He looked pained, Darcy decided. As if there was something he wanted to say but couldn't find the words. "If you knew—"

"If I knew, I would have stayed exactly where I was." Darcy turned back to the counter and tossed the ham and onion into the egg mixture determinedly. "You can never go back, Luke. Isn't that the saying?" She smiled grimly. "Actually, I think it's a good one. I don't want to go back and live through that horrible time. I want to move on."

"To what?" He asked it quietly, his eyes sad.

"To something better. I have a wonderful son. I want to show him the lovely things in the world. And that doesn't include any of my memories of this place." She turned on the burner and began making the omelette. "I'll stay here until things are settled, but then I'm leaving."

"And the ranch?"

"Will have to be sold to pay off their debts. I don't care about the money. Really I don't." She faced him defiantly.

"You mean you don't like sleeping safely in a warm bed with a full stomach and not having to worry whether someone will smash down the door, shoot off a gun or worse?"

He sounded angry and that irritated Darcy. Why couldn't he understand?

"Oh, I like it all right," she told him. "I'm not crazy, you know. I want all the best things for my son."

"But?"

"But the best things aren't always the things money can buy. And to tell you the truth, some things just plain cost too much. If anybody knows that, it's me."

The door closed softly several moments later, and she turned to watch as Luke crossed the yard. Clarice and Jamie were bent over a bale, earnestly discussing something. They waved at Luke, and Clarice nodded at something he said. Jamie's little face was red and glowing with good health as he scampered over to the big man who leaned down and scooped him up, hugging the little body close.

Darcy turned away to butter the toast and flip the eggs. She didn't know why, but she was certain that Jamie was perfectly safe with Luke and Clarice. They would encourage him to check things out, but make sure that he didn't get hurt. She'd seen the glow in Luke's eyes yesterday when he'd spoken to her son. The big, solid cowboy had answered every question as patiently as any father.

"Why didn't You give *me* a father like that?" Darcy glared at the ceiling, thinking of a God who would stand by while children suffered. "Why couldn't You give me parents that loved me like the other kids' parents did?"

Quick as a wink, the answer raced through her mind.

You didn't deserve that kind of love. You lied, cheated, stole and hurt people. How could anyone love you?

Heartsick and weary, Darcy tugged open the door and called the others to lunch. Why, oh, why had she ever come back?

Chapter Four

"Come on, son. Let's walk over here." One week later and Darcy was still nervous about being home.

Darcy grabbed Jamie's hand and hurried down the street, anxious to get to the lawyer's office and then run back to the safety of the farm. Funny, thinking the farm was safer than the town. Neither one had been exactly a haven of peace five years ago.

The hardest thing was listening to the speculation that whispered behind her.

"…Isn't that the Simms girl…?"

"…That's her kid? Cute little guy. Looks a little like Martha…."

"…Wonder how old he is…?"

They'd know soon enough, so there really wasn't any point in trying to hide the facts of his conception. But she had no intention of having his name dragged through the mud either, Darcy decided grimly.

"Hello, Darcy. Back in town, I see." Marietta Follensbee stood peering down at Jamie. "Is he yours?" she asked with a grim tightening of her lips.

"Yes. This is my son, Jamie, Mrs. Follensbee."

"Hmm. Looks a might peaked." Marietta reached out and pinched the skin of Jamie's cheek between two gnarled fingers. "Needs some good outside work and a few early nights to toughen him up, I'll warrant."

"He's only four! And Jamie is not *sickly* at all. Good day!" Darcy marched down the street to the drugstore as the knot of tension tightened its band around her forehead.

"Darcy." Elroy Spiggot stood behind the counter in his white jacket—the same one he'd worn for the past thirty years. His spectacles perched on the end of his nose and he peered through them haughtily.

"Hi, Mr. Spiggot. How are you and your wife doing?" Darcy did her best to sound interested in the two elderly hypochondriacs.

"Mrs. Spiggot died three years back. Food poisoning, it was. I don't suppose you knew, since you never made the effort to come back and see your own folks." There was condemnation clear and present in those tones, and Darcy shrank inwardly from the malice that glowed in the pharmacist's eyes. "Too ashamed of yourself, I expect. Be sure your sins will find you out, the Good Book says. I reckon they did just that." His gaze slid to Jamie, one eyebrow tilted meaningfully.

"No, Mr. Spiggot." Darcy enunciated each word clearly and precisely. "I was not ashamed to come back. I didn't want to return to a place where there were so many people waiting to take God's place as judge and jury. I apologized to you for stealing that candy bar and I worked for you without pay for two weeks as my parents wished. The debt is paid."

She wasn't going to go away silently, Darcy decided

bitterly. They wouldn't intimidate her as they had in the past.

"But just for your information, this is my *son*. His name is Jamie. He's a wonderful little boy who is innocent of anything I might have done." She turned toward the door, tugging Jamie along. "I think I can get whatever I need in the city, Mr. Spiggot. No need to bother yourself." She pulled open the door. "And, believe it or not, I am very sorry to hear about your wife. As, I'm sure, you were sorry to hear about my parents. Goodbye."

"We didn't get nothing, Mommy. You said we had to get something." Jamie stood frowning up at her, his little face curious.

Darcy sucked in a deep breath and let it out slowly between her teeth. That had been a tough one. And there was worse to come, if she knew the good citizens of Raven's Rest. And she did!

"No, sunshine boy, we didn't get anything. I decided it was too cold in there and I didn't want to stay very long." Which was a major understatement, Darcy admitted to herself grimly. But there was no way she wanted to color Jamie's view of the town with her own bad experiences.

"I didn't think it was cold in there. I thought it was hot! But I didn't like that man, Mommy. He looked too grumpy."

Darcy burst out laughing at this very accurate assessment, and hugged Jamie close. "I love you, sweetie. More and more every day."

Jamie's cold little lips brushed against her cheek as his chubby arms tugged against her neck. "I love you, too, Mommy. This much." And he squeezed for all he was worth.

"Let's go get some new crayons from that store over there." Darcy urged him across the street, but when they reached the other side, she was surprised to see Mr. Spiggot still standing in the window of his store, watching them. She deliberately turned her back on him.

"I think we need some really bright colors," she murmured to Jamie. "Something to brighten up this place a little."

"Still trying to change things, eh, Darce?" asked the tall man who stood before her.

"Todd? Todd Barlow?" Darcy studied the bearded face, frowning.

"Yeah, it's me."

"You sure look different. Kind of…older, I guess." It wasn't exactly complimentary, but the man in the brown button-down suit with the color-coordinated tie and shiny wingtips was a far cry from the blue-jeaned hoodlum she'd chummed around with years ago. "Are you still living here?"

"Yes, of course I live here. I run the store with my father. I'm married to Sara Higgins." He brushed a hand over his mustache with a self-satisfied smile that made Darcy only too aware that Todd felt superior to her.

"You and Sara? Well, congratulations. I didn't realize you even liked each other."

"Of course we like each other. We're married. Sara teaches at the school. In fact she's the vice-principal." Todd glanced down condescendingly.

"Oh, that's nice. You were dating Annette when I left.

Oh, this is my son, Jamie. Jamie, this is an old friend of mine from when I lived here."

Jamie thrust out his hand. "Hello."

"Hello." Todd's fingers barely brushed the child's before he thrust his briefcase into his other hand. "Did your husband come too, or are you just here long enough to settle up the ranch with Luke?"

"I'm not married, Todd. And no, Jamie and I haven't made any plans. We're taking things one day at a time."

"Yes, I remember that about you." Todd glanced at his watch. "You never did like to be scheduled into anything, did you, Darce? Always the rebel. Well, times change, and we all get older. You need to think about the future now, just like the rest of us. We can't stay children forever, Darcy. It's time to be an adult." He shifted impatiently.

"Yes, I suppose I should take a leaf out of your book, Todd. You always were the one who planned out our schemes so well. For years I wondered how the rest of us always got caught while you managed to make a getaway. Must have been that planning you did so carefully, right?" Darcy stared up at him, wide-eyed and innocent, watching in satisfaction as his face flushed a deep, dark red.

"Maybe I'll go and see the lawyer, while I'm here. Might as well get on with disposing of things so I can move on. You know, Todd—plan for the future."

"Yes, well…" Todd edged around her carefully. "I suppose I'll be seeing you at the adult fellowship meeting on Saturday night, then."

"Oh, I don't think so. I'm not too sure that I fit in

around here anymore. Do you?" Darcy didn't wait for his words, but turned and walked into the store with Jamie skipping along behind. "Here we go, Jamie. Nice bright crayons, lots of them. How about this?"

She swallowed her anger and frustration and tried to forget the contempt in those silky-smooth tones. She wouldn't be suckered into Todd's petty one-upmanship games—not this time.

She paid for the crayons out of her few remaining funds and, with a smile, handed Jamie the bag. As they walked along the street searching for the lawyer's office, Darcy focused on the future. Her future. One far away from here.

Her mind was so intent on her mission that she didn't even see Luke heading toward them until she bumped right into him.

"Darcy? I didn't know you were coming into town today. I could have given you a lift after I finished the chores." Luke carefully set her away from him with a grin. When she didn't return it, he stood on the curb frowning. "Is everything all right?"

"No," she told him through clenched teeth. "Everything is not all right. I feel like I'm making a spectacle of myself standing here, even *being* here, in this one-horse town!"

"How did you get into town?" He picked up Jamie's mittens and handed them back to the child.

"Clarice came in for her ladies' meeting, and I thought maybe I could get some business done. The lawyer's offices have moved." She glanced around. "A lot seems to have changed in Raven's Rest."

"I did tell you that, remember?" His face creased

in that grin that lifted the corners of his eyes. Darcy couldn't help but smile back.

"Yes, you did. Thanks. And I told you that a lot had stayed the same, too." She spared a glance over her shoulder to check for Mr. Spiggot's presence. "I was also right. Now, if you can just tell me where Mr. Pettigrew's office is currently located, I can go see him. I assume he is still my parents' lawyer?"

"Hey, Lucas! Who's the babe? Pretty cool!" A pair of teenaged boys winked at Luke as they gazed at Darcy.

"Randy. Caleb. No school today?" Luke was cool but friendly, his fingers tightening fractionally on Darcy's elbow.

"Yeah, there's school. There's always school." Caleb, at least, wasn't intimidated by Luke's warning glance. "You gonna introduce us, man?"

"This is Darcy Simms. And her son, Jamie."

"You're kidding? Martha's long-lost daughter? Pleased to meet you!" Caleb shook her hand as if he'd waited a lifetime, and would have kept on except that Darcy finally pulled her stiffened fingers away.

"All right! So you did it, eh, Luke? Lester'd be happy as a clam that you brought her back."

"You knew my parents?" Darcy was stunned at the looks on the faces of these two less-than-handsome youths. Neither one seemed exactly clean. Their stringy long hair, ragged jeans and gold earrings were about as acceptable in stodgy old Raven's Rest as leaving your garbage on the street.

"Sure we knew 'em," Randy told her. "We spent more hours out at their place than anybody else's in town.

Lester was helping us build a stock car. It must still be there." He looked to Luke for confirmation.

"And your mom was the best listener we ever had. She's the one who got me to talk to my dad about building the car. I don't think he would have coughed up that cash except that Martha got Lester to match my dad, dollar for dollar."

Darcy couldn't believe it. They were talking about *her* parents? The Martha and Lester Simms who had refused to take her to the local fair because it might corrupt her?

"How could you leave such a great place?" Randy wanted to know. "If I had parents like that, I'd stay home all the time!"

"Yeah, me, too. You didn't even write at Christmas. Martha told me one day when I was sitting with her. She felt bad about that." Caleb's eyes were filled with curiosity.

"They weren't always like that," Darcy burst out, unable to listen to any more of this. "I had perfectly good reasons for leaving home, you know. And my parents were two of the best." Darcy clamped her lips closed.

She shouldn't have said it. She should have shut up about the past, kept it bottled up inside rather than spilling out the pain of her childhood all over these kids. They didn't need to have their memories tainted with her ugly past.

"I'm sorry, boys." Luke broke into the conversation. "Darcy hasn't been back all that long and she just found out recently that her mom and dad passed away. Maybe you could talk to her about it all another day."

"Sure, man." Randy frowned at her. "I didn't mean to upset you. Sometimes people say things that hurt other people and they don't even realize it. I'm sorry if that's what we've done."

"It's all right. It's not your fault. I shouldn't have said anything." Darcy clutched Jamie's hand a little more tightly and stepped off the curb. "Goodbye."

Luke stayed behind talking quietly to Randy and Caleb.

Darcy didn't know what they said, but she could feel the scrutiny of their eyes from a block away, where she stopped to catch her breath. Miraculously, Percy Pettigrew's office was right in front of her. Darcy shoved the door open and went inside, pulling Jamie along.

"Hi, I'm Darcy Simms. I wonder if I could speak to Mr. Pettigrew. I believe he was the lawyer for my parents' estate."

"Darcy Simms, as I live and breathe!" A bustling woman of about fifty-five whipped out from behind the desk and rushed forward. "How are you, dear?" she asked, enveloping Darcy in a perfumed hug. "You've certainly lost weight since high school."

"Uh, yes. I suppose so." Darcy studied the stylish blonde for several moments. No enlightenment came. "I'm sorry, I..."

"You don't remember me?" The blonde laughed in a twitter that set her dangling earrings bouncing against her cheeks. "Of course you don't. I myself weighed a lot more in those not-so-happy days. And of course, I was a brunette. I'm Mary Pickens, Darcy."

She couldn't help it. Darcy stared at the woman who

had once embarrassed her so thoroughly that she had doubted she would ever live through it all.

"Hello," she managed in a choked voice.

"It's all right." Mary smiled. "I know I've changed quite a lot. Good thing, too. I was pretty pathetic before."

Darcy didn't know what to say so she kept quiet, waiting for the slam she knew would come. Mary had never chosen her words with regard to the other person. Just one more thing that hadn't changed.

"Is this your son?" Mary asked, glancing down at Jamie. "He's almost the same age as Annette's Jordan. Do you remember Annette?"

Who could forget the bossy manipulative Annette? Darcy wanted to demand.

"No, I see you don't." Mary sighed. "I wish some of us could forget the Annette from the past. She could use a little forgiveness."

"Is she ill?" Darcy asked perfunctorily, not really wanting to know how the town's spoiled brat was faring.

"No, she's healthy enough. She's just trying to sort out some problems in her life and it's not easy. I should know. I helped create some of them by forcing her to be someone she isn't. Please sit down, Darcy."

They sat in the pretty plum chairs. Mary handed Jamie a coloring book, and he took out his new crayons, immediately engrossed in the cartoon characters.

"You know, I've waited such a long time to do this," Mary murmured, tears forming at the corners of her eyes. "I should have the words memorized."

"Waited to do what?" Darcy stared at the woman. What was this all about?

"I've been wanting to apologize to you. For saying those things after the prom that year. It was none of my business and I should never have listened to gossip. I wanted Josiah for my Annette, you see. He was the best-looking boy in your group, and Annette claimed she was in love with him." Mary sighed.

"I got myself all worked up when the two of you started dating, and that night I'm afraid I lashed out. If I could take those horrible words back, Darcy, I would. Please believe me."

Time rolled back and it was six years ago... Josiah Pringle loved her and she was the luckiest girl in the world. They'd spent every dance holding each other, relishing the special time together.

Until Mary Pickens had ruined everything by telling the whole gymnasium that she had seen Darcy and Josiah necking on Lookout Point. Those awful, hateful words had stripped Darcy of every bit of joy, and left her standing, empty and lost, as her school chums looked on.

Her parents had been horrified as they'd driven her home, refusing to listen to anything she tried to say. Thanks to Mary Pickens, Darcy's reputation as the town bad girl had solidified in everyone's minds, but especially in her parents' minds.

"Can you ever forgive me?" Mary's pale green eyes were full of tears. "I know my words were what sent you down the path to self-destruction. I was the one who tore you apart. I could see how much you loved that kid, yet I went ahead and did it anyway—took away the most wonderful thing in your young life. I'm sorry, Darcy. More sorry than I can ever say."

"It doesn't matter," Darcy mumbled, clenching her purse in her hands as she stared at her feet. "It's in the past."

"It matters to me. I needed to apologize. I told your parents what I'd done, too. Last year. I needed to clear my conscience."

"You told them that you'd made it all up? That Josiah and I weren't anywhere near Lookout Point that night?" Darcy frowned. "What did they say?"

"Not much. They thanked me for telling them and said they'd have to pray for forgiveness themselves." She shrugged. "I'm sorry I didn't do it years ago. My only explanation is that I wanted the best for Annette. I guess every mother does."

"You'd think so, wouldn't you?" Darcy stared down at Jamie's glossy bright head. How much, she wondered idly, would Martha have been willing to forgive, knowing that Jamie was on the way six months later? And that he was a product of exactly the type of scene Mary had described to the entire town?

"So were you needing something specific?" Mary's face was a question. "I know you aren't here to see little old me."

"Actually, it's really nice to see you again." And to know that not everything around this town has stayed the same, Darcy added mentally. "But I was hoping to see Mr. Pettigrew. I want to get some of the details about the ranch sorted out. I'm sure Luke and Clarice would like to move on with their lives also."

"Move on?" Mary had a strange look on her face.

"Oh, you mean figure out how to handle things from hereon in? Yes, I can see that you would need to set that up. But I'm afraid Percy's out of the office for a while. He's had some heart trouble and is in Denver right now. I'm not sure just when he'll be back."

"I'm sorry to hear that. I hope it's not serious." Darcy felt her heart sink to her shoes. So, no quick flight. She was going to be stuck here for a while, trying to settle everything. Well, at least the ranch was far enough out of town that she wouldn't have to endure all the gossips.

"I don't think so. He always calls these trips his 'tune-ups.' He has a pacemaker, you know, and I guess from time to time it requires adjusting."

"Then perhaps you could give me a call when he returns. I'd really like to get everything ironed out as soon as possible." Darcy gathered up Jamie's crayons and helped him on with his jacket. "It's a little hard to know just what to do next."

"Everything has been set up quite well, Darcy. Please don't worry about a thing. Martha and Lester knew what they wanted, and Percy's very good at making sure it's ironclad. Just have patience." She patted Darcy's hand sympathetically. "So easy to say and so hard to do. Believe me, my dear, I know all about it. But the Lord is in control. He'll deal with it all."

"Thanks, Mary. I'll try not to hassle you too often."

"Nonsense! If you need anything, I'm right here. Just let me know. I'm glad you came back, Darcy. I've missed your wonderful happy spirit." Mary's voice was soft with—what? Compassion? Caring?

Darcy could hardly believe this was the same woman who had caused her so much pain. And yet, if Mary got the chance, wasn't it possible that she might do it all again? It was better for Darcy and Jamie if she didn't give in to her need for a friend. Not in Raven's Rest, at least.

"Thanks again. 'Bye, Mary." As she walked out of the office, and back to the seniors' hall, Darcy shook her head in wonder. It had been a very strange day. But the true test was still to come.

"Hello, you two." Clarice beamed as Darcy led Jamie into the huge room. Every elderly woman in the town was there and every one of their nosy probing eyes focused on her.

"Hi, Clarice. I'm sorry. I thought you would be finished." Darcy tried to ignore the curious stares and barely controlled herself from hiding Jamie's scared face in the folds of her jacket.

"Almost done. Deciding on a project. I vote for the boxes." She leaned over toward Darcy, who'd seated herself on a hard wooden chair nearby. "Those boxes. Some kind of purse, they call it. Never remember."

"It's *Samaritan's Purse*," Edilia Weatherby sighed. "I've told you three times. And it's a very worthwhile Christmas gift idea for children who are needy."

"It sounds lovely," Darcy murmured, peering into the display box with interest. There was an assortment of pencils and erasers, a writing pad, some toothpaste, a roll of hard candies and three windup toys. "What ages are they for?"

"You can choose 'em," Clarice was muttering as she gathered up several of the boxes into her arms. "If you don't want to do it, I'll send these myself."

"Now, Clarice," Harriet Heppworth chided. "We

didn't say we didn't *want* to do them. We haven't really decided. We have to take a vote. All in favor?" About fifteen of the twenty-five hands went up.

"Carried," Clarice announced in smug satisfaction. "Move adjournment."

"Really, Clarice! Must you rush us so? We want to have coffee yet, you know." Edilia preened. "I brought a cheesecake that's simply to die for—triple chocolate," she announced proudly.

"Can't eat chocolate. Too rich. Sure wouldn't die for it!" Clarice dropped the boxes into a cavernous bag she'd produced. "Coffee's okay, though."

"Do I take it we're adjourned then?" Harriet glanced from one nodding head to the next. "I do wish we could do things in an orderly fashion, ladies. Next meeting in two weeks." She smacked the homemade gavel against the table and watched morosely as the ladies who were serving shuffled over to the counter.

Darcy took it all in with a smile as she served some cake to Jamie and helped herself. She'd seen the same thing hundreds of times when her mother had been alive and she'd called in after school. The ladies of the community had good hearts for the needy souls who lived outside Raven's Rest. It was the ones inside the town boundaries that they had problems with.

"Darcy! How are you, dear? And this is your son, is it? He looks just like Jo—"

"Esther! Come and serve the tea."

"How old is the boy, Darcy?"

"He's four and his name is Jamie." As I'm sure you already know, she added mentally. "He'll be five in January." She said it stiffly, scrutinizing the faces carefully.

"I expect it will be good for the child to be around Luke," Harriet murmured with a sly smile. "He's already had some practice at fathering, and I'm sure little Jamie here could do worse. Him being without a father and all."

"Luke needs a new family," Olivia Hernsburg added, nodding thoughtfully. "He's been alone long enough now. It's time for him to look to the future. Especially with the ranch and all."

There was a long drawn-out silence then that made Darcy stare. It was as if everyone were holding their breaths, waiting for her to say something. But what could she say? She had no idea what they were talking about.

"I expect that's why you sent Luke to fetch her, isn't it, Clarice? Kind of kills two birds with one stone, if you know what I mean?" Edilia winked at everyone in general.

"Stuff's okay," Clarice butted in, holding her fork aloft from the piece of cheesecake she was tasting. "Bit too much salt, though."

"As if you'd know. You never bake anything to bring to these meetings. It's always from the bakery!" Edilia smirked nastily, and Darcy knew she didn't like the comment about her prize cheesecake. But in actual fact, Darcy agreed with Clarice. There *was* too much salt. And the chocolate was grainy.

"Bringing something next time," Clarice muttered, shoving away the rich, almost untouched dessert.

"Like what?"

"Don't know yet. Whatever strikes my fancy." Clarice brazenly outstared them all, and Darcy wanted to cheer her on.

"You're just trying to get them off the track, Clarice," Esther chirped into the conversation. "And it won't work. I know why she's so suddenly back here, rubbing our noses in her past. Darcy doesn't have a father for her child. You know it as well as anyone in this room. If she's telling the truth now, she was pregnant when she left here." Esther smoothed down her coiffed silver hair with a graceful hand that glittered with rings. Her eyes were hard with disdain.

"But I can hardly imagine that Luke Lassiter is prepared to take another man's leavings just to get his hands on all of that ranch. That seems a bit too much of a sacrifice, even for a kindly man like him."

Darcy had always wondered what nonplused meant. As the blood drained from her face and twenty-five nosey parkers stared at her, she suddenly knew. She couldn't believe anyone had actually said the words out loud. Even here in Raven's Rest, people usually still pretended to have manners.

Thousands of thoughts poured through Darcy's mind, and none of them, not one, was kind. Fury boiled like acid in her veins, eating her up with anger and indignation. How dare they!

"I didn't come back to find a father for Jamie, if that's what you're implying, Mrs. Fairfield. And I highly doubt that Luke suddenly feels the need for a family to replace the one he lost." She swallowed her tears and strove to strengthen her voice, determined that none of these vicious old biddies would see her cry.

"In fact, there is really only one reason why I would come back to this hotbed of gossip and discontent, where people spread scandal for the fun of it." She bundled up Jamie, wiped his face on a napkin, and slipped on her own jacket, her eyes meeting Clarice's. Luke's elderly aunt smiled and nodded approvingly, and Darcy straightened as a rush of courage bolstered her.

"I came back because my parents died and I owed it to them to see that their last wishes are carried out. But I don't owe anything to you. Neither does my son." She snatched up the purse that Clarice had given her and marched across the room.

"Neither does Luke," she snapped and swung out the door.

Behind her, Clarice was speaking. Darcy stopped just long enough to hear her words to the startled ladies who sat with their mouths hanging open.

"God has forgiven some of you even *your* terrible sins," Clarice said in a clear clipped voice that conveyed her displeasure. "Ought to think about that." There was a dearth of noise in the hall as she stomped across the room, boxes in tow.

"Idle tongues—" she muttered, tossing everything into the trunk and slamming it closed. Her eyes sparkled like black bits of onyx as they met Darcy's. "—Most dangerous member in the whole human body. Bad news in this town."

Darcy couldn't stop the laugh that burst from her throat as they drove away.

Chapter Five

Luke smiled as he watched Darcy chase a squealing Jamie through the drifts of snow. Just this once he allowed himself to enjoy the scene without harking back to the past. Maybe he really was healing. Maybe he *would* be able to face life without his family beside him. But he would never forget them.

"Nice," Clarice murmured from behind him. "'Bout time the girl laughed. Far too serious."

"Yes, she is," Luke agreed, sipping his afternoon coffee. "And thank you for making her feel welcome. It took a couple of weeks but she's thawing."

"She's hurting." Clarice stated the fact in a loud clear voice. "Runs herself ragged to stop thinking. Don't expect she'll stay around long."

"She's going to have to stay a little longer. Percy's stay in Denver has been extended. I don't know if it's his heart." Luke's glance moved back to the window. "She won't like it."

"Needs to get involved in something away from here." Clarice studied him seriously. "Got any ideas?"

Luke shook his head. "I tried to suggest the local ladies'

group or maybe helping out with the choir, but she blew me off with some drivel about spending more time with Jamie. As if she doesn't spend all day with him now."

"Needs time with him," Clarice remarked sagely, nodding her gray head. "Probably missed a lot of his babyhood, what with working and all. I could give Lester Simms a good tongue-lashing right about now!"

Luke leaned back from her waving fingers. Aunt Clarice in this mood was not to be trifled with. Still, he'd like to know what she was talking about. "Why?" He asked it carefully.

"Man was a niddling," she told him shortly.

"A what?" He frowned, trying to remember if he'd heard this particular descriptive before.

"A niddling. Pay attention, boy. Don't you know the English language?" She took a huge gulp of coffee. "Means he was a fool not to see the potential in that girl."

"Oh." Luke decided to look the word up later, once Clarice went to bed. He was pretty sure he wouldn't find it in any dictionary. Clarice's words often weren't. "Maybe—" he shrugged, unwilling to get into that discussion again "—but that was then and this is now. What are we going to do about it?"

"Get her busy, involved with somebody besides those old tabbies that harangued her last week," Clarice informed him as she marched to the door to call the others in. "Less time to dwell on the past, more time to think about the future."

And so it was that Luke found himself reading stories to Jamie in front of the fire that night while Clarice and Darcy buried themselves in the basement.

"Need your help," Clarice mumbled as she moved past the cold storage room with its jars of canned preserves safely stowed away. She opened the door at the end of the hall and flicked on a light, illuminating a small room lined with plastic. A huge sturdy workroom stood at one end, and above it shelves full of dried or drying pottery pieces.

"You're a potter?" Darcy gaped in amazement. Clay vessels of every shape and description sat on the shelves, on the tables, even on the floor. "I didn't realize."

"Lots don't." Clarice donned a big denim apron. "I have a class with the third graders tomorrow, and I figured you could help."

"Me? I don't know anything about pottery!" Darcy protested, running a curious finger down the smooth, wet clay that Clarice uncovered.

"You can learn, can't you?" Clarice pulled a wire from her pocket. She hung onto the two wooden ends and pulled the hair-thin wire through the clay in a deft motion that left a piece free at the top.

"I don't know." Darcy pulled off a small piece from the larger hunk and squeezed gently. "I don't think I'm the type. I never did well in art class."

"Clay isn't just a piece of delicate white paper that you have to throw out if you mess up," Clarice snorted inelegantly. "It's clay. If you don't like what you've made, you squash it up and start again. Nothing as forgiving as clay. 'Cept maybe the Lord." She seemed to think about that for a moment.

"What are you going to demonstrate?" Darcy watched as the other woman kneaded the huge lump of clay into a sort of fat cone shape with the swift action of her hands. "It looks like you're working bread dough."

"Same idea," Clarice nodded. "Have to get the air bubbles out." Apparently she wasn't satisfied that they were all gone, for she lifted the great grayish hunk in both of her small hands and slammed the mass onto the table. "Good. Now, flatten it."

Darcy wasn't sure whether the woman was talking to herself or to her assistant, so she stayed where she was and watched. In a matter of moments Clarice had a section of the clay flattened out on the table and was rolling an old wooden rolling pin over it.

"Your parents let me set this studio up down here after Luke and I moved in," she told Darcy. "I've been working with this stuff for so long, I just couldn't give it up now."

"Oh." There had been so many surprises lately that Darcy let this one go. "Why are there plastic sheets covering the walls?" Darcy studied the room curiously. "It looks like there's clay on them, but you couldn't make that much mess."

Clarice let out a cackle of mirth, her widow's peak giving her a wicked, witchlike look in the glaring overhead light. "You think not? Missy, when I get my wheel going, there's clay flying all over the place." She flipped the sheet of clay over as deftly as Darcy's mother had once flipped a pie crust.

"I thought of showing them how to make a box," she explained as her fingers moved nimbly. "The girls could make theirs into gifts for Christmas if they wanted. The boys, too. Or they could build coil pots." As she spoke, Clarice rolled out long rolls of clay and began laying them on the slab with a dab of water along the joining edge. Within seconds, she had the beginnings of a large box.

"Why don't you just flatten more clay and cut out the sides? It would sure be quicker."

"Quicker isn't necessarily better when you're working with clay." Clarice grunted as she worked. "Kind of like life, too, I guess. Patience is a virtue."

"You mean you can't do it?" Darcy curiously studied the rapidly building box.

"Sure you can do it. But you have to wait until the sides are dry enough to stand up by themselves and not too dry so that they'll crack. Touchy business. Too difficult for twenty-five third graders to tackle all at once." She glanced up to wink at Darcy. "Always reminds me of the way God has to carefully work in our lives or we get toppled because we're not prepared for His mighty touch."

"Can I try coiling something?" Clarice motioned to the rolls of clay, and Darcy picked one up, twirling it carefully around her finger. "What do I do?"

"Dip your finger in the water and then moisten the two seams," Clarice explained as she worked. "Push them together a little bit, too. Otherwise you end up with a perfectly shaped pile of coils that usually comes apart."

"Are you supposed to preserve the shape of the coils or make it look smooth, so you can't tell where the joins are?" Darcy frowned at the tilting form in front of her.

"You are the potter, Darcy. You have to make your own choices and then work to carry them out." Clarice stopped working, her green eyes shining. Her words were soft but full of meaning as she stared at Darcy. "It's exactly the same as life. You get a picture of what you want your life to be about and then you work to create that."

Darcy thought about it while she fiddled with her pot, placing coil upon coil. Clarice was mostly silent and Darcy found the words that she'd just said rolling around her brain.

Get a picture of what you want your life to be about...

Well, she'd had that for a long time, she decided, adding more water to the clay and smoothing away the bumps of each coil until the outside of the pot was smooth and glossy. She wanted her life to be about love and caring—the things she had missed out on.

"So how are you going to make the picture happen?" Clarice's voice abruptly broke the spell, and Darcy jerked, knocking over her pot. "Oh, sorry," the other woman muttered, reaching over to try to right it.

"It won't hold its shape now," Darcy muttered in frustration, her fingers clumsy against the wet, slippery surface.

"Too much water. Too much of anything weakens a person just like it does a pot. Too much trouble, a body can't abide it. Not enough and he gets complacent." Clarice took out her wire. "Just like a pot. Too much water and it sags away into nothingness." With a flick of her wrist, she cut through the pot from top to bottom leaving two halves standing on the table.

"Why did you do that?" Darcy asked, more curious than angry at the ruination of her creation.

"A good potter wants his work to look just as good inside as it does outside," Clarice muttered, pointing one bony finger at the obvious lumps and bumps. "It would have leaked here eventually," she explained. "Or fallen apart in the kiln. It's not strong enough, not connected with the rest."

"And I suppose you're going to say that it's the same with life," Darcy muttered in frustration, squeezing the squishy mess between her fingers. "If people don't stay connected, we lose our solidarity." She looked at Clarice defiantly. "Right?"

"Not just my opinion, either," Clarice told her happily. "Says so in The Book." She scooped up Darcy's sloppy mess and massaged it in with her own leftover bits.

"If it's no good for anything, why don't you just throw it out?" Darcy washed her hands in the big sink, grateful for the warm flow of water after the cool clay.

"Hardly ever throw clay out," Clarice informed her. "Mix it in with some more, let it dry, add some water. Whatever it needs, it can usually be used again. It's only after you fire it that clay can't be changed."

"What about when it's dried out? Say someone neglected it, left it out in the elements?" Darcy challenged her deliberately, meeting that all-knowing look. "What about then?"

"It can still be used. But it's got to go through a lot of painful processes first to make it serviceable again." She stopped what she was doing and met Darcy's stare head-on. Darcy knew that, once again, she wasn't talking just about the clay.

"And I suppose you think that's what I have to do. Mull over the past some more."

"Nope." Clarice covered her box with a bit of plastic and began straightening the counter.

"Then what *do* you think?" Darcy prodded, growing irritated with the conversation.

"Think you've thought enough about the past. Time to get on with your life. Meet it on the chin and keep going."

"And you think I should do this how? By immediately joining a bunch of gossiping ladies' groups? As if they'd let me! Or maybe I should go to church on Sunday and sit in the front row so I could beg everyone's forgiveness for not being here when my parents died." Darcy stomped upstairs behind the older woman and followed her into the kitchen, her anger growing. "I think you're forgetting just who's in the wrong here."

"Does it really matter anymore?" Clarice poured out two cups of coffee and set them down on the table, adding a plate of cookies before she dropped down on a chair. "What difference does it make?" she asked in a kind voice. "The past is past, done, over with. You can't change it. God doesn't expect you to."

Darcy frowned at the repeated reference to some heavenly interest in her mundane life. "So what does He expect?"

"He expects you to use this new opportunity He's given you." Clarice's black eyes shone back at her. "He expects you to deal with the past and move on. Or are you going to let it poison your mind forever?"

"My mind isn't poisoned," Darcy hotly denied. "But I can't just ignore everything that happened!" She gestured at the familiar room. "Being here, in this house, reminds me of it all over again."

"I imagine it does. So face it," Clarice challenged. "Look it square in the eye and say, 'Yes, I got a rough deal. Some of it I deserved, and some of it I didn't. But it's over now and I'm moving on.' Can you do that?" The words were harsh, but her voice was soft and full of compassion.

"You think I deserved to be treated the way I was?" Darcy demanded, her cheeks warm with anger. She couldn't believe it. Clarice was just like everyone else in this hick town, blaming her for all the problems. It was the past all over again.

"Oh, Darcy!" The bony hand reached across to enfold hers, squeezing gently when Darcy would have pulled away. "I'm not saying you should have been treated the way you were. And I'm not denying that this treatment caused a lot of problems in your life. What I am saying is that we humans are often the authors of our own misfortune. Some of the things you did added to your problems. Am I right?"

In all fairness, Darcy knew she couldn't deny it. She had accepted everyone else's opinion of her and played on that because she had half believed it herself.

"The wild parties, staying out so late, playing those rather nasty tricks—didn't they all contribute to the reputation you say you didn't deserve?"

"I wanted to have friends," Darcy muttered, loath to recall those painful years. "I just wanted to fit in, to belong."

"And the troublemakers were the only ones who let you." Clarice nodded. "I know. But you see, it's just a vicious circle, like a hamster on one of those wheels. They did this so you did that and then they did this.

Around and around and around. The same territory. Never goes anywhere. Never makes any progress." She clapped Darcy on the shoulder.

"You're not a hamster, my dear. And it's time to get out of the rut."

"How?" It sounded wonderful; it would be great to get rid of this awful burden of guilt and anger. But Darcy had no idea how one accomplished that.

"Just step off," Clarice asserted. "Refuse to let yourself fall into the rut and dwell on the past again except to use it to figure out how to make the future better. Otherwise, you'll just get more and more bitter. And Jamie doesn't want a bitter mother."

"Jamie! Gosh, I forgot all about him for a moment." Darcy jumped up and hurried toward the door.

"He'll be fine. Luke knows how to handle children. Used to have one of his own."

The words stopped Darcy dead in her tracks. Now she'd find out more about the mysterious man who was always in the background, smoothing her way. She whirled around and peered at the older woman. "He's divorced?" she whispered.

"No." Clarice stared at her coffee cup, her face losing all of its angularity. "He's a widower. Lost his wife and daughter in a house fire three years ago. Your parents saved his life."

When it was clear that Clarice would say no more, Darcy crept from the room, her head whirling with what she'd just learned. The scars on his neck, she remembered. How did he get them? And what did Clarice mean that her parents had "saved" his life? Was that why he was here, living on this farm? Had Luke

Lassiter become the son that Martha and Lester Simms had always wanted?

"Mommy, look!" Jamie's high-pitched voice penetrated her foggy brain, and Darcy glanced into the living room to find her son seated beside the ranch foreman; a huge book rested on their laps.

"Mister Luke is teaching me about cows and stuff." He beamed up at her, his little face shining with happiness. "This is a steer," he told her carefully, one chubby finger pointing to the photograph. "It's like the daddy. And this is a cow. She's the mommy."

"Yes, darling," she murmured. "But it's time for bed now. You'll have to talk more about ranching with Luke tomorrow." She held out her hand.

"But I can't go, Mommy. Mister Luke said he'd read me the story about all the animals going on a big boat." Jamie's earnest little face peered upward. "It's about when there was a flood," he whispered, eyes wide as saucers.

"Perhaps another time," Darcy murmured, helping him off the old worn sofa. "I'm sure Luke is busy with other things."

"Not too busy to read that," Luke murmured. "Would it be all right if I came up after he got into bed? I promise, I won't keep him up long."

He must miss the little nighttime rituals, Darcy thought, staring into those warm brown eyes. She couldn't imagine how hard it must be for him. How hard it would be for her to go on if anything ever happened to Jamie! Surely she couldn't deny Luke this small comfort.

"All right," she agreed at last. "But just for ten minutes. It's already way past your bedtime."

"I know," Jamie agreed, walking along beside her and into his room. "And there's a lot of work to do on a ranch. You have to get up really, really early." He stood still while she tugged off his T-shirt and jeans, his blue eyes pensive. "I like it here," he declared at last.

"You don't mind staying in this room all by yourself?" With a pang of regret for the past, Darcy glanced around the space that had once been hers. The rock star posters were gone, of course. And the navy walls she'd insisted on had been painted over with a clean ivory. But there, against the closet, along the baseboards, she could still see the indentations of heel marks put there in frustration over a world that didn't give. There were too many memories, and Darcy concentrated on slipping on Jamie's pajamas.

"Nope, I like it in here." Jamie shook his tousled brown head firmly. "'Sides, Mister Luke is right over there." He pointed across the hall. "An' he promised he'd make sure no bad people came. I don't like bad people." A frown marred the smooth forehead. "I wish there was some kids, though. New York had lots of kids to play with. 'Cept Jeffrey Peterson. I hate Jeffrey Peterson!"

"Jamie," she scolded, "we don't 'hate' people."

"You do. I heard you on the airplane. You told Mister Luke that you hated this place and everybody in it. I dunno why." He glanced around. "I like it. It's nice and quiet. There's no bad men here, are there, Mommy? I don't like bad men."

Trapped in the web of her own words, Darcy searched

for an explanation. "Listen, sweetie. I didn't really mean that I hated *everybody*. I was just upset."

"Why?" His blue eyes were quizzical. "Mister Luke said this used to be your home. Didn't you want to come home no more?"

"Anymore. And no, honey. I didn't. I felt like nobody loved me or cared about me when I lived here, Jamie. I got into trouble, and people got mad at me and that made it worse." She took a deep breath. "I felt like I was all alone."

"But nobody's alone." Jamie patted her hand consolingly. "Everybody has God watching them. God loves you, Mommy. Me, too!" He threw his arms around her neck and hugged for all he was worth, and Darcy hugged him back, tears rolling down her cheeks.

"I love you too, darling. Very much." She let him pull away a bit and met his puzzled stare.

"Why are you crying? Do you have a hurt?" He searched her face seriously. "I could kiss it better, Mommy."

"You already have," she whispered, hugging him close once more. "You're the best medicine in the world."

"An' I don't taste yucky, neither." Jamie grinned happily. "Do I brush my teeth now, or after Mister Luke reads the story?"

"Oh, now I think." Darcy told herself to regain some control. Her son wasn't going to have an emotional, out-of-control mother to look back on. "Come on, I'll watch. Be sure you do the back ones."

Ten minutes later Jamie was tucked up in bed, face shining, eyes huge with anticipation. "I'm ready, Mister

Luke!" he called out. His smile grew when Luke stepped through the door.

"Are you sure it's all right?" Luke asked, glancing at Darcy for confirmation.

"*I'm* sure," Jamie answered for both of them. "Smell my hands." He held them up as Luke obediently bent over and sniffed the small fingers. "They smell like flowers. That's how you know I washed with soap and water. If you can't smell the flowers, you didn't wash," he quoted, grinning at Darcy. "Right, Mom?"

"Right, Love Bug. Into bed now."

Seconds later Luke launched into his story of Noah and the ark as Darcy listened from the hard-backed maple chair that matched her desk. She'd forgotten many of the details that Luke elaborated upon. Like a sponge, Jamie soaked in the old Bible story. Luke was a wonderful storyteller, and the boy's face glowed with amazement.

"Two of *everything?*" He frowned at Luke's nod. "But wouldn't the snakes eat the birds and the tigers gobble up the giraffes?" Jamie loved animals, and Darcy had read him thousands of books over the years. The little boy prided himself on knowing the eating habits of many of them.

"Well, you see, God had everything arranged, and I think He must have had a plan to prevent that. He wanted a mommy and a daddy of every kind of animal so that after they got out of the ark, they could have lots of babies together. Anyway, He kept His eye on them in that ark just like He does now, and helped Noah make sure that each one got enough to eat and drink."

"Does God wear glasses?" Jamie stared innocently up at Luke.

"I don't think He needs them," Luke answered thoughtfully. "Why?" There was a twinkle in his eye that Darcy didn't miss.

"You keep saying He kept his *eye* on them," Jamie explained patiently. "I guess He must have pretty big eyes to see everything like that. I can't understand about eyes that big."

"That's right, son. People can't understand God. Not even if they try very hard. The Bible says He's unfathomable. That's a big word that means we can't imagine what He is like."

"Why?"

"Because we don't have anything to compare God with. God just is. He's big and great and powerful. He sees everything and knows everything."

"Oh." Jamie appeared to be thinking that over, so Luke continued on with the story.

Darcy sat listening, her mind on those Sunday School sessions she had attended so long ago. She'd heard the stories a hundred times, knew some of them off by heart, and yet they'd never made as much sense as they did right now with Luke's explanation.

"But why did all the people do the wrong things?" Jamie wanted to know.

"Everybody does wrong sometimes, son. There's no way we can help it because we're human. God made us and He knows that we're going to goof up." Darcy saw the tall man edge the quilt up a little higher on the bed, and smiled when Jamie wiggled out.

"But He doesn't care, right?"

"Oh, He cares all right, Jamie. Very much. And He understands. But He wants us to learn from our mistakes so we can get better at doing what He wants." Luke brushed the tousled curls back off the boy's face. "It's the same as if you took something from Aunt Clarice and then went and told her you were sorry. I'm sure she'd tell you she forgives you. But if you did the same thing tomorrow and then again the next day, I'm sure she would wonder if you were *really* sorry, or if you were just saying the words without meaning them."

"Uh-huh." Jamie's lids were drooping down, and Darcy rose from her chair.

"I think it's time you went to sleep, sunshine," she murmured, bending down to tuck him in once more. "Morning is going to come pretty early you know." She waited while Luke accepted another hug, and then took his place on the bed, snuggling her little boy in her arms. "Good night, Love Bug."

"She just calls me that—" Jamie yawned up at Luke "—I'm not really a bug. Good night, Mommy. I love you."

"I love you, too, sweetheart. Very much. Sweet dreams," Darcy whispered, watching until the soft deep breaths of sleep told her that Jamie was resting in dream world. She clicked off the lamp and slipped out the door, checking first that his night-light was on.

"He's a wonderful little boy," Luke murmured as he followed her down the stairs. "Full of love and so ready to give it out. I can't imagine how you've managed to do such a wonderful job raising him all by yourself and in such difficult circumstances."

"I had help at first," Darcy told him as she cleared

up Jamie's blocks and toys from the living room floor. "I met an old lady named Mrs. Pearse on the train the day I arrived in New York. She needed someone to stay with her so she could continue to live in her house, and I guess I looked pretty healthy. We agreed that I would live in, do the housework and make the meals in return for board and room." Darcy sighed. "She was so kind about my pregnancy, even took me to see a doctor. After I had Jamie, she insisted he and I remain with her. She loved him like a grandmother, and he adored her. I was able to spend the first fifteen months of his life with him."

"What happened then?"

"She died, and I had to go to work. It seems ironic, but I got a job as a nanny. I had to send my own son out to someone else so I could look after this woman's children every day. I stayed there until I could get a job at a day care. That way Jamie was always nearby." Darcy stared out at the snow blowing across the yard and remembered those first years.

"God was certainly there with you, protecting you," Luke murmured.

"Was He?" Darcy laughed bitterly. "I wonder." She thought of the scrimping and saving she'd done, the desperate search for a place to stay when the Pearse family insisted that she move out. "I don't think He even noticed."

"Why do you doubt it, Darcy? He sent someone to watch over you. He gave you a healthy baby and time to bond with him before the world intruded. He was there, watching out especially for you, His child."

"And when the day care was taken over by people who insisted you needed certification to work there?

Where was He then? Or when we got evicted, or when I had to move to keep from being attacked? How about that hole you found me in? Where was He when men stopped me on the street and harassed me and my son? Can you tell me that?" She yelled the words, furious at dredging it all up again.

"He was there, Darcy. All the time, He was there. You just had to call on Him."

"Don't you think I did?" Darcy felt the words explode from her as her fingers clenched into fists. "Don't you think I begged and pleaded for Him to help me find a way out? But it just got worse and worse until I was hanging on by a thread." She shuddered. "Do you know how many times I had to put Jamie to bed hungry because we didn't have anything and I was too afraid to leave my room at night?"

"I know it wasn't easy. And I admire you more than I can say for hanging on."

"Admire me?" She laughed bitterly. "Do you admire the fact that I've walked out of a place knowing I'd never be able to pay the rent I owe? Do you admire my stealing from someone's grocery bag so Jamie could have some milk?" She caught the sob in her throat and swallowed, refusing to give in to the tears.

"I came this close to giving him up for adoption, you know." She shivered at the memory, her voice ragged. "This close." She held up thumb and forefinger, less than an inch apart.

"Why didn't you? It would have been much easier on you." Luke's voice was calm, as if he wasn't the least bit stunned by her revelations. "He might have had a wonderful life with some couple."

"And he might have been miserable, wondering why his mother had abandoned him. Wondering if I didn't love him anymore." Darcy shook her head vehemently. "I wasn't having my child grow up thinking I didn't care about him! Besides—" she made a face "—I'm not known for taking the easy route." Darcy sighed miserably. "I tried to tell myself that it would be the best thing for him if I gave him up for adoption. But I couldn't, I just couldn't walk away and let him go."

"Why not?" Luke stood just three feet away. His eyes were clear and focused on her, waiting for her answer.

Darcy laughed, a hard brittle sound that resounded in the room. "Because I loved him from the moment he was born. I loved watching him look at me with complete and utter faith that I would do the right thing. Jamie never imagined that his mother would leave him alone to face life—"

"Darcy, I didn't mean…"

She ignored his interruption, determined to make him understand that Darcy Simms was not who the good folk of Raven's Rest thought she was. "I couldn't do it," she whispered. "I just couldn't give him away, as if he was something I didn't want. He was the one good thing in my life, and I wasn't going to hand him over without at least trying to be his mother." She sniffed, remembering the wash of feelings as if it were yesterday.

"Jamie loves me. He gives that love freely just because I'm his mother. He doesn't care if I don't always do what everyone else expects. It doesn't matter to him if I bleached my hair in high school, or cheated on a math test, or broke Hettie Arbunson's picture window. He just loves me. How could I hand that over to someone else as if it didn't matter?"

There was silence in the room. Luke must be digesting her past misdeeds, and he must be shocked, Darcy decided sadly. The upright, law-abiding Simms family had failed to control her again. The reprobate daughter was impossible to repair. As the seconds ticked by, she shifted nervously from one foot to the other, gnawing at her bottom lip.

"Darcy?" Luke's voice was full of something. Was it—sympathy? No, not that. He was smiling as if she'd done something wonderful.

"Y-yes," she stammered, afraid to look any deeper into those chocolate-brown eyes. Afraid to believe what she saw there.

"How can you say that you got nothing but pain from life in Raven's Rest? You left with Jamie tucked under your heart. How much more could God have done than give you that precious gift? You wouldn't or couldn't understand His love, so He gave you the kind of love that you *could* understand."

"No." She shook her dark head adamantly. "I didn't love Jamie's father. I never deluded myself that our relationship was about love. Not after the first few minutes anyway. It was about me searching for someone who wanted me for myself, as a person, worthy of loving. And it was about a boy who saw me as an opportunity." Her lips tightened. "And then he dumped me like yesterday's news, just as his mother wanted."

"I'm not talking about that kind of love," Luke told her. "I'm talking about Jamie's kind of love. You made a mistake, trusted where you shouldn't have. We all do that. But out of that mistake came a wonderful little boy."

"That pregnancy was why I had to leave," she explained cooly. "It was the final straw, and my parents were disgusted by me."

"It doesn't matter what they thought, or what you thought they felt. God put you in charge of something so special. He entrusted Jamie to you. And then, far from abandoning you, He stayed right there to smooth the way." Luke shook his head in amazement. "A thousand terrible things could have happened to you and your son, Darcy. Unspeakable things. But you were kept safe, thank God. Secure in His tender care. Jamie told me he even had a personal babysitter that last week in New York."

Luke slowly ambled to the doorway, his eyes shining with a peculiar light as he tugged on his sheepskin jacket. His face was thoughtful as he crammed his Stetson onto his head. "I don't think that's the sign of a God who doesn't care about you, Darcy. I think that's the sign of a God who loves you more than you know."

The house was quiet when Darcy finally went to her room. Clarice had long since retired, and as the old house creaked and groaned in the wind, Darcy thought long and hard about what Luke had said. One by one, she recalled the coincidences that had kept her from becoming one of thousands of street kids who were barely surviving while trapped in the deepest of troubles in the middle of a city that neither knew nor cared about one girl's problems.

Maybe You were there, she conceded, staring at the ceiling. *Maybe You did care about me. But, oh, God,*

*what is going to happen when I go to that school tomor-
row and the rest of the town finds out that Darcy Simms,
local bad girl, is just as rotten and lousy a daughter as
she ever was?*

Chapter Six

"All right class, now let's listen to the next directions."

Darcy watched as the giggling group of kids obediently put down their crafts and watched their teacher. Clarice slowly demonstrated how to put a little slurry—the watery mixture of clay—on each coil before gently joining it to the next one. In the back row, a little girl sat struggling to fit the pieces together.

"Here, honey. You dip your finger like this into the jar and mix it against the clay a little." Darcy hunched down to show the child and found a big pair of gray eyes peering up at her.

"Thank you," the child murmured politely. "Sometimes my hands don't do what I want them to do. Or my feet."

Darcy tried not to glance down at the heavy braces on the child's legs. "What's your name?"

"Ginny. Ginny Jones."

Darcy took a second startled look and chided herself for not realizing it immediately. "Are you Jesse's daughter?" she asked softly, aware of the sudden silence in the room. Clarice and Hilda Ridgely both stared at her.

"Yes. Do you know my daddy?" The child's red curls glowed in the late afternoon sun.

"I used to," Darcy told her. "We weren't in the same grade, but he used to help me with my science projects when I went to school here." She grinned down at the little girl. "I'm afraid I was never very good at science." Or a lot of other things, she almost added.

"Mommy says Daddy is too smart for his own good. And then Daddy says, 'René, you've got to forget the past. I don't want to move away from Raven's Rest with Dad so low.' Then they get all sad and Dad goes outside." Ginny carefully pressed another ring onto her "sculpture."

It was an intimate look into someone's personal life, and Darcy knew she had no business listening. But she did, just the same, curiosity overwhelming her good sense. René Carter had been voted the girl most likely to succeed. Last Darcy recalled, René had been intent on pursuing a scholarship that she'd won at a prestigious fashion design school. Darcy could well imagine that being stuck in this little town hadn't been her first choice. Ginny's obvious physical difficulties would have made life here even more difficult.

A towheaded boy down the row claimed her attention then, and Darcy put the past firmly out of her mind. By the time the bell rang, Clarice and Hilda had managed to organize things so that all the students' work was carefully stored under a big plastic sheet, ready for tomorrow's lesson.

"You have quite a rapport with children." Hilda peered over the tops of her bifocals to study Darcy with the same calculating look she'd used back when Darcy had misbehaved in her class all those years ago. "I don't suppose you've taken any training?" That disapproving look was back in her eyes. Nothing had changed in Miss Ridgely's class.

"No," Darcy admitted dryly. "I didn't have the money to go to school. Actually I never even thought of teaching. But I did enjoy today. Thank you for letting me help."

"My dear girl," Hilda puffed as she lifted a stack of books off a shelf. "In this place we never turn down an offer of help. And you have a natural gift with children. You always did."

Darcy stared at her. "I did?"

"Of course. That's why I asked you to help out the others so often. Surely you haven't forgotten Birdie McBride?"

Darcy searched her memory. "Birdie McBride? I don't think...wait a minute, you mean the little girl who wore those heavy leg things? She'd been in a car accident or something."

"It wasn't a car accident, it was polio. Her parents were missionaries and she contracted it as a baby, which meant she missed a lot of school." Miss Ridgely's dour face almost cracked in its smile. "You handled her better than I ever could have. I always feel pushed to get through the curriculum, and I just couldn't spare the time to go back over things that she should have learned before. But you sat with her, noon hour after noon hour, helping her to read."

The words were a balm on Darcy's aching heart. At least she'd done one thing right in her sojourn here. "But you never said anything," she muttered, frowning at her former teacher. "You never told me that."

"I wanted to. So many times I wanted to stop you and say 'Well done!'"

"Why didn't you?" Darcy asked bitterly. "It would have meant so much to know that I was doing something right in my mixed-up life."

"I tried to. I even called you up several times to suggest some colleges you might want to look into." Hilda shook her head sadly. "But you said you were too busy. Do you remember? I knew you were running with a bad crowd, and I was sure that if only you could get involved in planning the future, you'd forget those ne'er-do-wells and get back on the right track."

"I didn't know. I thought you wanted to bawl me out for something, just like everyone else." Dismay filled her at the missed opportunity. "I was so desperate for somebody to say something nice to me that I think I would have done anything to get some attention."

"But, Darcy," Hilda protested, laying a hand on her shoulder. "Your parents loved you very much. You must know that."

"Yeah, I should have known, shouldn't I?" Darcy refused to get maudlin about the past. She would deal with the here and now. "Anyway, thanks for the afternoon. I actually enjoyed it."

"There's a teacher's aide job that has been open for the past two months. No one seems to want to take it on." Hilda studied Darcy as if assessing her. "It's a good way to find out if that's the work for you. If you're interested, that is."

"But I don't know anything about teaching." Darcy

stared at her. "I've never done anything like that before."

"And never will if you don't try it out," Clarice muttered, coming up behind them. "Get your application in to Hilda. She'll look after the rest."

Sheer panic swept over Darcy. She wasn't ready for this, her mind screamed. She didn't even want to stay in Raven's Rest.

"I…that is, I was hoping to spend more time with Jamie," she managed at last and then quelled a shudder as Hilda's hawklike glance moved over her. "He's my son," she said defensively.

"Job only involves two afternoons a week." Clarice offered the words quietly. "Jamie's lonesome. He might want to go to the preschool and play with other kids on those afternoons."

"Yes, I'll have a talk with the principal, get her to call you. She'll give you the specifics." Hilda grabbed her purse and a pen off the desk. "I have to run now. Staff meeting. Thanks so much, Clarice. And you, too, Darcy. It's nice to see you again."

Darcy followed Clarice out of the school in total bemusement. Hilda hadn't said a word, not a word, about Jamie. Of course she was probably going to mention it in the staff room, telling everyone about the Simms girl. But at least Darcy didn't have to witness it.

Luke and Jamie were waiting outside the school in Luke's big truck.

"Hi!" Jamie leaned out the window, grinning from ear to ear. "We came to get some parts, and Mister Luke said we could stay and have coffee with you." He smiled at Clarice. "I never had coffee before."

"And you're not having any now, either." Darcy grinned as she kissed his cheek and ruffled his already messy hair. "I'm ready to go home."

"Have to get some things first—" Clarice chanted a list of destinations as she searched in her bag for her list "—the general store, the hardware store, the post office... You can go ahead if you like."

"Actually, I think we'd better stop at the grocery store." A picture of the almost-empty fridge flitted through Darcy's mind. "We need some milk, fresh fruit and vegetables for a salad."

"Okay, okay, ladies! But can't we stop for a coffee break first?" Luke's voice chided them plaintively. "I'm starved and cold. We were out mending fences all morning and my feet are numb."

"A bit parched myself," Clarice murmured. "Must be all that talking."

It was probably true, Darcy decided, watching the other woman run her tongue over her lips. She'd never heard Clarice say so much at one time since she'd met her.

They all trooped over to the café and Darcy found herself under Luke's steady gaze. "I'm buying," he told her firmly. "It's my treat."

There was nothing she could say but thank-you, since she had hardly any money. A job would come in really handy right now, she decided, thinking over Hilda's words once more. At least she'd have pocket change.

"I forgot my gloves in the staff room." Darcy gave them a frustrated glance. "You guys go ahead and order. I'll catch up."

She hurried back to the school and rushed inside,

heading for Hilda's room. But there were voices inside, and she stopped in her tracks at the familiar grumbling tones.

"I'm not having that *tramp* come into this school and work with impressionable children."

There was no mistaking the biting tones of her arch-enemy Annette Pickens.

"She's not a fallen woman," Hilda replied. "She made a mistake, and that was nearly *six years* ago! I daresay, we've all made a few of those—you included. And somebody managed to forgive us."

"Maybe. Still, she sails in here as if she's the queen of the castle, ready to show all us peasants how lucky we are to have us among her subjects. Well, I'm not giving her the job. Besides, she doesn't have any qualifications." Annette sounded triumphant over that, and Darcy almost laughed at the ridiculousness of it all. Surely after all these years, Annette wasn't still jealous?

"We need an aide, Annette. And Darcy Simms would make an excellent one. She's always done exceptionally well at teaching the younger children. Obviously that's carried over into her adult life. If you won't at least take her application and interview her, I'll speak to Roger about last Thursday."

"Hilda, that's blackmail! You can't tell him I went out with Lenny Turbelo for dinner on Monday! He'll kill me!"

Darcy flushed at this personal knowledge of Annette's private affairs, wishing she'd never stopped, but unable to walk away.

"Maybe he will. Or maybe you two will have to sit down and make some compromises. It's ridiculous the way you keep battling each other for the upper hand in this relationship. Why don't you try working together by setting some common goals? That's the way a marriage is supposed to work."

"As if you know anything about marriage," Annette replied. "You've never been married, so how would you know?"

"No, I haven't been married. But I've seen a lot of failed marriages, and I *do* know that the wrong thing to do when you're having problems is make your husband think you're two-timing him."

There was the scraping of a chair, and Darcy held her breath as she backed carefully away from the door. Then she turned, racing down the hall and back out the door she'd entered only moments ago.

Of all the hateful people to run into, Annette was just about the absolute worst. She'd hated the fact that Josiah and Darcy had grown so close in high school, and she'd never forgiven Darcy for taking him away from her. And now she was going to try to prevent Darcy from taking this job as an aide?

"Over my dead body, Annette." She muttered the words to herself, stomping through the snow to the café. "I *want* that job, I *deserve* that job—and I'm going to *have* that job."

"You look mad about something." Luke raised one curious eyebrow as he relieved her of her jacket and ordered another coffee. "Did something happen? I see you didn't find your gloves."

"No, I didn't. I guess I'll just have to go back. Maybe I can do it when I go in to fill out the job application." She explained the aide position to him.

"Sounds like a good opportunity." He grinned. "Go for it."

"I just might. Hey, maybe we can see the lawyer while we're here," she murmured, accepting the coffee mug and a thick piece of blueberry pie. "I'd like to start getting things sorted out."

"I don't think he's back yet, but we'll stop and find out." Darcy didn't miss the glance that Luke shot across to Clarice.

"Is there something I should know?" she asked quietly. "Something about the ranch? Is it in trouble?"

"No, it's not in trouble." Luke sipped slowly from his steaming cup. "These last few years, the ranch has done very well."

Darcy bit into her pie with gusto, relieved to hear that she wouldn't be any further in debt. "Then there shouldn't be any trouble with the will," she mumbled, relishing the sweet fruity filling that had never tasted so good anywhere else. But then she saw a strange look pass over Luke's face. "Should there?" she asked cautiously.

"Not trouble exactly. Darcy, there's something I've been meaning to say—"

He stopped when a tiny round woman toddled up beside them. "Hello, Mrs. Lancaster. Chilly day, isn't it?" He waited a moment for her response and lost total control of the conversation.

"My word, Clarice, don't you look spiffy! I haven't seen you in anything but pants for so long, I wasn't sure you owned any skirts." Her narrowed eyes slid over Clarice and settled on Darcy. "Finally made it back, did you? And a bit late at that. Where were you anyway, that you couldn't come home to see your parents when—"

"I'm sure Darcy appreciates your condolences, Mrs. Lancaster." Luke interrupted the conversation in a loud voice. "But I think she's just a bit overwhelmed with everything since she arrived. Things have changed quite a bit in five years."

Darcy glared up at the one person in Raven's Rest who could distort fact faster than any other. "This is my son, Mrs. Lancaster. His name is Jamie. He'll be five years old in January." She laid out the facts deliberately, waiting for those black eyes to count backward and figure it all out.

"Your son? But your parents didn't say anything about a child." Mrs. Lancaster peered down at Jamie, who sat placidly tolerating the scrutiny.

"They didn't know. And yes, I have been raising him on my own in New York from the day he was born. We managed just fine, thank you. But now we're back. For a while." She dared the woman to ask anything more.

"He does resemble your mother, rest her soul." The woman's eyes shifted to meet Darcy's glare head-on. "And I suppose you've come home to find a father for the boy. Sensible, my dear. Very sensible. And Luke is perfect, what with him being half owner of the ranch and all." Ella Lancaster gathered up her bags of groceries.

"I must say, however, that there will be a few broken hearts left around here. Jalise Penner won't be at all happy that yet another man's been taken off the market. She had her cap set on Luke there, and she won't take kindly to rearranging it at this late date. Ta ta." And with that bombshell, she scurried away.

"Of all the rude, overbearing people," Darcy seethed. "I can understand how her husband needs to disappear into the mountains, alone, for weeks at a time. It's a wonder he doesn't stay there permanently." She glanced round the table, her eyes settling on Luke's whitened face.

"What a pile of hogwash. As if my parents would leave half the ranch to you—" the shocked look on Clarice's face stopped her from continuing "—what's the matter?"

"Darcy, you need to hear something before this gets any further." Clarice's tones were soft but firm, and the hand she laid on Darcy's was compelling. "Promise me that you'll listen to Luke. Please?"

Darcy stared at first one, then the other. Enlightenment dawned slowly. "Then it's true?" she gasped as an arrow of sheer pain stabbed straight into her heart. "My own parents chose someone else over me to leave their worldly goods to?" The shadows chasing over Luke's brown eyes told her the truth.

"They didn't know where you were, Darcy," Luke told her. "And they were afraid that if they didn't set something up, if someone wasn't in control, the ranch would get eaten up by the banks or be left to run down. They didn't want that to happen."

"No, what they didn't *want* was Disappointing Darcy to get one thin dime of theirs without paying the tune! Tell me," she demanded bitterly, "do I have to live here for a year or two before I have legal claim to my half?" At the expression on his pale face, Darcy laughed, her voice full of unshed tears. "I thought so."

"Not a year," Luke murmured. "Six months. I'm sorry. I was trying to tell you."

"Of course you were! Sooner or later, right?" She studied her son, who was happily playing with his little car. "Tell me, Luke—what happens if I walk out that door and never return to Raven's Rest?"

His eyes widened, but he answered in the same calm tones. "You lose your right to half."

"Just like that. As if I'd never even been here." Darcy snapped her fingers. "Isn't that something? Even in death, five years after the fact, they're still trying to manipulate me."

"It isn't like that," he protested softly. "They just wanted you to come home one last time. To see that things had changed, that they had changed. It is only for six months. After that, you're free to leave if you want to. And I'll buy you out."

"Yes, with my other half of the inheritance!"

Darcy rolled the whole messy situation around in her mind. Free to leave? That was a joke! She didn't have enough money for the bus fare to Denver, let alone enough to rent a place and start over again. No job, no prospects. And a child to look after. Leaving Raven's Rest now wouldn't be the simple affair that it had been the first time around.

Fine. If they had wanted her back here, her parents had finally gotten their wish. She was here. She was staying, for a while at least. And she intended to find out everything she needed to know about how to get what was rightfully, *by birth,* her legacy.

"I want to see everything," she told him fiercely. "I want to see the books, the bank statements—everything."

He nodded curtly. "Have you been drawing a salary since they died?"

"Yes, the same as when they were alive. Nothing has changed."

Darcy ignored that. For her, *everything* had changed. Forget about love, forget about trying to make amends. There wasn't any point now. It didn't matter. What did matter was getting some security out of this fiasco for herself and her son. She didn't begrudge Luke any of what her parents had left. He could have it with her blessing. But she would take her fair share, too. After all, they owed her that much. Didn't they?

"And Clarice?" She hated saying it, hated the ugly, greedy way it came out. But she had to know exactly where she stood and how many other surprises there were waiting in the wings.

"I'm just staying for Luke's sake," the other woman replied. "I helped your mother out, but since she died, I've been keeping up the house and providing meals as best I could." Her thin angular face was intent. "I don't want any money, Darcy. I have my pension. But I would like to help out on the ranch if I can. Maybe I could watch Jamie for you once in a while."

Darcy nodded, but her mind was busy sorting it all out. "I want you to set up a bank account for me," she informed Luke in a cold hard voice. "And I want the same salary as you." She held up a hand to forestall his protests. "I'm perfectly willing to work for it, but I need some money to support Jamie and myself until this will thing is settled."

"I don't have any objections." He nodded, his eyes soft and compassionate. "It's not that much, actually."

He told her the amount and shrugged at the skepticism on her face. "Your dad and I had a deal. He helped me learn ranching, and I helped him with the physical stuff. I got my room and board free and a couple of head for my own at the end of the year, if we made a profit."

"Fine." The sum Luke had mentioned wouldn't go very far in New York, Darcy knew. If she wanted to get out of this place and back on her own, she'd need to supplement it somehow. Hilda Ridgely's words rumbled across her brain. The teacher's aide position might help. And it would look good on a resume.

"If you would rather Clarice move to her own place…" Luke began, his mouth pursed into a narrow disapproving line.

"No, not at all. I'd appreciate it if she could stay and watch Jamie for me two afternoons a week. And maybe an evening or two—I'm not sure about that right now." If Hilda knew what she was talking about, Darcy should be able to find out how to start the courses necessary to teach. She would not leave this town defenseless and ill-equipped to earn her living. *Not again.*

"Darcy, we had no intention of deceiving you." Luke leaned across the table, his hand touching hers until she yanked it away. "We just didn't know how to tell you."

"I can imagine." She held his steady gaze, daring him to look away.

"It's true, honey. Lucas didn't want any part of it, but then when we couldn't find you and things needed handling…well, someone had to step in." Clarice stood from the table. "I don't want to put upon anyone. I'll pack my things and be out by tomorrow morning." She left so quickly, in those jerky sparrow-like movements, that Darcy didn't have time to stop her.

"You've hurt her feelings." Luke's warm gaze had cooled somewhat. "You didn't have to do that."

"I never meant to! I just don't want any more secrets." Darcy swallowed the angry thoughts of her parents' deceit and concentrated on the glossy tabletop. "I can deal with hard reality, you know. It's not knowing what's coming next that gets to me."

"I never set out to get half of your ranch, Darcy. But when your father asked me if I'd run things and watch out for you, I agreed because I knew he needed the help and it would take a worry off his mind." His face tightened. "He had enough pain, Darcy. Agreeing to take over the ranch and run things with you was the least I could do."

"Pain? What pain?" Darcy frowned. "You keep acting as if he was sickly or something. My father was always as healthy as a horse."

"Are you certain you want to hear the truth, Darcy? All of it? Because I guarantee that it isn't pretty." He waited for her nod before drawing in a deep breath. "Your father had liver cancer. A lot of the time he was in agony, and the painkillers couldn't seem to touch it."

"Liver cancer? Oh, no! I never knew—didn't even guess." She felt the color drain from her face and clutched the edge of the table for support. Then she rushed blindly for the door. Outside, in the cold brisk air, she headed for the park, drawing in deep cleansing breaths. *Cancer?* Her father?

"Are you all right?"

She was startled to see Luke standing beside her,

Jamie at his side—both of them out of breath from trying to catch up to her. For a moment, she'd even forgotten about Jamie!

"Yes." She walked down the pathway between the overhanging boughs of pines that sheltered them from the wind. "Thanks," she added belatedly.

Jamie spied the playground equipment and raced off to climb on it. When he was safely out of earshot, Darcy turned to Luke.

"Okay, tell me all of it."

"It was a real blessing from God that he died when he did, Darcy. He was on his way to another chemo treatment. They were going to stay in Denver overnight and come home the next day. Your mother insisted on going along to keep him company, even though she couldn't possibly have handled the car. Clarice went to drive him back."

"Why couldn't my mother drive?" Darcy felt a frisson of fear. "Why?" she demanded when he didn't speak.

"She was too crippled by arthritis then, Darcy. I think she went along just to spend more time with him. Your father said riding in the car with your mother was more soothing than all the pain pills the doctors could prescribe. Your mother had her own medication for pain by then."

"She was bad, then?" Darcy whispered the words, not wanting to hear it confirmed, yet somehow needing to.

His arm curved round her shoulders, hugging her close for support. "She'd had several operations to try and straighten her joints, but nothing seemed to take." He handed her a tissue and took another deep breath.

"Clarice came because I asked her to. I interviewed some home-care people, but no one wanted to stay when they found out how far we were from the city. I was desperate for someone to help. Clarice sold her house on a moment's notice and came without asking any questions. She and your mother bonded the moment they met."

Darcy gulped down the sobs that rose in her throat. She'd been so thoughtless to the one person who had made her mother's last days tolerable. How could she look Clarice in the eye again?

"How did they die?" It hurt to ask, and Darcy clenched her fists to maintain her control.

"Your dad always felt good for a few hours after the treatment. Relatively good, that is. Then the nausea kicked in. Lester said that while he was feeling good, he wanted to look at the fall colors. Your mother insisted on going along. They begged Clarice to relax, leave them alone together for a bit." Luke kicked one booted toe against the grass. "He said he was well enough to drive."

Darcy could hear the regret tinging his voice, and knew then how much he had truly cared for her parents. "And?"

"A semi was coming from the opposite direction. Apparently its brakes failed and the driver couldn't stop. Your dad didn't have a chance to get out of the way." He glanced at her. "I'm sorry."

"It's all right," she murmured, clenching her jaw. "I had to know. I suppose it was better to hear it from you."

"Maybe. Anyway, that's what happened." His look told her that he didn't quite know what she would do with the information. "They're buried in the graveyard by the church," he said. "Harvey Withers told me they'd chosen the lots a long time ago."

"I figured as much." Darcy smiled grimly. "They always did put the church first."

"Not the church, Darcy. *God.* That's the way it should be, don't you think?"

But Darcy didn't know what she thought anymore. She only knew that her parents were gone and she felt alone. More alone than she had in years. And now the ranch—the one thing of theirs that they could have trusted her with—didn't belong to her. Not really.

"I have to go over to the feed store. Is it okay if Jamie comes with me?" Luke's eyes met hers with a sympathetic look. "You could go on over to the church, if you wanted," he suggested diffidently. "I'll be ready to leave in about an hour."

It was better than sitting in his truck, having the entire population staring at her, Darcy decided. She stood watching Jamie as he slid down the curly slide, his face glowing from the cold. Nobody could make her feel guilty about him, though. Jamie wasn't a mistake. Her child was the one good thing in her life.

"All right." She agreed finally, ignoring the reservations she felt. She would have to go to the cemetery sooner or later.

"I'll meet you back here at five." She headed toward the far side of the park. But something stopped her. Turning, she cast Luke a glance. He was standing where she'd left him, his dark eyes following her. "Thanks," she murmured.

He nodded. "You're welcome." His big wide smile

made her feel strangely comforted, and Darcy set off again, determined to at least look at the new graves.

As she went, her mind replayed his words. *They put God first. Isn't that the way it should be?*

Maybe, a nasty little voice inside chided her. But they should have put you second. Instead you came in dead last.

That was enough to send her racing across the grass, forcing herself to move so fast that her lungs begged for relief. At least it stopped the tears from coming.

When she got to the church, there were people in the adjoining graveyard. Darcy had no intention of wandering around looking like a fool as she hunted for her parents' graves, so she walked inside the church to wait. Someone was practicing on the organ and the light melodic notes carried through the building, hanging suspended from the cathedral ceiling as they resounded around the sanctuary.

It was a familiar room. She'd been here hundreds of times, often not of her own will but out of a sense of duty. Her parents had always sat in the pew at the front. And over there was the pew she'd shared with her friends a long time ago. Darcy knew that if she kneeled and looked under the bench, she'd find her initials carved into the seat. She could still feel the sting of punishment for that misdeed.

And there, by the altar, was where she'd prayed long and hard. With her whole heart, she'd begged God to change her, to make her into the kind of person someone could love. Too bad He hadn't answered. At least not in the way she meant. The one intimate experience Darcy had shared with another human being couldn't possibly be called love.

"Hello! I didn't hear you come in."

Darcy whirled around to find a tall, slim man behind her. He wore faded denims and a tattered cotton T-shirt, and his hair looked as if he'd been raking his fingers through it for hours.

"I don't usually practice when anyone is around. My mom says I need to ease up on the loud pedal. Anyway, most of the people in this congregation don't like my kind of music." He grinned, his face wreathed in boyish charm.

"That wasn't church music," she pointed out carefully. "It was too fast."

"I know." He grinned again. "I do it that way on purpose, just to keep up my fingers. If I only played the way they sang, my hands would have rigor mortis by the end of the first verse." He thrust out his tanned arm. "Kenny Anderson."

"Darcy. Darcy Simms." She shook his hand quickly and then pulled back when the look of sympathy flooded his face.

"I'm sorry about your parents." His voice hinted at her loss without becoming maudlin. "They were really nice people. Our youth group went out there lots of times. They sure did like kids."

All except their own, Darcy felt like telling him. But she only smiled and nodded. "Thanks. Do you know where they're buried? I thought I'd take a look."

"Yeah, sure." He sent her a funny look that Darcy couldn't interpret. "We were all here, you know. The youth group, I mean. My dad let us take part in the funeral."

"Your father did?" Darcy wondered why the man had organized her parents' funeral.

"David Anderson. He's the pastor here." Kenny watched her for a moment before leading the way outside. "We've been here for about two years. The Pringles were gone long before we got here." It was a nonchalant comment meant to convey a friendly bit of information, but it sent a clench of fear to her stomach.

"Wh-where did they go?" Darcy asked, moistening her lips.

"I forget." The boy, Kenny, wrinkled his forehead. "Someplace west, I think. Did you know that the oldest boy and girl were married before they left?" When Darcy didn't say anything, he nodded. "Yes. Joe married some girl from Denver. I think they're missionaries in Brazil now. And Brenda met some guy at Bible School. They're pastoring down south."

"Oh." It was the most she could get out.

"Here they are. Right beside each other. They liked to be together, didn't they?" Kenny smiled at the two mounds placed side by side on the hillside. "We came with fresh flowers every day before it got so cold."

"That was nice," Darcy murmured, unable to stop staring at the two graves. She was alone, all alone in the world.

The wind whipped down the hill and tugged at her hair, tossing it wildly. Stabbing cold hit her full in the face, stinging her eyes. Kenny murmured something and walked away. But still Darcy couldn't leave. She stared at the final resting place of her parents as bitter tears coursed down her cheeks.

"If I had known you were ill, I would have come back," she whispered, sinking to her knees. "I don't know what we could have said that hadn't already been said over and over, but I wish I'd known."

The wind was howling now, tearing through the almost bare trees and driving the dry, crunchy leaves into a whirling frenzy. The sun shone, its watery yellow doing nothing to dispel the chill that held her there, unmoving on the hard ground.

"I have a son, you know. Your grandson. His name is Jamie. He looks like you, Mom." From somewhere on the other side of the hill, there were voices, but they quickly died away. "He's a wonderful little boy and I will never regret that I kept him. He loves me." She said the words boldly.

"Jamie doesn't care about people's rules. He doesn't know that I'm bad. He just loves me because I'm Mommy. The same as I loved you."

It hurt to say the words that had been jammed inside for so long. Her throat clogged with emotion. There was no answer from them. There couldn't be. They had gone to a place that she couldn't reach, and never would. And they'd gone together, leaving her behind. *Alone.* Alone with the memories of their bitter recriminations.

Do you think you can just stay here? Act as if there's nothing wrong with a single girl having a baby? How can you do that to us? Do you think everyone will just forget your transgressions? Remember, there is a cost for every crime. You've chosen to have a child without a father. You'll have to explain that to him someday.

*You can tell him why his mother wouldn't give him the
chance at life in a happy family where two parents
would provide for him. We won't be part of your deceit,
Darcy. It's time to face your sins.*

The feeling overwhelmed her like a black cloud of
smoke. Every word inside begged for release and yet the
ache was so great. But there was so much that needed to
be said. She *needed* to say it, to let go of the bitterness
that had festered inside for five long years.

"Why didn't you love me, Mom and Dad? What did I
do that was so terrible? Didn't you want children?" The
thought suddenly occurred to her, but was just as quickly tossed away. They'd loved having the youth group,
Kenny had said. Clarice—or maybe it was Luke—had
said much the same thing. So it was just her. There was
something wrong with her.

"I've felt it for as long as I can remember," she said
quickly, tracing a tiny cross in the dirt with one finger.
"It wasn't that you didn't try. You provided for my physical needs very well, better than I've done for Jamie
sometimes. But I didn't belong in your heart, and I knew
it. The two of you made a circle and I couldn't get in no
matter how hard I tried." She pushed the hair out of her
eyes.

"I know you were disappointed in me. I disappointed
myself long before I got pregnant. But Jamie is a wonderful little boy and I could never have given him away.
He's a part of me.

"All I ever wanted was love. I wanted to know that
no matter what happened, you would always love me
just because I was your child. Was that so wrong?"

Still, the two graves lay silent.

"Darcy?" The word was almost whispered. She could hear it even though the wind had gained force, pulling and tugging at the down-filled jacket she'd left undone. She glanced up, noticing the tiny snowflakes dancing in the air.

Luke stood behind her, his sheepskin jacket tugged up around his ears and his hands protected from the weather by thick leather gloves. There were twinkles of light coming from behind his head, and Darcy stared, mesmerized by their colors.

"It's pretty," she murmured. "Like a kaleidoscope. Can I see?" She reached out to touch the glittering lights, striving to warm herself in their heat before the world went black.

Luke grabbed her as she swooned, and swung her up in his arms. She weighed next to nothing, he noted absently, striding across the grounds to where the truck sat purring by the church. He set her carefully inside, one hand brushing over the pale thin cheek.

"Lord, she's frozen!" he whispered as he did up her seat belt and slammed the door closed.

Luke raced around the truck and clambered in, flicking the heater up another notch in the already warm cab. In one swift movement, he'd shed his jacket and wrapped it around her.

There was nothing else in the cab to cover her with. Nor was there anything in the back. He was just going to have to head for home, Luke decided grimly. He hoped the storm that he could see brewing in the west would hold off until they got there. At least Clarice and the boy would be safe on the farm by now. He offered a word of thanks heavenward that he'd found his aunt outside the drugstore and sent the boy home with her.

Darcy moaned a little and shivered, hunching herself into her jacket. "C-c-cold," Darcy whimpered.

He didn't think she was awake. Just in case, he slipped his hand over hers and squeezed.

"I'm here, Darcy. I'm taking you home. We'll get you warm pretty soon."

She didn't respond, so he concentrated on his driving for a few minutes, then he tried again.

"Darcy," he called gently. "Darcy, can you wake up now?" He eased around an even bigger pile of snow and made the last turn toward home. "Darcy?"

He maneuvered his way through the gates, giving thanks as he drove up to the porch with a song of praise on his lips. *Thank you, Father.*

Luke jumped out of the truck, not caring that the cold ripped through his thin woolen shirt. He stalked around the powerful engine, through the drifts, and pulled open her door, gathering Darcy's lax body into his arms.

"Come on," he murmured tenderly, easing her out. "We're home now. You can have a nice hot bath."

"Home?" She opened one eye and peered up at him. "I'm cold, Luke, and my throat hurts. A lot. Could you get me some blankets?"

"Sure I will. Soon as we get inside. Just stay put now." She snuggled against him, and he sighed in relief, heading for the front door that swung wide open at their arrival. "Thanks, Clarice."

"It's me!" Jamie peered out from behind the door, smiling proudly. "Why are you carrying my mom?"

"Just close the door now, will you? That's a good

boy. Where's Auntie Clarice?" Luke searched the living room as he deposited Darcy on the sofa.

"I'm looking after her. She's sick." He stopped talking and smiled as a faint voice hailed him from down the hall. "I gotta go," he said gravely. "Aunt Clarice wants a drink."

"Could I take it to her while you stay here and make sure your mommy doesn't fall off the couch? She's not feeling very well either, and you and I will have to get her to bed after I tell Clarice I'm home. Okay?" he asked quickly, as Clarice's voice called out again, more frantic now.

"I guess so." Jamie nodded in agreement as he perched himself on the floor beside his mother's feet.

Luke raced down the hall to find Clarice, white-faced and shaking, trying to lever herself out of bed. "You're sick, Clarice. Get back into bed."

"Never get sick," the woman denied angrily. "Tough old bird like me doesn't cave in like that. My back's out is all. Medication makes me so tired. I was afraid Jamie was in trouble."

"He's fine. But if you don't cave in and lie down, you're going to fall down." Luke grinned. "Now, get in to bed or I'll have to report you to Jamie."

"Just for a minute," she finally agreed, flopping back on the pillows with obvious relief. "Till I get my sea legs again. Or my back straightens out." She was exhausted, and Luke knew she'd be snoring before he left the room. He headed back to the living room.

"Mommy?" Jamie whispered, watching as Darcy tried to stand.

"Darcy, it's Luke. Easy, honey. Just sit down. That's

a girl." He grabbed her hand from behind and held on tightly in case she fought against him. He needn't have worried. Darcy sagged against him as if her stuffing had been removed. He kept his voice low and soothing, knowing Jamie was watching everything.

"Sit down, Darcy. You're sick and you need to rest." He sat down beside her, curving one arm around her shoulders when she laid her head on his chest.

"I'm not so bad, Luke. Am I? Doesn't God care about me at all?" The sad, defeated words stabbed him to the heart with their plaintive request for reassurance.

"Of course God cares about you! God loves you. He always has. You just wouldn't let Him for a while." He brushed the silken strands off her forehead and pressed his lips there, cradling her tenderly in his arms.

"I wouldn't?"

"No. But He didn't go away. He's still here, loving you. Because He's your heavenly Father and you are more precious to Him than anything else in the world." Jamie was staring at them, and Luke patted the seat beside him, inviting the boy closer.

Darcy shook her head. "God's mad at me."

"Oh, Darcy!" He felt his heart wrench. How had it happened that this beautiful woman felt so unloved? "God isn't mad at you. He knows you've been through some really tough times, and He's been there all along, waiting for you to ask Him for help."

She sighed miserably. "I've just goofed up one too many times. I wish it was true, though." Her eyes were wide and unfocused. "I'd like someone to love me."

"There is no limit to God's love. And I know He

wouldn't refuse to forgive you, if you asked. He loves you, Darcy."

"No." She straightened, shaking her head vehemently. "Three times you're out." Her voice was higher now, and Luke could hear the frenzy building. "I struck out way more than that."

"Listen to me, Darcy. This is a verse from the Bible. It tells us about what God is really like." Luke heard the words whispered in his head even as he recited them: "'The Lord your God is a merciful God; He will not abandon you or destroy you.'" He cleared his throat. "It's a promise, Darcy. And God doesn't go back on His promises."

"Are you sure?" Her scared voice broke the long silence that dragged between them.

"I'm positive. 'He who is the Glory of Israel does not lie or change his mind; for He is not a man, that He should change His mind.' You see, when God says something, He means it."

"But you don't know what I've done—the things I've said. Nobody could forgive all that." She coughed, trying to clear her raspy throat.

"No, a person couldn't," he agreed, threading one hand through Jamie's soft fall of hair. "But this is God and He is very clear about loving us just the way we are. He doesn't leave any room for maybes."

"I can't think," she told him. "I feel funny. And my throat hurts again." Her blue eyes lit up as they focused on her son. "Hello, sweetheart. Did you have fun with Clarice?"

But Jamie merely stared at her, his frown wrinkling the smooth skin of his forehead.

She tried to stand in order to move toward him, but she wavered and grabbed Luke's arm.

"Oh, my. The whole room is spinning. Jamie, did you see those stars?"

She sagged against Luke, and he caught her close, his fingers slipping to her forehead. She was warm and he guessed she'd developed a fever.

"I'm cold," she muttered, snuggling against him. "Why is it so cold? I just have a little sore throat. Nothing to get silly about."

Luke wondered privately just how long she'd been nursing that "little" sore throat. Probably for weeks, if he was any judge of things.

"I don't see any stars. Where are the stars, Mister Luke?"

"Jamie, we need to get your mom to her room. She's sick." He scooped the slight form into his arms and started for her bedroom.

"My mom doesn't never get sick," Jamie proclaimed, trailing along behind. "Not never."

"Now where have I heard that before, Lord?" Luke grinned wryly as he set her on the bed.

"Jamie, could you get my nightgown?" Darcy asked. "It's in the bathroom. L-luke, you can leave now," she chattered, shivering.

Luke left the room and flicked up the thermostat in the living room. After a few minutes he went back into Darcy's room, where she was huddled under the covers, shivering even harder than before. "Why can't I get warm?"

"Because you sat outside, on the ground, in the middle of a Colorado blizzard, with nothing to protect you from that icy wind," he pointed out. "How long were you there?"

"I don't know. It doesn't matter." She closed her eyes and snuggled under the blankets. "I'll be fine in the morning."

"I'll go get some aspirin and hot water bottles. Jamie, want to help?"

"I want to stay with my mom." The child had perched himself on the side of the bed and was staring at Darcy with a worried frown. Luke knew her condition had affected him, but right now there was nothing he could do to reassure Jamie. Watching his mother for a few moments might help. Once she fell asleep, though, Luke would try to comfort the child.

But a few minutes later, as he tucked the warm bottles against her icy toes, Luke couldn't help wondering who would comfort the woman who lay dozing on the bed.

All I ever wanted was love, she'd said in that hurt little-girl voice out there by her parents' graves.

Luke couldn't help thinking that the needy child inside was still searching for the thing she had missed out on so long ago. And he had no idea how anyone would penetrate those barriers she kept so firmly in place. How could he help her find what she needed?

Only You, Lord, he prayed in his mind, sinking into the hard-backed chair that sat near the window. *Only You know the way out of this.*

Chapter Seven

"I have a lot to do," Darcy croaked, her throat on fire. "I can't afford to lie around like this."

"You're not going anywhere." Luke glared down at her.

"And I suppose you're going to stop me?" Darcy would have liked to scream her frustration, but the pain that would cause wasn't worth thinking about. "Look, I'm a partner in this place. I need to do my share." She coughed a little, trying to catch her breath as the pain seared her chest.

"You will. But not today." His tone was matter-of-fact. As if someone had appointed him her guardian, she fumed inwardly.

"Darcy, you've been fighting this thing for three days and just missed getting pneumonia. Yesterday a thaw set in outside, but this is the first morning you've been lucid for more than thirty minutes. The doctor said bed rest—and that's what you're having."

"I have to look after my son. Where is he?" She glanced around the room, trying to see past the tall bossy man standing in her doorway.

"He's eating breakfast. Then he's coming with me. I've got some cattle stuck up on the north ridge and I have to go round them up. Jamie will be fine. My concern is you."

"You're not taking him on some expedition into the hills?" She choked it out, incensed by the very idea of her small defenseless son out in the frigid winter weather. "He's just a little boy!"

"He's a smart little boy who wants to learn more about ranching. And I'm going to teach him while you lie in that bed and regain your strength."

"There's nothing wrong with my strength," she burst out, unable to control her temper one moment longer. "I'm fine."

Darcy flipped the bedclothes back and swung her pajama-clad legs over the side, wincing at the aches and pains her body was rapidly relaying to her brain. She grabbed the night table and stood…for about thirty seconds, until the room began to whirl around crazily and she sat back down.

Tears formed on her lashes and dropped down her cheeks. Why did nothing in her life ever go right? She'd intended to apply for that job at the school and now she couldn't even stand, let alone deal with thirty rambunctious kids.

"The doctor said your reserves have been drained, Darcy. He thinks you've been running on nerves for far too long. So do I. You need to focus on recharging those batteries you've run down. And then you can worry about looking into schools." Luke's voice was more gentle than she'd ever heard it and Darcy couldn't help staring at him.

"How did you know about my plans to study?" she demanded in her squawky voice.

"You've been mumbling about them for the past three days," he said, smiling. "Between that and ranting about some broken vase, you had quite a time. Personally, I think it's a great idea to plan for the future. But you can't do anything until you get yourself strong. And that's going to take time."

Darcy peered up at him. There was admiration in his tone, as if he approved of her plans. Not that it mattered, she reminded herself.

"You don't think it would take too much time away from the ranch? After all, I want to pull my weight." She frowned. "I can't take the wages if I don't do the job."

With a start, she realized that she had just admitted she fully intended to hang around for a while.

"Darcy, I don't need help with the animals or the fences. I've got a hired man for that. But it would be nice to have hot meals at night and clean clothes for the morning. Not that I'm asking you to be a maid or anything!"

Darcy rolled her eyes. "Good." She chuckled. "I'm not a very good maid. But that's hardly doing enough when you're outside working all day. There must be something else."

He bit his lip, wondering whether or not to suggest it. It would give her a clearer picture of what he was trying to do with the ranch, and he wouldn't mind passing it over to her.

"I could show you how to keep the books," he said at last, watching for some sign that she hated the idea.

"It takes me far too long to balance the statements, and the ledger is way out of date."

Far from being dismayed, Darcy seemed pleased that he would ask. "Books I can do," she said. "I'll get you to show me how you've been handling things and take over right away. Then I'll keep them up after Jamie's in bed or when my other work is done."

"All right, I get the picture!" He held up his hand, laughing at her sincerity. "But you can't do it all right now. You're as weak as water. Yesterday you could barely sit up in bed for more than twenty minutes. You're not quite ready to take on the world today."

"You mean you've been looking after me?" The thought brought a flush of embarrassment to her cheeks. "Why? Where's Clarice?" She needed to see the older woman, to apologize for her unkind remarks. "She's not gone, is she?"

He shook his dark head. "No." His eyes glinted in the morning sun that flooded the room. "She's flat on her back in her room. Clarice pulled something she shouldn't have on the day of the storm and she's had to stay put."

"Oh, I'm sorry," Darcy murmured, genuinely distressed at the thought of that strong wiry woman having to stay still. "What happened?"

"What happened is that she's as stubborn as you! She insisted on lugging in a great big box of clay that she'd picked up earlier. Apparently she got it into the house all right, but going down the stairs, she missed a step and wrenched her back."

"Why didn't she just leave it till the blizzard was over?"

"Good question. I asked her that yesterday." His tone was unrepentant. "Apparently raw clay cannot freeze or it's no longer any good for throwing or firing. When she got home, the thermometer was in the low thirties, so she didn't want to leave it out in the car. It costs quite a bit to get the stuff shipped up here because it weighs so much. No way was she going to waste it." He snorted indignantly. "As if it was worth all the trouble it's caused. I'm so tired of people doing stupid things to save a dollar."

"Maybe that's because you have so many dollars. Or maybe it's because you've never had to watch them leave faster than they arrived." Her voice cracked and almost gave way. "When you get a dime, you learn to stretch it out and make every penny count. Believe me, I know."

"Frugality is fine. But I can afford to buy my aunt another box of that stuff if she needs it."

"Maybe she didn't want to ask you," she countered dryly. Her voice was going fast. At this rate, she soon wouldn't be able to speak at all, she thought grimly.

"Of course she didn't! She's got to be independent. As if it would hurt her to lean on me once in a while." He started to leave the room.

"And who do you lean on?" she asked in a croaky whisper.

Luke turned back, his forehead wrinkled in a frown as he stared at her, brown eyes pensive. "I'm fine," he muttered.

"I see." Darcy shifted in the warm cocoon, feeling the tiredness wash over her in waves. She yawned. "It's all right for you to be independent because you're a big strong man, but it's not for us because we're weak little women. Typical male chauvinist." She snuggled down in her bed and let her eyelids droop, knowing he wouldn't let that comment pass without a rebuttal.

"No one could ever call you weak, Darcy Simms. I don't think I've ever known a stronger woman," he whispered. "Hang onto that inner fortitude, Darcy. You're going to need it around here."

Luke watched as she sighed once and then resumed that steady, even breathing pattern that told him she was asleep. It was true, he decided, staring down at her beautiful face and rich dark hair spread across the pillow. Darcy Simms was one very strong lady. She reminded him a little of Macy, his wife.

Macella Davies had pushed, pulled and dragged him through most of his teenage years. She'd coaxed him to finish school, waited for him while he flirted with a variety of careers, and then quietly advised him to return to ranching.

"It's hard work," she'd laughed up at him. "But that never hurt anyone, did it?" It was a philosophy she'd applied to their married life as well. If there was a job to be done, Macy tackled it head-on. He could still see her in the labor room, face white and strained as she breathed through the contractions.

"Gracious me," she'd puffed, her eyes sparkling with that fire of determination. "This is hard going. They should give women overtime for this." And then she'd dived back into her whooshing as another spasm gripped her body. Luke stuck by her through the whole thing, trying to help in any way he could.

Who had stayed with Darcy? he wondered suddenly,

glancing down at the sleeping woman. Macy's labor hadn't lasted more than six hours. He wondered if someone had been there to hold Darcy's hand and encourage her through the various stages until Jamie appeared. Surely she hadn't handled that alone, too?

He shook himself, clenching his teeth in annoyance. What business was it of his what Darcy Simms had done? He wasn't interested in her past—or her future. In fact, once she was better and the will settled, he hoped she'd let him buy her out.

With a twinge of guilt, he remembered Darcy's litany of grief in the graveyard. When she hadn't moved, even after he honked twice, Luke had become concerned about her. Besides he'd lost a wife and child, and understood her feeling of loss.

Martha and Lester, as kind and as sweet as they'd been to him, had somehow never gotten through to Darcy. She still didn't realize that they had missed her so terribly that they'd been willing to go looking for her themselves, and when that was no longer possible, had spent thousands on a private search for her. The physical drain on them had been obvious to him, and he had never doubted that they loved their daughter.

Darcy had sounded bitter and so hurt, as if she were aching for someone to wrap their arms around her and hold her. He knew that feeling. He'd had it the day Macy and Leila had been killed simply because they'd gone to visit a friend in Chicago and been on the wrong street at the wrong time. He'd woken up a happy contented father and gone to bed realizing that his life, as he'd known it, was over.

"Mister Luke?" Jamie stood in the doorway beckoning, his finger to his lips. "Is my mommy all better?"

Luke ruffled the nut-brown hair with a grin and pulled the door almost closed. "Not yet, sport. But she's getting there. She was arguing with me a few minutes ago. Said she wanted to get up." He snickered. "Of course, she fell asleep right after that, so I guess she changed her mind."

"Know what?" the little boy said, "My mom an' me used to play games," he confided with a glint in his eye, changing the subject with a rapidity that Luke was coming to recognize.

"What kind of games?"

"I Spy games. And travel games. We'd put our clothes in a big bag and we'd go on a trip to see a different part of New York. It was fun." The blue eyes sparkled with happy memories.

She'd shielded him, Luke realized. Poor and alone in the huge city, Darcy Simms had managed to protect herself and her son from the ugly side of life. She had absorbed the difficulties of moving from one place to the next to avoid unwanted attention, without him even guessing the reason. Not only that, but she'd given him happy memories. Luke's admiration grew for the feisty woman lying upstairs.

"How would you like to go for a long horseback ride today, Jamie?" Luke found his gloves, plucked two big red apples from the basket on the counter, and grabbed his Stetson.

"Really?" The boy clapped his hands with glee. "Can I have my own horsey?"

Luke burst out laughing at the glow of happiness on the child's face.

"I think we'd better wait to ask your mom's permission for that." He grinned, bending to place a cap on Jamie's head. He hunkered down and quickly slipped off the brown boots, exchanging the right for left. "Today you can ride with me on Thunder. He's very strong, and I'm sure he can carry both of us."

"*Thunder?* Really?" Jamie threw his arms around Luke's neck. "I love you, Mister Luke."

The embrace and the heartfelt emotion behind it threw Luke. He hadn't expected to feel this warm rise of affection for Darcy's son. But as the chubby arms squeezed his neck, Luke realized how much he'd missed by losing his daughter so young. His arms came up of their own accord and held the little body tenderly against his chest, experiencing feelings he'd long held in check.

For once in his life, Luke didn't care if he was being sentimental or maudlin. He didn't even allow himself to feel unfaithful to his daughter's memory. He simply stayed where he was and enjoyed the moment for all the joy it held. And then in a voice choked with emotion he murmured, "Thank you."

They spent two hours finding the reluctant cows and directing them, with the help of Shep the dog, back to the rest of the herd. Jamie giggled and laughed and clapped his hands, apparently not feeling the cold as he rode in front of Luke, his excited blue eyes taking in everything.

"I like ranches," he announced as they munched on their apples. "I'm glad I can live here. Can I stay here forever 'n' ever, Mister Luke?"

Luke didn't know how to answer the child. If it were up to Luke, Jamie would stay for a very long time, growing stronger and healthier day by day. But that meant Darcy would stay, and Luke wasn't so sure how that made him feel.

He half suspected that before long, she'd be digging out all his secret feelings of betrayal, and he had no stomach for raking over them again. Once he'd had it all…and then he'd lost it. Now there was this ranch to run, Aunt Clarice to take care of, and a future that he'd have to think about. Someday. But not yet.

By the time they returned home, Luke was ready for lunch. He heated some soup for the four of them, and with Jamie's help, made up a tray for the two ladies.

"I didn't give my mom a good-morning kiss," Jamie told him seriously. "She always gets a good-morning kiss or else she can't get up." He put his hand on the edge of the tray in a proprietary manner that made Luke smile. "I can help," he insisted.

Darcy blinked awake as they came into the room, her gorgeous blue eyes widening with joy as she caught sight of Jamie. "Hello, Love Bug!" She helped him up on the bed and accepted his hug with open arms.

"I came to give you the good-morning kiss," he told her seriously. "So you can get up after you eat the lunch me an' Mister Luke made. It's good," he promised, placing a resounding smack on her cheek.

"Thank you, sweetheart." She sipped a bit of soup and nodded. "It's very good. You've done a wonderful job. Have you been a good boy?"

"O' course! She's not getting up yet." Jamie frowned

at Luke. "You better give her a good-morning kiss, too."

It was the last thing he'd expected and Luke's startled glance flew to Darcy's. She was beautiful, even after three days in bed with a fever. Her hair flowed away from her face, leaving him with a perfect view of her wide forehead, almond-shaped eyes, thick brown lashes and high, pink-tinged cheekbones. She was blushing, and the sight of it warmed something cold inside Luke.

Her stubborn chin tilted up a fraction as she stared at him. "Jamie, I don't need any more kisses. I'll get up in a little while. Maybe this afternoon. After I have another nap."

"No!" Jamie held his ground. "The daddies have to give the mommies a kiss in the morning. That's the rule."

"Sweetie, Luke isn't your daddy. He doesn't have to kiss me." Darcy's blue eyes darkened with something— what was it? Pain? Remorse?

"He's the daddy in this house," Jamie persisted, his forehead creasing in a frown. He turned to stare at Luke. "You kiss my mommy now, Mister Luke. Then she can get up." He waited patiently.

"Jamie, I told you. Luke isn't—"

"It's all right," he murmured, bending close to Darcy. Luke didn't want to hear the words again. He knew he wasn't a father. Not anymore, at least. But the kid was so intent on getting his mother up. It wouldn't hurt anything, would it?

"There now," he told Jamie, straightening. "Your mommy can finish her lunch and have another nap.

Then, maybe, if she feels like it, she could get up for a little while this afternoon. Okay?"

"Yes." Jamie hopped from the bed, almost upsetting the tray in his rush to leave. "We gotta go now, Mom," he explained. "Aunt Clarice needs her good-morning kiss, too. All the ladies in the house get one."

"I see." Luke studied Darcy's rosy cheeks as the child whooped his way back to the kitchen. She looked so young and defenseless sitting there, Luke couldn't help the surge of protectiveness he felt. She didn't deserve the problems she'd had in life.

"I'm sorry." Her husky voice whispered across to him. "He's got a one-track mind at times. Lately it seems to dwell on fathers and their duties."

"It's only natural. Anyway, *I'm* not sorry." Luke grinned down at her with a wink. "He gave me the opportunity to kiss a beautiful woman, and it's barely even noon! I kind of like traditions like that."

If it was possible, Darcy flushed an even deeper shade of pink. Her eyes avoided his as she fiddled with the blankets.

"It's not something I think we should continue," she muttered darkly, peeking up at him quickly before her blue eyes slewed away. "I'm sorry if he's bothering you. I should be able to look after him this afternoon—"

"You can't." Luke didn't even realize he'd said it until he spotted the surprise on her face. "I mean, we planned to go into town this afternoon. I said I'd get him a treat if he behaved this morning—and he did. It's okay, isn't it? He's safe with me, you know. I won't let him out of my sight."

"It's not that," she murmured, looking away from

him, her fingers weaving together in agitation. "It's just that, well, I don't want him hurt."

Luke frowned. "No one in Raven's Rest is going to hurt him, Darcy. They probably won't even notice him."

"Oh, they'll notice, all right." She stared up at him piercingly, her eyes blazing with anger. "The illegitimate son of that tramp, Darcy Simms." She mimicked a high-pitched woman's voice. "What a nerve. To dare bring that child back here where decent people are trying to raise their families with values." She clamped her lips together and knotted the sheet, her frustration evident. "That's what they'll say, you know, and I don't want Jamie to hear any of it. My mistakes are not his fault."

"I promise I'll look after him, Darcy. He'll be fine. Can't you trust me?" Luke kept his voice low and soothing. It must be hard to let go, he thought. She'd been alone, fending for herself and the boy for so long that it's natural she finds it hard to release Jamie into someone else's care.

Luke took a step forward, covering her small white hand with his. She started in surprise, but he stayed where he was, his gaze steady.

"I'll watch him as if he were my own," he promised quietly. There was a battle going on in her eyes, one that made him wonder if Darcy Simms had ever really, truly trusted anyone. Her fingers tried to pull away, but Luke held on just enough to let her know that he meant what he said.

Finally she leaned back on her pillows, her eyes closing as she whooshed out a sigh of resignation. Her eyes were darker, more intense, when they opened. They studied his face thoroughly, scrutinizing every detail, before she nodded once.

"All right, he can go. But I'm holding you to your promise."

He smiled. "You won't be sorry, Darcy." With a pang of remorse, Luke suddenly realized just how pale her skin really was.

"Don't worry about supper," he said quietly. "I'll bring something from town." She tried to argue, but Luke cut her off. "Just take it easy today," he ordered brusquely. "Maybe by tomorrow you'll feel like moving around."

He turned to leave, shifting the tray to the side where she could reach it if she needed anything. His glance took in the barely touched soup and the grilled cheese sandwich he'd prepared, now missing only two tiny bites. She'd hardly touched a thing.

"Luke?" He turned at the door and glanced over his shoulder. "Thanks," she whispered, a tiny smile curving her lips.

"You're welcome," he returned, smiling back. "Now get some rest."

"Yes, sir." But it was a playful comment, and he took no offense. After all, how did one argue with a woman who looked like that?

Chapter Eight

Raven's Rest was bustling with folks gathering in town to shop for their annual Thanksgiving supplies. The number of turkeys leaving the grocery store made Luke grin.

"Hey, Luke!" Reverend Anderson slapped him on the back, grinning from ear to ear. "Here to pick up your Thanksgiving supplies, are you? I never knew you could cook."

"I can't, and you know that very well!" Luke smiled back. "But with both Darcy and Clarice laid up, I need a few more TV dinners." He stopped, feeling the tug on his jacket, and glanced down at the little boy hugging his leg. "This is Jamie," he said, lifting the child in his arms.

"Hi, Jamie! My goodness, do you look like your grandmother!" The pastor's booming voice caused the boy to shrink back a little. "She had that same stubborn tilt to your chin."

"I don't gots a grandma," Jamie told him, frowning. "Nor a daddy neither. I just gots my mom and me.

An' Mister Luke an' Auntie Clarice," he added after a moment's thought.

"I know." The minister nodded, directing a surprised look in Luke's direction. "But that's a pretty good family to start with, don't you think?" When Jamie nodded, Pastor David turned back to Luke. "What did you say is wrong with the ladies in your house?"

"Darcy's down with a real bad cold," Luke told him, setting the little boy back on the floor and reminding him to stay nearby. "And Aunt Clarice carried a box of clay downstairs and strained her back. We've been nursing them both back to health."

"You? A nurse?" A bubbling laugh burst from the minister. "Somehow, I just can't imagine it," he chortled.

"How about if I round up some folks who'll come out to help with dinner on Thursday? That way your ladies can still get their rest without missing a good meal." He studied the stack of TV dinners in Luke's basket, shook his head, and carefully removed them, shoving them back into the freezer. "No cardboard at Thanksgiving," he muttered, shuddering. "It's against all the rules."

"That would be really nice, David, but I don't know how Darcy would feel about it. She's a little nervous about meeting people."

"Afraid of the gossip, I imagine." The Reverend shook his head, frowning. "Nasty thing, gossip. Never does anything but tear people down. As if anyone wants to be reminded of their past—"

"Reverend Anderson! Surely you're not buying *canned* cranberries to go with that turkey I gave you?

My word, I didn't think your wife would allow that prepackaged stuff at her table." Ella Lancaster tut-tutted. "Surely you'll be using some of those *fresh* cranberries from the Hansons?"

"I really don't know, Mrs. Lancaster. I'm just following orders."

The Reverend looked a little green around the gills, Luke noted, grinning. "Oh, Reverend Anderson doesn't eat cranberries," he muttered, knowing the old woman would have to make something of it.

"And why not, might I ask? They're very healthy. Clean the gall bladder out wonderfully."

Luke snickered under his breath, wondering how long David could maintain his pasted-on smile. The man had the weakest stomach of anyone Luke had ever known, and the dirty-socks smell of cooking cranberries made him physically ill. Fortunately, Mrs. Lancaster let the subject drop when she spied Jamie.

"Now who is this?" she cooed, chucking the boy under the chin.

Jamie, of course, found sanctuary by hiding himself in Luke's legs, keeping his face firmly hidden. "This is Darcy Simms's son, Jamie," Luke introduced them. "He's a bit shy at the moment."

"Why in the world would he be shy of me?" Ella blurted out. "Come on, boy. Shake hands like a little man."

But Jamie was having none of it. Lifting the boy into his arms, Luke let him keep his chin tucked into his chest.

"How long is she staying?" Ella's mean little eyes

focused intently on Luke. "Looks like she's got you all wrapped up."

"I don't know what you mean." Luke kept his voice low. He wasn't going to stand here with Darcy's son and listen to a lot of innuendo. Neither would he allow her to malign the child's mother over her past.

"Well, you're looking after her kid while she's off doing who knows what!"

Luke heard the pastor suck in his breath as the spiteful words left the woman's mouth. There was a glimmer of sympathy in David's face as he watched Luke get himself under control.

"My mom's sick!" Jamie's little voice broke the tense silence. "She's been in bed for three days. Mister Luke said she's getting better though."

"And how would he know?" Ella demanded, snorting indignantly. "He's a rancher, not a nurse!"

"I called the doctor. He said Darcy had a serious cold. She spent a little too long outside at her parents' grave site." Luke said the words deliberately, reminding the woman of Darcy and Jamie's recent loss.

Luke turned to the minister. "David, would you help Jamie pick out some of those nuts? We're going to have them while we watch a video tonight." He waited till the two were safely out of earshot, his hand reaching out to grasp Mrs. Lancaster's arm before she could scuttle away. "Just a minute. I want to talk to you."

"Let me go."

Luke held his ground. "I will in a minute," he grated. "But first I have something to say to you."

"I imagine it's about bringing something out to the

farm for Clarice," Ella muttered. "I suppose I can take time out of my schedule—for *her*."

Luke shook his head angrily. "Clarice doesn't want your help," he hissed. "And neither do I. Not if you intend to go on maligning Darcy in this way. The ranch is her home, and she has every right to be there."

"She doesn't belong there! Not after the way she's behaved. Look how she ran away and left Lester and Martha to manage on their own. Ungrateful child! Maybe you don't know the grief she caused them, but I do. And then to come home with that, that fatherless boy!" Words seemed to fail her here, and Luke was glad of it. He couldn't listen to any more anyway.

"You don't know anything about it, Mrs. Lancaster. How can you possibly understand what Darcy's life was like, or what made her decide she had to leave? Do you think it was easy for her to manage, alone in the city, with a child?"

"She chose her bed."

"And she's paying for it, if it makes you feel any better," he said. "And I'm sure it does," he muttered under his breath. Luke ached to wipe that smug look off the woman's face. "What gives you the right to go around acting like judge and jury, Mrs. Lancaster? Haven't you ever made a mistake? Or is it just that nobody in Raven's Rest knows about it yet?"

"Of all the nerve!" If the woman didn't vent some of that rage, she was going to burst a blood vessel.

"I quite agree," he muttered grimly. "It takes a lot of nerve to condemn someone you know nothing about, whose problems you couldn't possibly understand. The world would be a whole lot better if people kept their self-righteous noses out of other folks' lives. Good day!" He turned away and marched down the aisle to find Jamie, rage boiling through his blood.

Was it any wonder Darcy Simms had stayed away from this place for five long years?

"Luke? Luke!" An urgent hand grabbed his sleeve.

"What? Oh, hi, Jalise." He said it apologetically, his eyes busily searching the store. "I'm sorry I didn't see you."

"I'm not surprised!" Jalise Penner blinked up at him curiously. "You were stomping away as if something was chewing at your heels." She glanced back down the aisle to where Mrs. Lancaster stood frowning, watching them together. "Don't tell me Ella was on your case."

"Not mine. Darcy's. That woman doesn't have an ounce of humanity in her!"

"Darcy? Darcy *Simms?*" Jalise's brown eyes sparkled. "You mean she's back? Great!"

Luke searched for some hint of hidden meaning in the words, but Jalise seemed genuinely pleased about the news. "Do you know her?" he asked carefully, preparing himself for another onslaught.

"Of course I know her. We were in the same class at school. Darcy and I used to be best friends." Her eyes clouded. "Until she found someone she preferred more than me." Jalise seemed lost in thought for a moment. "How is she?" she asked at last.

"She's been sick. That's why I brought Jamie along today. Darcy's son, Jamie."

"I didn't realize she had a son," Jalise murmured.

She studied him, her silver-gray eyes speculative. "It doesn't bother you to have him around?"

"No." Luke shook his head, only then acknowledging the truth. "In fact, I've been enjoying Jamie. He's so curious about everything on the ranch."

"Where were they living?"

"New York. This isn't for publication, Jalise, but I'm really glad I found them when I did. I don't know how much longer she could have lasted." He glanced around at the familiar surroundings that he'd begun to take for granted. "The people in this little community have a lot to be grateful for."

When Luke finally caught up with Jamie in the candy aisle, the boy was busily explaining to the minister how they'd moved the cows earlier in the day. His eyes danced merrily, and it was obvious that he hadn't missed Luke one whit.

"All finished your shopping?" Pastor Anderson asked.

"Just about. Thanks, David. Come on, Jamie, my boy. We've got work to do."

Jamie peered up at Jalise, his eyes admiring her white-blond hair. "My name is Jamie Simms," he announced loudly, holding out his hand. "I'm four-and-a-half years old."

"Four?" Jalise stared at him, her eyes darkening as she puzzled that one out. Luke's fears for the boy's sensibilities renewed themselves ten times over before Jalise seemed to get herself under control enough to respond. "Oh. Well, hello, Jamie. My name is Mrs. Penner, but you can call me Jalise. I'm a friend of your mom's." She shook the little hand gravely and gave that smile that Luke had seen soften the hardest heart.

Jamie peered up at her frowning. "My mom don't gots no friends here 'cept Mister Luke and Aunt Clarice. She tol' me."

"Is that right? Well, maybe she forgot about me then. I used to go to school with her, and your mommy was my best friend in the whole world." Jalise seemed to think for a moment and then crouched down beside him. "Do you think you could remember to tell her that I said 'hello'? I'd sure like to visit her when she's feeling better."

"I guess so." Jamie studied her, reaching out one hand to delicately touch the glistening fall of hair. "It's pretty. Do you gots any kids?" he asked quietly.

"No, Jamie, I'm sorry but I don't. I wish I had a little boy like you, though. Your mommy is very lucky."

Luke could hear the tears in her voice. He knew how much it hurt Jalise that she had no child to live on after Billy's death.

"Yes," Jamie agreed in a loud, satisfied voice. "I'm a good boy." He tugged Luke's hand. "Come on, Mister Luke. We gotta go home and look after the pay-shuns." He smiled, delighted with his new word.

"I've got to get going, too," David Anderson told them. "I've got a sermon to prepare for Sunday." He rubbed his chin thoughtfully. "I believe it's time to discuss the Bible's stand on idle gossip."

"Gossip?" Jalise stared at him. "There aren't any scriptures that talk specifically about gossip, are there?"

David winked. "You'll have to come on Sunday to find out, Jalise. See you later."

"Yeah. Thanks, David. I appreciate your… intervention." Luke shook his hand gratefully.

"You're welcome," David chuckled, thrusting his hands in his pockets. He ambled off to his car, his gait slowing again as he approached another parishioner.

"I've got to go, too," Jalise added, glancing at her watch. "I've got Junior Choir tonight." She patted Jamie's head and turned to Luke. "Please tell Darcy to call. I'd love to see her again. It's been too long."

"I'll tell her," Luke promised, but he wanted to tell Jalise not to get her hopes up. Darcy didn't seem willing to allow anyone past the barrier she'd erected, and if Ella Lancaster was any example of the reception she'd receive, he couldn't say he blamed her. "Okay, kiddo!" he said to Jamie. "Let's finish shopping."

By the time Luke got through the checkout and loaded his supplies, the sun was long gone and the wind howled, tossing around stinging bits of icy sleet. He took the road home carefully, grateful for his four-wheel drive, and pulled into the yard with relief.

The warm yellow glow raised his spirits, and he felt a renewed energy course through his veins as he and Jamie lugged the groceries into the house, sniffing appreciatively as the fragrant smell of roasting beef floated out to greet them.

"Something sure smells good," Jamie chirped, tossing off his coat and boots. "My mom musta made something."

Privately, Luke thought so, too, and he was grateful for it. But he wished she'd taken a little longer to rest. The shadows under her eyes and sunken hollows below her cheeks told him that she needed freedom from stress, sleep, and some decent food to get back to good health.

"Hi, Mom," Jamie squealed, racing across the room to where his mother sat snuggled up on the sofa. "Are you better?"

"Lots better, sweetheart." She accepted his hug readily, returning it with obvious pleasure. "Were you a good boy?" she asked, softly brushing the hair off his forehead.

"Uh-huh. I met a man who works in a church who tol' me I could go there sometimes—if you'd let me—an' see some other kids that come to hear about God. Can I go?"

Luke saw the frown that creased her mouth. "He was talking to David Anderson." He said it quietly, watching for signs that the wall was back up around her once more.

"I meeted a lady, too," Jamie crowed, wiggling away to stand in front of Darcy. "She said she was your friend. I didn't know you had friends here, Mommy."

"Your mom has lots of friends here," Luke told him quietly, flopping into the easy chair. "She used to live here, remember? Jalise and your mom were good friends before your mom had to go away."

Jamie nodded, bent to pick up his airplane from the coffee table and raced from the room, swooping up and down. Luke hoped that the message got through to Darcy: *Not everyone is like Ella Lancaster.*

"You saw Jalise?" Darcy's blue eyes searched his face. "How...how is she?"

"She's lonely. With Billy gone, it's been tough. She tries to fill up her time with meetings and stuff, but I think rattling around in that big old farmhouse must be awfully solitary. She could use a friend."

"I'm sure Billy left her well provided for. He never had a shortage of cash."

Luke gave her a stern look. "Money doesn't buy friends or happiness, Darcy. And the one thing Jalise Penner could use right now is a friend. You were very close once. Maybe you could be again. Why don't you call her?"

"And say what?" Darcy glared at him. "Would you like me to fill her in on my terrible past? Or maybe we could discuss my parents' deaths. That ought to lighten things up!"

"Stop feeling sorry for yourself," he burst out, angry that this woman he was coming to admire couldn't dig herself free of the misery of a past that was dead and gone. "Why don't you try asking her about herself, about some old friends, about her plans? You can give her something no one else can, Darcy."

"I haven't got anything to give. I'm flat broke in case you hadn't noticed." Darcy surged to her feet, the quilt draping around her ankles. "Jalise doesn't need anything from me."

"She needs you to be her friend. That's all. Can't you do that for her?" Luke held her gaze, concern rising as he saw the fear welling up in her eyes, giving her that scared-little-girl look she'd had in New York. She finally broke his stare and tried to move away.

"Sometimes you have to take a chance on people, Darcy," he murmured, gazing down into her expressive eyes, his hands on her narrow waist. "There are some *good* souls out there who will stick with you through thick and thin if you give them a chance."

She made no effort to move away, and frankly, Luke was glad. He enjoyed holding her like this. It had been a long time since he'd felt such a rush of protectiveness flow over him. When she buried her tired head against his chest, he realized how much he'd missed sharing this warmth and closeness with someone.

"I'd like to believe in your pipe dream, Luke," she whispered. "I really would. But reality is a whole different ball game. I know what the people here think of me. I've known it all along. And I don't care." There was a tinge of loneliness to that statement that made it ring false.

"I think you're a strong beautiful woman who's taken on life determined to prove a point." He let his arms tighten around her just a fraction. "You've proven it, Darcy. You can handle what you're given. But doesn't it get lonely doing it all by yourself?"

She dropped her hands from his chest. "That's the only way I know *how* to handle things."

"You aren't alone. God is there, waiting for you to lean on Him. If you want to." He stared into her eyes. "I'm here, too." Luke met her gaze. "If you want me," he added softly, unsure himself of exactly what he meant. All he knew was that she was hurting and he wanted desperately to help, to take it away. To make her world good and happy again.

"I guess I *could* use a friend."

The whisper-soft words brushed over his skin as she spoke, her pink lips tantalizing him. It was inevitable that he would kiss her. As a friend he wanted to reassure her, to ease the load a little. But as his mouth brushed across hers and she returned his kiss, Luke mentally admitted the truth. Darcy Simms touched his heart in a way that had nothing at all to do with sympathy. And from her response, Luke was pretty sure that he'd moved up a step from interloper-ranch hand. Which was a good thing.

Wasn't it?

Chapter Nine

"Miss Ridgely? I was wondering if you still had that job of teacher's aide open? I'd like to apply for it." Darcy forced a note of calmness into her voice and ignored the twenty or so other people in the staff room who sat peering at her.

"Yes, dear, I have. And the job hasn't been filled. Oh, it will be lovely to have an extra set of hands around here! Come with me, Darcy. I'll just get the forms from my desk. I was hoping you'd be back." The benevolent smile of the older woman sent Darcy's spirits soaring.

The few early-bird students that had already arrived were still outside playing in the newly fallen snow. Darcy could hear their cries and giggles through the huge glass windows in Miss Ridgely's room.

"This is wonderful news, Darcy. I just know you'll be so good at this job. It's too bad you didn't go on to college. You would make a wonderful teacher."

It was the second time she'd heard it in as many weeks, and Darcy couldn't help but wonder if she would be any use as a teacher. In New York it *had* been she who had shown the other girls the routine—that was true. And she did enjoy explaining things. But teaching? That was a whole different ball game.

"Here we are." Hilda held the form up triumphantly.

"You're sure you think I can do this?" Darcy studied the woman's shining eyes. "I've never tried anything like it before, but it *is* interesting."

"Darcy, you're a natural teacher. You have an innate ability to hear all the things people don't say. That's going to stand you well when you deal with these children. I wish you'd think more about taking those distance courses. It wouldn't take you that long, and you could really have a good basis to work on your degree."

"I don't think I could afford college," Darcy told her, feeling a private sense of loss. "Not with Jamie, and helping out on the farm."

"But you don't have to pay for it all at once. It's not as if you'd be taking a full load."

"No, but it still means money. How much is a full-credit course now?"

"They vary, naturally, but I happen to have a calendar here…" Hilda held it out so Darcy could see the fee structure.

"I could probably afford that," Darcy began doubtfully, "but the work might be beyond me." Still, the dream of herself in a classroom tantalized her.

"Of course you could do it. With your hands tied!" Hilda's voice was refreshingly reassuring, and in the face of such enthusiasm, Darcy couldn't help but grin back.

"I don't know. It seems like such a big project. And

I can't guarantee just how long Luke will continue with this arrangement. He might decide he wants to move on somewhere else." Or that he wants me gone, she admitted to herself.

"That's the beauty of distance education. Doesn't matter where you are. And I'd be happy to have you in my class to do your internship."

Darcy couldn't help it—she was catching this positive spirit. "I can't thank you enough, Hilda. This will be so wonderful."

"Yes, it will. I enjoy my classes each day, but it will be so nice to have someone to share them with. I wonder…" She tapped the tip of her nose as her thick bushy eyebrows drew together. "You may be able to claim some of the time you spend as an aide as a credit—apprenticeship or something. I'll check into that." She made a note to herself and stuck it on the side of her filing cabinet.

"Um, Miss Ridgely?" Darcy wondered just how to word a touchy question. "I was wondering, that is, well, what about Annette? I know she doesn't really want me here. Mostly because of the past, but still, I don't want to make things uncomfortable for you."

"Annette's stubborn, but she's talked to the board and they feel that you should be given a chance at the position. Since we're so short of help, she can hardly object." Hilda patted her shoulder comfortingly. "Don't worry about Annette, Darcy. Just concentrate on the task before you."

"I will," Darcy promised. "Now, would you like to show me what I'll be working on if I get the job?"

"God is more than a judge to His children."
Reverend Anderson's topic for a sermon struck Darcy

as unusual. Everyone knew that God judged people for their sins. And goodness knew, she had a pile of sins to make up for. Everyone knew that, too.

"It's not that He doesn't know we've done wrong. And it's not that He doesn't care." The pastor's face was alive with the excitement of his faith as he spoke to the congregation packed into the tiny church. "But God is not like human beings. He doesn't dwell on someone's mistakes, hashing and rehashing them over and over, always standing in judgment even after we've asked His forgiveness. God says that once you've repented of the wrong, He remembers it no more…"

Several people in front of Darcy shifted uneasily in their seats. She felt particularly uncomfortable herself. Perhaps it was the heat; so many people crowded into such a small area was bound to make it warmer than usual. It was funny, though. Clarice didn't seem to notice it. Nor did Luke, who sat facing the front with Jamie comfortably seated on his lap.

"…As members of God's family, can we do less than God does? Can we afford to hang onto the past and constantly harangue ourselves and others about it? Isn't it time we faced up to our shortcomings and got on with the life we've been given today?"

There wasn't a sound in the sanctuary. Not a single baby cried, not one teenager shifted. Every eye was focused on the man standing behind the pulpit, speaking a truth so painful that it hurt the listeners to hear.

"The Bible tells us not to judge anyone, lest we ourselves be judged by the same harsh measure. Dearly beloved, is that how you want to spend your time, criticizing everyone who has made a mistake?" His voice dropped. "Then you'd better start your judgments by looking in the mirror. *Let the one who is blameless cast the first stone*."

Darcy glanced down at her hands, shamed by her own judgmental attitude toward the people who sat in front of her and behind her. If she had a bad reputation, there was a reason, wasn't there? She'd deliberately played the part of town brat and fed into people's impressions. What goes around comes around, she reminded herself bitterly.

"My dear family, our heavenly Father is concerned with the future of His children. He wants us to get beyond all the pain and mistakes of the past. God wants to move into the future and show us such hope and joy, we can't imagine it. Forget the hurts and the disappointments. Put them away."

The words floated around Darcy's head. So easy to say, she thought sadly. So difficult to do.

"The past cannot be changed, dear ones. It's dead and gone. But we have a whole new canvas in front of us. We can paint whatever we wish on that. Choose!" Everyone sat straighter, startled by the peremptory command.

"Choose right now whether you will make your life a picture of joy, happiness and sharing, or whether you will drag all the old ugly disappointments of the past onto that pristine blank page and dirty it up with what God has already forgotten. He's given you the opportunity to sparkle and shine. Will you ignore that and rust away in your past?"

Darcy stood with the rest of the congregation and halfheartedly sang the words to the closing hymn. The pastor's words rang in her head as she shook hands with a few old friends—and walked past those who turned their backs.

"Good sermon." Clarice shook the Reverend's hand vigorously. "Right to the point. Top-notch."

"Thank you, Clarice. I only hope it sinks in."

"Takes a while. A body needs to meditate on the right path. Better not to make quick decisions."

"Yes, you're absolutely right." David Anderson grinned in satisfaction. "So many people just let the days roll by without realizing that they won't get a second chance. How's your back?"

"Still there," Clarice quipped, her prim mouth stretched wide. "Been getting lots of walking in. Helps." She nodded once and then marched down the steps to the group of ladies huddled on the lawn.

"Darcy. How are you? I understand you've also been ill." There was sympathy in those eyes, as if they saw everything that was in her heart, and understood.

"Just a cold. I'm fine now, thanks to Luke." She sent a smile his way.

"Well, that's good to hear. And I'm very happy you came this morning." Pastor Anderson squeezed her hand. "Very glad."

"I'm afraid that's due to Luke, too. He's awfully hard to say 'no' to! Not that I wanted to," she amended with a blush. "Not after everyone was so kind about Thanksgiving. That was a lovely meal you brought out. Clarice and I could never have managed it in our conditions. And Luke isn't exactly…handy when it comes to cooking."

Darcy couldn't help the smile that tickled the corner of her lips at the sight of the frown on Luke's handsome face. He'd been adamant that she had to make a public appearance today, especially after the townsfolk had driven out with a wonderful array of turkey, ham and all the fixings. But Darcy hadn't missed the four TV dinners he'd secreted at the back of the freezer. When the pastor arrived at the farm, she'd deliberately heated them up for lunch yesterday. His dour look now reminded her that he wasn't going to let it slide.

Still, in spite of feeling uncomfortable during the service, and even though she knew all the old hens were cackling even now, Luke had been right about this service, she conceded. In spite of everything, she was glad she had come, if only to listen to the lovely music.

"See. You lived! Next time, don't bother arguing," Luke murmured in her ear as they went out the door. "It wasn't that bad, was it?"

"Bad enough. I felt like every pair of eyes in the place was staring at me for a while. Thank goodness the junior choir had that presentation." Darcy watched as Jamie spoke to some children racing around the parking lot. The other kids seemed to accept him for what he was—a little boy who wanted to make friends. She heaved a sigh of relief as her son joined the group.

"Dar, is that you?" Jalise Penner raced down the stairs in the most unladylike fashion and stopped in front of Darcy, panting. "You haven't changed a bit. Welcome home!"

Darcy found herself wrapped in welcoming arms and hugged for all she was worth. She couldn't do any less than return the greeting as her eyes filled with tears.

"Thank you, Jay," she said at last, holding the other woman at arm's length. "It's nice to be back...I guess."

"Oh, the old tabbies have been having a go, I suppose?" Jalise glanced from Luke to Darcy and then back to Luke, who inclined his head. "Forget about them," she advised, glaring at Mrs. Lancaster as the woman stared rudely and then leaned over to whisper in her neighbor's ear.

"Remember, Dar, this is Raven's Rest. They have to talk about something other than—"

"—the weather, crop prices and Joe Blow's new haircut," Darcy finished with a grin. She burst out laughing at Jalise's pained look.

"At least it takes their tongues off me." Jalise pitched her voice in a loud, rather squeaky tone that Darcy was sure would be heard by the other women. "That girl needs a man and a passel of children," she cackled. "Billy shouldn't have left her with so much time on her hands. Why she's wearing herself out with that café!"

Jalise reverted to her normal tones. "As if he just wandered off without thinking that he was going for good and I might want a child before he left. Honestly! But you know, Dar, I think what bugs me more than their nasty gossiping is that they call my lovely, wonderful restaurant a café! Even though I specifically called it The Coffee Klatsch."

"Luke told me about Billy. I'm so sorry, Jalise." Darcy hugged her old friend once more. "How are you managing?"

"I'm okay. I've had some time to deal with it and even though I wish he'd hung around for a little longer, I can't wish him back. God has a plan. I know that." She grimaced. "I just don't know what it is."

"Join the club." Darcy studied the face she'd known

so well. It was thinner now, older. Sadder. But then, weren't they all?

"Why don't you drop in for coffee some afternoon?" Jalise invited. "I usually take off between two and four. I've been needing someone to confide in."

Darcy was so relieved that Jalise didn't want to talk about the past that she agreed to meet her friend for coffee the next day. "I have to see the lawyer anyway," she murmured with a telling glance at Luke. "I want to know how things stand."

"Well, Old Man Pettigrew is back home, so that'll probably work out," Jalise agreed. "If you're looking for something to do, I can always use someone to help out in the *café*." She grinned playfully.

"Oh, Jay! That's so kind of you. And thank you. But I'm going to start as a teacher's aide and I don't want to be away from Jamie too much right now. Next year he'll be in school you know."

"Yes, I know." There was a strange note in Jalise's voice that Darcy was afraid to analyze. "You are so lucky. He's a wonderful little boy."

"Yes, he is," Luke put in softly. "And if we don't get him out of that snowbank, he'll probably freeze to death. You girls can chitchat all you like, but I'm getting Jamie and we're going to the truck. I'm not needed here anyway!"

Darcy burst out laughing at his mock offended expression, and heard Jalise join her. Together they watched Luke coax Jamie away from his friends and into the cab.

"I guess that's a hint," Darcy mumbled. "I see Clarice is already sitting in the back. I'd better go."

"See you tomorrow. And be prepared to hang around. We've got a lot to catch up on." Jalise waved at Luke before scurrying across the lot to her own little car.

As Darcy strode over to the truck, her mind whirled with the activities of the morning. It hadn't been nearly as bad as she'd feared. No one had said anything out of the ordinary, and some folks had certainly gone out of their way to make her feel welcome.

Maybe Clarice and the good minister were right, she reflected. Maybe this was a new beginning and maybe—just maybe—she could start over again. She resolved to put the past behind her, and then wondered exactly how one went about doing that. Especially when one had a four-year-old reminder of exactly what the past entailed.

Chapter Ten

"Don't envy me, Jay. It really wasn't all that glamorous. While you were here getting married, I was scrounging for my next meal and dodging every lecher in the city!"

Jalise reached out and squeezed her hand. "I'm sorry you had to go through all that, Darcy. And I'm sorry that I wasn't there for you. Not that you needed me. Not with God on your side. Besides, you're very strong, you know. It's something I've come to admire about you."

"Really? I guess I've never thought of myself as being particularly strong. Rebellious maybe, but not strong." Darcy fidgeted in her chair. "I suppose you know about the ranch?"

"You mean about Luke inheriting half?" Jalise nodded. "In this kind of place you can't avoid the gossip, and much as I hate to admit it, there's usually some part of it that's true. Are you upset?"

"I was at first. Furious. But then I realized that my parents probably just wanted to protect their lifelong work. And I wasn't around to see to it. Luke was here—

he was like their son. He has a right to whatever they wanted him to have. I don't really deserve anything."

"Of course you do, Darcy! Don't sell yourself short, kid. You do know your parents tried to find you? Your dad spent a lot of time chasing down leads. That's why he needed Luke. Then, of course, he got sick and he couldn't spend as much time as he wanted to. But for a while there, Lester and Martha would take off every weekend, driving here and there to find out if anyone had any news about you."

That was the last thing Darcy'd expected to hear, and she could hardly believe it. "They tried to find me?"

"Of course they did, Dar! They were worried about you when you didn't answer their ads."

"I never saw any ads," Darcy murmured, staring at her. "But then, I didn't have much money for newspapers, either." She frowned. "Jay, I can't quite believe this. You're saying that my parents actually tried to find me and get me to come home?"

Jalise nodded. "But after your dad got so sick, the doctor told him he had to take it easy, stop worrying. By then your mom couldn't do much more. I used to go out and see them quite often. To cheer them up, you know?" Darcy closed her eyes, trying to absorb all this information. "I think if Luke hadn't coerced Clarice into coming here and shaking things up, your mother would have just given up. Clarice convinced them to forget about what they couldn't fix and concentrate on what they could."

"And that's when the air-conditioning and new appliances came in?" Darcy guessed, watching Jalise closely.

"Uh-huh. It wasn't that they forgot about you, Darcy. They had to do something for someone else or go crazy with guilt."

"Guilt?" Darcy whispered the word, somehow afraid to hear what Jalise would say next.

"They felt a terrible guilt. Your mother told me once that she'd been given a gift from God when you were born and that she had only just realized that she had messed things up by trying to make you perfect. It took your leaving for her to see that she'd ruined that gift."

"You can't *make* a child do anything. Not in the long term. You can only teach them and care for them and let them know how much they mean to you." Darcy whispered the words as she stared at her hands. "Jamie taught me that. He's my child and I love him more than life. I have hopes and dreams for him—but I don't own him. He is his own little person."

Jalise nodded. "I know. You seem like a great mother. But it was a lesson that it took your mom so long to learn, maybe because of her own childhood. I don't know. But she always thought you knew how much she loved you, Dar."

"She never said it—not once that I can remember." Darcy hunched over in her chair and stared at her friend. "I *ached* to hear them say that, and they never did."

"Are you sure, honey?" Jalise wrapped her long slim fingers around Darcy's arm and squeezed. "Are you sure they never said it? Sometime when you're alone and have time, try to remember more than the rotten times. I think you'll find that your parents tried to tell you in a hundred different ways that they loved you."

Somehow Darcy managed to get through the next

few minutes without bawling. But later, as she walked down the street toward the church, her mind flew back to a past she would rather forget. Had there really been love there, and she'd missed it?

"Darcy, good morning. I hope you're feeling well."

"I'm fine, Reverend Anderson. And thank you again for the wonderful Thanksgiving feast. I don't know how you managed to get so much into your car. I hope it wasn't damaged from the trip," she teased.

"You know how those dents got in the side, don't you? A turkey leg popped out and struck an oncoming vehicle." His face was perfectly serious, and Darcy couldn't help smiling. "Actually, I was hoping I'd meet you. I wanted to ask you something."

"Go ahead," Darcy said.

"It's about the Christmas pageant. Jalise Penner will be leading the junior choir while the rest of the Sunday School students are putting on a play."

"Sounds lovely." She kept her voice carefully noncommittal.

"Actually, it's a pretty good way to make sure no children are left out. Not everyone can be counted on to recite a poem or a story. But with the music and just a few recitations, I think we can make it an evening of praise and worship to the King."

"I'm sure it will be wonderful."

"The thing is, we haven't any costumes. René Jones did design a few things, and Bettina Bensen donated the fabric from her store, but no one has time to sew them up. And those who are willing simply don't have the expertise needed to translate René's ideas into reality."

"And you hoped I'd be able to help out?" Darcy finished for him, wondering if the whole world knew that she'd been working in the garment district. "Ordinarily I would. I'm sure René's costumes are wonderful. But I've just agreed to take on the teacher's aide position at school, and I said I'd help Luke with the ranch book-keeping. I don't think I'd have time for anything more." She felt a pang of regret and wondered why it was suddenly important to her to do this.

"The pageant isn't until Christmas Eve, Darcy. And we don't need the costumes until right before that. Isn't there some way you could manage it?" He sounded so earnest that Darcy found herself reconsidering. "I'm sure Jalise would help. René might even be talked into lending a hand. Please?"

Darcy frowned. She didn't owe these people anything. The past was gone and she intended to focus on the future as Clarice had suggested. So why did she feel somehow beholden?

"It's a big night for Jalise," Reverend Anderson continued softly. His eyes glowed with some inner secret. "She's been planning this for months."

Three days later Darcy had to bite her lip to keep from rescinding her silly offer to help. Mounds of white gauzy "angel" fabric sat waiting for the scissors. There were rich velvets for the wise men, bark cloth for the shepherds, and wooly "sheepskins" to be shaped and stuffed with wriggling little boys and girls.

"Why do I let you get me into these things, Jalise?" Darcy moaned as her friend quickly shaped wings from wire coat hangers. "We'll never get through all of this!"

"Oh, don't be such a pessimist! These are only for the manger scene. The rest of the play uses everyday clothes."

"Yes, but look at these sketches! They're so elaborate." Darcy spread the drawings over the huge cutting table in the seniors' center, studying them with a groan. "I don't know how to make patterns for this headgear!"

"So, let's call René and get her to come over and show us." Jalise walked to the phone and dialed before Darcy could object.

Five minutes later René was explaining the historical significance of the garments and how each would fit the actor.

"You must know a little about this stuff, Darcy. You worked in a clothing outfit in New York, didn't you?" An envious note crept into René's otherwise dull voice. "Surely you got to see them design the patterns?"

"Yes, I did. But I never had to translate pattern to fabric. I usually worked in other areas." Darcy forced herself to remain calm and unruffled. "I heard that you won yourself a pretty prestigious place at Chelan's. I envy you that. They've got some of the best designs in the city."

"Yeah, I did. But I never got to finish it out. That's been a regret of mine."

"I know what regret is like," Darcy commiserated. "I have a few of those myself."

"It's weird, really. When you're eighteen, you're ready to take on anyone and anything and you think you have all the time in the world. And then one day you wake up and find out that your window of opportunity has vanished, that it's all over and you've missed your chance."

"You haven't missed anything, René," Jalise burst out. "You've got a wonderful husband, a nice home, a beautiful daughter. Some women would kill for that."

"I'm not 'some women.'" René's voice was full of hurt, and Darcy suddenly felt compassion for the vivacious redhead. "To me, Raven's Rest is the end of the earth."

"I know what you mean," Darcy murmured, thinking of her own situation. "When I left here, I was full of plans for the future. I wasn't going to even come back until I could show my parents that I didn't need them."

"I only ever wanted to stay here with Billy and raise my family." Jalise stared at the quilt hanging on the wall as tears formed at the corners of her eyes. "I thought I'd done all the right things and yet still I didn't get my heart's desire…."

They worked steadily, quietly. Darcy organized each pattern piece with the others until she had three complete wise men outfits. René started on the shepherds' costumes, and Jalise continued to wrap white gauze around the angel's wings she'd formed.

"It sort of makes me think of this," Jalise said after a long contemplative silence. When the others frowned at her, she grinned and waved a hand at the mess surrounding them. "Well, look at this chaos! Someone who walked in would think that there isn't rhyme or reason to what we're doing. René's just hacking away at that, and you're picking up her leftovers."

"And?" René slit a neckline in the sheep's head.

"I know what she means." Darcy grinned. "It might look like a mess, but actually we *are* organized and there *is* a method to what we're doing."

"Exactly!" Jalise beamed with satisfaction.

"So what?" retorted René. "How does that help me know what to do with this craving I have? It doesn't. This omnipotent plan you're so infatuated with is Greek to me. I can't see the point of it. Why couldn't Jesse's father have found someone else to run his ranch? Why did we have to come back here?" There were tears in her beautiful eyes.

"You really mean, why did Ginny have to be born with her disease?" Jalise added softly, and patted the slim shoulder as René burst into fresh tears. "I don't know the answer to that, sweetheart. Nobody does. But it's what we've got to work with."

"I don't *want* to work with it. I want things to be the way I want them."

Darcy smiled to herself at the tone of rebellion in René's voice. It sounded like her own voice, she decided grimly. René was saying exactly what Darcy had felt for years. And the answer that she was getting wasn't any more satisfactory to her than the one Darcy had come up with for her own situation.

"The thing is, René—" Jalise's forehead furrowed in thought "—we don't know how your ideas would have worked out either. We know what we want to happen, but maybe that wouldn't have been the case either. Maybe if you'd stayed at in-training, you wouldn't have had Ginny. Or maybe Jesse would have been hurt or gotten mixed up in something evil. We just don't know."

"Or maybe everything would have gone along

perfectly, and I'd be set up as a designer right now, showing the world my creations." René's lips tightened.

"And I'd have gone to school and gotten a really good job somewhere with people who cared about me," Darcy added.

"And maybe I'd have six children by now and be happily at home, raising them! It's useless to 'what if' all the time. It didn't happen—and we have to get on with what *did*."

"How?" René glared at the others fiercely. "By pretending that what we really want doesn't matter? It matters, Jalise. It hasn't just gone away."

"And it won't. God made you the way you are, honey. He doesn't want you to deny the very desires that He's given you. He just wants you to find a new way to use them."

"And what about Darcy?" Darcy wanted to know the answer herself.

"I don't know what God's plans are," Jalise admitted. "I'm just speculating that if we didn't go down one trail, maybe it's because God meant for us to do something else. Maybe Darcy had to come home to face her demons before she can move on."

"And you?" Darcy studied her friend's thoughtful look. "What do you see as God's reason for your situation? Didn't He want you and Billy to be married? Is that why Billy died?"

"No! Billy and I were meant to be together. I knew that from long ago. And we did have a wonderful married life. But it wasn't all pain free. We disagreed on a lot of things. And Billy suffered terrible bouts of depression. It wasn't all roses, you know."

"So what's the point?" René frowned. "What's the reason?"

"I don't know," Jalise repeated. "I just know that I'm supposed to pick up the pieces and go on. Billy's and my dreams of a family are gone. But I'm still here, and I'm alive. I have to wait for God to show me the next step."

"All I have to say is that it's pretty frustrating!" René gathered up the scraps and shoved them into a garbage bag.

"That's for sure," Darcy agreed grimly. "I no more wanted to come back here than fly to the moon. It's been really hard to deal with all the nasty remarks and speculation. People wondering about Jamie, talking about him. What good does that do me?"

"It's made you stronger, for one thing." Jalise's silver-gray eyes sparkled. "The old Darcy would have retaliated if someone dared to say something she didn't like. Remember those eggings you carried out so frequently? The old Darcy would have tried to get back at anyone who got on her wrong side. You've grown beyond that because you faced the past."

"And I've seen you with Luke Lassiter several times lately," René added with a gleam in her eye. "The two of you seem pretty cozy. I remember a time when you wouldn't let anyone but Josiah Pringle within forty feet of you." She grinned. "I guess that's all changed if that kiss you and Luke exchanged in the park yesterday was any indicator."

Darcy flushed, studying her fingers. "It was just a thank-you kiss," she murmured. "He helped me get all the papers in for a course I'm taking. It didn't mean anything." But she knew she was lying. It meant quite a lot to her to be held in those strong arms and treated like someone special, someone who mattered.

"No, of course not. How silly of me! Didn't mean anything, my foot!" René smirked. "So that's why Luke's been floating on air for days on end. I knew he liked you, of course. But I only half speculated that he was interested in you romantically, too."

"He's not! We're just…friends." Darcy searched for an out; whatever was between her and Luke was too new to bear this scrutiny. "He's just been helping me."

Jalise looked at René, who nodded her red head smugly. "Uh-huh." They grinned happily. "Friends—*right*."

"Oh, for pity's sake!" Darcy packed up her fabric pieces and, with the others' help, loaded them into Clarice's little car. But as she drove home, she considered in a whole new light her relationship with the tall dark cowboy.

Luke was not like any man she'd ever known. He didn't pay any attention to what other people thought, for one thing. He just went ahead and did what he felt was right. Jamie was no relation and yet the man had tucked the child under his protective wing by introducing him to all the wonders of the ranch. They'd spent hours talking about the livestock, the land and the jobs that needed doing, when Luke must have longed for some peace and quiet.

"You can do this," he'd encouraged her when she stood trembling in front of the distance education building in Denver. "You're smart, you know what's important and you love children. You'll make a wonderful teacher." And with those words ringing in her ears, she'd walked into that building and answered hundreds of questions without the least bit of hesitation. She'd even had enough spunk to ask for concessions and—wonder of wonders—the faculty head had agreed to give her credit for her hours of aide work.

Darcy steered the car through town and out onto the highway.

"Is there really some point to this coming home business?" she asked herself, thinking of Jalise's words. "Has it all been part of some master plan?"

Clarice's words from the battered, worn Bible that she insisted on reading out loud every morning came back. *"The Lord longs to be gracious to you; He rises to show you compassion."*

"Why would God show me compassion? What am I to Him?"

Like the fluttering wing of a dove, the answer flew straight to her heart and landed there with assurance. She was God's child. He cared about her!

"I didn't know," she whispered in awe, staring at the darkness that surrounded her. "I didn't know that You were there, worrying about me."

Suddenly Clarice's words made sense. God hadn't abandoned her. He'd just let her go off on her own tangent for a while. Hadn't she done the same thing with Jamie when he'd been dead set on doing things his own little way? Wasn't that a way of educating him, just as her own self-centered journey had taught her much about life?

"Why did the bug die, Mommy?" She remembered his dismay when he'd insisted on keeping the worm in his pocket.

"Because worms can't live in pockets. They need soil and light and air. I told you that, remember?"

"But I want it to live, Mommy!"

Darcy suddenly accepted that she had been acting like Jamie—demanding that God rearrange things to suit her instead of seeing that there was a better path to follow. If she had only let go of the anger and the doubt a year ago and come back sooner, maybe she'd have seen her parents one last time….

Darcy pulled into the yard, but sat with the motor running, staring up into the night sky. *I'm sorry,* she whispered brokenly. *I've done it all wrong. I didn't know, didn't understand. I'll try to do better. I'll listen before judging. I'll pay more attention. I'll get it right somehow. I can do this. I can make up for the past.*

And feeling more confident than she had in days, Darcy hurried into the house, intent on Christmas, Luke, Clarice and Jamie. The future. Their future.

Chapter Eleven

❧

"Something smells wonderful," Luke said, his nose in the air, sniffing.

Darcy smiled as she lifted a pan from the oven. Two weeks till Christmas and she was worse than Jamie. She could hardly wait to enjoy everything.

"It's Christmas cookies. Mommy an' me are baking cookies and butter tarts." Jamie's face was covered with an assortment of flour, cookie dough and icing. "See, I made an angel." He held up a crooked little figure with distended wings and a halo that had bent down over one eye.

"It's a very pretty angel, too." Luke smiled, his eyes meeting Darcy's with a question. "Why is it purple?"

"'Cause I like purple. An' they told us at Sunday School that when people wore purple in the Bible it was 'cause they were royal. This is a royal angel." He sounded slightly offended that Luke hadn't known.

"Yes, now that you mention it, I can see that," Luke agreed solemnly. "Can I have one to eat?"

"No!" Jamie looked shocked at the very idea. "These are for Christmas."

"But sweetheart, we have lots. I think Luke could have just one, don't you? After all, we let Clarice taste one." Darcy had to look away from the admiring glow in Luke's dark brown eyes, hoping he would assume the flush on her cheeks was from the oven. "I just warmed some mulled cider if you'd like to try it. It was my mother's favorite recipe."

"Mulled cider?" He shook his head. "I don't think I've ever had it. But I'm willing to try some." He sat down at the end of the table, waiting patiently while Jamie chose just which cookie he should have.

Darcy poured a bright red-and-green mug full of the steaming cinnamon-scented drink, her heart pounding a little faster as she set it before him. His fingers brushed hers and from the glow in his eyes, Darcy was pretty sure the touch was no accident.

"Thank you," his low voice whispered in her ear as she straightened.

Darcy smiled back shyly. "You're welcome."

"Here. You can have this one. It's got its wing broked." Jamie handed over the damaged cookie, and watched soberly as Luke's white teeth bit into the glossy red icing.

"Why didn't you give him one of the better ones?" Darcy asked, studying the head bent so seriously over the table. "When we give someone something, we always want to give them the best and keep the broken ones for ourselves," she lectured, wondering if he was too young to understand.

"But, Mommy!" Jamie protested indignantly. "You said they all taste the same, whether they have a bit missing or not!"

"He's got you there." Luke's laughing voice was for her ears alone, and Darcy grinned back. "Anyway, we have to keep the really special ones for when people come to visit us, right, Jamie? We don't want our company to eat broken cookies."

Our company. It sounded so…familial. As if they were a cohesive group working together. A family. It was surprising just what a warm glow spread to her heart at those offhanded words of Luke's.

"How about if you and I build a snowman, Jamie? The snow's just wet enough that it might stand up overnight."

"Yes!" Jamie jumped down from his chair and rushed to the bathroom to wash his sticky hands.

"He sure moves," Luke chuckled. "Energy to burn."

"Don't I know it!" Darcy swept up the flour from the floor, then set about scrubbing the table. "He's got icing everywhere."

She could feel Luke watching her, and it made her strangely nervous; she had to pay special attention when removing the last pan of cookies. Then, with a deft movement, she slipped in two pans of butter tarts and reset the timer.

"Do you have anything special planned tonight?" he asked.

She turned to find his eyes fixed on her, his mouth tilted upward at one corner in a secretive smile. "I've got an assignment due on Thursday that I should do a little more work on."

"I thought you said you'd finished that. And I know you've done the books up to date because I checked.

Can't you take just a few hours off? You'll enjoy it, I promise."

His words were so persuasive and his eyes so hopeful that Darcy couldn't have denied him even if she'd wanted to. And she didn't want to.

"What time?"

"Oh, after supper. Clarice and Jamie can come, too."

Now why did that disappoint her? Darcy wondered. She loved her son and Clarice, too! But it would have been nice if Luke had asked to spend just a little while alone with her.

Darcy forced herself to think of supper, and cleaned the kitchen with enough elbow grease to make it sparkle. Once she had the chicken potpies cooking, the potatoes roasting and the table set, she wasted a few moments peering out the window to where Luke and Jamie were building their snowman.

They look so good together. Like a *real* father and son, her mind whispered as she watched Luke help Jamie lift the head onto the snowman. Luke was patient and gentle, even when Jamie grew cranky and tired. And despite the boy's constant questions, Luke managed to teach him with a calm understanding and forbearance that Darcy found sadly lacking in herself at times.

And Clarice was the perfect grandmother for Jamie. She didn't seem to mind when he crawled up on her lap with sticky hands, spilled his milk on her best shoes, or cut up the catalog she'd ordered specially from the pottery store. She read him Bible stories constantly and expanded on their principles by using ordinary everyday events that seemed to stay in his little mind long after the story had been forgotten.

In fact, both of the Lassiters had been a godsend, and Darcy found herself asking "why" less and less. It may not have seemed like it at one time, but this was indeed her *home*. And she was happy to be here in spite of all the bad memories that she had once held. Now, inch by inch, day by day, she was building new memories with Clarice and Luke.

She felt confident about the decision she'd made to put her trust in God and His plans. And somehow, with the acceptance of that decision, all of the terrible bitterness and hate that she had carried for so long was slowly but surely ebbing away.

"He loves that little boy." Clarice's voice came over her left shoulder. "We both do. It's going to be a wonderful Christmas. It's been so long since I've had a little one to watch and fuss over."

"You fuss over him too much." Darcy grinned, slipping her hand into Clarice's. "He's going to be spoiled rotten." And she didn't mind in the least.

"Nonsense. He has far too much character for that. And he's been so good for Luke. I know the boy hasn't said much, but Jamie fills a hole in his heart that's been aching for a long time. Ever since Leila and Macy died."

Leila and Macy. Now, at last, Darcy had names for the two people who haunted Luke's past. She felt sorry they'd gone; sorry that she never knew them. But she was glad if Luke took a little comfort from her son. After all, he'd already given them so much.

The buzzer rang, signaling the readiness of the

biscuits. While Clarice went to call the others in, Darcy lifted out the golden-brown rolls. She'd worked especially hard to make this meal—one of Luke's favorites—extra festive. And judging by the gleam in his warm brown eyes, she'd succeeded.

"Wow! All of my favorites. I'm a lucky man, Jamie, my boy. Thank you, Darcy. This is wonderful." He never failed to compliment her on her cooking, and Darcy couldn't help the little glow that bubbled up inside. It was nice to be appreciated.

"They're all *my* favorites, too." Jamie eagerly helped himself to one of the biscuits. He dropped it quickly as Clarice bowed her head, following her lead and waiting for Luke to say grace: "Father, we thank You for Your bounty to us. And we thank You for the season of Your son's birth. Thank You for sending Him to take our punishment. Help us to be a blessing to others. Amen."

"Amen," Jamie added loudly, and then made sure all eyes were open before buttering his biscuit.

The four of them enjoyed a lively meal, complete with wonderful food and conversation—and lots of laughter. Darcy was beginning to realize how much these things had been missing from her life in New York.

"I hope you are all full and warm," Luke murmured softly after the main course, eyeing the double-decker chocolate cake Darcy had brought to the table. "Because after supper, I want to take you all for a sleigh ride."

Darcy stared at him. "A sleigh ride? I haven't been on one of those in years."

"Well, it's the perfect night for it. And there are a bunch of us who are going to take the lumber trail up to the spruce grove. Maybe we can even pick out our Christmas tree while we're there."

"Are we gonna have lights 'n' everything?" Jamie's huge blue eyes grew even bigger at Luke's nod. "And an angel on top?"

"Oh, yes, we have to have an angel. It was an angel that brought the good news to Mary, remember?" Clarice's voice was full of…what? Darcy asked herself. *Love and caring and happiness,* came the swift response as she watched that craggy face shine. And the funny thing was, she knew exactly how Clarice felt. She couldn't imagine her life without these people here to share in it. This Christmas *was* going to be special.

"All right, everybody in? Here we go then." Luke touched the reins and the horses set off down the road, their hooves clip-clopping at a steady, even gait.

"It's a perfect night, isn't it?" Darcy tilted her head back to stare at the stars above. "I can see the constellations as clearly as if the sky were a page in a textbook. Look, Jamie. There's the Big Dipper."

Jamie leaned forward in his seat behind her and beside Clarice. "We already found that, Mommy. An' I seed Cassy—what's it called again, Aunt Clarice?"

"Cassiopeia. And there's Orion's Belt." A lot of giggling and whispering ensued, and Darcy glanced at Luke.

"Thanks for thinking of this," she murmured. "Jamie's thrilled and so am I. The sleigh bells are just the right touch, too."

"Your dad got them. And made the sleigh, too—at least part of it. I just finished it for him." He glanced sideways at her. "I'm sorry. I didn't mean to upset you."

"You didn't. I'm beginning to realize that a lot of what I remember was due to my mind-set. I let old hurts eat away at me until I'd manufactured them into something so monstrous that it took over my life."

"You mean, it wasn't as bad as you remembered?"

"To tell the truth, I don't know. Jalise asked me a while ago if there weren't some happy times here, and when I got started thinking about it, I realized that I'd only ever dwelt on the misery. I still don't remember a lot of good times, but every once in a while, a tickle of something happy twigs at my mind and I find myself smiling."

His gloved hand enfolded hers and squeezed. "I'm glad." He smiled, his breath a white foggy cloud around them. "You're too smart to let yourself be dragged down by the past."

"It's not all rosy," she warned, threading her fingers through his. "I still have days when I can't help asking why. Why didn't they love me? Why did they let me leave? But I'm beginning to realize that I may never know the answers to that. And I have to move on."

"I like the way you're moving on." His voice was low and feathered against her ear, his lips brushing her cheek. "You've done extremely well at school, I hear. The kids love you and even some of the teachers are singing your praises."

"It's just a matter of organization." But the warmth around her heart couldn't be denied.

"And you're a *master* at organization. The office has never looked so good. It was a mercy you took it all in hand before Percy started asking for documents. I knew they were there but—"

"Where?" she finished for him, laughing at his embarrassed look. "It's actually not that difficult if you file something as soon as you're finished with it."

"I'll try," he said in a humble, little-boy voice that made her giggle. "How are your courses?"

"Well, I must confess, you were right. I was an idiot to take two at one time. Especially *those* two. But I love the psychology reading. It's fun. And English has always been a favorite of mine, although I must say I'm getting a little tired of Dickens. That's one paper I'll be happy to turn in."

"Mommy, it's starting to snow!" Jamie's excited voice cut through their conversation, his voice ringing with joy. "Look, Mommy. Look!"

"I'm looking, sweetie." And Darcy was looking, a huge grin lifting her mouth. The whole world was like the inside of one of those glass snow domes that you shake to get the snow to whirl around. Fat white lacy flakes drifted down slowly, settling on the ground in a silent blanket of pure white.

"It's perfect," she whispered, catching one of the flakes on her tongue. "Like a single frame of a memory that you have tucked away in your mind and pull out on special occasions to make you feel better."

"It is nice, isn't it?" Luke agreed as his arm wrapped around her shoulders. "I'm awfully glad you're here to share it."

"So am I." This was where she belonged. God had given her this one absolutely perfect night to help her understand that He was there, in control. Whatever happened, she could rest in His love and know that He would handle it all.

They glided on farther, and soon came upon other sleighs packed full of people traveling up the pretty path, fronds of overhanging evergreens shielding them from the snow.

"Let's sing," Clarice called from the back, and started off "It Came Upon A Midnight Clear." Seconds later the others joined in, their voices blending in an *a cappella* harmony that resounded through the valley.

"Why are we stopping?" Darcy whispered a few minutes later at the end of "Silent Night."

"There's going to be a campfire here. Someone came up earlier and cleared a site. The Andersons brought hot chocolate, and I brought that pan of chocolate fudge you had cooling in the porch." His voice held a hint of laughter, but Darcy could see the question in his eyes.

"Good," she said, smiling when he squeezed her hand. "I want to contribute something, too." She pulled out the tin of shortbread she'd tucked under the seat and lifted the lid to show him. "We can set this out, too."

"It's not shortbread, is it?" He breathed, inhaling the buttery fragrance of the shapes. "I love shortbread!"

"My mother's special Scottish recipe. It'll melt in your mouth. Here, try one." Without a second thought, she popped the confection into his mouth and waited, her cheeks burning as his warm brown eyes rolled upward.

"Do we have to share that?" he teased in a whisper, his breath wafting across her ear. The faint motion sent a flurry of ripples up to her brain. "Maybe you and I could disappear into those woods with a thermos and this tin. No one would even notice." He jerked his head toward Jamie and Clarice who were already rushing toward the fire that glowed brightly in the darkness.

She followed his glance, her eyes noting that they were indeed alone. The others had abandoned their sleighs and were laughing and giggling round the fire.

"If I ask Clarice to watch Jamie, will you come for a walk with me, Darcy?"

She nodded, tucking a few cookies into her pocket, and the cookie tin back beneath the seat. A thrill of pleasure coursed through her. She couldn't believe she was with such a wonderful man.

He helped her down from the sleigh, placed a finger over her lips and, after tucking her arm through his, led her away from the others. Soon they were scurrying along a logging trail that Luke insisted, in a hushed whisper, he knew very well. Gradually, the voices of the others faded away until the forest closed around them, silent and waiting.

Which was exactly how Darcy felt. She didn't know what to expect next. Luke had always been warm and friendly with her. Lately he'd been more than friendly, and she'd welcomed the increasing warmth of their friendship. But tonight there was a special glow in his dark eyes that made her unexpectedly nervous. And happy. And excited.

"If we keep following this, we'll circle around the fire and eventually come back to where we left the sleigh. I came up here last year to get a Christmas tree for your parents, but we had tons of snow and I had to turn back. We ended up with a scrawny little spruce that I found over by the river." He smiled. "It didn't matter to your mother, though. She fiddled with it for days, and by Christmas Eve it was the most beautiful tree around."

"I'll bet she made little cinnamon gingerbread hearts and hung them on ribbons," added Darcy. "And potpourri sachets. She loved those. And mistletoe cookies. She used to make dozens of those to give away with the Christmas baskets that the church handed out."

"She didn't do a lot last year. She wasn't feeling all that spry. But she did manage to get something pretty special for those hampers. I asked her why she didn't just order something from the store and have it tucked in, and she said that it was important to—"

"—give something of yourself," Darcy finished. "She often said that. I remember a Christmas Eve when I went with her." Darcy stared up at the sky, remembering. "She used to disappear after the service, you know. Dad and I would stay at the church or go to the pastor's for a hot drink, and Mom would leave. She'd be gone about an hour and when she returned her whole face was lit up. I never could figure out what she was doing."

"I suppose you bugged her about it until she finally agreed to let you come along." Luke's tone was indulgent.

"Yes, she did. But only if I saved my allowance and got three gifts that I wanted but would give away. It had to be something I really wanted for myself, you see. Otherwise she said it wasn't worth giving."

"What did you get?"

"The first two were easy. Mason's in town had a huge bar of chocolate that I *really* wanted. I suppose you know that I like chocolate…."

"*Like it?*" Luke rolled his eyes, teasingly.

She grinned. "Anyway, I bought that. And they had a little sampler box with seven different perfumes in tiny little bottles that had gold tops. I'd coveted that for a solid month, and although there were only two left, I bought one of them. But it was the third gift that really caused problems."

"Because you didn't know what to get?"

"No, I knew what to get. But I didn't want to buy it just to give it away. Not at all—" she glanced up, feeling embarrassed "—greedy thing that I was."

"You could never be greedy," he murmured gallantly, his fingers tightening around hers. "What was this wonderful item?"

"You'll laugh," she warned, her cheeks growing warmer in the chilly air. Darcy stared at her boots. "It was a ten-piece manicure set."

"Files and stuff?" He frowned.

"A manicure set," she told him belligerently, wishing she'd never started this. "The kind of set that comes with all the trimmings including a bright red polish that I knew I'd never be allowed to wear around the house. Everything a younger girl needs to look glamorous." With her eyes, she dared him to say a word.

"I see. So did you buy it?"

Butter wouldn't melt in that innocent, bland mouth, Darcy noted. "Oh, I bought it all right. And a stuffed toy. I was going to keep the manicure set and give away the toy. I had everything wrapped and ready to go before the Christmas Eve service, and my mother called me into her room. She asked if I was certain that I was giving the three things that I most wanted for Christmas."

"And you told her?"

"I told her 'yes.' But before we left, I felt so guilty that I raced upstairs and exchanged the toy for that lovely set. It really hurt to wrap it up and carry it out to the car, and I spent the service praying that God would perform some miracle so that I wouldn't have to give it away."

Luke walked along beside her, her smaller hand nestled in his as they trod along the trail. Darcy was thankful for the silence as she organized her thoughts. He seemed to know that she needed the time and space to plunge on and finish the tale.

"After the service, my mother and I drove over to the east side. In those days it was a rundown area of Raven's Rest and a lot of people were suffering because the mill had closed down. She parked away from the houses, sort of in the dark, and took some things out of the trunk. I didn't know what they were, but I recognized some of the plates and tins as ones she'd frozen her baking in. There were gifts with name tags carefully spelled out on them and covered in bright foil paper with glittering bows. I could hardly believe it."

"Why?"

"Because I'd always been told not to waste money. My gifts usually came wrapped in newspaper or a piece of fabric with a hair ribbon on top. This was extravagance that I'd never seen before." Darcy swallowed past the strange lump in her throat, and continued.

"I followed her as she crept up to the doorstep and laid everything out on it. It took several trips at most of the houses, and I knew that was because there were so many people living in each. When we were all finished, she went back to the car. I was to knock on the door and then race away as quickly as possible. That part of it was fun."

She gulped down the tears that wouldn't stay out of her voice, and whispered so softly that no one else could possibly have heard. "They couldn't believe it. The parents turned on all the lights and everyone was so excited!" Darcy smiled. "I'll never forget those looks. I stayed hidden, you see. Disobedience again. But I wanted to know and so I hid in a bush or climbed up a tree. I remember the kids treated those gifts as if they were gold. They carried them so carefully, and I could see how stunned they were. It was amazing!"

"It must have been. It's a wonderful expression of Christmas spirit to pass on to a child." Luke's voice was full of meaning, and, for once, Darcy didn't take umbrage.

"Yes, it was."

Darcy could hardly bear to go on. "And I understood that what she was doing was important, believe me. I just couldn't accept that it wasn't right for me to have a little of that gold paper and ribbon that she lavished on everyone else. Now I wonder if perhaps there wasn't enough money to do both."

After a long silence, Luke's low voice broke the hush of the forest. "And the manicure set?"

"I was hoping you'd forget that," Darcy mumbled, keeping her face averted. "I left it at the last house we stopped at, and believe me, it was just about the hardest thing I'd ever had to do."

"Why? Surely you were resigned to giving it away by then?"

"Yes, but it was who it was going to. I knew who lived

there, you see. Mary Pickens was the town's biggest gossip in those days. She spread a ton of rumors about me that I tried desperately to live up to. Her daughter, Annette, was my worst enemy at school, and she did every single thing she could to get me into trouble." She smiled bitterly. "Actually, not much has changed. She's still trying to get back at me through my job at the school now."

"And she's the one who got it?"

"Yes, Annette's the one who got my lovely Nail Galore kit. And showed her nails off every time I was around. She thought she was pretty hot stuff, and I would have liked nothing better than to tell her I'd given it to her because she and her mother were poor. Fortunately, I never let on. But the day she showed off her glamorous red nails, I was devastated. I'd dreamed about the difference it would make in my life, how beautiful I'd be. That kit had cost me every dime I had saved for weeks on end."

Luke wrapped an arm around her shoulders and hugged her against his chest, his genuine concern for her obvious. "I'm sorry you had such a hard time, Darcy."

She felt silly—but at least Luke seemed to understand how hard it had been to give the gift away.

"Yeah, so am I. But I guess it taught me a lot, too." Darcy searched for something to take the focus off her as she stood in the circle of his arms. "How about you? You must have some good memories of Christmases past."

He kept one arm strung round her shoulders as they resumed their walk. His voice was quiet in the waiting stillness.

"You mean with Macy? We only spent two of them together. The first one was at her parents'. We were engaged, but they didn't want her to marry me. It was not a happy occasion. By the second one we were expecting Leila, and Macy was feeling pretty rough. We were in California at the time, so we didn't even have snow. I suppose it wasn't the best of circumstances, but I didn't mind. I figured as long as we were together, everything was wonderful."

"She must have been very special." Darcy had gleaned a few details from Clarice—enough to know that Macy Lassiter had spunk enough to weather out the rough patches. She felt sad that Luke had lost his wife, but then, that loss had brought him here, to her. She couldn't, no, wouldn't be sorry about that.

"She wasn't perfect. Macy had her faults, but I loved her anyway. I couldn't believe it when they told me she'd died. And Leila, too. It was inconceivable to me that God would let such a thing happen."

"It does seem hard, doesn't it? Not to know why, and yet to have to accept it and go on." Darcy squeezed his fingers. "I'm sorry, Luke."

"I was, too. For a long time. That feeling sorry for myself was what got me into trouble. I just sank deeper and deeper into my self-pitying world. Eventually I came to two conclusions."

A silence stretched between them. "Well, are you going to share them?" Darcy prodded gently. "It's only fair. After all, I've told you my personal stuff," she reminded.

"It isn't all that earthshaking. Or maybe it is. It's just that God is still God regardless of what happens.

Nothing I can do or say will ever change that. He's always in control."

"And the other conclusion?" Darcy murmured, considering his words.

"The other is simply that I can either trust in that and follow His lead or I can trust in my own understanding and hope I scrape through somehow. When you get right down to it, it's not much of a choice, is it?"

"No, it's not much of a choice," she whispered, thinking of her own difficulty in accepting God's way.

"Anyway, I ended up here, working with your parents. They and Clarice helped me see that I'd been fortunate to have what I had. And they showed me that God was greater than my circumstance. I can't resent that. Besides, I met you and Jamie." He smiled down at her. "Meeting you was quite an experience."

"It was? Why?" Darcy frowned, wondering if she should have asked. There were some things that it was better not to know.

"At first I thought you were just some spoiled brat. You know—a teenager that couldn't get along with her parents and ran away."

"I was." Darcy grimaced at the truth of it.

"But there was more to the story. I've watched you face up to the townsfolks' small minds and grow from the challenge. You've raised a wonderful little boy who isn't afraid to explore things and, even better, has no idea that his life was full of hardships. Jamie treats problems like puzzles and that's due to you. Your love and nurturing have helped shape a child who will tackle life full-force. You're a very special woman, Darcy Simms, and I appreciate you more each day."

Luke stopped on the path, his hand on her elbow halting her amid the fresh pine-scented boughs. A hint of wood smoke reached them, but Darcy was oblivious to everything but the warm glow in those brown velvet eyes as Luke gazed at her. His head tilted down just a fraction, his lips mere inches from hers.

"I want to kiss you," he murmured, his mouth hovering above hers. "Is that okay with you?"

"More than okay," Darcy replied, raising herself on tiptoes as his lips slanted down over hers.

It was a soft kiss, a gentle, exploring kiss that asked questions and gave answers. Darcy couldn't help but respond to the thrill of it, her arms slowly moving around his neck as her fingers smoothed the silkiness of his dark nape.

When Luke buried his lips in her hair, Darcy leaned her head on his chest and breathed in the scent of horses and smoke and the fresh outdoors that lingered in his jacket. She linked her arms around his waist and stayed nestled in his arms, content.

"You're very special to me, Darcy," he whispered, tilting her head back so that he could see her eyes. His thumb stroked her cheek. "I think I'm falling in love with you."

Darcy stared at him, unable to doubt the sincerity of his words. His eyes shone with joy and his lips were tender as they found hers once more. But what could she answer? She liked Luke; liked him a lot if the truth were told. And she enjoyed living on the ranch, watching him work with the animals, and share Jamie's little hugs.

Was that love? She'd thought she was in love once before, and it had turned to ashes in her hands.

How could she know?

"It's all right," he murmured, setting her carefully away from him. "You don't have to say anything. I apologize if I've offended you." He turned away to walk down the path.

Darcy caught up with him in several steps, amazed to see that they were now close to the campfire clearing.

"No, Luke. It's not that." She caught at his arm, forcing him to a halt. "I like you, too. Very much."

"But…?" He smiled sadly.

"But I'm not sure about the rest. Not yet." She sank onto a log. "I'm finding out things about my parents that I never suspected. And I'm learning things about *me* that are almost overwhelming. I never dreamed I'd be good at teaching—and yet I love it." She studied him, trying to gauge whether or not he understood her confusion.

"I feel like I'm uncovering a whole new me, sort of like digging for treasure and finding the contents of the chest aren't what you expected at all. And I like this new me. But I don't want to mess it up."

"And loving me would do that?" he asked.

"No, of course not. I just meant I don't want to blow it. Again." She drew in a deep breath. "I've made so many mistakes, Luke. I've done things wrong all through my life because I tend to rush into action before logically thinking things through. I don't want to rush anymore. I want to plan and take each step after I've carefully considered everything. No more rash behavior for Darcy Simms. Can you understand that?"

Luke sat down beside her, his legs thrust out in front.

He was silent for several moments, his face inscrutable. Darcy shifted uneasily, wondering what he was thinking about, but deciding to let him sort through his thoughts in peace. When he did speak, she sat up straight, prepared for rejection.

"I guess it is all rather new," he agreed, turning to face her. "For you, anyway. I've known my own mind for a while now." He picked up her hand and enfolded it in his.

"I understand that you don't want to rush into anything. And I appreciate this new maturity you've gained. I think you never gave yourself enough credit before." He squeezed her fingers. "But, Darcy, I don't want to take any of that away. Love isn't about taking, it's about giving. I'm going to enjoy showing you that. So don't expect me to give up and go away. I won't. I'm here for the long haul. For you. Anytime you need me."

"Thank you," Darcy whispered, tears blurring her vision as she realized again what a wonderful man he was.

The only problem was her. Was Darcy Simms back in Raven's Rest permanently, or was this just another side road on her journey? And if it was, how could it include Luke Lassiter?

Chapter Twelve

When Darcy and Luke arrived back at the campfire, they met a very excited Jamie. The little boy told them that he and Clarice had invited a few people back to the ranch for some hot chocolate.

"Do you mind?" Luke stared at her intently, obviously gauging her reaction.

"No. No, I don't mind." The idea of visitors wasn't as repugnant as she would have thought.

Sleighs all followed Luke's, and soon the house was filled with guests. Christmas carols played on the stereo and the fireplace burned with a bright dancing flame as young and old milled around, sipping hot chocolate and punch that Clarice had hastily prepared.

"Haven't had folks over in a while. Thought it would be fun to have the place alive again." Clarice stopped suddenly and looked back at Darcy. "Should have asked," she muttered frowning.

"Of course you shouldn't! This is your home. And a Christmas get-together is a great idea. Thank goodness we did the decorations yesterday," Darcy said.

"It's very kind of you to have us out here like this,"

Elroy Spiggot mumbled, and she turned to see him behind her, his eyes downcast. "'Specially with the things—"

Darcy cut him off, not wanting to hear about the past. This was the present and maybe, just maybe, her future. "Of course you're welcome, Mr. Spiggot. And you also, Mrs. Lancaster. Christmas is a time for friends and family, don't you think?"

Hilda Ridgely stood behind Ella Lancaster, a broad grin across her stern face. She winked at Darcy, and Darcy winked back, feeling happier than she had in years.

"Darcy? How are you?" A tall, slightly graying man stood, hand outstretched, his smile quizzical.

"Jesse? Jesse Jones?" Darcy noticed that René stood behind him. "Oh, no wonder René told me she's worried about you. You're old, Jesse!" It was a timeworn taunt, and Jesse didn't let her down. He swung her up in a bear hug that threatened to crack her ribs, his laughter ringing out.

"If that isn't just like you, pip-squeak! Still so wet behind the ears, you don't know enough to respect your elders."

"Not so wet, Jesse," Darcy murmured, watching as Jamie showed another child his train set.

"No." Jesse's voice dropped a bit, a hint of sadness running through it as he glanced at his wife. "I guess we've all aged a bit since those days."

"Well, hopefully *some* of us have learned something." Darcy, striving to recapture the merriment, said to Jesse, "Wait till you see the costumes René's designed for the Christmas pageant. I'll bet you could market her patterns and retire from farming."

Given Jesse and René's history, it was the wrong thing to say—and Darcy knew it immediately. She waited for René to burst into tears or race from the room. She could already see the white lines radiating around Jesse's pinched lips. Surprisingly, René seemed deep in thought.

"I never thought of that," she murmured, her eyes far away. "The patterns and instructions are quite simple— even amateurs could assemble them. I could work out an assortment of themes—you know, English caroler, a Dickens's village."

"She's off!" Jesse grinned, but Darcy could see the relief in his eyes. "Now there'll be no rest for days while she ponders this."

"Do you good to stay up late once in a while." Luke playfully punched the other man in the arm. "You're getting staid in your old age."

"Staid? Ha! I can out-toss you in darts any day of the week, *old* buddy." They bickered playfully back and forth as they headed for the study, and Darcy knew they'd be engaged in a game shortly.

"It's a good idea though. Don't you think?" René asked. "I wonder if I couldn't work up something for a layette, too?"

Darcy stared at her. "A baby layette? Those are really hot right now. I've seen them in catalogs—the drapes, crib bumper pads, change table, quilt, pillows and a whole bunch of other things specifically designed to match. They cost a mint!"

René smiled, stroking her hand down her cheek.

"Exactly," she whispered, eyes shining. "And I could do it, Darcy. I could put together a package that would out-shine anything that's out there right now." She grabbed the telephone pad and pencil, sank onto a kitchen stool, and began to jot things down. Darcy could only stare at the change in the unhappy woman's features.

Jalise entered the room and tapped Darcy on the arm. "Earth to Darcy! What's wrong with her?"

"She's decided to design a costume line and a layette line. I think." Darcy grinned. "Isn't it great?"

"It's great to see her so animated," Jalise agreed as she and Darcy moved into the hallway. "I just hope the layette idea takes root at home."

"What do you mean?"

"Jesse's wanted more kids for so long now, but René's always said Ginny's treatment had to come first."

"But Ginny does her exercises herself now," Darcy said. "You mean, it was just an excuse?"

"I think so. René always wanted lots of children. It's only since she came back that she's been so negative. And speaking of couples, what happened to you and Luke? You were both noticeably absent when I arrived at the campfire."

Darcy blushed. "We just went for a walk, Jay. Nothing unusual in that, is there?"

"That depends." Jalise's gray eyes narrowed. "What happened on this *walk* of yours? And spare me no details."

"We talked."

"And?"

"And Luke kissed me."

"Even better! And?"

"Do you have to know every detail?" Darcy glanced around, hoping everyone was busy with their own conversation. She had no desire to have this spread around.

"Yes, I do. Now tell me!"

"He said he loves me," Darcy whispered, a little in awe of the words herself.

"Finally." Jalise hugged her, enveloping Darcy in a cloud of flowery perfume. "It's about time."

"You mean…you knew?" Darcy felt as if her knees would give way. "How could you know?"

"It's perfectly obvious to anyone who's watched him watching you. He gets this calf-eyed look whenever he's with you. As if he's the proudest man in the world. What did you tell him?"

"That I needed more time. Well, I do," she insisted, ignoring Jalise's raised eyebrows. "I'm tired of messing up, Jay. If I'm going to settle down here, it has to be for the right reasons. I can't just use Luke as a way out. Do you understand?"

"Only because I know you and the convoluted way your mind works." Jalise's acerbic tones jolted Darcy. "You think you're not good enough or something silly like that, don't you."

"He's just lost his daughter and his wife. I've just lost my parents. We're both in a state of upheaval. We need time to sort through this, decide what we want."

"He's already said what he wants." Jalise tugged her into a corner, away from any potential eavesdroppers. "Macy and Leila have been dead for three years now. Luke's dealt with their loss. And now he wants to live again. With you. Isn't that what you want, too?"

"I like him, Jay. I like him a lot. He's so gentle and tender and yet he always knows exactly where he's going. And Jamie adores him." Darcy wrung her hands together. "But I was crazy about someone else once. And I made a terrible mistake. I'm a mother now. I can't afford to make another one."

"Another mistake like Josiah Pringle, you mean?" Jalise met Darcy's stare unabashed. "I guessed about him a long time ago, sweetie. But that's the past. And you are looking at the future. Aren't you?"

"Past, future—it all comes together eventually, Jay. Anyway, I'm going to turn it all over to God and let Him show me the way. And that means waiting on His timing, doesn't it?"

"Yes, I guess it does. I'm sorry, Dar. I didn't mean to push. It's just that I want you to be happy, and I think Luke would make you happier than you've ever been."

"Can I tell you a secret, Jay? I think he would, too."

I think he would, too.

A week later the words he had overheard still sent a tingle of joy to his brain. And Luke hugged the knowledge close to his heart. He hadn't blown it, hadn't overstepped himself. Darcy Simms did feel something for him. She just hadn't sorted it all out yet. But he intended to help her do it.

"You goin' to town again?" Clarice studied him as if he had a fever.

"Yes." He said it defiantly, to bolster his courage. "I told Darcy I'd take her out after she finished her exam. It's near that time now. I thought maybe dinner at that Greek place that just opened. Can you manage Jamie?"

"Jamie and I been managing quite a lot lately. One more night won't hurt." Clarice stared at him. "You *mean* to wear one blue sock and one gray?"

Luke felt like an idiot as he scurried back up the stairs. Talk about acting like a teenager! Half an hour later he felt the same way as he sat outside the church waiting for Darcy. Pastor David had agreed to monitor her exam so she wouldn't have to go to Denver, and he knew that she was relieved not to have to travel. Thoughts of tonight occupied his mind for long moments after that.

Luke held his breath when she finally emerged. She looked okay, not as if she had been crying or anything. Wasn't that a good sign? He climbed out of the truck and walked the few steps to meet her, praying for the right words.

"Well?"

"I'm finished."

He rolled his eyes. "I know that. How did you do?"

She smiled at his angst. "Pretty well, I think. The questions weren't as difficult as I thought and I didn't skip one." She climbed in the truck, waited until he closed the door and came around to the other side. "I'm basically happy."

He frowned. "What aren't you saying?" he demanded after a moment, knowing something was hidden behind those deep, dark blue eyes.

She grinned a big happy grin that set her face alight. "I think I did really, really well," she said finally. "I couldn't believe it. I just kept working my way down the page, thinking it's going to get worse. But it didn't."

"I knew you'd do it." He hugged her close, breathing in her scent as he did. "So now it's time for dinner on me. How about Stratos'?"

"I'm kind of keyed up. Do you think we could walk in the park for a little while? I need some exercise."

Luke shrugged. "I'm not really dressed for it," he told her sheepishly. "But I could use a little exercise myself." Especially since he seemed to be all thumbs at getting the key in the ignition. "Good thing they clear those walks for the joggers."

"I noticed you were all gussied up." Darcy's blue eyes teased mercilessly. "It's a good thing Jamie didn't see you. He'd be asking you all kinds of questions about that tie." She burst out laughing at his pained expression.

"It is a little loud, isn't it?" He laid one finger against the vivid tie. "Clarice gave it to me last Christmas and I don't want her to feel bad, so every once in a while I wear it."

"I think that's very nice of you. Most men would shove it in a drawer and try to forget it was there." She peered out the window as he drove through town. "Isn't it pretty? I love the way the lights sparkle on the snow."

"Christmas is special no matter where you spend it. But I guess it's always nicer at home." He let that sink in for a moment and then changed the subject. "I was talking to Jalise while I waited."

"How is she?" As soon as he pulled into the parking lot, Darcy was out of the truck and pulling in deep breaths of the chilly air.

Luke came around to her side and took her hand. Under the giant pines and huge spruce they walked, laughing together as a squirrel dashed across in front.

"Rooting for you. Also extremely curious. I had to answer a lot of nosey parker questions." He made a face to tell her how little he'd enjoyed the experience.

She giggled. "I can imagine."

"She wondered if you'd ever told me what made you leave Raven's Rest. You never have." He stared down into her eyes.

"Oh, Luke. I'm so happy, so excited. I don't want to ruin all that by dragging up the past again. This is a beautiful day, a wonderful season. Can't we just enjoy that?"

"Sure." He kept pace with her. "But when you want to talk, I'm here. I won't judge, I promise. We've all made mistakes, but those errors made us who we are today. And I really like who you are, Darcy Simms."

She smiled, a genuine, heartrending smile that made him forget everything but the fact that he was falling in love with this woman.

"You're so sweet, Luke. I know that I can trust you, that you wouldn't condemn. And I promise, I'll give you all the details. But not today, okay? Let's just enjoy this beauty." She whirled round and round in a circle, her arms embracing the world as her hair spun in a curtain of black.

"This is a perfect day. A wonderful, fantastic, deliciously perfect day." In a burst of ecstasy, she hugged him and then danced off down the path to return moments later with an icicle in her hands. "Look at this. Did you ever see such a big one? I knocked my two front teeth out when I was six trying to reach an icicle just like this."

He shivered, fully aware of just how insubstantial his dress clothes were for a walk in the park.

"I'm turning into one of those," he muttered to himself.

But Darcy heard him. Giggling, she tossed the icicle away, took his hand and hurried him back to the truck.

"You ranchers," she taunted. "You're such sissies. Us tough city girls outdo you every time."

He helped her into the truck and then switched it on, setting the heater to high. This teasing, laughing woman was such a change from the scared girl he'd first encountered, Luke couldn't help but join in the teasing.

"You city girls are full of hot air," he complained, backing out of the lot. "And you're no more a city girl than I am. Are you hungry yet?"

"Starved."

Ten minutes later they were seated at a table of a very nice Greek restaurant. After placing their orders, Luke began to tell Darcy about his youth.

Darcy giggled throughout the evening until Luke thought she'd burst. He knew she'd never imagined him as a bratty kid who got into everything.

"Didn't the teachers ever suspect that it was you who set the lab on fire with your experiment?" she asked. "Oh, these ribs are delicious!"

"Well, yes. Later. Actually, they were so excited that I won the state competition, they didn't even reprimand me. I was Mr. Trip's pet student until the day I graduated." He regaled about his other antics while dessert was served.

"Brag, brag, brag." Darcy shook her head, pushing her plate away as she leaned back in her chair. "I am stuffed. Thank you, Luke. That was a wonderful meal. They certainly know how to cook here."

He nodded. "Yes, they do. And I like coming here because the booths give you a little more privacy than Jalise's café in town."

He'd no sooner uttered the words than an elderly couple stopped to speak to him about their horses. Moments later a neighbor followed, chatting about everything. He was followed by a group from the ladies' group who duly noted Luke's companion. They moved away, their whispers floating back.

"They're out together?"

"So much for a quiet dinner together," Luke said.

"It doesn't matter what they say," she whispered as he helped her away from the table. "We know that it was perfect."

Luke paid the bill, helped her don her coat and escorted her out of the restaurant. Outside, the sky was dark and bright with stars shining overhead. They ambled across the parking lot to the truck.

"It's funny," she mused, staring up. "I don't think I ever even noticed the stars in New York. Here they're so bright."

"They sure are." But Luke was staring at the stars in her eyes. "Darcy," he murmured, his hands drawing her closer, "would you mind very much if those old girls happened to catch a glimpse of me kissing you?"

"They're gone," she whispered, holding his gaze with her own. "I saw them pull out a few minutes ago."

"Oh." He was disappointed with her answer.

"But, no, I wouldn't mind a bit. In fact I'd really like you to kiss me right now."

"Oh!" Luke saw the flicker of a smile waver across her lips and knew that she was as nervous as he. That made him feel a whole lot better.

He bent his head and kissed her, his lips touching hers, his breath melding with hers. As her arms slipped around his neck, Luke tugged her closer.

This was right. This was beautiful. This was what he wanted to last. He didn't need to know any more about her. He already knew everything that mattered.

He was deeply in love with Darcy Simms.

Darcy was walking on air. No, she was floating. Her exams had passed without a hitch and she felt certain she'd done well. School was out for the Christmas break, and life was wonderful. Of course, most of the reason for that feeling came from the man seated across from her, trying desperately to wrap his gift for Jamie.

"I detest gift wrapping," Luke muttered, tearing the pretty paper as he tugged his fingers away.

"Especially when you leave it till right before Christmas." Darcy giggled at the flecks of silver that had come off the paper and stuck to his nose where he'd scratched it. "Why didn't you ask for a box?"

"What kind of a box would fit this?" he demanded, glaring at the huge metal crane with a rotating arm that transported a bright yellow bucket on the end.

"Anything would be better than that. Why don't you

hide it and put little scavenger-hunt notes under the tree? He'd love that."

Luke brightened at that idea. He wrapped the bulky item in a huge bath sheet and lugged it up to his room. Seconds later he was back with a pad and pencil, and busied himself scribbling.

"You shouldn't have spent so much on him, though. He's not used to it all." Darcy stifled thoughts of her own extravagance in the form of a shiny red-and-chrome bicycle she'd purchased, which now lay hidden in the barn. It was going to be the best Christmas Jamie had ever seen.

"And what do *you* want for Christmas?" Luke's hands tightened on her waist as he turned her into his arms with an ease that had become very familiar to Darcy. His mouth grazed hers in a light kiss.

"I have everything I want right here." Darcy ignored the niggle of conscience reminding her that she had one wish that wouldn't see the light of day—to know forgiveness. Instead she tightened her hands around his neck and kissed him back with abandon.

"Do you now? Well, then I might as well return your gift. It's pointless to try to improve on perfection."

Darcy giggled as his eyes danced with secrets. "Oh, you won't take it back," she assured him smugly.

"How do you know that?"

"You couldn't stand it. You can barely keep it a secret now." She kissed the tip of his nose and then wriggled out of his embrace. "Go do something, Luke, and leave me alone. I've got to get supper on. Clarice and Jamie will be back from their shopping trip soon, and we have that caroling party tonight."

"Are you sure you have warm enough clothes? It can get pretty chilly going door to door."

"Yes, I have some wonderful things, thanks to Clarice." Darcy smiled in reminiscence. "You know, that's one of the things that helped me decide to come back."

"Clothes?" He sounded amazed.

"Yes, clothes! You know very well that I had nothing nice and I didn't want to show up looking like a bum. Clarice's wonderful gift gave me a sense of dignity that I hadn't felt in a long time. It was as if I could hold my head up again because someone cared about me enough to think of that small detail."

Darcy turned on the oven and slipped a casserole inside. "Clarice is the most perceptive woman I know. She manages to make you feel needed and wanted without emphasizing how much you need her. I think it's a special gift. I only hope I can pay her back someday."

"She's happier than I've ever seen her, and that's due to you," Luke told her. "You have a knack for helping people find themselves."

"Rather strange, don't you think? Especially since it's taking *me* so long to find myself." Darcy rinsed off her salad ingredients. When Luke's hands closed over her shoulders, she jumped in surprise, but allowed him to turn her to face him.

"You're finding yourself right on God's schedule," he murmured. "And you've touched lives along the way. René Jones is thrilled about the idea you gave her. I talked to Jesse yesterday and he said it's as if she has a new lease on life."

Darcy blushed, but the warm glow that spread through

her body wasn't entirely due to Luke's presence. For the first time in a very long while she felt proud of what she was doing.

"Well, if I helped, I'm glad. I like René. Speaking of which, I have to get the last bit of braid sewn on that costume. I'm going to take it and that baking into town when we go tonight."

Luke stopped munching on his carrot. His eyes narrowed. "You're not giving away the shortbread, are you? I never did get to taste that—"

"As I recall, I offered you some—" Darcy set the table, hoping he would ignore her red face "—but you were too busy."

"Yes, I was. Too busy falling in love with you." His lips brushed the top of her head. "You're quite a woman, Darcy Simms."

"I'm glad you think so." She slipped out of his arms and sank onto a nearby chair to tack the thick gold braid onto the wise man's costume. She drew a sigh of relief as Luke went whistling out the door, and let the fabric fall to her lap.

Chapter Thirteen

"The caroling was fun, wasn't it?" Luke tucked her hand into his and held on as he negotiated the highway drive home.

In order for him to hold her hand, Darcy had to move closer. Which wasn't a hardship, she decided happily.

"It was lovely. The seniors in the apartment complex were so excited to have someone come and sing to them. It must be lonely." She thought about her parents together on the farm, and was glad that they had had each other.

Luke turned the truck into the yard. Darcy escaped out of the truck before he could catch her and raced across the yard laughing, almost making it up the stairs before his fingers caught hers.

"Hey, don't I get a good-night kiss?" he demanded, his arms going about her waist.

"You sure have a lot of reasons why I should kiss you." Darcy considered them all. "There's the good-morning kiss, the breakfast kiss, the kiss at coffee time, the just-because kiss, the dessert kiss after lunch, the help-me-make-it-through-the-day kiss, pre- and post-dinner kisses..."

"But this has to be the best one of them all," he whispered as his mouth neared hers.

Darcy held her breath, waiting, but when he didn't kiss her, she asked the question that lay uppermost in her mind. "Why?"

"Because this one has to last me until tomorrow morning." And then he gave her the most tender kiss. "I love you, Darcy," he murmured at last, his lips buried in her hair.

Darcy couldn't hold in her response. It surged up from the depths of her heart and she could no more have stifled it than stopped breathing.

"I love you, too, Luke. Very much."

He pushed away gently to peer down into her eyes. "You do? Really? I mean—I always knew you would someday, but I just didn't expect—that is, I thought you needed time, and I was going to give it to you—"

"Lucas?" Darcy interrupted.

"Yes?"

"Do you think you could stop talking and kiss me again? After all, it is a very long time until my good-morning kiss."

And Luke proceeded to do as he was told.

"I'm going home!" René Jones clapped a hand to her head. "Everything that can go wrong is going wrong with this Christmas pageant. I knew it would."

Jalise seemed to be of the same opinion. "It was just too grandiose. We should have known that."

Darcy glared at both of them. "Jalise Penner, don't

you dare cop out on me now. I need you to go and get what's left of those Christmas pageant props into place. René, if you're going to be sick, go to the bathroom. Has anyone seen Luke?"

"I'm sorry, Darcy. I haven't felt well for days. It's usually just in the mornings, though. I'm always fine by this time of the day." René's greenish-white face had Darcy searching for Luke. "I don't know what's wrong with me lately."

"I do." Darcy glanced from one to the other of her friends. "Oh, brother! You two were the science brains. Don't you know anything about pregnancy?"

"Pregnant? René?" Jalise gaped.

"Pregnant? Me? But I wasn't even trying!" René abruptly sat down, her face losing what little color it had.

"Yes, well, trust me. Sometimes it happens that way." Darcy was amazed that she could joke about the past this way. But then again, someone had to do something. The whole play was going to flop if they didn't!

She called to Luke, who was on the other side of the stage. "Find Jesse, will you? René needs him." When Luke didn't move, Darcy went over to him and whispered in his ear. His face wreathed in smiles, Luke returned moments later with a stunned Jesse.

"René? Are you sure?" The tender look on the big man's face brought tears to Darcy's eyes. How could René doubt that this man loved her?

"No, I'm not sure. Not at all." René patted Jesse's cheek. "But Darcy is."

"I pray that it's true," he said in wonder.

"Well, for now you're going to have to assume it

is, and get her out of here. Go find a seat in the audience if you must hang around. We've got a show to put on." Darcy squealed when Jesse enveloped her in a bear hug. "Jesse, it's ten minutes till show time! Get out of here."

"Oh, it's so wonderful!" Jalise wept as she watched Jesse usher his wife from the crowded and rather hot stage.

"Jalise, get hold of yourself! We've got to get these children lined up. Now, the choir goes out front first, right? Luke, you make sure they've all got their bows and cummerbunds on. Then line them up in the hall. There should be thirty-two of them." She squeezed his hand and let him go. "What comes first, Jay?"

Somehow they had everyone in their place by seven, and the curtain went up on time. Cheery little voices carried the timeless hymns off without a hitch, and even "Joseph," who'd been sick ten minutes before, played his part regally.

"It was a wonderful evening!" Ella Lancaster shook Darcy's hand after the performance. "Just wonderful."

Darcy finally had to pull away to nab one of the wise men, and get him to remove his shimmering velvet robe. But she deliberately remained behind the curtain to allow Jalise and René their moment in the sun.

"Tired?" Luke helped her hang up the costumes and fold away the last of the bright red cummerbunds. "It's okay if you are. You've earned it."

"Mommy, I liked your show." Jamie stood sucking on a candy cane beside Clarice's tall, spare form. "Did you like our class song?"

"Thank you, darling. And I loved your song."

Darcy hugged him tightly. "I need to stay here and clean up. Would it be all right if I imposed once more, Clarice?"

"Not an imposition! I love Jamie. We'll go home and sit in front of the fire, and I'll read him the Christmas story. When you come home, you can tuck him in."

"Thank you, Clarice." Darcy hugged the older woman with a heart full of love. "You are very special to both of us."

Seconds later Darcy and Luke were alone, packing away the items to leave the platform free for the next day's service.

"I thought if I got it all put away tonight, I could have Christmas and the following day off without stirring from the house. I'm worn out."

"You look pretty good to me," Luke said, taking her in his arms.

Reluctantly, several moments later, Darcy pulled herself away to finish her work. "That's it! Let's go home."

Luke silently helped her on with her coat and waited as she switched out all the lights. At the truck he held open the door and Darcy climbed in.

"I like the sound of that," he murmured as he climbed in the driver's side, letting the engine idle while he studied her.

"The sound of what?" Darcy could barely lift her eyelids.

"Home. A real home. For you and me. And Jamie. And Clarice, too, if she wants."

Darcy's eyes did fly open at that. She stared at him.

"I'm talking about the future, Darcy. Our future.

Together. Will you marry me?" Luke didn't wait for her answer. "You said you loved me. And I love you more than I could ever tell. There was pain in each of our lives until God brought us here together. I'm glad He did because I want to marry you. I want us to be a family. I don't care about the ranch. It's yours to do with as you see fit. We can go anywhere you want. All I ask is that we go together."

Wild unbridled joy brought tears to her eyes as she stared into that dearly beloved face.

"Darcy? Is it too soon?" Luke's voice was hesitant. "I'll understand if you need more time. Maybe you need to think it through more clearly. I know you wanted to be sure you are doing God's will. Maybe—"

"Luke?" Darcy waited until his dark fathomless eyes focused on her. Then she whispered her answer. "Yes."

He seemed stunned. "You mean it? Really? But I thought—no, never mind all of that. Yes?"

He wrapped his arms around her and kissed her, his heart filled with joy. And then, while Darcy sat beside him, he drove home singing "Joy To The World" in the flattest, most off-key voice she'd ever heard. But it sounded beautiful to her ears.

Darcy was amazed at his ability to get Jamie into bed without a protest. And she watched, amused, as Clarice huffed off to her room after an unsubtle hint from her nephew. But Darcy wasn't prepared for the small black velvet box he handed her as they sat before the fire.

"Merry Christmas, Darcy. With all my love."

She caught her breath at the beautiful solitaire dia-mond perched high on the thick gold band. And she still wasn't sure that she was breathing when he slipped it onto her finger.

"When can we get married?" he demanded. "When can we tell Jamie? Will he mind? How about giving him a wonderful Christmas and then telling him after things quiet down. Then we can reassure him how much we both love him." Darcy started laughing as tears flooded her face. "Darcy? Oh, my. Here, mop up, darling. I'm sorry."

He held her close, and soon Darcy did stop crying. But she couldn't stop the smile that spread across her face. "I love you, Luke Lassiter. And every day I thank God that He sent you to bring me back here." She kissed him, returning his love with her own.

Luke leaned back against the sofa, Darcy cradled in his arms as he stared into the fire.

"What are you thinking about?"

His eyes glowed in the firelight and he traced one finger down her cheek to her mouth.

"I was just wondering if that was my good-night kiss, a thank-you kiss or an I-love-you kiss. I do like to keep them all straight." His mouth quirked in a tiny grin.

"That was a just-because kiss," Darcy informed him, rising to her feet as she lifted Jamie's stocking down from the mantel. "And if you help me get these filled, I'll show you my good-night kiss. That way you won't get mixed up again."

Luke complied with a swiftness that had her giggling uncontrollably when she finally went to bed. She held her hand up in the shaft of moonlight shining through the window and admired her ring for the umpteenth time, even though a big wad of tape kept it securely on her finger. They'd have it sized and then, after New Year's, they'd tell the world their news. Meanwhile, it was their special secret and she would hug it to herself.

Thank You, Lord. Thank You very much for Luke Lassiter. I'll try to get it right this time. I'll try not to make any mistakes. But if I do, could You please forgive me? I'm not very good at this loving thing yet. But I will be, she promised. *I will be.*

It was the most wonderful Christmas Darcy could ever remember. Fresh snow left the sunny world outside glistening and gleaming with a brightness that almost hurt her eyes.

Jamie was ecstatic over his bicycle and insisted on riding it once around the living room, much to Darcy's dismay. At least the training wheels prevented any falls.

Clarice seemed delighted by the bright teal-and-royal-blue angora shawl that Darcy had crocheted. "I've never had anything so lovely," she murmured, brushing her knobby fingers across the gossamer softness. "It's perfect."

"It's nothing compared to the wardrobe you gave me when you didn't even know me." But Darcy accepted her hug. "And I love these dishes. I didn't know you could fire so high and still get such a bright glaze. I'm going to enjoy using them. And Jamie's wooden spoons will be perfect for stirring." She knew her son had earned the money helping Luke, and she let her eyes express her thanks to him.

But it was Luke's face that she focused on and Luke's smile she waited for as he opened the last gift under the tree. As he pulled out the rust-colored cardigan she'd made, Darcy felt a glow of satisfaction. She'd thought to buy him something as a gift, but this was straight from her heart, and, somehow, she thought he would appreciate it the most.

He caught her under the mistletoe later that day to tell her how much he appreciated the labor of love. "I'll wear it often. It'll feel like your arms around me," he whispered, just as his lips covered hers.

They enjoyed a relaxed fun day which included a sleigh ride through one of the meadows. And when they took a few minutes to renew their pledges of love, Jamie and Clarice didn't seem to mind. The turkey, plump and golden and dripping with succulent juices, sat in the middle of the table. And as they joined hands around it and bowed in prayer, Darcy couldn't help glancing around at the ones she now called family. She echoed Luke's words.

"Father, you've blessed us abundantly. Not just with physical gifts, but with each other. Most of all You gave us Your son to show us the way to You. Bless us now and keep us ever mindful of your great sacrifice. Amen."

"Amen," Jamie added, beaming from ear to ear.

Chapter Fourteen

Darcy glanced at the roomful of six rowdy children and blew her bangs from her forehead. Maybe having such a large birthday for Jamie after the Christmas rush hadn't been such a good idea. She'd planned a sledding party but worried that it was too cold.

"Get 'em outside in that air and let 'em run," Clarice advised dourly. "January's a good month to get fresh air."

"And it *is* fresh!" Darcy glanced at the thermometer and shivered. "You don't think it would be too cold for them?"

"Not likely! These are hardy children and they're dressed for the weather. Let them go sledding for a while and see if that doesn't tire them out."

"Okay, kids. We're going sledding. Get your snow pants and jackets on." With Clarice's help, Darcy got them dressed, one by one, and outside. Jamie led the way to the ridge behind the house that provided the perfect incline for a toboggan ride.

"Now listen to me. We have to go on this side. Nobody

is to go over there. It's really dangerous because of the trees."

She shepherded them to the left, and watched as Jamie hurtled himself down on the racer Clarice had given him. In a matter of moments he was at the bottom, and Darcy let out her pent-up breath in relief.

Down they went, some on plastic sheets, some on sleds or toboggans and some on the seats of their pants. Their hilarity was a joy to behold, and Darcy grinned as she watched Jamie land upside down in a soft puffy snowbank.

"Looks like a pretty good time," Luke murmured as he came up behind her, his arm sneaking around her waist. "Want to try it?"

"Me?" Darcy stared at him. "I'm a little too big, don't you think?"

"No, I don't. Nobody is ever too old to go sliding. Come on." And before she knew it, Darcy was seated behind him, flying down the hill on a flat piece of waxy cardboard. They fell off near the bottom, much to the amusement of the kids, and Darcy couldn't help but laugh as she dusted herself off.

"Now comes the hard part, old girl. We have to climb all the way up that hill," Luke said with a laugh.

"Hey! Who are you calling *old?*" And Darcy raced up the face of it just to prove that she could, gasping and wheezing when she finally reached the top.

The group of six whooped and hollered their way back to the house and descended on the table like a herd of locusts. Clarice kept them in line until Darcy could light the cake and supervise the singing. And Luke stood ready with a camera, snapping pictures wildly as Jamie blew out all five candles. Watching the happy kids gulp down cake and juice, Darcy leaned back against Luke, relishing the feel of his arms around her.

"It's hard to believe he was born five years ago. He's so grown up. I wish my parents had met him, held him. I was so stupid to go running off. But I couldn't think of any other way." She roused herself, determined not to cling to the past. "At least he's healthy and happy. Thanks to you and Clarice."

"And you." Luke's eyes darkened. "You're a wonderful mother, Darcy."

"Thank you."

"How long till we take these guys home?"

"I promised they could watch the rest of that video. About twenty minutes more," she vowed. "Then the bedlam will be over."

Twenty minutes almost to the second, Luke returned to watch as the tape ended and then called for the group to get their coats.

"Can I help take them home, Mommy?" Jamie asked.

"I don't think so, sweetie. There wouldn't be enough seat belts for everyone. You could help me clean up, though."

But once the other children had left, Jamie wasn't inclined to be helpful. He wandered here and there, unable to settle to anything. When Clarice offered to play a game, he snapped at her, and Darcy was forced to send him to his bedroom.

"When you can speak politely, you can come out. Birthday or no birthday, we remember our manners, son." He blinked up at her tearfully, his mouth tipped down, and Darcy felt her heart contract with love.

"Why don't I have a daddy, Mommy? The other kids all do. But I never had one. Not even one. Jimmy Wiggins has two!"

Darcy sucked in her breath. How could she ever tell Jamie about his father? Whatever happened, she wanted to shield him from the truth.

"We talked about this before, son. Remember? Some children don't have a daddy. But that's okay. Because we have a Father in heaven that loves us very much."

"It is *not* okay!" He glared at her. "It's not fair. I want a daddy to do things with. I want my own daddy so he can tuck me in at night, an' play baseball an' lots of stuff." His voice had become shrill. "Why can't God get me a daddy, Mommy? Doesn't He love me enough?" Jamie was sobbing loudly, his little body stiff and unyielding as she tried to hug him.

"Honey, I need to tell you…" Darcy prayed for some heavenly help, searching her mind for answers. Maybe she could tell Jamie that she and Luke…but no. Luke wanted to do that when they went out for dinner. It would be his very special birthday gift. "Jamie, there's something—"

"No!" Jamie jerked away from her restraining hand and threw himself across the bed.

Unable to reason with her son, and knowing that he was tired from all the excitement, Darcy ignored the outburst, brushing his forehead with a kiss before she went back downstairs.

"Everything all right?" Clarice had the table cleaned off and the dishes half washed.

"Yes, he's just tired. He asked me about his father."

"And?"

"What could I say?"

"You could have told him that Luke would be his new father," Clarice said. "You could have told the whole town when you told me."

"I would have, but Luke wanted to tell Jamie first, once the Christmas rush and the excitement of his birthday were over. We were planning on doing it tonight. Oh, well. He'll sleep a bit and be back to his cheerful self."

But when Darcy went to get her son for supper, his bed was empty. She searched every room, scoured every closet and hunted under every bed to no avail. Jamie was nowhere to be found!

"Where could he be, Clarice?" A shaft of fear shot through her heart as she noticed the empty hook by the door. "His coat is gone!"

"Probably went out to the barn," Clarice guessed. "He loves to sit with those animals."

Darcy raced back into the house seconds later, breathless from her search. "I called and called and he didn't answer. Where *is* he, Clarice?"

"I don't know." The older woman paled visibly. *Lord, we need Your help and we need it now.* She looked up as Luke drove into the yard. "I'll get my coat on. You go get Luke to help you start looking outside. I'll check all around in here one more time."

Luke insisted on searching the barns, workshop and garage, and, unable to think of another solution, Darcy tagged along. But it was dark in each building, and outside the wind had stiffened, icy particles stung their cheeks.

"I don't know, sweetheart. I just can't understand where he'd go. But we'll find him, don't worry. Thankfully, they finished sledding before this sleet hit. The hill would be sheer ice by now."

Darcy stopped in her tracks, grunting when Luke careened into her. "Luke—the sled! Do you think he would have gone sledding by himself?"

"Let's see if it's missing."

It was.

"Call him and keep calling," Luke ordered. "I'm going to get the truck and a rope. If it's as icy as I think, we'll need something to hang onto. Besides, the truck lights will help. Meet me at the hill."

"Jamie! Ja-mie!" She called, but the wind tore the words away before she'd reached the hill and peered down into the little valley below. Darcy screamed it out again and again, but no answer came.

Luke drove up behind her in the truck. "Okay, Darcy, I've got a rope on and I'm going down. You stay here."

"I'm not staying here! That's *my* son we're looking for."

"I might need help to get him up. If I tell you, you can come down, but put a rope on first. There's one on the seat." He kissed her hard and then rappeled over the edge, his boots clacking on the ice.

Darcy watched as he moved through the headlights. *Please God, don't let Jamie die. He's just a child, an innocent little boy. Don't make him pay for my sin. He's been such a joy to me, such a gift when I needed someone special. And he loves it here. Please God, don't let him be hurt.*

She continued to pray even while fearing that it was doing no good. Every so often she paused to call out her son's name, but there was no answer. Clarice came out shortly after, her face grim.

"I've searched every nook and cranny. He's not inside."

"Darcy, I've found him!" Luke's voice came faintly up the hillside. "He's been injured."

Darcy swayed at the words, her heart in her throat.

Lord, this mother and son need Your mighty touch right now, Clarice prayed. *Stay near, Heavenly Father and keep that child safe in Your hands.* Clarice hugged Darcy close. "He'll be all right," she promised. But there was a starkness to her voice that Darcy recognized as fear.

"Darcy? I need another rope. Tie it onto the front and then toss it down. Make sure it's tied tight. Get Clarice to help you."

"I'm here, boy." Clarice moved with purpose, urging Darcy out of the way as she found the coil of rope and fixed it firmly to the front of Luke's half-ton. "Always hated trucks. Changing my mind tonight." She grunted with the effort of tossing the rope over the edge, then walked back and climbed into the cab.

"Did you get it?" Darcy was unaware of the cold or the wind except as they would interfere with the rescue of her son. "Can you get him up?"

"No. He's unconscious, I think. And it's too slippery for me to climb back up. I'm going to tie him to the sled. When I give the word, tell Clarice to back up very slowly. I'll try to get a foothold as we go. Got it?"

"Yes, we've got it." Darcy nodded at Clarice.

Why should her child have to pay for all the stupid, senseless mistakes she'd made? Why hadn't she told him about Luke when she'd had the chance? Why was God letting this happen?

New knowledge seeped into her brain slowly. God didn't want her to marry Luke! She wasn't worthy. This was His judgment on her for the many times she'd rejected Him and scorned to follow in the path He'd directed. It was a lesson, that's what it was. A lesson in what might have been if she hadn't ruined it all with her stupidity.

It was pure agony to wait for Luke's return up the hill. With every creak of the truck, Darcy shook in fear, berating herself for her folly. Pleading and promising, the words rolled toward heaven mindlessly, each one begging for mercy for Jamie. But God's mercy seemed a long way off as she caught sight of Luke and her son moving into the truck's glare.

Jamie lay still and white on the sled, his head tilted to one side. She sucked in her breath at the huge, purplish lump on his forehead. With dread dragging at her conscious mind, Darcy knelt and brushed his hair back.

"Honey, it's Mommy. Can you hear me? I was so afraid. You weren't supposed to slide near the trees, son. It's too dangerous. Jamie? Please wake up."

"Come on, Darcy. We've got to get him to the hospital. I don't know what other injuries he may have." Luke was trying to undo the ropes that held the little boy to the sled, but his fingers were cold and clumsy. Clarice brushed them away and undid the knots with her bare hands, her voice soft.

"It's all right, Jamie. Auntie Clarice is here. I'll help you. And so will Uncle Luke. And your mommy. You don't have to be afraid. We're not mad." But even for his beloved Clarice, Jamie would not wake up.

Darcy's black curtain of despair would not be lifted, not when they reached the hospital, not when the attendants lifted Jamie onto the stretcher, not when the doctors shut her out of his room, and not when Luke's arms wrapped around her.

"He's in God's hands, sweetheart. And God loves little children. Jamie's going to be fine."

She jerked away, and Luke let her go, his arms falling to his sides. He watched as she walked over to the window and peered mindlessly out at the falling snow. "He'll be fine, darling."

But Darcy wouldn't listen, wouldn't allow herself to be consoled. She knew the truth. God was a just God, a fair God. He couldn't let a sinner like her get away with all her misdeeds just because she was sorry for them. How many times had her parents told her that every sin had a price?

She watched as an ambulance pulled up to the entrance, her mind grappling with the situation.

"All right," she whispered brokenly. "I'll do whatever it takes to keep Jamie alive."

Including leaving Luke and Clarice? Leave this place, turn your back on everything? Darcy could hear the question reverberate through her mind and she turned to glance at the man she had come to love so deeply. *Will you give up everything you've found, as a*

*punishment for the wrong you've done? Will you leave
here and never return?*

The very thought of it made her gasp with agony, but
Darcy resolutely turned away from Luke's frowning face
and stared out into the blackness.

Just let Jamie be all right, God, she murmured. *I'll
leave here right after that. I'll go back to New York. I'll
manage whatever You send. Just let him live.*

As if in direct response to her tearful plea, the doctor
walked into the waiting room, his eyes darting from
Luke to her. "Miss Simms?"

"Is he all right? Is Jamie going to be okay?" Darcy
sent up one last prayer.

"I think so. We're reasonably certain that your son
has suffered a concussion, but since there is some swelling at the back of the head, we'll have to wait until
he wakes up. The sooner he does that, the better I'll
feel." He smiled encouragingly. "In the meantime, I've
ordered some tests, just to be certain."

"Can I see him?" Darcy started for the door.

"Miss Simms, we've moved him into 108. I, er, that
is, don't be too concerned about the equipment you'll see
in there. We're monitoring everything, just to be sure.
Also, he has a broken arm." She nodded and stepped
past him, hurrying down the hall to her son's room,
her heart filled with joy. A broken arm—what did that
matter? It would heal. As long as he was all right....

But how could she do it: tear herself away from
everything that had become so precious in these past
few months? How could she just leave, as if nothing
mattered? As if she wouldn't leave behind a piece of her

heart with the big, lanky rancher who'd come to mean so much to her?

"I can deal with it," she kept telling herself as she walked. "As long as Jamie is okay, I'll handle the rest, no matter what."

Jamie lay on the narrow bed, his body covered by a sheet. The lump on his forehead was blossoming with color, but his eyes were closed. Darcy noted the rhythm of his chest, assuring herself that he was still breathing.

Thank You, God. She inhaled, her fingers closing around his still ones where they stuck out below the edge of the cast. *Thank You for looking after my son.*

Tears welled as she listened to the steady *beep* of the heart monitor. Near his head, a machine scribbled a wild variation of lines on a continuous piece of paper. *Oh, dear Lord, please let it be okay.*

"Mommy's here, Love Bug. Right here beside you. You're all right. I won't let anything hurt you." She pressed a butterfly-soft kiss against his cheek, sucking in a tortured breath when he didn't respond.

"Darcy? Don't cry, honey. He's going to be all right! The doctors think he'll wake up pretty soon now." Luke turned her in his arms and let her bawl, his hands gently soothing on her back.

And for several long moments, Darcy let him, storing up the memory for the future. It was all she would have to remember of him. Then she tugged herself away, dashing the tears from her cheeks.

"He'll get better by leaps and bounds when he finds out we're getting married, Darcy! I just know—"

"We're not getting married, Luke," she said, ignoring the stab of pain the words brought.

"Sure we are. We'll have to wait till he's better, of course. But that won't be long. And then we'll be one big happy family."

"No, Luke." She shook her head adamantly, fingers closing in a fist of determination. "I'm sorry, but I can't marry you."

"What?" He frowned, staring at her. "Why?"

"Because this isn't the place for me. It never has been." She used the old argument, knowing that he wouldn't try to compete against what he thought of as the bright lights of the big city. "I can't live in a one-horse rinky-dink town for the rest of my life. There are places I need to go, and things I want to do before I die."

"And you're just figuring that out now?" His face was a mask of self-control. "After all this time, you've suddenly forgotten exactly what your life in New York was like?"

"No." She couldn't meet his gaze and so she turned and focused on her son. "But that's not going to happen again. I have some references now. I can work in a school during the day and finish my studies at night. Besides, I'll have my half of the money from the ranch. You can buy me out. Jamie and I'll be fine."

"And it doesn't mean anything to you—leaving the heritage your parents gave to you?" His tone was sour. "What about Jamie? What about your son's future? Doesn't he deserve a life of security?"

"I'm doing this for him," she whispered brokenly. "So that he doesn't get driven to the same lengths I was, so he doesn't have to make the same mistakes." She swallowed. "And I'm doing it for you, too, Luke. You have no idea of the things I've done, the mistakes I've made. If you did, you wouldn't want to have anything to do with me. You should be glad I'm sparing you the pain. I'm doing it to help you."

"No, you're not." Luke laughed bitterly, the sound harsh in the quiet room. "You're leaving because you're running scared. Why not admit it? You can't, or won't, let yourself trust in God and wait to see what's in the future for us. *You've* got to be in control, Master Planner Darcy Simms!"

His scorn chipped away at her hard-won control.

"You don't understand," she croaked.

"Sure I do. I love you and Jamie both. I thought you loved me—that you and I would make up for the pain of the past. But at the first hint of trouble, you bolt, just like you've always done." His eyes hardened. "You say you loved your parents, but I'm beginning to wonder about that. Love doesn't stick its tail between its legs and run scared when the going gets tough, Darcy. Love endures."

"I do love you, Luke. But I'm leaving out of love, too. Please don't be angry. I just have to go."

"No, you don't have to!" He strode across to the door and yanked it open. "That's the saddest thing about it. You could have waited until Jamie woke up. We could have told him what we'd planned and he would have been ecstatic. But you won't wait and see what happens. You might get hurt or things might turn out differently than you think."

He sighed, lowering his voice. "When will you learn

to trust, Darcy? To trust me? To trust God? To trust that the whole world isn't out to get you before you get them?" He studied her face sadly. "Our future could have been something great, you know. It still can be. Please, just think things out a little more clearly. Pray about it."

"I have prayed, Luke. Long and hard. And I've never been as sure as I am right now that I made the right decision." She stared down at Jamie's dark head on the white pillow. "As soon as the doctors say he's able to travel, we'll be leaving Raven's Rest."

Chapter Fifteen

That Jamie was well and had been released from the hospital was wonderful. But with it came the knowledge that Luke's precious Darcy would be leaving. Before she did, Luke had to tell her something important.

Please God, show me the right way to do this.

"Darcy, can I talk to you?" he said after dinner the next night. She glanced at him warily. "In the office would be the best. I have something I need to give to you."

He was relieved when she said nothing, but simply followed him into the perfectly organized room. Dully, he wondered how long it would be before everything was a mess again.

"Yes?"

"Darcy, I know I should have given these to you long ago. Your parents asked me to make sure you got them. I was saving them for a special occasion, but I guess this is the best time." He removed the brown envelope from the filing cabinet and held it out. "Your mother left this in my care, to give to you when you came home."

She took it, her fingers careful to avoid his. He saw

the way her face blanched as she stared down at the familiar writing, and he felt the pain all the way through his heart.

"I'll leave you alone to read them. Jamie's watching the television. I'll stay with him."

Darcy nodded, then slit the envelope and slipped out the pages covered in her mother's perfect script.

My dearest Darcy,

For so long we've searched for you, longing for the day when you would come home and be with us again. Now it looks like we're not going to find you in time. So I'm writing this as our apology. Dad and I know we made many mistakes raising you. But dearest girl, we just wanted the best for you. And we thought that if we were very strict and instilled a sense of responsibility in you, you would rise to the wonderful life God had planned for you. In our concern to do everything by the book, we forgot the most important part of parenting—love.

Darcy stared, unable to believe what she was reading. Could it possibly be true? Were Clarice and Luke and even Jalise right when they said that Martha and Lester had loved her?

These past five years, I've wondered so many times if things would have been different if we'd told you from the beginning that you were adopted. Would it have explained anything to know that my youngest sister, Dora, got pregnant with you by a man who hadn't told her he had a wife and a family? Would you have understood how badly we wanted to keep the stigma from you by ensuring that you had a strict upbringing, by making sure that you never knew how much that one incident wrecked her whole life? We were so scared of the sins of the mother being visited on you that we overcompensated. I know now that the circumstances of your birth weren't that important. You were ours. Loving you should have been our main concern, and we failed miserably.

God gave us you, Darcy. You are our child and we will never stop loving you, no matter what has happened or will happen. Nothing can change that, my dear. Not anything.

Dad and I are so proud of you. We never told you that, I know, but it's true all the same. We felt that whatever good you did was because we'd raised you right. Now I see that your success in school was due to you and you alone, Darcy. So many times these past five years I've heard my nagging, nasty words echoing through my head, and wondered why I said them. My only excuse is that I wanted to love you and I didn't know how to tell you that. I do now. I love you, Darcy.

I tried to talk you into the adoption because I felt your baby would have a better home with a couple than with you. I was so scared. But I was wrong, Darcy. You will make an excellent mother because with you the person inside will always come first. It's strange to think of ourselves as grandparents and yet everyday we thank God for this small life He has entrusted you with. We're confident that the Lord has a special plan for your life, one we know nothing about but that is all the more wonderful because it's from Him. And He will lead you through paths I couldn't begin to understand five years ago. I think I understand them better now.

Don't feel sad when you look around, Darcy. Rejoice and be glad. If you are reading this, we're in heaven, and though I desperately wanted to hold you just one more time, to tell you that you are my very special daughter, I'm glad you're not here. I couldn't bear for you to think of me like this. Ah, my old vanity again. When will I learn that it's what is on the inside that counts?

Darcy smiled through her tears, remembering how her mother hated to have anyone see her without her nails filed, hair neatly combed, her clothing covered by a spotless white apron.

When God gave you to us, we were so happy and proud. Today I feel like that, too, because I know that the Father is watching out for my little girl. And He will be there, beside you, for the rest of your journey in this life, in spite of our mistakes.

I love you, my dear daughter. More than life itself.

Your very proud mother.

"Mommy? Why are you crying, Mommy?" Jamie patted her arm carefully, his round little face peering up in concern. "Are you sad, Mommy?" The bruising around his eye had turned to a faint yellow now, but he was walking and talking—and that's all that Darcy cared about. That and the fact that she finally understood.

"Sad—and happy, sweetheart. But I'm fine." She kissed his forehead, hugging him to her breast.

"You're squishing the paper, Mommy!" Jamie tugged out of her arms and held out a single sheet of paper. "You dropped it on the floor."

"Thank you, darling."

"Welcome." He grinned and skipped out the door to watch the end of his program.

Darcy stared down at the solid black writing, added on at the end of her mother's words. She'd never known her father to sit down and write a letter. The fact that he had apparently taken enough time to do so told her that he wanted to be sure she understood him.

> Luke Lassiter is a good man, Darcy. I trust him to manage the ranch. In return for his faithful service to your mother and me when I couldn't pay him, and for all the wonderful care he and Clarice have given to us, I've deeded half the place over to him. I had hoped that one day you two might meet and that Luke would be my son-in-law. He needs someone to take care of him and you would do that very well. But I know that it's up to God and He is able to take care of you far better than we ever could. Your mother and I pray for you every night, knowing that God is watching over you and our grandchild.
>
> We love you, Darcy.
> Dad.

They loved her! The tears flowed steadily down her cheeks as she tried to absorb everything. They hadn't cared about what she'd done, or the fact that she had run away.

Thank You, Lord, she whispered, carefully folding the precious words and secreting them inside her purse. *Thank You so much.*

She fingered the sparkling diamond that Luke had given her. She'd tucked it into her purse for safekeeping, but now she pulled it out and set it on the desk. *Thank You for giving me this bit of solace before I leave here.*

She was so tempted to stay, to fulfil her parents' wishes.

But she needed some time to think.

Darcy tugged on her coat and took a walk down the lane. She needed to move on. But how?

"Darcy?" Jalise stared at her from inside her car. "Didn't you hear me honk?" She stared at her friend's tearstained face. "What's wrong?"

"Hi, Jalise. Nothing. *Everything.* I'm leaving Raven's Rest. Again."

"But you can't!" Jalise's eyes darkened. "Your whole life is here. Clarice, the ranch, the school kids. Luke. He loves you, Darcy."

Jalise motioned Darcy into the car, where it was warm, and Darcy got in before answering.

"I love him, too. But I can't stay here, Jay. Not now."

"But why? Surely you realize that God has been leading you back? He's provided you with a home, people who love you, and work that you're very good at. Why would you want to leave?"

"I have to. I'm not worthy of Luke's love." It hurt to say it, but it was the truth. "Besides, I promised."

"Promised who?" Jay frowned. "I don't understand."

"I know. I guess that's been the problem all along. How to understand Darcy!" She laughed harshly, the pain welling up inside.

"Honey, Luke doesn't care about what you've done in the past. Nobody does. All he wants is a future with you and Jamie. That's all he's wanted for months."

"He has?"

"Listen, Dar, once I thought Luke would make a good husband for me. Lord knows, I'm lonely and I don't want to spend the rest of my life alone. Running the restaurant has just been something to fill in the hours." She cleared her throat. "But Luke told me long ago that he wasn't interested. And when I see him with you, I know his love for you was meant to be. You can't run away from that kind of love any more than you could run away from your parents' love! It's right there, just waiting for you to accept it."

"I thought I could. But now I realize it was just wishful thinking." She tried to laugh and ended up sobbing. "Besides, I made a deal with God. I promised to give up everything I thought I'd found if God would just heal Jamie. He kept His part, and now it's time for me to do the same."

"Oh, Dar!" Jalise laughed in relief as the tears welled up in her eyes. "You can't make bargains with God. Nobody knows that better than me. Believe me, I tried with Billy." She hugged her friend close. "God had a plan then and He has one now. He loves you, sweetie. He's laid it all out so perfectly. You've returned home, you've won over the naysayers. You've found a place where you can serve in the community. And you found Luke."

Darcy tried to concentrate on the words, seeing the big picture form, but knowing the one fatal flaw.

"And most of all, you found love, and Jamie found a daddy. Do you think He planned all that for you to have you just walk away? God loves you, Darcy. You're His daughter, His child! He wants everything good for you. And He's given it to you. But you have to take it and do something with it."

The words hit a chord inside that had died sometime in the distant past. She was loved, in so many ways. It was what she'd always longed for, dreamed of, and it had been right here all along. Could she just throw it all away again?

"But you don't understand. I've spoiled things, made so many mistakes. I have an illegitimate child."

"You have a wonderful son, Dar. A little boy that God gave you when you needed someone to love. And you've asked for God's forgiveness, haven't you?" She waited till Darcy nodded. "Well, when God forgives, the Bible says He remembers *no more*. You're dwelling on something that God has already forgiven and forgotten, girl. He doesn't want you to do some kind of penance for the rest of your life just because Jamie is alive and well!"

"But can Luke forgive and forget?" The dreaded fear grew inside her brain. "I don't think so. He'll be reminded of my ugly past every time he looks at Jamie."

"Oh, Darcy," Jalise murmured. "Luke doesn't care about the past. He's too busy thinking about the future."

"He might care. If he knew the truth." Darcy could hardly bear to think about the awful things she'd kept locked away inside. Just like her parents had hidden their secrets.

"I don't think his love is that shallow. But if *you* do, test him. Tell him the truth and see if it matters to him or not. What have you got to lose?"

Darcy thought about it for a moment. "All right, I'll tell him. It won't be easy. I've never told anyone else."

"But won't it be worth it to have him in your life for good?"

"Yes. Thank you, Jay." She threw her arms around Jalise and hugged her tightly. "You always were the best friend in the world."

"It took you long enough to notice," Jalise laughed, hugging her back. "Now don't you have something to do?"

"Yes, I guess I do." Darcy got out of the car, closed the door and waved goodbye. Then she headed back toward the house, her mind busy. She wasn't going to hide the past anymore. If anyone knew better, it was her. Too much pain and sorrow had come from keeping secrets.

She hardly dared imagine that Jalise was right. Would Luke forgive her? Did God really mean for her to have it *all?*

"Mommy?" Jamie's little face peered up at her curiously, from the open front door.

"What, sweetie?"

"Are we going looking for a new home?" The blue eyes were wide and innocent, and Darcy gave thanks again to the Father who had watched over them so carefully.

"You know something, Love Bug? I think we've already found our home." Darcy glanced around, searching for some glimpse of Luke. *Please God, let me finally be home*.

"Clarice, could you keep Jamie busy for a while? I have something I need to talk to Luke about."

The older woman's face shone with an inner light as she wrapped her arms around the two of them, squeezing for all she was worth. When she let them go at last, her eyes sparkled with unshed tears of joy.

"He's out in the workshop, love."

Darcy hurried to Luke's private workshop. He was inside, bent over something on the worktable. She slipped through the door soundlessly and waited, content to watch his big, capable hands tenderly sand the hard wood.

"Luke."

He whirled around, his face anguished-looking. "Darcy? I thought you were packing. Did you forget something?"

She heard the pain in his words even though he strove to hide it. Her heart ached for the trouble she'd caused him and she vowed to make up for it. For the rest of her life.

"Yes, I did. I forgot a lot of things." She stood where

she was, imprinting the strong features on her mind forever. "I forgot to trust God. I forgot to trust you. I forgot that the truth kept hidden can only hurt. And, worst of all, I forgot about love. I was hoping you could listen to something I need to say."

He nodded, his eyes brimming with curiosity.

"I know you don't understand why I thought I had to leave, so I'd like to explain something. It happened a long time ago."

"It doesn't matter, Darcy. I don't care about the past. I've got my hope in the future. But if it will make you feel better, go ahead. I'll listen."

"Thank you." She drew a huge breath, plopped down on a stump and began. "You already know that I was the town brat. It seemed to me as if everyone hated me, and I could understand that. I hated myself. But Josiah Pringle was the one boy who saw through my bad-girl image to the insecure child underneath. He took time to talk to me, encourage me, hold me when I cried. I thought he loved me.

"We spent a lot of time together. Secret time when my parents thought I was locked up in my room. They had grounded me because of some gossip by a woman in the church. They didn't care that I was innocent, or maybe they knew better. Anyway, one afternoon I snuck out and met Josiah at this secret place we had in the woods." Darcy forced herself to meet his gaze.

"I was so angry, and so *hurt*. How could they believe that I was a tramp? My own parents? Josiah comforted me as he always had, only this time he got carried away. I thought, 'Well, why not? Maybe it will make him love me more.'" She laughed bitterly.

"It didn't. He ran off and left me there, and I suddenly realized that I had become everything they'd called me." She felt the tears rolling down her cheeks, but ignored them, needing to get it all said. "Several weeks later I figured out that I was pregnant. I sent Josiah a note, which his mother read. She brought him along to our meeting and proceeded to tell me that Josiah wasn't going to be tied to the town 'harlot.' Besides, she said, how could they be sure the baby was his?"

"What did he say?" Luke's voice was full of anger.

"Nothing. He stood there staring at the floor and let her tear me to shreds. She threatened to tell my parents the whole story unless I had an abortion."

"What!"

"I couldn't do it. I knew I'd done wrong. And I knew I had to pay for it. But I couldn't take my baby's life!" She remembered the agony of decision. "Josiah promised we'd get married after graduation. We could have another baby. He'd be free then—of legal age. So I agreed. Or pretended to. His mother never said a word to me. He probably told her that I'd had the abortion."

"But you didn't." It wasn't a question.

"No, I couldn't. I kept thinking that the baby hadn't done anything wrong. I had. I should pay, not the baby. When we graduated, I made sure I was top of the class. I poured myself into getting those grades, as if that would help. But I was still pregnant, and I knew it wouldn't be long before I showed. I talked to Josiah just once, the last time I saw him. He said he had met someone else. A 'good Christian' girl. They were serious. So I went to my parents and I told them I was pregnant."

Luke frowned. "They never knew whose baby it was?"

"No." She shook her head.

He moved toward her, his hand gentle on her shoulder. "But Darcy, none of it matters, don't you see? It's the past. And thanks to your grit, you have Jamie. Was that *his* middle name?"

"James was his father's middle name. I had some dream of a tradition, you see." She smiled grimly, mocking her own foolishness, as her fingers wrapped tightly around his. "I was a fool."

"So who isn't?" He kissed the top of her head, his arms around her. "But why did you suddenly decide to leave? Was it something I said?"

"No!" She snuggled her head into his shoulder. "It was something I felt. Guilt. A great big load of it. I thought Jamie's getting hurt was God's way of getting even with me for my sin—sort of a payback. I reasoned that if I agreed to give up everything I loved, God would forgive me enough to let Jamie live."

Luke gently pressed her away, his eyes serious. "Sweetheart, God doesn't treat His children like that. He's forgiven you for the past. I think it's time you forgave yourself."

Darcy smiled up at him. "I was kind of hoping you'd remind me." She waited expectantly, praying that Jalise hadn't been wrong.

"Are you sure this time? Really sure, Darcy?" His arms moved up around her, gently cuddling her closer.

"I'd like to take you up on your offer of marriage, Luke. If you still want me, that is."

"For how long?" he whispered, drawing a shaky breath.

"I thought maybe—" she paused "—for the rest of our lives. I've finally come home, Luke. I'm not really Martha and Lester's daughter. I'm just me, God's child and Jamie's mom. And maybe, just maybe, your wife."

His melting brown eyes slid over her, absorbing every detail, before his arms tightened. "Thank God!" And then he kissed her with a thoroughness that left her in no doubt of his feelings on the matter.

And Darcy, with her heart singing heavenly music, kissed him back.

Epilogue

"Darcy, you've got to stand still if you want me to get this hat on straight. The veiling is lopsided," Jalise murmured in frustration.

"I don't even care if I *have* a veil," Darcy replied. "I don't know why I let Luke talk me into all this fuss anyway. We could have been married without all the hoopla. I only ever agreed to marry the man—not to let the town watch!"

"That's about to happen in less than five minutes, so you'd better make the best of it." Clarice straightened the ivory lace that trailed behind. "Besides, my nephew wanted you to have this special day to look back on for years and years. And I think he was right."

"So do I." Jalise nodded, satisfied with her work.

"You look lovely, dear. I'm sure your mother is looking down from heaven, smiling right now. She always meant for you to wear her dress." Clarice fingered the old silk gently. "She'd be so proud of you today."

"I know. I wish Dad was here to walk me down the aisle." Darcy smiled, feeling the thrill in her heart that the hurt was finally gone. "I guess he probably is, even if I can't see him."

"Everybody's here," Jalise said, glancing between the curtains. "Even Mrs. Lancaster!"

Darcy peeked, too. The music changed and Luke's brother, who was serving as the best man, entered the church, followed by Jamie and then Luke. They looked so handsome as they lined up in front in their matching black suits and bow ties.

"Come on, woman! It's time for us to meet that fiancé of yours and his bossy brother." Jalise spread the short wispy tulle over Darcy's shoulders and smoothed the full ruffled skirt. "You look beautiful, Dar. I love you." She pressed a kiss against Darcy's cheek and accepted a hug in return.

Darcy took a deep breath, relishing the words. *I love you.* It was so wonderful to hear that. She would never tire of it. Never. And she was learning to give as good as she got.

"I love you, Jay. And you, too, Clarice." She smiled mistily. "I feel like I'm overflowing with love."

Jalise grinned. "I think that big lug at the front feels the same way. Look at his grin." She made a face. "It's too bad his best man couldn't smile a little more. Cade Lassiter is nothing like his brother!"

"Now Jay, no fighting. It's not nice. Besides, I don't want to play peacemaker between you two."

"You won't have time. That's the prelude Gertie's using to signal you. Get moving. Go on out there and tie up that groom nice and tight before someone else does." Clarice pushed them out the door, grasped the usher's arm, and marched beside him to her seat near the front.

As the chords of the "Wedding March" resounded through the small building, Jalise gave Darcy's hand one last squeeze, picked up her bouquet of daffodils and started down the aisle. Little Ginny Jones followed her, walking carefully with her new braces. When she reached the front, Darcy tightened her fingers around her own bouquet of spring iris, lilies and daffodils, and stepped out slowly, her eyes firmly fixed on the tall, lean man with the glowing brown eyes that twinkled a secret message.

"Hi, beautiful." His fingers gathered hers in a squeeze of reassurance. "You look wonderful, Darcy."

"So do you." More than wonderful, she wanted to say. Like a dream come true. And her heart sang praises to God.

The old-fashioned vows were savored and repeated all through the congregation as the bride and groom promised their love to each other. René Jones's poignant solo left not a dry eye in the church. And the townsfolk of Raven's Rest spent many an hour after the reception discussing how wonderful it was that Darcy Simms had come home at last.

* * * * *

Dear Reader,

Isn't it awful to be left hanging, wondering if you matter to anyone at all? To wait, day after day, for some sign of relief from those problems that just won't quit? We moan and groan, blame other people and push ourselves to find a way out when all the time God is there, waiting for us, revealing His perfect will. I hope you've enjoyed Darcy's story and learned with her that God hasn't turned His back on you. Please watch for a return of Darcy with her friend Jalise Peters and Luke's rebel brother Cade.

Until we meet again, I wish you the steadfast assurance and calm certainty that no matter what your life brings, you are God's dear child and He will heal your heart's deepest ache.

Lois Richer

HIS ANSWERED PRAYER

This is my commandment,
that you love one another, as I have loved you.
—*John* 15:12

This book is for kids everywhere, big or little,
who hurt because Mommy or Daddy isn't there.
Your Father above is waiting with open arms.

Chapter One

"Mommy?"

"Yes, Daniel."

"Where is my daddy?"

"Uh…"

"I'm gonna pray really hard, so God will send me a daddy."

Blair Delaney sighed, her son's earnest question from last night still ringing in her ears. Daniel hadn't waited for the answer she didn't have—or at least, one he'd understand—but had bluntly petitioned heaven with his heartfelt demand.

She shoved her hair behind her ear and deliberately pushed the problem of Daniel's absent father out of her mind. It was procrastination of the worst sort, but she couldn't deal with it now. She had to focus on the tasks at hand. Her family depended on her. They needed her to be strong, to keep things on track, to take care of them.

She picked up the shortwave radio and pressed the button.

"I'm heading for the hives in the west field, Mac. If

I'm lucky and things are as good as they seem out here, I won't have to feed the bees sugar for much longer now."

"That's good, Busy Bee."

The old nickname drew a grin. Trust Grandpa to put a smile into her day. She wasn't going to let him down. Somehow she'd manage Daniel and all the other little problems that kept creeping up, demanding her attention.

"It'll be nice for you to stop making these runs every day." Mac's voice came strong and clear, proof positive that he was once more feeling up to snuff.

Blair let out a breath of relief. That lingering winter cold that had rattled around in his chest since December scared her. Maybe it was finally gone. Blair heard him ask how long she'd be.

"The thing is, I'm not sure, Grandpa. Daniel will be at kindergarten till three. I should be back long before the bus gets there. Can you check on Aunt Willie for me, make sure she takes her medication on time?"

Mac's ready answer sent a shaft of pleasure straight to her heart. Sometimes it was nice to be needed, to do things that really mattered to the ones you loved.

Blair snapped the radio into its holder seconds before she had to grab the wheel and force it right on the rutted, muddy road. Spring in the valley made it tough to negotiate the unpaved foothill roads that bordered Colorado's famous Rocky Mountains. But when the valley sprouted this bright vibrant wash of color, she couldn't wish herself anyplace else. This was home.

Ten minutes later Blair surveyed the first blush of green that tipped the branches surrounding her field.

Below her feet, tiny plants forced their way through the soil and stretched to meet the sun. It was fresh, it was good. It was hers.

Or it would be one day.

Blair strode across the meadow where she'd set out her beehives, the same meadow she'd worked so hard to make a profit on. As she walked, her mind focused on Daniel's upcoming field trip. The class kitty was still short of the requisite funds. His teacher needed her to organize one more fundraiser before the end of May. Blair would have to come up with a plan. Just another little job to see to.

The hives seemed in good repair, once she removed the outer insulating wraps. A quick check inside proved the durability of this particular strain of bees, and she pushed away any lingering doubts she'd had about spending so much on them.

"With any luck at all, this will be a banner year for Mind Your Own Beeswax." The words brought a satisfied smile to her lips.

The company had been her idea over six years ago, just after her life had fallen apart. She'd run home to Grandpa Mac and his sister Wilhelmina. Even though they were barely scraping by on the tumbledown ranch they'd chosen for retirement, they welcomed her, and Daniel when he'd arrived, with open arms. They needed her, and Blair had willingly pitched in. Her fledgling honey and beeswax candle business really took off after Daniel's birth and now consumed most of Blair's time.

With a practiced eye she studied the field. The Merrihews always planted early. That was one of the reasons she chose to rent to them. That and the fact that their clover crops provided exactly the environment her bees needed.

Blair mentally calculated how much her earnings and Mac's pension brought in and then subtracted the costs of Willie's special expenses and the costs involved in helping their friend Albert Hunter. He had a predilection for inventions that never quite took off.

"It's going to be a stretch," she muttered, unwilling to even consider what would happen if her grandfather were no longer there. She didn't love him just for his pension, though he'd teased her about it often enough!

If I could just expand a bit, she thought, turning to survey the hilly terrain beyond. But where?

A movement to the left caught her attention, and she frowned. Someone was out there. Blair walked to the truck, trying to identify the lone figure perched atop a mound of dirt, studying the southern portion of her valley through a surveyor's transom.

"Not another one! Why won't these guys take no for an answer? We're *not* going to sell. This is part of Daniel's heritage." The land wasn't as good as a daddy, of course, but next to love, it was all she had to give her son.

She scrambled around the edge of the field, hiding herself in the bushes and trees that surrounded the area so she'd be able to sneak up behind the intruder. She needn't have bothered. He didn't seem to notice her or anything else around him, lost as he was in his scribbling on the small notebook he'd pulled out of his pants pocket after checking his sighting once more. He was so totally immersed in his own world that the snap of a twig beneath her feet didn't break his concentration.

When she was about fifty feet away, Blair left her cover and moved into the open.

"You're trespassing," she called loudly, hoping to startle the interloper.

He jerked upright, his body tall and lean and still. Then, ever so slowly, he turned around. Blair gasped.

"You!" She clenched her fists against her thighs as all the hurt of the past welled up inside. "What are you doing here, Gabriel?"

Gabe Sloan stood there in his sand-washed silk shirt, designer jeans and Italian leather boots, a twisted smile rolling across his handsome face. His hair, jet-black and poker straight, lay in its familiar style, cut close to the head. Eyes, those piercing mossy green eyes, took in every detail of her appearance.

"Blair," he murmured, his lips barely moving. "The trusting, always truthful, *disappearing* Blair Delaney." His mouth slashed a chilly grin. "To what do I owe the honor of your sudden return to my life?" He stared at her like a hawk sighting a mouse. But his voice exhibited total disinterest in her answer.

"I'm not in your life, Gabe," she whispered, unable to believe what she was seeing, though the sinking in the pit of her stomach assured her he was there. "In fact, I never was. Not the way I wanted to be. You never needed me, remember? You don't need anybody."

His face tightened, and his eyes hardened. His wide mouth pinched in a stiff little smile. He avoided her glare.

"Part of that is true. Though why you had to take

off, run away like a scared young rabbit is beyond me."
Gabe sighed, his whole body shifting. "It doesn't matter
anymore, does it? You were too young—for a lot of
things. I should have known that." He shook his head,
eyes hard but with an underlying rueful glint that flashed
to meet hers.

"I had a duty to protect my company, Blair. Whether
you liked it or not."

She tossed her head, angry that he was still using his
company as an excuse to push her away. "Uh-uh. You
wanted me to sign that prenuptial agreement to protect
yourself. It was obvious you had no intention of putting
everything into our marriage. You'd already provided a
way out!"

He laughed, a short harsh bark that told her he hadn't
changed his view of her, or people in general. Gabe
always believed someone was out to cheat him. She
watched as he turned that suspicion her way.

"You don't understand because you never had a head
for business, Blair. You were too deep into your chemistry formulas and theories. So go ahead. Pile all the guilt
you want on my head. I've been through it before. You
won't say anything somebody hasn't already left at my
door. Fortunately, you got away in time, before regrets
got the better of you."

A lot he knew! She regretted so many things. Blair
shook her head. She wasn't going back to that misery
of self-doubt. She wasn't ever going back. He wouldn't
do that to her again.

"The only thing I'm interested in chewing you out
for is your presence on my land. I'd like you to leave,
Gabe."

"Your land?" The great Gabriel Sloan frowned, obviously confused by her protest. "This is my land. And I have the papers to prove it."

"Don't be ridiculous!" Blair snapped, furious that *now,* at this stage of the game, he was still looking for an ulterior motive. "We hold the deed to all of this property."

"We?" His body stiffened, eyes alert as he digested this bit of information. "Are you married?"

"It's none of your business." She returned his stare with a glare that usually made people look away. But Gabriel wasn't like other people. "No," she finally admitted.

"But you always said, uh—" he thought a moment "—that your parents were dead." He peered at the ground, frowning, obviously sifting through what little he could remember as he kicked at a clump of dirt.

Blair could almost hear that computerlike brain of his clicking through the file of information he had about her, deleting this byte, updating that one. Finally he spoke.

"The only people you ever talked about were your grandfather and some aunt. I don't remember anything about Colorado."

"That's hardly surprising."

Blair swallowed the rest of her snappy comeback at the impaling glint of those now-emerald eyes. She remembered how those eyes changed color to suit his mood. That intense scrutiny, that ability to look right through her, they all combined to send twitching jitters skipping over her nerves.

"Should I have asked, Blair?"

Blair fumed at the spin he put on her words. She'd

forgotten how good he was at twisting what she said. He made it sound as if she'd woven a web of deceit instead of opening her heart up to him, only to have it thrown back in her face!

"I never lied to you, Gabe." At least, only by omission.

"Does that mean you and your family live around here now?" He studied her curiously, his eyes roving slowly over the top of her head to the tumble of lopsided curls she'd raked her hair into this morning on her way to the truck.

Slowly his gaze flowed past the big bulky sweater, ragged jeans and muddy cowboy boots. Then he glanced across the fields that would soon blossom with flowers.

"I never took you for the down-home, country type, Blair."

"You never really knew me." She let the sharp words pour out, angry that Gabe even imagined he'd known the person inside of her. "That much was obvious from the way you used me."

"I didn't use you!" His face washed in a red tide of anger. "It wasn't my fault you expected too much."

"I did, didn't I?" she agreed quietly, turning to stare at the gorgeous blue sky that sparkled over the snow-capped mountains in the distance. She squeezed her eyes shut, forcing down the lump in her throat. "Way too much, as it turns out."

Please help me, she prayed desperately. *I never thought I'd see him again. I thought You would lead me to someone else. I don't want this!*

"Blair? What are you doing? Open your eyes!" His

hand on her arm helped wake her to the fact that her reality had changed. The peace she'd always found in this valley was shattered, shifted into something ominous that could turn on her if she wasn't careful.

Blair jerked her arm out of his grasp and whirled away, anxious to put as much distance between them as possible.

"I'm fine. There's nothing for you here, Gabriel Sloan. Nothing! This is my family's land. I'd like you to leave."

He stayed where he was, saying nothing. And when Blair couldn't take his silence for one moment longer, she headed for her truck.

"Blair?"

His softly voiced request made her stop in her tracks.

"It's my land now. At least part of it is. I did buy it. Free and clear. No encumbrances."

She shouldn't be surprised. It was the way he'd always preferred to live—never let anyone get too close. The words pricked a nerve in her mind. Blair whirled, her forehead wrinkled in a frown. He sounded so positive of his right to be here.

"Not possible, Gabriel. You must have the wrong place. This particular quarter section is my grandfather's. He's had it in his family for years. He's willing it to me when he dies."

Gabe seemed unabashed by her assurance. He simply shrugged, then pulled out a piece of paper from his pocket.

As he read the legal description to one of the three

quarters Mac owned, Blair felt the bottom tilt out of her world.

"No." She shook her head stubbornly. "Someone has made a mistake."

"Perhaps you?" His mouth tilted in a questioning quirk. Blair took the document and scanned it, her eyes halting abruptly when they fell on the signature at the bottom.

"Mac?" she whispered. "Mac actually sold you this?"

"Mackenzie Rhodes." He nodded. "He wrote to me, offered to sell me a little bit of heaven about four months ago. I had someone check it out, then decided to buy. This is the first time I've seen anything other than the videos and snapshots that were taken." He stopped, one eyebrow quirked upward. "Is it a problem?"

Blair sucked in a deep breath and concentrated. Hard.

"It's a mistake," she mumbled at last. "It has to be. He wouldn't do this to me. He wouldn't. Not Mac." It was the only solution she could some up with. "Not my own grandfather," Blair asserted, giving a vigorous shake to her head. "He knows how much I depend on this land."

"You do?" Gabe surveyed the area with interest. "Why does a chemist with your qualifications depend on this particular land? And for what?"

Her *qualifications?* If he only knew.

"I need it for my business." She saw the jerk of his head and compressed her lips tightly, stemming the diatribe that ached for release. "I have to earn my way, you know."

"Don't we all." There it was again, that sardonic twist that manipulated his attractive mouth into a mocking sneer. "Are you doing a field study or something?"

"I have hives all around this field." At his skeptical look she lifted a hand and pointed. "There, see those white boxes? And there?" Gabe squinted into the distance, then finally nodded.

"That's only a small number of the hives that provide the honey I sell. I also make candles, though I doubt you've heard of my company." She told him the name and shrugged when his eyes didn't light up. "I didn't think so. We're pretty new on the scene." She shifted uncomfortably. "What are you staring at?"

"You. I can't seem to see you sticky with honey." His smile begged her to see the joke. "You always looked so elegant, so refined. If Eunice Standish could see her model for women's fashions now, what would she think?"

Anger snipped at Blair. How dare he malign her for making an honest living? How would somebody as rich and spoiled as Gabe ever understand how hard it was to provide just the daily bread for four other people?

"I only took that part-time job because it paid so well. And to please you, so I'd look the way you wanted." She shrugged carelessly. "Now I don't really care what you or Eunice or anyone else thinks. This is *my* life." She straightened to her full height and frowned. "As interesting as this is, Gabe, I do have work to do. I'd appreciate it if you'd leave now."

"What *work* do you have to do today?"

She jerked her head at his curious tone, but could find nothing derogatory in his eyes. Maybe she's misjudged him. Maybe he had changed. She shrugged and grudgingly told him.

"I'm going to unwrap the last of the hives. I've done most of the ones on the south side, but I left a few hives in this field till today because that part of the hill takes longer to thaw out."

"Can I watch?"

Blair sighed. Why now? Why here? Why today? Couldn't he have gone hunting for land somewhere else? Why did he want land, anyway? The Gabriel Sloan she knew scorned any place that didn't boast all the amenities of his deluxe L.A. condo.

"Blair? I promise I won't interfere."

"If you do you'll get stung!" That made her smile. She wondered if he'd understand her hidden meaning.

"It's happened before. A certain college student used to do it quite often, as it happens. I missed her."

Blair got caught up in the storm of sea foam that swirled in his eyes. Her breath caught, reminding her how easily Gabe Sloan could draw her in, make her believe she was the most precious thing in his life. It wouldn't happen again.

"I doubt you even noticed I was gone," she returned sourly. "I'm sure you were too involved in the latest gizmo and high-tech security to keep it under wraps." She wished it wasn't true, but reality was hard to ignore.

"I noticed, Blair. Especially when I had to cancel that elaborate wedding." His voice growled low, full of mocking innuendo. "Caterers, church, flowers, it took a lot of time."

And money. Blair heard the words even if he didn't

say them. She forced her foot not to stamp. He was thinking about the money again, she just knew it. The one thing that had managed to uproot a love she was sure they'd share until eternity.

Gabe studied her, head tilted to one side in that familiar pose, and Blair smiled at the gesture so exactly a mirror of Daniel's.

Daniel!

"I—that is, I have to get busy. You can trail along if you want. Or not. I don't care." She stalked through the bushes, ignoring the whoosh of mud as her boots found firm passage through the spring runoff.

She could hear Gabe following her but ignored him.

It didn't take long to get to the last few hives and undo their insulated covers. She folded them carefully, then turned to face him.

"That's all there is to the show for today, Gabe. I've got to get home and get to work. There's a lot to do. Goodbye."

He said nothing, simply stood there, studying her as if she were one of the oddly hewn pieces of smooth alabaster he'd collected so avidly six years ago.

"Can you find your way out of here?"

She tossed the hive wrappers into the back of the truck then turned to face him, hands clamped to her hips.

"Blair, I have legal title to this land, and I'm not backing out. This is exactly the kind of place I've been looking for." His lips clamped shut, the expression on his face changed, hardened. "Perhaps the best thing to do is check it out. Now. Before things go much further."

"What things?" She gaped at him, her mind numb.

"An excavation crew is set to come in here Monday morning."

"Excavation?" Blair blanched at the thought of her beautiful valley, destroyed. "Why?"

"I'm building a house. I intend to live in this valley, Blair. It's going to be my home."

She couldn't take it in, couldn't understand what kind of a joke he was playing.

"But you live in Los Angeles," she reminded him, depicting the picture she remembered late at night when she should have slept. "You crave bright lights, fast cars and people you can impress by ignoring them." Yes, that was the real Gabe. "Why would you move *here,* to the middle of nowhere?"

It didn't make sense. None of this did. Gabriel Sloan was as city as they came. Going out with starlets, winning at squash, traveling on the big showy jet, those were the things he needed to prove himself. Gabe craved all the glitz and glamour of the nightlife that L.A. offered. There was nothing around here that would interest him.

His voice roused her from her introspection.

"I'm experimenting, Blair. Isn't that what you used to encourage? I want something different from my life. The company just isn't enough anymore. It bores me. I've hired a manager. I want to take some time and relax for a while. Consider what's next."

"You've let go of the reins?" She squeaked in disbelief. "You? The guy who thinks everybody's out to take him?" It was a direct quote. He'd said it over six years ago on that fateful morning when all her dreams had died.

Oh, God, where are you? Does he know about Daniel? Is that why he's here?

The very thought made her head spin, and all the blood rushed to her feet. He was going to steal Daniel! And he had money and power enough to do it.

"Blair? Sit down." He pushed her onto a huge granite slab of glacial rock whose quartz sparkles flashed in the bright sun. His hands rubbed hers, his surprisingly warm and gentle. "You're still as thin as a reed," he muttered, pausing to brush a ringleted tendril from her cheek. "And this hair is still a riot of curls. I didn't think it was possible, but you're thinner. Are you still so busy taking care of everyone else, you don't take care of yourself?"

She pulled away, but she had no energy to get up. Not yet.

"I'm fine. I'm just busy. I guess I forgot to eat breakfast." As if that would have changed anything. She glared at him. "Why now, Gabe? Why here?"

"I wanted a change. And I was intrigued by his description. Heaven on earth. Who wouldn't want that?"

There was a bitter tilt to his lips that made her wonder if Gabe had suffered some financial setbacks she didn't know about. Or perhaps he'd lost the edge that put his company out in front.

"Who indeed?" She was going to strangle Mac when she got hold of him. How could he have sold this land out from under her, especially to Gabe? How could he have set this all up when he knew the risks? And it was a setup. She had no doubts about that.

Gabe picked up her hand. "You've got calluses here," he murmured as his thumb brushed across her palm. "You shouldn't work so hard, Blair."

Yeah, right! Like how else would she live? Blair shifted away from him and clambered awkwardly to her feet. Why was she always so ungraceful whenever he was around? Why did he make her so nervous?

Because of Daniel.

But she hadn't had Daniel to think about back then. In the old days just the sound of Gabe's voice had made her skin prickle with anticipation.

She shoved the memories away. "I'm going home to talk to my grandfather," she murmured. "Something isn't right here."

"I assure you it's all perfectly legal. I don't do business any other way." He sounded angry that she'd suspect him of subterfuge. "You should at least remember that much."

Blair didn't respond. Instead, she walked to her truck and climbed in, mulling the whole thing over inside her tired brain.

"No, I know. It's just that Mac said—" She glanced at him, vaguely surprised that he'd followed her. "Never mind. I'll sort it out. You'll probably get a letter canceling the whole deal."

Gabe shook his head and shoved her door closed. "No, the deal's already been finalized. I'm not allowing anyone to back out now. If you wait a minute, I'll get my vehicle and follow you. I'd like to know the answer to a few questions of my own."

Blair glanced at her watch, then nodded grimly. Daniel wasn't due home for at least another hour. If she hurried, she could get this all sorted out and have Gabe on his way before kindergarten was dismissed for the afternoon.

Twenty minutes later they pulled up in front of her grandfather's old house. She couldn't help contrasting its ramshackle appearance with the elegant, glossy glass-and-chrome condo Gabe had lived in seven years ago. Her battered brown half-ton sat rusting on the spot while his polished black and silver sport utility screamed money. Night and day.

Still, what did it matter? He'd always known that she wasn't in his league, didn't have money to burn. Her part-time job had been a good one, and she'd been comfortable sharing digs with Clarissa Featherhawk and Briony Green. But every extra cent she hadn't needed for college went home to Mac and Willie, to repay them.

"Having second thoughts about introducing me to your family?" The mocking query brought her to the present.

Without a word Blair tripped up the stairs to the back door. She opened it, then moved back to allow Gabe in. He stepped out of his expensive boots first, then through the doorway and into the kitchen, his eyes curiously appraising the old farmhouse.

"Mac? Can you come in here? Now?"

Blair stepped out of her boots and grabbed the coffeepot. Without wasting any movements, she poured two mugs of the steaming black brew, set them on the table and motioned Gabe to sit down.

Gabe raised his eyebrows at her silent order, but took

his seat without speaking. He took one sip of the coffee, coughed, then added a generous measure of cream and sugar.

Blair sat and pretended to ignore him.

"Hey, Busy Bee. You're early. How were the hives?" Mac strolled through the hallway and into the kitchen, his eyes widening as he caught sight of Gabe. "Hello."

"Mac, this is Gabriel Sloan. He thinks he's bought the south quarter from you. Gabe, this is my grandfather. The infamous Mackenzie Rhodes of your letter."

Her grandfather flicked an eyebrow at her acid tone, then turned his attention to their guest. The two men silently sized up each other, shook hands and then sat. Blair glanced from one to the other.

"Well?" she demanded of her grandfather. "Aren't you going to tell him that it's a mistake?"

Mac smiled tenderly and reached out to fold her hand in his.

"No," he murmured. "I'm not. I sold Mr. Sloan the land. It was mine, I had a right to and I did it." His face showed no sign of repentance.

"But, Grandfather, you know that I depend on that land!" Blair felt the sting of his betrayal to the soles of her feet. "How could you sell it to *him?* Why not to me? I would have bought you out!"

She glared at Gabe, who kept his head bent, studying his coffee as if it would metamorphose into his favorite mocha latte. Blair switched her focus to her grandfather.

"Why?"

"You know why," he returned evenly, his face stern.

"We've discussed it before. I think it's the right thing to do. It's time. You know that."

Blair pursed her lips, mindful of the heated arguments she'd had with him for months now. Mac believed she owed it to Gabe to tell Daniel's father he had a son. She thought she'd made him understand how foolish it would be to expect Gabe to accept the boy, to believe Gabe could father his child the way Mac had fathered her.

Apparently none of her protests had touched him.

"How can you do this to us?" she said under her breath. "This is my business. You have no right to interfere in my private life."

Mac didn't back down, his dark eyes glossy with unshed tears. "I have the right of a man who loves his granddaughter more than life." He reached out to pat her cheek. "I'm not young anymore, Busy Bee. I won't be around forever. I want to know my family is okay."

"And this is how you do it? By going against me, behind my back, selling this land out from under me? I can manage for all of us. Haven't I done fine so far?"

A thin high-pitched voice wobbled out a few notes from a well-known hymn. The sound grew louder as Willie entered the kitchen.

"Ooh, what a handsome fellow!" Willie's cooing voice spoke behind Blair's right ear.

Blair sighed. *Not now,* she prayed. *Please don't let Willie blurt out the truth.* "He's yours, isn't he, Blair."

"He's—"

"Mac sold him some land, Willie." Blair broke in, desperate to keep her grandfather from spilling the beans. "The south quarter."

"You *sold* our heritage, Mackenzie?" Willie coughed delicately into her lavender lace handkerchief as she fluttered around the kitchen. "Have things become so bad that we must sell off our birthright to live?"

Blair was about to set her straight, to add further explanations, when she heard a noise outside. Her grandfather sat up straight, her aunt collapsed into a chair and Gabe frowned at them all. Blair couldn't move a muscle as her son came bounding through the door.

"Hi, Mom! The bus came early 'cause the school had a fire." Daniel let his jacket, backpack and lunch bag fall where they would, his gaze fastened on the tall, dark-haired stranger who sat staring at him.

"Hey, you an' me got the same hair," Daniel declared, his mouth stretched wide in a smile. "My mom has a picture of you. Are you the answer?"

Blair gulped down a sob, unable to say a word, though her hands closed over her son's shoulders as she hugged him close for one brief moment, prolonging what she somehow knew would change irrevocably from this moment on.

"The answer?" Gabe swallowed, his eyes swinging from Mac to Blair to the little boy. "I don't know what you mean."

Daniel wiggled himself free of his mother's hold and went to stand in front of the big man. Two pairs of eyes, the same startling green, inspected each other.

"The answer," Daniel explained, "to my prayer. For a daddy. I'm almost six an' I really need a daddy. Are you gonna be him?"

Chapter Two

"Gabe, this is my son, Daniel. Daniel, I'd like you to meet Gabriel Sloan."

Gabe almost laughed at the words. She didn't *want* the boy to meet him at all. And he knew why. This child was his son!

Gabe stared at the mirror image of himself at five. The little boy in front of him solemnly shook his hand as the truth smacked Gabe squarely between the eyes. He had a child. He was a father!

"So I was wondering, Mr. Gabriel, are you the one?"

Gabe jerked back to reality with stunned surprise as a small hand carefully patted his arm.

"The one?" he repeated blankly. His eyes sought Blair and he swallowed hard at the pain and worry he found swirling in the depths of her molten chocolate eyes. He focused on the boy. "Uh, I'm not exactly sure just yet."

"Oh." Daniel's mobile face fell with disappointment, but brightened a moment later. "That doesn't mean no," he insisted. "My mom says she's not sure lots of times. It means maybe."

"Right." Gabe swallowed, the thought of parenthood engulfing him in a wash of anxiety. *Not yet,* his brain screamed. *I'm not ready for that yet, God! I've only just taken the first steps to changing my life.*

"It's okay. You can think about it if you want." Daniel smiled, then leaned near Gabe's ear. "But could you hurry up? My teacher says we're having parent-teacher day pretty soon, and Joey Lancaster is bringing his dad. I don't like Joey Lancaster."

Gabe got the implied message loud and clear. *My dad is better than yours.* Poor little tyke! Belatedly he wondered how long Daniel had been praying for a father.

A wave of anger washed over him as he considered how much he'd missed. A baby, a toddler, hugs, goodnight kisses, Christmases and birthdays. He'd known none of that. But Blair had. And she'd kept him in the dark. On purpose. That hurt more than he'd ever imagined, though Gabe didn't understand why. He knew he wasn't daddy material. He was a loner. He didn't need anyone. He couldn't afford to.

But she could have told him.

Gabe turned to stare at Blair and immediately rethought his position. He had no rights when it came to Daniel. None. He'd lost them all when Blair, sweet, innocent Blair, walked out of his life with her childish dreams ruined. By him.

"You need me, Gabe," she'd sobbed that morning. He cringed, remembering his furious response. "I don't need anybody."

"I thought you loved me enough to believe I'm not like the others. I've tried so hard to be what you want, but you still can't see the real me. You can't see beyond the security of your business and your money. You can't see love."

That memory could still make him ache for her shattered innocence. Blair, backing away from him, hair tumbling around her shoulders in that glossy riot of curls that he'd touched only moments before.

Once, just that once he'd let himself desire something more than security. Daniel was the result. The knowledge ate at him like acid on an open wound.

He'd sent her away with his child.

"You'd better do your chores, Daniel. Maybe Albert will help you." Blair's soft voice broke through his reverie.

Gabe looked up. Who was Albert? Someone Blair was interested in? Was that why Daniel needed a father, to ward off the unwanted attentions of this Albert person?

"Okay." Daniel grabbed two cookies from the nutcracker cookie jar that perched on a low shelf. He whirled to grin at Gabe. "See you later," he offered.

"Yes, you will," Gabe returned evenly, refusing to look at Blair. "I'm glad I met you, Daniel."

"Me, too." Daniel raced out the door, jacket forgotten as he sang a new song.

"You're the child's father, aren't you?" The woman Blair had called Willie stood surveying him with watery blue eyes. "Anyone with vision can see that you're Danny's daddy. It's about time you showed up and took some responsibility. Now the first thing will be to get the child a decent home."

"Don't, Willie. Daniel isn't going anywhere. He's going to stay right here with me." Blair's chocolate eyes dared Gabe to say any different. "I've got things to do. Mac, you and Mr. Sloan no doubt have your *deal* to discuss. I'm going out."

She was gone in a rush, those russet-tipped curls flying behind. Gabe stood and watched her through the window. He heard two voices speaking, saw an older man hug her close and kiss her cheek before the derelict old truck rattled down the road.

"She's not too happy with me, son. And I can't say I blame her. It was a nasty trick to play on my grand-daughter." Mac's sad voice was resigned.

"Then why did you?" Gabe could see no remorse on the lined, worn features.

"Because I love her. And I love that boy. I don't want to see either one of them hurt. I'm not as young as I was, you know. I'm afraid of what will happen to her when Willie and I aren't around for her to devote herself to. Blair is killing herself trying to look after us all."

"Look after you?" Gabe returned to his seat and thoughtfully sipped his coffee, aware that the ethereal Willie had drifted into another room. "Why should she look after you? Are you sick?"

"Willie is, though she won't admit it. Her medicine costs something terrible. I've got a heart condition, but it's nothing serious. Not yet. As long as we've got my pension, we can manage, but what happens when I'm gone? Albert can only do so much."

There it was again. "Albert?" Gabe fixed the older man with a severe look and waited.

"Albert Hunter. He's been our friend for years. Keeping busy around here is about the only thing that makes him forget the bottle. He's an inventor. Blair brought him home one day, asked me to help him sober up, and she's been taking care of him ever since. That's what Blair does—takes care of people. She needs to be needed."

"Oh." Gabe digested it all with a nod, his mind busy as he tried to merge this information with the woman he'd known. "Are you sure Daniel is my son?" he blurted. It was a stupid question.

Mac apparently agreed. He favored him with a severe look. "You know that right well enough, without me telling you. We were supposed to fly out Saturday morning for the wedding that night. But just as we were heading out the door, Blair phoned and said it was off. Next thing we knew, she'd dropped out of her last year of college. She came home at the end of October. Boy turns six at the end of May. You work it out."

Gabe didn't have to. He knew without doing the math. Hidden away in a trunk he hadn't opened in years was a picture his mother had put in an album just days before her death. His first day of school. He and Daniel could have been twins.

Gabe couldn't stop the questions. "Why didn't she tell me? Let me know?"

"Don't be daft, son! You pushed her away." Mac sniffed, his face scrunched up in anger, eyes blazing. "This is going to hurt her a lot, and I don't like to see my granddaughter hurt. Goes against everything I believe. The Rhodeses take care of each other. Always."

"So why drag me into your wonderful life?" Gabe couldn't stop the sneer from coloring his voice. This man would know soon enough that he wasn't the person to direct Daniel's young life. Gabe was totally wrong for that job. Suspicion dawned. Was this just another taker, the latest in a long list of people after his money? "What do you want from me?"

Mackenzie Rhodes fixed him with a fierce glare. "I want you to be a father to that little boy. It isn't right for him to grow up without a dad. Children need a man in their lives."

"What about you? And Albert?" Gabe almost laughed at the glower on Mac's face.

"I'm half dead! I can't be around for the boy forever, much as I'd like to. My rheumatism acts up in the winter so's I can barely get out of bed." He swiveled his arm as if to prove that it was damaged. "Albert's a good man, but he's not the boy's father. You are. Daniel needs someone to love and protect him and his mother. You owe him that."

No doubt he was right, Gabe conceded. He did owe the boy. But he couldn't be a father. He didn't know how. Even the prospect of it made him jumpy. Suddenly it was as if he was ten again and his dad was laughing at him.

"Swim, boy. Be a man."

Gabe could feel the doubts swirling overhead, waiting to cover him, to suffocate him just as the water had filled his lungs. He couldn't do this! He wasn't father material.

"I, uh, that is, I'm not…"

"Anybody can learn to be a father."

"But I don't…" Mac's steady gaze kept Gabe pinned to his chair, stopped the words that would express his doubts.

"You just have to look beyond yourself to someone else's needs." The wise eyes narrowed. "You told me in that letter your lawyer wrote that you wanted that land to build a house on. Said you were going to settle down, give up the city. That all true?"

Gabe nodded slowly, remembering his dream. A home of his own, a place to find out exactly who he was behind all the pretense.

"Why?" Mac's back straightened. "Why what?"

"Why does a big, important computer fella like yourself want to run away from his life?" Mac tipped back in his chair and considered Gabe from that perspective.

"I'm not running away." Gabe wished he'd had some warning, some preparation for this inquisition.

"Aren't you?" Mac munched on one of the cookies he'd appropriated from the jar. He handed the other one over. "She can sure bake cookies," he muttered happily.

"Blair?" Gabe waited for the other man's nod. "When I knew her she didn't bake anything. She wore exotic outfits and crazy makeup. She reminded me of a butterfly whenever we went out."

"You didn't know the real Blair. Never played dress-up in her life. She likes things casual, comfortable. So what about now?" Mac's question was abrupt, to the point.

"She's still beautiful, but in a different way. She looks more fragile, and yet somehow stronger." Gabe tried to puzzle it out. "I can't say it properly."

"I wasn't talking about her looks. I was asking how you feel about my granddaughter."

Gabe flinched under the scrutiny, his mind whirling a hundred miles an hour. "I don't know. I don't know anything! How can I? All of a sudden I see a woman who walked out on our wedding years ago. And I find out I have a kid, a son I've never even heard about before. It's a little overwhelming." He frowned, his mouth as sour as if he'd just eaten a dill pickle.

Mac barked out a laugh. "That's life for you. Want some advice? Get used to it. Fast. And make a decision."

"A decision?" Gabe frowned, wondering if the old fellow was hinting at something. "What kind of a decision?"

Mac straightened, his chair banging to the floor with a snap that had Gabe flinching.

"Be a man! Figure out if you're going to break that boy's heart by walking away from him. Decide if you're gonna take on the role of father and be the best darn father any kid ever had, or if you're going to run away from your responsibility. Make a choice."

For a moment, Gabe heard his father's tones, his father's mocking reminder that he'd never quite measured up to the standard. He surged to his feet, tension coiling inside him faster than lightning. And he'd thought running his company was pressure! "I have to think." He spat the words out.

Mac shook his head as he set his cup on the counter. Then he turned and faced Gabe, his eyes tired, his expression sad.

"Don't know why I bothered," he muttered. "Guess I figured you'd have some spunk and gumption and wouldn't let a woman do all the work. But, on second thought, you're not the kind of man my kin needs, Mr. Sloan. You like to run away from your problems instead of facing them."

"Not true." Gabe shook his head. "I like to figure out what the situation is before I make a move." He met that stern gaze unflinchingly, his voice cold. "And I'm not letting you renege on this contract. That land is mine." He patted his chest pocket and the paper beneath.

"Only if you build on it within the six months," Mac reminded him. "Anything else and the whole thing reverts back to me."

"I know that." Gabe pulled his boots on, then straightened and looked the other man in the eye. "I'll need to think it over," he repeated. "That's the way I do things."

Mac nodded, but his face showed worry. "Just don't run away," he ordered. "That doesn't do anyone any good."

"I'm not the one who ran. Blair did that, the day we were to be married." The bitterness still rankled. She'd dumped him, made him look a fool in front of his colleagues and associates, shown him up as a failure. He couldn't quite forgive her for that. Not even all these years later.

Mac's hand closed around his shoulder, his eyes piercing. "What other option did you give her?" he demanded quietly. "Blair loved you completely. I know that for a fact. She wanted to be your wife, she wanted the two of you to build a life together. She believed God sent you into her life, and she was ready to do whatever you asked of her. What did you do to spoil that?"

Gabe returned the stare, his temper sizzling. "I didn't do a thing any other businessman in my position wouldn't have done. If you knew anything about business, you'd know you have to protect yourself and your work. It didn't mean I didn't care about her. It was only a preventive measure."

Mac smiled sadly. "Protect yourself, eh. Who protected her, this young fiancée of yours? Did you?" The condemning words echoed around the room as Mac turned and walked away, his shoulders slumped in defeat.

There wasn't any more to be said. Gabe had failed then, and he knew it. He stepped outside, pulling the door closed quietly. He climbed into his truck and started it. As he left the house, then the yard and finally the valley, he couldn't help but admire the beauty laid out before him. It would be so nice to live here, to get away from the constant, petty demands on his time, to go back to just fiddling with things, daydreaming of new ways and means. He had only just begun to learn who was beneath the facade of successful computer designer. How could he take on a kid, do all the things a loving father should? Where did you go to find out how to love?

Gabe drove five miles into the minuscule town of Teal's Crossing and returned to his hotel room. Five minutes later he was lying on the bed, reaming out his lawyer.

"Why didn't you tell me about this goofy deal, Rich? I walked right into it. If I don't build a house here, I lose the land and the money. Whose interests are you protecting, anyhow?"

Richard Wellington was well used to his boss's anger. He snickered loudly over the line. "I *did* tell you, Gabe. At least six times. But you were so hung up on getting the plans drawn for this dream home that you completely ignored my warnings."

"And are they? Finished, I mean?" Gabe licked his lips at the mention of the plans he'd secretly reveled in for weeks. A place that would prove he was far more than anything his father could have dreamed of. A place that would show the world he didn't need any of them. A place he could hide.

"Ready and on the way to you by courier. Contractor says he'll start digging right away. Got some materials coming in the first of next week." Rich sounded very smug. "Pool should be ready right on time."

Those words sent a shiver up his spine, but Gabe ignored it. He'd deal with the past one step at a time. He couldn't ignore it any longer.

Gabe didn't know how else to broach the subject so he asked it straight out. "Rich, what happens if I get married?"

Silence. "Well, uh, I guess you get a wife. Why?" The tentative response verged on suspicion.

Gabe swallowed, then dove in. "Remember Blair?"

Guarded silence, then a whoosh of air. "Yeah, I remember. Had you tied up in knots for months after she left town. Why?"

"She's here. It's her grandfather who's selling the land."

"Uh-oh." Papers rattled. "Why didn't I know that?"

"I don't know." He waited a moment. "She's raising my son, Rich." Gabe was stunned at the measure of satisfaction and pride he felt in saying those words. Son. Child of mine.

"What!" Rich burst into a volley of questions, which

he proceeded to answer himself. Then he trotted out a list of things Blair could do to lay claim to the company, which he could prevent by suing for custody. "I'll have the papers to you in two days."

"I don't want to sue her for custody," Gabe murmured as an idea grew, taking shape and form in his mind. "I think I want to get to know my son. His name is Daniel."

"Daniel? Your father's name." Rich's voice was sharp. "How did she find out?"

Gabe smiled. Rich had learned distrust the hard way. Gabe had taught him all about it every time the young lawyer handled another deal. Now the man was as paranoid as he. The thought was not comforting.

"I don't know that she has found out anything. But that doesn't matter right now. I just know that this kid thinks he needs a father, and I can't turn my back on that. I remember what it was like too well."

"I suppose you do." Rich was silent for a long time. But when he finally spoke, his voice was filled with ominous warning. "Gabe, are you sure this child is yours?"

"Oh, yes. He's mine. That is not in question. Besides, Blair wouldn't lie." Though, if he remembered correctly, Blair hadn't told him anything about Daniel. His lips tightened. "So, buddy, how do I go about forcing her to let me get to know the boy?"

"You're sure you want to do this?" Rich's voice urged him to reconsider.

"I'm sure. His name will be Daniel Sloan, but he's not going to have a childhood like mine. Not if I can help it."

Rich appeared to accept this, for he offered no further objections. Instead his voice softened, bounding over the phone line with enthusiasm.

"I think you'll make a great father, Gabe. And Blair always did worship the ground you walked on. If I remember correctly, she was ready to marry you. Why would she object to your presence now? I never did understand why she took off like that. You never said." A pregnant pause offered the opportunity.

Gabe swallowed, but he wouldn't lie to himself or his friend. He'd lived his life by dealing in cold, hard truth. He wouldn't stop now.

"It was my fault, I demanded she sign that prenup when I knew deep down that she wouldn't. I used her, Rich. I took her love and put my own conditions on it. And then I let her go as if it didn't matter. Yeah, she loved me once. I don't think that's going to be an issue now. She *might* agree to marry me, if I pushed it, but it would only be for Daniel's sake."

He remembered her sad, mournful words when she'd phoned him the morning of their wedding day.

"I planned a white wedding in the church. My grandfather was going to walk me down the aisle. My great-aunt is bringing a big, showy cake. I was going to promise to love you forever. I was going to make sure we had lots of pictures so we could tell our children how happy we were."

Gabe could still hear his caustic laugh. "Forever is in the movies, Blair. It doesn't happen in real life. And I won't be having any children. Not ever." He let her hear the steel in his voice. "I'm not the father type. That part is nonnegotiable."

She'd gone silent then. He could almost see her face pinch tightly. Her voice, when it came at last, was soft, broken, brimming with tears.

"Goodbye, Gabriel Sloan. I love you. I'm sorry you won't believe that you're capable of more than making money."

"Gabe? Gabriel!" Rich's worried tones kicked him to the present.

"I'm here." He sighed. "I don't think marriage is an option anymore, Rich."

"Are you sure you don't just want to sue for custody? Take the kid away. With your bankroll, you'd win hands down."

Daniel's bright, expectant face rolled into his mind's eye. Gabriel shook his head.

"Daniel's lived with her for over five years," he whispered. "She loves him and he loves her. I won't destroy that." *I just want to stay on the edges, feel the warmth, understand what makes a family.*

"Up to you, buddy. Okay then, if you're determined to get close to the kid, I guess the surest way is to threaten custody. If she's as good a mother as you think, she'd marry you rather than lose her kid."

Gabe laughed, but there was nothing amusing in the thought. "I don't think she'd ever marry me, Rich. And I sure can't marry her. You of all people know I'm not a family kind of man." He swallowed hard. "Six, almost seven years, but, after all, what's really changed?"

"Then you bluff. Threaten everything you can think of. I know you, Sloan. You'll think of something to make her see you're better suited to raising the kid than her."

Gabe hung up with the advice still ringing in his ears.

But you're not better suited, not at all. It's just another lie you let people believe, his conscience reminded him. *You couldn't possibly take that boy from the one person who loves him more than life. You have nothing to offer him. At least, nothing that really matters.*

"What do I know about being a father?" he whispered, worry overtaking his brain. "How can I be sure that I won't do something wrong? That I won't scar him or cause something that will make him unhappy years down the road, after I'm gone?"

It was a prospect he had to deal with. He knew how easily that could happen. His father hadn't wanted to leave his son the memories he carried. At least, Gabe told himself that, hoping it was true. But Daniel, Sr., hadn't been able to accept the son he'd fathered, either. Gabe simply didn't fit the baseball and fishing mold his father had set.

In fact, Gabe hated sports. All he'd ever wanted was to create things, to build things. To use his brain. Being sent to his room in punishment had provided hours of solitude to do just that.

"I won't force Daniel to be a replica of me," he assured his tired brain. "He doesn't have to like computers. If he wants to fish, I'll fish. I can learn that stuff. The company's okay, now. I've got all the money I'll ever need. I owe it to myself to take some time off—to see if Blair and I can make a go of it." He thought about Mac's letter. Why had it arrived when it had? Was God giving him a second chance?

"I owe it to him to do better than my dad did for me."

Which shouldn't be hard, given the past.

You owe him love.

That word sent a shiver of worry through his brain. Love? Gabe didn't think he had it in him. Not the kind of love the songs were about, the kind of love he'd read about in stories and poems. Certainly not the emotion that required you to give away everything you valued for the sake of someone else, the kind of love that made you vulnerable and weak, prey to others.

"He doesn't need to see that part of me," Gabe told himself. "He'll never know about that. I'll make sure of it."

But as he lay in his hotel room thinking about a black-haired little boy and his too solemn mother, Gabe wondered how he'd keep that shriveled-up, scared part of himself locked away when he'd spent such a large part of his life wondering where the next con to get his money would come from.

"One day at a time," he reminded himself. "With God's help, I'll face this one day at a time. That's what Pastor Jake said on Sunday."

Surely if you kept your eyes on the future, you couldn't get caught up in the past?

"Daniel's my only chance to make amends," he whispered, eyes closed as he prayed for help. "At least if I mess up, and I probably will, I know that Blair will make sure my son gets all the love he needs. He won't end up like me."

Please, God, don't let him end up all alone like me.

Chapter Three

I don't understand how You could do this to me, God. Mac's always loved me, I know he has. Why did he have to find Gabe, send him that letter, stir things up? Why couldn't he have left well enough alone? Why did You let it happen?

Days later, and it was still a silly question! Blair knew the answer, at least the one Mac had given this morning when she'd asked.

"I'm old, honey. Some days I get tired and feeling down. I miss your gran, God rest her soul. Lots of times, all I want is to go to Heaven and rest, talk to God about things, give Myrtle a hug and kiss. But I couldn't ever die peacefully if I thought you and Daniel weren't cared for. It wouldn't be right."

"We're fine, Grandpa. We're managing really well now. I have the business and it's growing, Willie's doing better with those new pills and Albert hasn't had anything to drink since a year ago at Christmas."

Mac had snorted derisively. "Ha! You're lying to yourself, Busy Bee. We're scraping by and just barely doing that. What happens if the bees don't produce their usual this year? Or if some of those orders get canceled? We'll be in hot water then, and no mistake." He'd patted the pocket that held his bankbook with smug satisfaction. "At least this way I can be sure you'll have a nest egg to fall back on, and you've got the right to leave your hives in place for the next three years. He paid a lot for that land, you know."

"He can afford it. And that's a bunch of baloney, Grandfather! You're as healthy as a horse! Selling that land to Gabe was just a way to manipulate him into finding out about Daniel, and you know it. I thought you loved us more than that."

She fixed him with a stern look, but Mac didn't back down.

"It's because I love you two so much that I did it. You and Daniel need Gabe. And he needs a chance to be the boy's father. He's ready to move ahead with his life. Leaving the city and that company prove that. I think he's changed."

"You don't know that, Mac. Gabe takes the company wherever he goes. And he doesn't *want* to be a father, not at all. It's just a duty thing." She shut off the piercing memory of that moment, that one single second of pure joy when he'd looked, really looked at Daniel, fully acknowledged that the child was part of him. She'd hoped to argue her case more fully. But Mac had shrugged and walked away.

Reality intruded as Blair dipped another taper into the wax and watched while it drizzled off, knowing that she was spoiling its finish by waiting so long. But today, business just didn't seem as important. She had to figure out what to do, decide how she was going to explain to Daniel that Gabe wouldn't be his father. Not ever.

"After all, he's had more than seven days to accept the idea. And he hasn't called, hasn't even spoken to Daniel. What kind of a father is that?"

No kind of father at all. Which was exactly why she'd never told Gabe about her son. He hadn't wanted to be a father, that much she was clear on. If she'd doubted it then, watching him avoid the children she worked with in her spare time would have been enough. And there were his words over the phone that last awful morning. *I'll never be a father.* The idea was repugnant to him!

The phone pealed a summons. "Hey, Blair!"

"Clarissa? How are you?" Blair grinned as she envisioned her formerly thin college buddy now hugely pregnant with the twins she'd been told to expect.

"I'm big, okay? Enough said." Clarissa's normally sweet voice halted, then continued. "I just read something I thought you might be interested in. Gabriel Sloan has handed over management of his company to a group of vice presidents."

Blair gulped, then nodded. "He's here, Pris. Mac sold him a piece of land, and he's apparently going to build a house on it. Some kind of castle affair, if the rumors are true."

Clarissa's voice wavered quietly down the wire. "Does he know?"

"About Daniel? Yeah, he knows."

Clarissa's mutter of protest left no room for doubt. She was mad. "They don't let women as big as me fly, Blair Delaney, but if you don't spill the beans, I'll sic Briony on you. And you know how inquisitive she is."

Blair giggled at the reminder of their friend and former college roomie, the third in their group who had also been dumped by her sweetheart. Bri had a scientist's mind. She liked the facts laid out clearly and concisely. She never accepted "no" for an answer.

"Nice try, Pris. But you can't. Bri's off somewhere in the Canadian Rockies doing the last bit of research for her thesis." Blair unplugged the kettle and poured herself a cup of hot water, dipping the lemon mint tea bag in and out rhythmically for several moments.

"I see."

Blair waited, a tiny smile nudging the corner of her lips. Clarissa didn't disappoint her.

"Wade? I'll need the van. I'm going on a little trip to see an old college buddy who's trying to hold something back."

"No, you are not traveling, Clarissa Featherhawk! You're staying right there." A mutter of threats rumbled across the line. "All right, already! Gabriel Sloan arrived a few days ago. He's staying in the hotel in Teal's Crossing and he's tearing up my land as we speak. That's all I know."

"Is he still as good looking?"

Blair closed her eyes, took a deep breath and admitted the truth. "Yes." She let her mind brood on the ultra short raven's wing hair, the hard jawline, the full mocking lips.

"Does he still have those glacial green meltwater eyes?" Clarissa demanded. "I've never seen eyes that could turn such an aquamarine color. He used to make my knees shake when he looked at me."

Still does, Blair wanted to yell. She quelled that schoolgirl response.

"I never understood why his Hollywood buddies didn't offer him a job. He's every woman's dream man." Clarissa giggled. "Except mine, of course. Wade's the one I dream of."

"Lucky Wade." Blair covered a rush of feelings by asking Clarissa innumerable questions about her pregnancy, her husband of almost one year, her ready-made family. Anything to keep the talk off of Gabe.

"You're stalling, Blair. Trying to throw me off the scent. That's always a good sign. I guess I'd better let you go so you can think about Gabe some more." Clarissa chuckled at her mumbled protest. "Keep me posted," she ordered before she rang off.

"As if there's anything to keep her posted on!" Blair said to herself. She emptied her cold tea into the sink and concentrated on work.

"So this is where you're hiding out?"

Blair whirled, shocked as much by the low, amused tones as by the sound of his rich, full voice echoing among the rafters of her bee barn.

"I wasn't hiding," she disagreed. "I have work to do. Unlike some people I could mention. Are all the little peons at Polytech too busy to miss you, Gabe?" She got back to dipping.

He didn't take offense. Instead he walked up and watched what she was doing.

"If you want the truth, they don't want me there anymore," he told her, a mocking smile tilting his lips. "It seems that I'm bad for their thinking. Their productivity goes way up when the boss isn't hovering around."

He watched as her hands suddenly became busier with a series dipper that held six wicks. "I didn't know you sold dipped candles, too. Can I try that?"

Blair frowned, but after studying his face, she found no hint of mockery. He looked genuinely interested in her work.

"I suppose." She showed him how to dip the wicks, then turn and redip to get the multicolored effects her customers loved.

Gabe tried several, lips pursed in concentration as he perfected the action. When she could stand the silence no longer, Blair took the rack out of his hand and set it aside.

"What do you really want, Gabriel?"

"I want my son."

Blair knocked the rack on the floor, completely ruining all her work. She ignored the mess and the expense as she stared at him, searching for an answer in his unfathomable stare. The words rocked her to the core of her being. Why, when she'd known it would come to this?

"You want Daniel? But you don't even know him!" She glared at him, daring him to deny it. "He's a little boy who's only ever known this place as his home. What kind of a father would rip him away from the only family he knows?" She chewed him out with her eyes, letting him see the contempt in them.

Gabe stayed where he was, his eyes watchful, swirling and slumbering with hidden menace as they studied her. "I don't want to take him away from you, Blair. I know how much you mean to him. I lost my own mother when I was young. I know what that's like."

She frowned. What did that mean, and why was he suddenly opening up now? He'd never given her much insight into his past when they were engaged.

"I came to ask you something," he murmured at last.

"Go ahead. I reserve the right to refuse an answer." She wouldn't let him see her fear. *Please help me, God. Don't let him take Daniel.*

"Will you marry me?"

Blair wanted to laugh. Or cry. Something. Her eyes studied him, shocked by his quiet words. "Marry you? Why, for goodness' sake?"

He looked innocent enough, his hands hanging at his sides, his feet crossed at the ankles as he leaned against the workbench in his natty designer clothes. Blair knew the pose was a disguise to conceal his thoughts. What was he planning?

"Why? Hmm." He frowned for a few minutes, then smiled at her, his eyes lighting up in the teasing glint she'd almost forgotten. "To keep a promise I made once, over six years ago."

"What promise?" She kept her gaze trained on him, refusing to fall for the diversion. "You never actually proposed. I did that, I think. You said okay." She looked away from his eyes, noticed the wax hardening on the floor. She bent to scrape it off the tiles, glad to avoid the speculation in his curious stare as the heat of a blush burned her cheeks.

"Maybe I didn't actually say the words, but I led you to believe that's what I wanted, too. Now it's pay-up time. So will you please marry me?" He waited till she'd straightened, then held out a black velvet box, and when

Blair didn't take it, snapped it open to reveal a glittering marquise diamond set on a narrow gold band. "Please, Blair?"

Blair's breath got tangled up in her throat, and she couldn't draw fresh air into her lungs. She stared at the gorgeous ring and wondered how he'd known she had always loved that particular setting. It wasn't what he'd chosen last time.

"I'm building a house, a home. That's why I bought that land from your grandfather. I'd planned to move here anyway. I'm leaving Los Angeles. For a while, at least."

"Why?" Her voiced croaked, her disbelief echoing around the room.

Gabe shrugged, but she could see him closing up against her probing, hiding his thoughts away, just as he'd always done. "Because I need to regroup, get a new game plan, figure out where I'm going from here."

She snickered, tossing the lump of misshapen wax into the garbage. "Yeah, right! You've always known that, Gabriel. Straight to the top. Business first. The biggest, the best, the brightest. That's always been your focus."

"It was," he admitted quietly. "But lately, it just doesn't mean as much. I feel like I'm missing something."

"So by marrying me, latching onto my son, you'll fill in some piece of your life that you didn't know existed seven years ago?" She shook her head, her ponytail flopping from side to side. "I don't think so. Thanks anyway, but we don't need your pity."

"It isn't like that." He sighed, leaning his narrow hips against her counter. He set the ring on the workbench as if it didn't matter a whit to him whether it got lost in the wax kettle or not. "Besides, he's my son, too. Why didn't you ever tell me?"

There was something in his voice, some plaintive yearning that made her stop fiddling with the wax and look at him.

"Would you have believed me?" she murmured. She could have wept at the hurt that darkened his eyes and made his lips pinch together. But it couldn't stop the questions.

"Can you guarantee that you wouldn't have tried to take him away or talk me into giving him up for adoption?" She made herself continue in spite of the torture contorting his handsome features. "You said you never wanted a child."

"That was before I knew, before I realized…" He stopped, brushed a hand across his eyes, scuffed a polished toe against the floor. "Maybe I'm just not saying this right."

Unreasoning anger flooded her. "You've said everything you need to say. You've done your duty, Gabe. Don't worry, I'll tell Mac you offered. But no, I won't marry you so you can try out your hand at playing father." She saw his mouth tighten and hurried on.

"Daniel is the most important thing in the world to me. I love him, and I won't let you hurt him. You don't want a gold digger for a wife, or the encumbrance of a child in your life. Remember?"

When he winced at the repetition of his own words, Blair felt a stab of shame. But she wouldn't take them back. Daniel was too important to be used as a pawn, no matter how much she'd once cared for this man. She would not weaken, wouldn't let him see that she'd never given up the dream of a husband, and a home where she was the most important person in her husband's world.

"You're turning this around, Blair. Making it ugly. And that's not what I'm saying. I want us to be a…a family."

"Why?" She pressed him for an answer, knowing he wouldn't have one. Gabriel Sloan had never wanted any encumbrances in his solitary life. Things couldn't have changed that much.

"Because he's my son and I owe it to him," he said, exploding, mouth tight, eyes hard as emeralds. "And because you're his mother and I owe you, too. I should never have…never mind that." His cheeks darkened.

So he felt guilty for that one night of indiscretion? Blair smiled bitterly. Well, it was as good a reason as any to suggest marriage, she supposed. It just wasn't *her* reason, not the one she'd dreamed of, anyway. Not when she remembered her grandparents' marriage, and from what Mac said, her parents had been happy, too.

"So tell me, Gabe, just how would this marriage work?" She'd string him along, pretend she would go along with it. For a while. It would be interesting to note just how far the great Gabriel Sloan was willing to go with this experiment at nobility.

But in the end she would turn him down cold. Daniel was *her* son, and she intended him to feel the love in his life. Gabe didn't believe in love, and she couldn't forget that.

"Blair?"

She glanced up, then at his hand on her arm. Though

he moved it immediately, Blair was only too aware of his touch and her reaction to it. How could she still feel this way? Especially now.

"I want the very best for Daniel," she began, trying to focus the conversation and direct it where she wanted it to go. "I know how much he's wanted a father. Especially lately. He keeps asking me about you, where you are, what you do, what you're like."

Gabe's face whitened. "He knows I'm his father?" His eyes were huge, his hands tight with tension as they clenched and unclenched at his side. "What have you told him?"

"He doesn't know *you* are his father." Blair fiddled with a tray of glitter that would accent the Christmas candles. "He doesn't know anything about his father. I've never said a thing."

"Then how—"

"They've been doing a series of projects at school about families." Blair shrugged at his frown. "This is a little community. Daniel knows the families of the kids in his class. He's seen two parents, a happy home, siblings. Some of the kids like to brag about their fathers." She shrugged. "I don't suppose his teacher thought of him as any different when they started on their family study unit."

"Which is exactly the scene you always wanted," Gabe muttered, peering at her. "Your ideal was always this happy home scenario, wasn't it? I can still hear you talking about how wonderful families were. I thought it was just a line."

And I can still feel how much you didn't want that.

Blair searched for some underlying meaning to his words, but could find nothing to show he was goading her.

"Yes, well, we all have to grow up sometime. That isn't going to happen for me. I've got Mac, Willie, Albert and Daniel to look after. I've learned to deal with my reality. The truth is, raising a child takes a lot out of you. I'm not sure I could handle any more of them."

"Wouldn't it be easier if there were two of us parenting? I could take over sometimes when you needed a break. Or vice versa. We could share our son."

It felt funny to hear him call Daniel that. And yet, Gabe *was* his father. He *owed* Daniel.

"We don't have to be married for you to be involved in his life," she offered, turning her back as she clicked off the switch controlling the wax warmer and began boxing already completed sets of candles. Surely she couldn't mess that up. "If you're so determined to stay here, fine. Build your house. Live in it. You can see Daniel, be around for him. But his home will always be with me."

"Why are you so dead set against marriage? Once you would have jumped at the chance." He stood opposite her, his hands mimicking her movements as he, too, boxed candles.

"I'm not against marriage, when it happens for the right reasons. You're mixing those reasons up just like you're mixing these orders up. You don't know the formula." She quickly redid the boxes he'd finished.

She wouldn't give in to the anger, wouldn't talk about the burn of distrust inside that still, after all these years, ate away at her. Let him think what he liked, she wasn't going to drag herself through it all again. She'd learned her lesson, learned it well.

Forgive and forget, Mac said. Very well. It had cost her dearly, but she'd forgiven Gabe. She had! But Blair Delaney wasn't so stupid that she would ever forget the shame or the sense of betrayal he'd left her with. Not ever.

Gabe stood, staring at her with an odd questioning look.

"Sorry. Did you say something?"

"The formula for marriage?" A twisted smile tugged at his mouth. "You always did bring chemistry into everything."

His wink reminded her of the past they'd once shared. A past she didn't want to remember. She shook it off like a nasty pest and focused on his next words.

"What reason could be more right than providing a home for a child?" His voice remained calmly reasonable.

Blair sighed, then turned and walked toward her office. She wasn't going to get anything done as long as he was here. At least she could sit down for a moment, even if she couldn't relax.

One glance told her that Gabe had followed. He folded himself onto one of her small, ratty chairs and tilted back, his eyes intent on her.

"I know women grow up with this fairy-tale idea about weddings and marriage. Fine, you can have all the white lace and orange blossoms you want. I'll even hire a white charger if that will help. But the bottom line is that I intend to be a father to my son, Blair."

Blair studied him with narrowed eyes, her fingers knotting in her lap, where he couldn't see them.

"It would only be a temporary father," she argued angrily. "As soon as somebody from your office calls, you'll go trailing back. And Daniel will be left behind, wondering why you don't call him or take him to his soccer games. I'm not allowing that." She held his gaze, daring him to say what she saw glinting in the depths of his eyes.

"The thing is, you can't stop it, Blair. I *am* going to have my son."

His mouth clamped in that implacable line she remembered so well. The emphasis was unmistakable. Blair could see the tiny white lines radiating from his lips and knew he meant business. *Oh, God, please make this stop!*

He leaned over and wrapped his fingers around hers, holding her hand carefully in his. Blair felt herself drawn by his eyes. Something glinted there, some shred of desolate rejection that she knew involved his past.

"I just want to spend some time with him, Blair. Is that so wrong?" His voice softened, cajoled. "You've had almost six years with him. I haven't had six minutes."

There was no condemnation in his eyes, but Blair felt guilty anyway. She'd deprived Gabe of seeing Daniel's first smile, his first step, of hearing his first word. Little joys that parents should have shared. He'd been robbed of them.

"I don't want to take him away, Blair. Please believe that I don't want to hurt you. I just want to put the past behind us and make something good for the future. Something for Daniel."

She tugged, and he let go of her hand, but stayed leaning across her desk, his face serious.

"Please? I don't want people gossiping about his parents, or the fact that we aren't married. I don't want him teased, mocked, ostracized. You said it yourself, it's a small town." He looked triumphant at having found this bit of wisdom to use against her. "Surely you wouldn't do that to an innocent child?"

Blair refused to trust in those softly spoken words. She'd trusted his honest intentions once before, and he'd disappointed her deeply. She wouldn't go that route again. Instead she cut to the truth of the matter.

"You're not in love with me, Gabe. You never were." She stated the facts baldly, ensuring that he knew she'd accepted the truth about their relationship.

"Wasn't I?" He shook his head, his eyes hooded, shading his thoughts. "I don't know what love is. I was infatuated with you, that's for sure. For a while you made me believe things I'd never thought possible, sort of like a Tinkerbell in disguise." He grimaced at those words and tried again.

"I mean, well, I guess I felt more alive when you came into my life. I haven't felt that in a long time, Blair."

It was an honest admission that she hadn't expected. But she couldn't allow it to sway her. Not now, not with Daniel to think about.

"That's nice of you to say, Gabe. But I don't want to base my son's future, my future, on something you *might* have felt a long time ago. It wouldn't be practical."

He leaned back, his mouth tipped in a frown as he studied her. "When did you become so practical?"

She smiled, letting the sarcasm tinge her words. "A little over six years ago," she murmured, then felt ashamed as a flush covered his cheekbones. "I've had to be practical. Otherwise my family and I wouldn't have survived."

Gabe jumped to his feet, shoved his hands in his pockets and strode across the room and back. He stopped right beside her.

"Look, I know I messed up. I was a jerk, an idiot, a creep. You can call me whatever you want and feel totally justified. But I didn't know about Daniel! Now that I do, I want to try to make things right."

Blair sighed, more weary than she'd been in months.

"You couldn't just jet back to L.A., back to your company and your life there? You couldn't just forget about him?" She breathed out the wish with a hope and a prayer, knowing as she did that it was futile.

Silence reigned. She glanced up curiously and found him staring at her, his jaw clenched, his eyes roiling with anger.

"Could *you* do that? I'm not my father, Blair. I'm not going to ignore my son, dump him in his room and forget him there. I know firsthand what that kind of life is like."

"I'm sorry." She didn't know what else to say. Gabriel Sloan had never shared his past with her, never allowed her to see into his childish hurts and disappointments. Oh, she'd had a few hints here and there, had known his adolescence had been less than perfect.

But this sounded like abandonment. Was that why he was so anxious to build a relationship with Daniel?

"I can't see how it would work." She fiddled with

the pens jammed into the tin-can penholder Daniel had given her last Christmas. "I have to take care of my grandfather and my great-aunt. I can't just leave them to fend for themselves. They're old, they need me. Albert, too."

"So we'll include them." Gabriel's simple statement shocked her into silence. "It could work, I know it could. We'll make the house bigger, include a place for them in our family. I've never had a grandfather or any aunts."

"Gabriel, you've always lived alone. You don't know what it's like to have people around you all the time." Blair almost laughed at the idea of it. "Daniel isn't going to go away just because you're thinking up a new computer gizmo. He's a child. When he wants attention, he wants it now."

A thousand problems filled her mind, and yet she didn't voice them. She couldn't. Not when she saw the shimmer of hope that transformed his face into boyish eagerness.

"I'm not involved with any project. I hire people for that. Polytech almost runs itself now. Besides, that guy, Albert, is working on this neat idea. I checked it out yesterday. It sounds crazy, but I have a hunch…" Gabe's thumb rubbed his chin, his mind consumed with a new problem.

Blair smiled, remembering the habit from the old days. How many times had he taken her for dinner and started talking about his work, only to end up scratching diagrams on napkins and completely forgetting his surroundings?

"Gabe?" He turned from his perusal out her window, his eyes far away. "This is exactly what I mean. Just when you're in the middle of something, Daniel will come and ask you to play. Or Mac will need help with something. Or Willie will burst into your room and relay some insight that sends everything else out of your brain. This isn't your L.A. condo. You won't be able to get into your jet and take off to some spa in the valley whenever you want. Parenthood is a full-time occupation."

He smiled, a huge, ear-splitting grin that begged her to share his exhilaration. "I know I'll have to make some adjustments." He rubbed his palms together as if he could hardly wait. "But I'll get used to it."

Blair scrambled for another route to dissuade him, frantically searching her brain. It was obvious Gabe was considering the idea of a family. She'd never have guessed that, and the knowledge made her question what other facets she'd missed in this complicated man.

"What would you expect from me? I mean, I've never been married, but I know I don't want to do it more than once. I couldn't do that to Daniel." She risked a glimpse at his face. "After all, we're not in love or anything. It wouldn't be the usual marriage."

Blair rearranged the items on the top of her desk again, her mind veering from the question she most wanted to ask.

"Blair?" He stood beside the desk, his hand stretched toward her. "Stop babbling and come here."

Blair looked at the floor, at her scuffed boots, at the messy desk, at her ragged fingernails. She looked everywhere she could until, finally, she looked at him. Then she slipped her hand into his and allowed him to draw her near him. Gabe's other hand clasped hers as he looked deeply into her eyes.

"It's not just Daniel I want," he murmured, his voice rippling over her taut nerves. "I think…I want all of it." He swallowed hard, his chest bulging as he took a deep breath. "All of what?" She couldn't believe she was hearing this.

"I'd like the chance to find out what being a family means. I'm thirty-five, Blair. I know for sure what I don't want, and I think I know what I want. I'm willing—no, excited about making us into a family, including your grandfather, your aunt, even Albert. The more the merrier, as far as I'm concerned. I never had that, and I'd like to experience it. I'd like to prove that I'm not the selfish, egocentric swine my father was."

"But—" His fingers brushed over her lips, and Blair immediately ceased speaking. This was important. She had to hear what he was about to say. His voice was faint, hesitant.

"You have to understand something. I don't need anyone, Blair. I can go on with my life the way it was, and I'll be just fine. I could give you money, support you and Daniel, and you'd probably do a bang-up job of raising him." He made a sad little face. "But I don't want to do that. It would be like walking away, wimping out when I know I owe you both more than that."

He shifted, raked a hand through his shorn hair. Clearly the words made him nervous.

"I don't understand this family thing you've got going here. It's not part of my experience. You say I've missed out, that I don't understand. I'd like to. I'd like to be the kind of man your grandfather is. I'd like to have Daniel look at me the way he looks at Mac—as if the sun rises and sets on his shoulders." His hands gripped hers.

"It's hard to explain, but I'd like to give the boy the things a father should, even though I don't know what those are. I want to be there to see him grow up and explore his world." His fingers tightened. "I'm not stupid. I can learn how to be a father. Maybe Mac will even help me. Just don't shut me out, Blair."

She hesitated, her mind swirling with doubts. "I don't know." He was obviously sincere, she could see that. But for how long?

"Please, Blair, give me a chance. Just say you'll think about getting married. I can wait, as long as you'll let me stay and get to know him. We can sort all the rest out as we go along. I promise I won't rush you, I won't push you, I won't abandon you. I just want to share Daniel with you."

Stymied by his admission of need when he'd just insisted he didn't need anyone, Blair sought for something to say. It was tempting, so tempting. To be able to share Willie's medical bills with someone who could shoulder them, to have some of the burden of her money woes lifted, to know Daniel wouldn't be short-changed because of her childish mistake—it was all there for the taking.

Maybe it could work. Maybe she could have someone to talk to, to share the problems with. Maybe Gabe could be the man she needed, the father Daniel wanted. Maybe she just had to ask.

And that was the problem. Blair didn't ask for help. Not anymore. She was the one in charge, the person other people depended on. She couldn't relax that guard.

What was it he'd said? *Share it with you.* He'd

sounded so forlorn, as if he'd never been able to share with anyone. And yet Gabe had been a member of the church, always chaired, hosted and funded a horde of projects, even spoken occasionally to the men's groups.

He's always stood alone among the crowd. The truth smacked her between the eyes. Was Gabe lonely?

"Well, Blair? Are you willing to do what we should have done years ago? Will you marry me?"

As she studied his resolute face, Blair tried to remember the cold, brusque businessman. She tried to recall his harsh words and the unflagging demands on his employees. But all she could see was a needy little boy who wanted a family around him—a man who wanted somebody to care for him, maybe even somebody to care about.

"I don't know," she whispered. "I have to think about this. And you should, too. It's a big step and it's irrevocable. At least for me."

As she said the words, she wondered if she'd done the right thing to let him hope. Daniel *did* need a father, but he needed a permanent one. Gabe wasn't permanent. Maybe, once he'd spent an evening or two with Daniel, he'd realize how demanding a child could be. Maybe he'd want to go back to his self-sufficient life. Blair shivered. Why did that thought bother her?

She wasn't prepared when Gabe leaned down and kissed her, his lips tender against her mouth.

"Please?"

She kissed him back. Partly because it was expected, but partly because she wanted to remind herself to be on guard. As the flood of emotion hurled through her body, she drew back and gazed into his eyes. She couldn't need him—not again.

"One step at a time," she cautioned. "We take it very slowly. And we don't mention one word about marriage to my grandfather or to anyone else. You need to get to know Daniel. His needs come first."

He threw back his head and laughed, his eyes sparkling like a glacial mountain stream tumbling joyfully over the rocks to freedom. Would fatherhood free Gabe? Or would it chain him to her for the rest of their lives?

"When?" he demanded. "When and how do I start being a father?"

Blair just stood there, her mind frozen as a picture of Gabe and Daniel together got caught in her brain.

"Right away," he decided, hugging her close, then setting her free. "After school today. After all, it will soon be summer. He'll have lots of free time then." He stopped, considered, then glanced at her sideways. "I want Daniel to have my name, Blair."

Blair gulped. "Uh, shouldn't we sit down and organize things first? I mean, you've got your house to build and I have my job. Eventually we'll have to tell the family so they can help. And Daniel." She closed her eyes, knowing how ecstatic Daniel would be to finally have a father. "I need to prepare Daniel."

Suddenly she realized what she was giving up. Daniel would no longer be solely under her authority. She wouldn't have the final say in his life anymore. She couldn't. If Gabe was to be an integral part of her son's life, Daniel had to learn to run to Gabe for some things, to depend on his father, to need him. Which was another reason to hold off this rushed marriage. The Gabe she remembered wasn't exactly dependable.

"Blair? You're not backing out? You're not going to change your mind, are you?" His eyes shone like emeralds. He studied her, concern glinting from their depths. "You will share him with me?"

She shook her head. "No, I won't change my mind. I'm just thinking. Let's ease into it one thing at a time. Then we'll talk about marriage somewhere down the road."

"Not that far down. I want him to feel like every other kid in his class. Secure. Normal." His voice was firm. "I'm prepared to wait a month, two at the outside."

Her mouth flopped open. "Gabe, I can't! There's a lot to see to. A lot to think about."

He shook his head, his face implacable. "You'll dither and fuss, and it will never happen. Two months, that's as far as I'm prepared to go. Unless Daniel puts up some objection." He frowned at the idea.

"You're still issuing decrees." Blair fumed out loud. "I'm not promising anything, Gabriel. I want Daniel to have a chance to get to know you first. He has to be comfortable with this, or it isn't going to work. So does my family." She held her breath and waited, praying that she hadn't made a terrible mistake. "If our marriage happens, it will be because everyone is comfortable with it. Not because you force me into it."

Finally Gabe's dark head nodded his agreement. "Yes, maybe you're right. The community will have a chance to get used to the idea, too. And the house will be done."

"In two months?" Blair almost laughed. "I think

you'd better be prepared to rough it out at the hotel, Gabe. It's going to take a lot longer than a few months to build the kind of house you're talking about."

"Where there's a will there's a way," he quoted gravely. He walked out of her office with a quick measured stride and returned moments later. "Keep this as a reminder," he murmured, holding out the diamond.

It caught her breath, sparkling and shimmering on his palm. But diamonds were for love. And he didn't love her. He never had.

Blair shook her head, wishing she could have at least tried it on. It was so lovely. She swallowed. "No. You keep it."

"If you don't like it we can get something else," he offered with a frown. "It's just that when I saw it, I thought of you."

"Willie would say that was God directing you." The brilliant stone caught the sun's rays and deflected them onto her shirt. "I've always loved this particular cut. And the setting is beautiful."

He let her admire it for a while. But when Blair finally glanced up, she caught a frown tugging at the corners of his mouth.

"I'll try not to mess up, Blair. I'm not very good at listening, but I promise I'll work on it." His voice brimmed with determination. "I think I could be a good husband and a good father. If I try hard enough." Before she could protest he slid the ring onto her finger. "Keep it as a symbol of our agreement," he murmured. "You can wear it when nobody's around if it makes you feel better."

"I'll try, too," she murmured, automatically threading

her fingers through his out of habit. She ignored a noise from outside. "But I'll pray for some heavenly direction, as well. Just so we don't get off track."

He nodded. "Did you hear something?"

"Course she didn't. Thunderstruck by that ring, I imagine." Willie surged through the door, her austere face wreathed in a smile as she wrapped Gabe in one of her smothering hugs. "Knew as soon as I laid eyes on you that you were the man for Blair. 'Those whom God has joined together let no man put asunder.'" She smiled at his stunned surprise. "Plain as the nose on your face. Told Mac that yesterday."

"Yesterday? But…I only decided for sure last night." Gabe tilted his head as he studied the older woman. His eyes stretched wide in amazement.

Blair couldn't help the giggle that burst out even as she scorned her aunt's matchmaking.

"We're not getting married, Willie. At least, not just yet. So don't get too worked up. We want to let Daniel get used to his father first. Besides, Gabe might change his mind before the time is up," she warned, then gave up as Willie teetered on her tiptoes and smacked a kiss against Gabe's cheek.

Blair's eyes met Gabe's glittery ones. She shrugged in apology. "We're not the usual assortment of family members."

"No, we're better." Willie let him go and picked up Blair's hand. "When we love someone, we don't give up easily. That tenacity will be important to you."

"Busy Bee, have you seen Wil—" Mac burst through the door, then stopped as he spied the three of them. "Oh. What's going on?"

"These two are getting married." Willie glanced at Blair and sighed. "Eventually," she added. She frowned at Mac. "Well, don't just stand there! Welcome him into the family."

But Mac's eyes were scrunched tightly closed. No one could miss his whispered prayer. "Thank You, God! I knew You and I could pull it off if I could just get them together."

As she watched the two men shake hands, Blair frowned, remembering Mac's words. Time would tell if her grandfather had done them a favor or foiled any hope for the future.

Please help us, she thought while everyone chatted. *Please show me if this is wrong so I can stop it before it's too late. I have to be strong. I can't let myself need him.*

She glanced up, her eyes snagged by the look on Gabe's craggily handsome face. For the first time since she'd met him, he looked content. Why was that?

Chapter Four

"Daniel?" Two days later Gabe gulped, prayed for courage, then knelt in front of the little boy. "Could we talk?" He felt the hairs on the back of his neck prickle, felt the burn of Blair's eyes as she watched from the doorway. Oh, why had she insisted *he* do this? She was far more qualified. She'd given the boy enough hints that Gabe figured he didn't need to say more. If she was so worried, why didn't she tell him all of it?

"Whatcha wanna talk about? 'Lectricity? I got a book about that." Daniel rummaged through the bookshelves in his room, finally locating the tattered volume. He held it out proudly. "We're learning about this at school. I can read most of it myself."

"Really?" Gabe allowed himself a small diversion. "Did you know that I learned to read when I was about your age?"

Daniel's head came up with a jerk, and he stared at Gabe as if he knew something big was about to happen. "Oh."

"I guess it's only natural that you and I would learn to

read early, you being my son and all." He held his breath and prayed for the wisdom to handle this properly.

"Yeah. Kids and dads have lots of things the same. Like our hair, 'cept yours is shorter." Daniel rubbed his hand over Gabe's shorn stubble. "An' you got eyes like mine, too. My mom's are a different color. Are you gonna stay my dad?"

Boy, the kid's mind was a maze. Gabe sucked in a breath.

"Yes, I sure am. Forever and ever. I bought some land from your grandfather, and I'm building a house across the valley." He waited for the questions.

"Dads usually live with their kids." Daniel's voice dropped to an almost-whisper. "Aren't you going to be staying around here? Is that why you need your own house?" He flopped onto the floor beside Gabe, the book forgotten.

"No, I'm staying. It's just that your grandpa's house is pretty full with him and his sister and your mom and you." He sat down and stretched his legs out, kneading the kink out of his knee as he searched for an explanation. "Besides, I have a lot of toys, and I need a special room for them."

"Toys?" Daniel scoffed. "Dads don't need toys."

"Oh, yes, Daniel. Everyone needs toys. That's what keeps our minds busy. My favorite toy is a big computer that I call Fred. I can do lots of stuff with him."

"Fred's a funny name for a computer." Daniel let that go, his mind obviously busy with something else. "Why did you wait so long?"

Gabe frowned. "Wait? What do you mean?"

"Felicia Cartwright gots a new baby in her house and

its dad is already there. How come you waited so long to come and see me?"

Behind him, Gabe heard Blair walk into the room, felt the whoosh of air as she sank onto the carpet in front of him and folded her legs into the lotus position.

"It took Gabe a while to find you, sweetheart. He didn't wait on purpose." She picked up Daniel's chubby little hand and cuddled it between hers. "I'll bet he's really sad that he missed seeing you play hockey this winter, but I know he can't wait until you start riding Mortimer. Besides, your dad is here now. Is that okay?"

"Yes. That's what I prayed about." Daniel's big eyes widened, and a beatific grin spread across his face as he turned to his father. "Mortimer's a horse. Grandpa Mac says he's coming to stay on my birthday. Do you want to come to my birthday party? It's not for a while, but I could remind you."

Gabe had to swallow the lump in his throat. "I would really like that."

"Cool!" Daniel's grin drooped a little. "Are you sure you can stay that long?"

"Daniel, I'm going to live here. That means I'm not going to go away again, except maybe for a day or two to do business."

"Oh, you mean like when my mom goes to the big show to sell her candles? That's when Willie and me get to eat lots and lots of spaghetti. When we're full as a tick, Grandpa Mac does the dishes, and Albert cleans the floor. Making spaghetti is messy." He studied Gabe for a little longer. "Can you and me do things?"

"I sure hope so. I'd like to do things with you." Gabe

shoved away the fear those words engendered. He would learn, he vowed. He'd learn it all. "There's just one thing, Daniel. I don't think I'm a very good dad. I've never been one, you see, and I'm not sure of exactly how to do it."

Daniel nodded sagely. "'Cause you didn't practice, right? Mrs. Jenkins says practice makes perfect. She's my teacher," he added in a confidential tone.

"She must know what she's talking about, then." Gabe made himself take a deep breath. "But just in case I do something wrong, you have to promise that you'll tell me so I can fix it. I want to be a very good dad."

Daniel nodded, then after a moment turned to play with his building set. Gabe sought Blair's eyes, wondering what to do next. She shrugged.

"Honey, are there any questions you want to ask Gabe or me? We'll try to answer the best we can."

Daniel glanced from her to Gabe. "What kinda questions?" he said.

"Oh, just things you might have wondered about. Things you don't talk about but would still like to know the answers." Blair spoke in an offhand tone, allowing the boy a chance to think his own thoughts on the subject.

Once more Gabe realized what a wonderful mother she was. She had a knack for knowing when to push ahead and when to back off, and he'd seen it at work in the past few days.

"I dunno." Daniel stopped what he was doing and cocked his head to one side. "What's his house gonna be like?"

Gabe understood this one. The boy wondered if it

would be full of don't-touch stuff. "I call it my castle," Gabe told him, grinning as the boy's eyes grew huge. "When it's finished, you'll be able to live there with the rest of us. If you want to see a drawing of it, I could show you that sometime."

"Wow! A real castle." Daniel jumped up and swung himself around the room in a series of acrobatic moves that had no name. They were the simple joyful outbursts of a happy boy. "I'm gonna live in a castle. Wait till the kids hear about this."

Gabe's glance flew to Blair. He caught the same stunned surprise in her face that he knew filled his own. Now what? he wondered. How was he supposed to handle this? Blair had been very clear in her insistence on a waiting period before she agreed to marry him. But how did you explain that to an excited five-year-old boy who'd only just found his father?

Mac's grizzled head poked around the corner. "What's all the racket up here?" he grumbled, a smile tugging at his lips. "Sounds like a herd of grumpy elephants."

"Grandpa, guess what? I'm gonna live in a castle with my dad." Daniel's eyes glittered with excitement.

"Is that right?" Mac's eyes moved from Gabe to Blair and back again. "Isn't that something? I suppose once you get all doo-dahed up in your fancy castle you won't want to come and see Willie and me in our rickety house?" He winked at Blair. "I'll be left all alone." His mournful face brought Daniel to his side.

"I'll always come and see you, Grandpa. Me and my dad are going to do lots of things together, but we could bring you and Willie to the castle, too. Couldn't we, Dad?"

The child's pleading gaze suddenly turned on his father, who was having trouble breathing after hearing himself called *dad*. "Sure, sure we could," Gabe managed to say, trying to recall what he was agreeing to.

"And Grandpa can show us about fishing. Grandpa's the best fisherman in the world."

"Danny, my boy, that's a wonderful compliment! Thank you."

"Welcome." Daniel glowed as Mac patted him on the shoulder.

"But I think it probably takes a while to build a thing like a castle. Until it's done and everything gets sorted out, I think Willie and I will stay right where we are. We need to be around for Albert, you see. And I kinda like my own place."

Daniel nodded as if he fully understood that sentiment. "Me, too. Maybe I could have two homes."

"Or three or four," Mac agreed. "No reason why not. A house is just a house, but a home is a home because of the people in it. Doesn't really matter where it is or how fancy it is. What matters is how much love there is inside it."

"I know, Grandpa." Daniel's hand slid into the blue-veined grasp, his fingers wrapping around the gnarled, bent ones. "An' we got lots and lots of love, don't we? We can make anyplace be home."

Mac bent over and kissed his tousled head. "That we can, laddie. Now maybe your mom and dad need some time to talk about things. How about if you and I go check out the creek? It's getting pretty high, you know. Albert's been trying out a new gizmo that counts how many fish go down the stream. Do you want to see it?"

"Yes!" Daniel danced from one foot to the other. Then he glanced at Gabe. "I can't do nothing with you right now, 'cause Grandpa and I gotta go look at somethin'. Maybe after lunch. Okay?"

Gabe tried not to laugh. "Very okay," he agreed. "I've got a few things to do myself."

"Cool." Daniel dragged his grandfather out of the room, talking a mile a minute as he went.

"Cool. The word of the week." Blair smiled, but there was worry lurking in the depths of her coffee-bean eyes.

"Thanks for stepping in." Gabe said it sincerely. "I got a little flustered there for a minute. He might look like me, but his mind works like yours, twisting and turning all over the place."

"Gabe, how long is it really going to take to build that house? I'll have to try and put it in some kind of time frame that he understands." She got to her feet, her eyes moving to the window.

"Don't look smug, but the two months has been extended. They've now promised no longer than nine weeks, and I guarantee they won't go beyond that because they'll forfeit a huge amount of money." He checked to make sure she wasn't laughing. "That puts us around the end of April. Might take a few days to get some furniture and stuff, but I'd think we could move in by the end of the month. Does an early May wedding suit you?"

"You're intent on going through with this?"

He nodded. "Oh, yes. I intend to go through with

all of it." She stood there studying him, so Gabe got up and wandered to the window. This was a nice enough site, but he had the better one, especially with that creek running alongside.

He heard the whisper of her movements, knew the exact moment when she stopped behind him.

"Are you positive? You're not missing the company?"

Gabe turned, wondering at the funny sound in her voice. A certain huskiness that usually meant she was emotional. But why?

"I told you, the company will do just fine without me. I'm not needed there. Not anymore. My staff is trained to handle almost anything." His breath caught in his throat when a hint of her perfume snagged on the breeze and wafted past him. A little bit spicy, a little bit flowery, very soft. It personified Blair, and Gabe suddenly realized that he'd never forgotten even that small detail about her.

"What's really bothering you, Blair? I've seen you giving me these little sideways looks when you think I'm not watching. What's going on inside here?" He tapped the tumble of curls she'd fastened to the top of her head with a huge yellow clip.

"You won't like it," she warned. "Probably not." If he knew Blair she'd blurt it out full speed, without worrying about his sensibilities. She was hopeless at prevarication. "Go ahead."

"It's not a criticism. You've done very well with Daniel. Better than I ever expected. It's just…well, I didn't expect you to fall in with Aunt Willie or Mac so easily. I kind of thought you and Albert had things in common, but Aunt Willie is different."

"She's a breath of fresh air. I can't imagine how anyone can't love her. She's like you." Blair's tiny frown made him smile. "She never lies or pretends what she doesn't feel. She doesn't try to stroke you."

"You always did despise that. Come on, let's get some coffee and relax on the veranda." She led the way to the kitchen and poured out two cups.

"I hate it because it's deceit. I can deal with somebody's anger or dislike, or most of the other stuff. But when they sweet-talk out of one side of their mouth while they stab you with the other, well, I get mad." He took a sip of the potent black brew and shuddered. "What do you people do to get it like this? It tastes like sludge."

Gabe emptied the pot and set about making a fresh one. When it was streaming through the filter, he turned to study her. "There's more, we both know it. You might as well say it, Blair. I can take it." He hoped.

"I wish you wouldn't listen to Mac so much." She let him take her cup, pour a fresh one.

"You don't like me to talk to your grandfather?" Gabe filled his mug and sat down. He tried to figure it out, tried to keep his cool. "Why not? What do I do that bothers you the most? Am I upsetting him or something?"

She wouldn't look at him, wouldn't meet his gaze. Worry snickered through Gabe. What had he done that was so awful? Was she going to rescind her offer about Daniel? Was she going to make him leave?

"Just say it, okay, Blair? You don't want me around them. You want me to go." Despair tugged at him, dark and overwhelming. He wouldn't stay where he wasn't wanted. He'd go. But just until he'd figured out something else. There had to be a way for him to be a part of this family. There just had to be.

Blair opened her mouth, but clamped it shut when her aunt breezed into the room clad in a frilly dress with big red polka dots and flounces that fluttered as she moved. It was something straight out of the good old days.

"Hello, darlings!" Willie picked out her favorite china mug with the sprigs of lavender painted on the sides. "I smelled freshly brewed coffee and, after our tête-à-tête yesterday, I knew it had to be yours, Gabe dear. No one else makes coffee as well as you. Thank you." She bent to ruffle his hair, her fingers gentle as they brushed his neck and over his shoulder. "I do love it when you come over."

Gabe squeezed her fingers and brushed a kiss against the powdered porcelain cheek she presented. "Thank you, Miss Rhodes. I appreciate the way you've accepted me into your home. I hope I'm not intruding. Mac told me you're preparing for a play."

"Darling, you're our Blair's almost-husband! And my almost-nephew. You belong here. As soon as I get that attic cleaned up, you can move in. Or were we moving out? That medicine gets things all muddled in my mind. I forget." She leaned to hug him close, covering him in a cloud of lilac fragrance. "Oh, well. Yes, I'm doing a bit piece in *Hamlet* with our little theater group next month. I hope you'll come."

"I wouldn't miss it." He watched her exit, then resumed his study of Blair. To his amazement, she had a frown on her face.

"I wish you wouldn't do that," she mumbled.

"Do what?" He was almost afraid to say it, afraid to hear her response.

"Get so friendly with them. Make them think you're always going to be here, that they can count on you." Her mouth clenched white, and her eyes flashed with anger.

Gabe's jaw dropped.

"Oh, don't act so surprised. You know what I mean. Letting them believe that everything's going to be wonderful."

"Isn't it going to be?" He challenged her to deny it.

"No. Yes. I don't know! You don't know, either." She ladled another two teaspoons into her already sweetened coffee. "You haven't been here long enough to know, and I wish you wouldn't keep up this pretense of loving the jolly backwoods. It's a lie, and we all know how much you hate lies, Gabe."

She was jealous of his bond with her family! Gabe breathed a sigh of relief. This at least he understood. If he had a family like this, he'd be jealous of somebody butting in, too. He followed her to the veranda.

"I'm not pretending or lying." He waited till she was seated, then took the chair beside hers. "I do like it here. It's so natural, so beautiful. Yesterday I saw deer. I didn't know there were any still around."

"The neighbors have a game farm." Blair wasn't slouched in her usual relaxed position. She crouched on the edge of her chair, like a cat ready to pounce. "And don't change the subject. You know very well that this isn't your usual setting. It's hokey and so totally *not* your style."

Gabe felt like a rabbit caught in her headlights. But

for once the scrutiny didn't bother him. Let her study him night and day. He didn't mind. He wasn't pretending a thing. He loved it here. He'd never felt so comfortable around anyone as he did with this family.

"What are you getting out of this, Gabe? A good laugh? A little payback? What?" Her eyes dared him to respond.

He couldn't tell her the truth. He couldn't explain that what he got here was unadulterated acceptance. Nobody thought it was the least bit strange when he sat in the barn and worked on his laptop for hours at a time.

Yesterday, nobody had called him a geek or raised their eyebrows when he forgot to get out of his car. He'd been so wrapped up in the idea for a new game that he'd scribbled as much as he could on paper. He remembered Mac brought him a sandwich and some chicken soup that he'd forgotten to eat. When it got dark, Willie came and tugged on his arm until she lovingly captured his attention.

"What makes you think I'm getting anything out of it, other than a chance to see my son every day?"

She sniffed. "As if you even notice him! I had to pry you away from that Fred thing to get you to kiss him good-night," she grumbled. "I could feel you itching to get back to it when Mac coerced you into that game of rummy. The way you look today, I'm pretty sure you spent most of the night peering at it."

"I did." He admitted the truth freely. "I got an idea for a new game." Gabe made himself shut down on that. What woman, newly engaged or otherwise, wanted to talk about computer gizmos? "But it's nothing I can't change. I just have to learn how to do it." He hunkered down, relaxing, his chin on his hands, elbows on his knees. "I'm not trying to steal them, Blair. They'll always love you best."

"What?" She stared at him. "I'm not jealous, you idiot! I just don't want them hurt."

"Neither do I. Believe me, that's the last thing I want. I think they're very special." He followed when she jumped up and scurried inside, pausing at the counter while she rinsed her cup. "I know you're looking out for them, Blair. I remember those little envelopes you used to mail every other Friday. Special delivery, priority. They were to them, weren't they? To help out? Even then you were taking care of them. Just like you always take care of everyone around you."

"Oh, brother!" She lunged away from the counter, but Gabe moved and blocked her escape. She glared at him. "You make me sound like Mother Teresa or something. I'm not a saint, Gabe. I just don't want to see them hurt. They're my family."

"I know." He leaned down and brushed his lips against hers, remembering the fire of her kisses from long ago. But this Blair was wary, more reserved. She stepped away from him.

"I have to go to work," she said softly. "Thanks for the coffee."

"You're welcome." Gabe watched the screen door wheeze closed. He saw her stop and listen to Daniel and Mac talking to Albert. Gabe walked outside, hoping to overhear their conversation. Maybe if he listened to them together, he'd get a better idea of what kids did with their fathers, what families talked about.

A wave of lilac assaulted his nostrils as a delicate

hand ruffled his hair. Willie's barely audible voice floated to him. "She's very protective."

Gabe jerked upright. He couldn't remember when anyone had ruffled his hair. Not ever. Tears burned in his throat. Why? he asked himself. Why did that little touch mean so much?

"Blair's made herself into our guardian. She talks a tough line, but inside she's afraid."

"Blair? Afraid? I don't think so." Gabe turned his head to stare at the willowy woman on teetering heels who seemed more like his almost forgotten mother every day.

Aunt Willie was adamant. "If you knew her better you'd see it. She's always trying to make up for something, go the extra mile, ensure she's done more than anyone would ever expect. She's trying to atone for her sins."

Gabe blinked. "Huh?"

"It's true. She's been like that since her parents died when she was four. I believe that deep down, Blair thinks that if she'd been better, more lovable, done more, said more, helped more, that her parents wouldn't have died. Somewhere inside she still clings to those beliefs. So she stretches herself thin trying to make up for her mistakes. She doesn't understand grace."

"Grace?" Gabe felt like a recorder, repeating whatever he'd heard.

Willie waved him into a chair while she made herself comfortable in her willow rocker.

"Grace," she asserted firmly. "It means something that's given freely, something you can't earn or deserve. It's like God's grace to us. We're sinners, all of us. We've done nothing to deserve His love. In fact, we should be punished. And yet God says, 'It's all right. I forgive you. I gave My son's life—I don't need yours. You're forgiven, no strings attached.' You see?"

Gabe nodded slowly. "I've heard about it, and I guess I understand it when it comes to God. But I don't see why you think Blair's stuck on it."

"Because she doesn't believe that she can just accept forgiveness." Willie lifted her knitting from a bag nearby. Her needles clacked rhythmically. "She thinks she has to pay, that she's too far for grace to reach."

"But what could she possibly have done that gave her such an idea?" He closed his eyes and listened to the song-drenched breeze as birds flitted in and out of the valley. He felt the sun on his face, warming him, the wind caressing him. And he waited for Willie's answer.

When it came, it drove every other thought out of his mind.

"Blair went against everything she believed in when she slept with you. She wanted to obey God's commands and keep herself only for her husband, but she made a mistake. When she became pregnant and had to drop her studies to return home, she believed it was because she needed to pay for her sins." Willie riveted him with her steady stare. "She's trying to atone for a mistake that's almost seven years old."

Chapter Five

A month later Gabe sat on the Rhodes' veranda again, but his thoughts were no clearer. He couldn't get Willie's words out of his mind, though he'd yet to face Blair with them.

The guilt gnawed at him. *He'd* done that to her. He'd made her abandon her beliefs, her principles. He'd been so desperate to hold onto her love, he'd rushed her, forced her into something she wasn't ready for. He'd taken it all away, and then added insult to injury with that stupid prenup. The guilt was his, not hers. He wanted to tell her that, to atone for it, to wipe her slate clean no matter what it did to him.

And yet, he was afraid to show his emotion. Afraid that if he let her see how much he wanted to keep what he had, how much he treasured the security of sharing this family with her, told her how inconceivable he found it that he could come and go at will and still be welcomed back, she'd take it all away from him. Their mistake was in the past. Wasn't it better to leave it alone?

"Hey, Daddy, want to come fishing? Grandpa and

me are going." Daniel stood in front of him, his knobby knees sticking out under the shorts he'd reluctantly donned when the weather had turned unseasonably warm.

"Son, I'd just love to go fishing. But maybe later on, okay? If this weather holds." Gabe swung the boy up and around, delighting in the squeals of laughter that resulted.

"You'll get his lunch all over him if you keep that up." Blair's voice held a hint of warning, and Gabe instantly set Daniel down. "How's the house?"

He turned to face her and sucked in a breath at her beauty. She wore no fancy clothes, no brand-name outfit. She had on a sleeveless white cotton blouse and a pair of denim shorts that left lots of golden brown leg bare to the sun. Her hair was caught up in a fluff of tumbling curls, bursting from two combs that followed the cap of her skull. Her bangs, long and wispy, curled with perspiration, and she swiped them off her forehead with a careless hand. The hand that wore his diamond.

"You're frowning. Is the place that awful?" She winked at him. "Did the castle thing turn out to be a bad idea?"

Gabe's heart relaxed as her chocolate eyes melted with laughter that spilled onto the lazy afternoon heat. For some reason, she'd refused all his entreaties to look at the progress he'd made. She'd sent Mac to check her hives and add more of the funny boxes she called supers. But she stayed away from his field. Gabe didn't know why, but he had a hunch it had to do with trust.

"It's not exactly a castle," he told her. "Everything's

moving very well. You'd know if you came and looked at it yourself." He dared her to refuse.

"Oh, I will, one of these days. Things are just so busy right now. And it has to be a castle if it's home for a computer king." She ignored his pleading look and turned to the house. "Gardens and flower beds wait for no man."

"You know very well they're both finished, for now." Willie shoved the door open with one foot, balancing a tray that carried a frosty pitcher of lemonade and six glasses. "Do you good to get out and relax for a while."

"No time like the present." Gabe added his two bits to the conversation. Not that it would sway her. She ignored him when she could, when he'd let her get away with it.

"Mommy, could we please go see the castle? My daddy's building it specially for us an' I want to see it. Please?"

The voice wheedled and whined, begging so sadly that Gabe wondered how Blair could keep from yelling her agreement. No doubt she was a far better parent than he'd ever be.

"All right, we'll all go. After I take a break and have some of Willie's lemonade." She tossed Gabe one stark, meaningful glance before moving across the veranda to lean on the balustrade. "You guys could have gone anytime, you know," she said, watching her grandfather climb the stairs.

"We wouldn't dream of looking at your future home without you present. Come on, Albert. Come and have a drink. Leave that contraption alone for a minute!"

Albert straightened slightly and pushed the gray strands out of his eyes before nudging his glasses up his nose. He looked like a tired old professor. "Oh. Yes. Of course." He darted up the steps like a rabbit pursued, accepted his glass of lemonade and drained it in one gulp. "Delightful. Thank you. Must be going now." He limped down the steps, favoring the leg Gabe knew he'd injured in the war.

"Albert?" Blair's soft voice stopped him mid-step. "We're going to take a look at Gabe's castle. Wouldn't you like to come and take the grand tour with us? We won't be long. After all, you'll all be living there one day, too."

"*Our* castle," Gabe muttered, but no one paid him any attention.

"Yes, of course. Lovely." Albert scurried across the grass toward his work shed, mumbling to himself. Halfway there, he stopped, turned around, a frown on his face. "Castle?"

"We'll come and get you when we're ready to go." Willie nodded when he stared at her for a minute. Then Albert gave a stiff little bow and resumed his stumbling gait to his workroom.

"What's he working on now?" Blair turned to Gabe, her manner telling him that she didn't want to ask but felt compelled to do so.

"A kind of dune buggy thing that's used for retrieval." Gabe accepted his glass with a smile at Willie and in return got an affectionate caress as her hand tenderly cupped his cheek.

"Surely that's not new?" Pointedly, Blair took a seat several feet away from him.

"It is when it's for use in the Arctic." He felt a smug ping of satisfaction at the startled looks on their faces. "It has every chance of succeeding, too. The parts are specially insulated so that they don't seize up when it's cold." He waited, and when no one spoke, looked directly at Blair. "Are you ready to go now?"

She set down her glass. Gabe reached out and pulled her from her chair. "I hope you like it." He couldn't help gazing into her lovely eyes. "If you don't, just tell me. At this stage we can change almost anything."

He could see the hesitation there, the words unspoken. "Almost anything," he repeated quietly, reading the unspoken words. "I'm not leaving, Blair."

A touch of sadness clung to him. This should be a happy time, a time they looked forward to. This, after all, would be their future home. Instead Blair's eyes swirled with secret fears and her fingers clenched in worry. She still didn't trust him. Not yet. But she would. Gabe was determined to prove himself.

He knew nothing about families, even less about unity and drawing together. But he could learn. If he just worked hard enough, he knew he could learn.

"It's beautiful." Willie spun around in the huge kitchen with its modern hearth. "Look at this, Blair. The breakfast nook is part of the turret. Those windows! My goodness, the morning sun will just light this place up."

"I like the dungeon." Daniel grinned at his father. "It makes me think of pirates and things."

"It's not really a dungeon, son." Gabe mussed his hair just as Willie had done his own. "It's a workroom. I'm going to be building some things down there."

"Can I help?" Daniel's big eyes pleaded for the chance.

"Of course. Albert's going to help, too. We'll call it the invention dungeon. How about that?"

Mac flopped onto a short ladder left behind by some workman. He thrust out one hand and grinned a huge, smirking grin. "I don't know how you've done it, boy, but you've certainly done it. This place is shooting up faster than a geyser in Yellowstone."

"Most of it was prebuilt to specs. It just needed a few alterations, then it was shipped in and assembled once the foundation was solid. I used those straw blocks for a lot of it. Good insulation in the winter and just as efficient in the summer."

Daniel peered through the windows that overlooked the back yard. The rough terrain had been torn apart by huge earthmoving machines, which had left a cleared space. But the creek and many of the trees still stood firm and untouched.

"What's that?" he demanded in a shrill voice, breaking through the conversation.

"Daniel, don't yell. Ask politely." Blair turned toward him. "I've been wondering that myself, Gabe. Why is that hole there?"

Gabe swallowed hard. "It's going to be a pool." Willie clapped her hands in excitement. Mac whistled. Albert went out to take a closer look. But Blair stood there, her eyes dark and curious.

"I didn't know you swam. I know you had your club and that you lifted weights or something. When we used to go to Santa Monica pier, you always insisted on staying on the beach." Pink streaks shot across her face. "Of course, that was a long time ago."

Gabe went for honesty. "I can't swim," he told her.

Blair frowned in perplexity. "Then why?"

"I'm going to learn." He shut out his father's mocking voice and faced four sets of curious eyes. "It's just something I have to do."

"And you couldn't do this in the community pool? You had to build your own?" Blair shook her head in disbelief.

He knew she thought he'd gone to excess on some things, but Gabe didn't care. This was going to be his home, and he wanted it to be perfect for everyone. Then maybe she would stay, settle down. Relax and build a future with him.

"It might take me a long time to learn. I didn't want to hog it." *Or have everyone gape and stare while I have a panic attack.*

"I might just take those lessons with you." Mac shoved himself upright and grinned. "Never did learn even the dog paddle. 'Spect I could take a dip or two with you. But not in winter. I draw the line there."

Gabe couldn't stop his mouth from spreading in a grin even if he'd wanted to. This was what he liked about them. No questions. Just acceptance. If he wanted to stick a big pool in his back yard, well, they embraced that just as they embraced him. No problem.

"I'm going to heat it, Mac. Maybe we could enclose it. You know, have an underground tunnel to the house, or something?"

"You can do that? You don't say!" Mac clapped him on the back. "Thought of pretty near everything, haven't you, son?" He shoved his hands in his back pockets, teetering on his heels. "I can always go to the old place to do my whittling. Wouldn't want to mess up this castle."

Gabe pointed a finger. "There's a workroom right over there if you want it, Mac. I had it put there specially. That way you won't have to take the stairs to get there." While Mac and Willie enthused over the room, Gabe moved closer to Blair. "Do you want to come and see the master bedroom?" He kept his voice diffident, absent of meaning so she wouldn't panic.

"It's on the main floor?"

He nodded and led her out of the kitchen, through the adjoining family room and the solarium to the rooms he'd insisted on designing himself.

"This is the bedroom, walk-in closets, bathroom. The Jacuzzi is through there, and there's a steam room, too."

"You'd think you were addicted to water," she muttered. "If the tub upstairs was a foot longer, you wouldn't have needed the pool." Her eyes were huge as she studied a tub set on a higher level against a bank of opaque windows. "Does this open?" She tried one and found that, indeed, it swung out onto a flagstone patio that was surrounded with a bounty of trees and flowering shrubs ready to be planted. At one end lay the beginnings of a rose garden.

Gabe spared a glance to notice that they'd already planted a few of the prickly bushes. He turned to the room he'd planned so carefully, then adjusted after she'd quietly agreed to marry him late one night last month.

"This will be a two-sided fireplace," he told her,

motioning to the roughed-in area that snuggled against one end of the hot tub, while the other looked over the bedroom. "Is it okay?"

He was beginning to worry. She hadn't said much, just walked around, touching a hand here, a finger there.

"It's very…romantic." Her voice whispered across the silence. "But I don't need it. I'm not a fancy person, Gabe. I'm not the socialite deb you thought I was. I'm a working woman, a mother, a plain, ordinary person. This is so—" she waved a hand, taking in the rich cedar beams, vast amounts of window space and glistening amenities "—so *much*. I don't need all this, Gabe."

He grinned. She was worried about spending a lot of money. He could handle that.

"Nobody *needs* this, Blair. And it won't bring us happiness or make us any more satisfied. There's always bigger and better. I know that." He tried to put it into words without letting her see the shadows that still lingered from so long ago. "But I wanted something special. I've never had a home, remember?"

"But your condo? What about it?" She sank down on one of the steps that led to the Jacuzzi and, after a moment, Gabe sat beside her. "It wasn't anything like this."

"It wasn't home. It was a stopping place. I needed a place to sleep and it did the job." That was all it had been. The knowledge hit him with amazement. It didn't have the warmth, the welcome that Mac's little farmhouse offered, in spite of the ridiculous cost.

"Gabe, don't take this the wrong way, okay?" She laid a hand on his arm in supplication, her dark eyes glowing in the fading light. "You've gone to a lot of trouble here.

And a lot of expense. You already know how much I love swimming. And that jungle gym area you had set up for Daniel is wonderful. I know he'll enjoy it, but…" Her voice trailed away, her forehead furrowed. "It's too much," she finished at last. "I don't want him to become, well, jaded."

"You mean jaded like me?" It hurt to have her say such things, but he needed to get it out into the open.

"No." Her head swung slowly, thoughtfully from side to side. "I don't think you're jaded. But a lot of your friends were. They had no pity left for a homeless person or a fellow who was down on his luck. They couldn't see past their own selfish lives to the bounty they enjoyed. I don't want Daniel to grow up like that. I want him to understand that love is more important than any of that."

Gabe thought about the little boy for a moment and let his lips turn up at the remembrance. "I think Daniel already has that fact firmly established. And I'm not trying to buy his affection, Blair. Please don't think that." Her hand was still on his arm, sending little prickles of heat straight to his chest. He shifted a bit so that he could entwine his fingers with hers. "Maybe I'm not saying this properly."

"Just say whatever's on your mind." Her perfume, soft and enticing, drifted across to him. "I'll try to understand."

He studied her beautiful face for a moment, then gave in to temptation and told her what was in his heart. "I don't know anything about building a family, Blair. I never knew what that was like. But, I think it's what I want." He swallowed hard, then pushed on.

"I thought if I could get this part of it right, the building, the rooms, the places for everyone so they'll be comfortable here, well—" he stopped, hating to go on, to show how much he needed her to help him with this "—I figured maybe you could do the rest of it." It came out in a rush.

Blair frowned at him, curling tendrils of her glossy hair tumbling about her face and down her neck. "I could do what?" she asked in confusion.

"The family part. Or at least, you could teach me. You and Willie and Mac. You're good at it."

Her fingers tightened around his for just a moment. He stared at them, then looked into her eyes. To his surprise she had tears glistening on her lashes.

"I can't make us a family, Gabe."

His heart sank to his heels at the death knell of those words. His head dropped to his chest. He'd known, deep down, that it couldn't work, that he was asking too much, giving too little. Blair didn't care about money. He'd always known that, though he'd pretended otherwise. Why would she be any different now? Why would his castle make any difference to her feelings for him?

"I understand." He eased himself away from her, preparing to get up as he loosened his fingers and let hers slip away. It was just like his dream—slipping out of his grasp.

"Gabe?"

He froze, preparing himself for her chastising. "Yes?"

"No one person can *make* a family. It's a give-and-take relationship. And it takes time. We can't just automatically be a family because you want it."

"I know." He didn't look at her, but kept his eyes on the rough floorboards, still unfinished. A work in progress—just like him.

"We'll have to work at it. Hard. We'll have to be prepared to give in sometimes. We can't run away when times get tough. We've got to keep working through the problems. That's how families are made. It's the rough times that make you solid, seal the bonds."

New life surged through his brain. Was she offering to help him? He waited, his heart racing a hundred miles an hour. Moments later her warm, dainty hand crept inside his.

"There aren't any guarantees with marriage, Gabe. I can't promise that it will always be sunshine or that you'll like everything that happens. I can't make the past all better."

"I know." He held her fingers fast, drawing air into his starved lungs as he listened to her words, heard the tentativeness in her voice.

"But I can promise that I'll stay here. I promise that I won't give up and run away. If you really want this, I'll do my best to make it work."

He fingered the ring on her finger, twirled it, caught a beam of light in it and let it play over the wood. And all the while he tried to control the emotion that made him want to bawl like a baby.

"I really want this, Blair." He forced himself to meet her steady regard. "I promise that I won't take off, won't fly into a tantrum, won't demand my own way all the time. I'll stick it out until you tell me to go. I'll be the best father and husband I can possibly be." He gulped down the fear. "There's just one thing."

She smiled that goofy, lopsided smile. "With you there always is. Well?"

"Don't expect perfection. I have no idea how things are supposed to work. I know diddly about family life and even less about being a father. If I'm doing it wrong, promise you'll tell me."

"Oh, I'll tell you." She smirked at him, then her face grew serious. "There's no 'supposed to' about this, Gabe. We make up our own rules as we go along. Nobody has all the answers except God, and if we trust in Him and keep pushing, we'll figure it out together. Okay?"

"Very okay." He slipped an arm around her waist and hugged her close, swallowing when she hugged him back in that free, generous, nondemanding way her family had. "Can I kiss you?" The words slipped out before he had time to think about the inadvisability of asking such a thing.

Gabe stared at her perfectly sculpted face and wondered when this need had begun to grow inside. He wanted to hold her close, to protect her, to keep her safe. But mostly he just wanted to hold her.

"I guess." She shrugged at his startled look. "Nothing has gone the way I expected lately. Everything seems bigger than life."

"Is this a bad time to tell you that there's going to be a hot tub at the end of the pool?" Gabe held his breath. To his amazement, she burst out laughing.

"Always full of surprises." She cocked her head, then slipped her arms around his shoulders. "If you're kissing me, you'd better get started. I hear the pitter-patter of Daniel's feet."

Gabe leaned forward and kissed her. As kisses went,

it wasn't a ten. For one thing, he almost missed her lips. For another, he felt choked up with emotions of all kinds, and he didn't want her to guess that her words had touched him so deeply.

But the beginning of the kiss didn't matter. When his lips touched hers, it was perfect, right. He knew she was everything he'd wanted in his life, beauty, joy and a zest for the future. Maybe with Blair he could finally find some measure of peace.

"They're kissin' again," Daniel chirped from the doorway, making it sound as if his parents did little else.

Which, as far as Gabe was concerned, wasn't a bad idea at all. Not half bad.

Three weeks later, Blair sat in the upper balcony of the little church she'd grown up in and listened as the organist practiced for the Sunday service. There was no one around, no one to take her mind off her thoughts. No reason to mask the guilt.

You don't trust Gabriel Sloan. You don't need him— not really. You don't believe he's going to stick around. Why act as if you do?

Her conscience kept asking the same questions over and over.

Why pretend you've forgiven him when you know perfectly well that you're still nursing a grudge?

Blair sighed, the old anger at his cavalier treatment of her youthful innocence welling up anew. She shifted uncomfortably, remembering those moments at the castle when he'd opened up to her just the tiniest bit. He'd done that because he thought she trusted him. And she didn't. Not as she should trust the man she was marrying in a few weeks.

"Is everything okay, honey?" Aunt Willie slipped in beside her and lifted one hand to brush away the tear that had fallen to Blair's cheek. "I know you think my pills make it so I don't see and hear a lot of what goes on, and maybe I don't. But can't you tell me why you're crying? I promise I'll try to understand."

"It's so hard, Willie." When Blair dashed a hand across her eyes she caught the flash of Gabe's diamond. The tears wouldn't stop. "He's done nothing wrong, nothing. He's really trying. He goes to Grandpa for advice, he's never angry or pushy with Daniel, he's really attempting to work through our problems."

"We're talking about Gabriel, of course?" Her aunt nodded her graying head. "And yet you still can't forgive him, can you?"

"It hurts, Willie. It really hurts. I loved him so much. I'd poured myself into that relationship, and he just threw it away. Now he walks back into my life and expects to pick up the threads. How can I do that? How can I just let it all go and say, 'Okay, Gabe, we'll be married. No problem. Let bygones be bygones'? I can't stop asking why. Why wasn't my love enough for him? Why did he need the protection of his money?" The words wouldn't stop. "Why did God let me go through that?"

"Because you needed to learn a lesson? Maybe to help you grow strong and rely on Him." Willie stared at the picture of Christ in the garden that hung above the choir section. "Honey, you know that Grandpa and I think the world of you, that we love you more than life, don't you?" She waited for Blair's nod. "And I would never purposely choose to hurt you, unless it was for your own good." Blair made a face. "Uh-oh."

"You know what I mean." Willie leaned back and closed her eyes. "You're one of those people who need to feel useful, who need to *do*. You know I'm right."

"Yes, you are. But there's nothing wrong with that. Somebody's got to do things." Blair rushed to defend herself.

"Of course they do, dear. I'm not saying it's bad. I'm just wondering if perhaps, well, you get so busy *doing* that you're starting to believe your works are what make you strong. I've seen you almost run yourself ragged these past few weeks, hurrying here and there, trying to keep so busy you won't have time to think."

"I guess I don't know what you're saying." Blair watched the sun flicker across the stained glass windows, highlighting scenes from Jesus's life. "You think I should just sit and do nothing?"

"I think you should lean on God instead of your own strength. I don't know what's changed in Gabe's life. I don't know why he suddenly feels he has to start over, begin a new life. Maybe we'll never know. But I believe this is an opportunity for you."

Blair frowned, twiddling one curl around her finger as she studied her aunt. "An opportunity to do what?"

"To get past the past. To believe that God has forgiven that sin and that He doesn't see it anymore. He's already done it, but you're acting as if you can't accept His gift of grace."

"I am?" Blair considered the words while privately acknowledging the sting they brought to her heart. So even Willie had seen her bitterness.

"Aren't you? Isn't that what this taking care of everybody is about? You're trying to make yourself worthy of love, and you already are worthy. God loves you just the way you are."

"But I get so mad at him. Why wasn't he like this before? Why wasn't I smarter? Oh, I mess up so much!" The tears welled as the secret grudge inside her shifted until it was under the microscope of her heart.

"Sweetheart, we all mess up. Me more than most. You think you should be perfect and you want to know why God doesn't make you more like Him." Willie waited until Blair nodded. "He is, my darling. Every day. He's just not finished yet. But until He is, His grace is sufficient to overcome all of your flaws."

"But I'm not worthy of loving. I know He died for my sins, but I just keep on sinning. I get angry at Gabe when he tries to fit into our lives, when he assumes that we can be a family just because he wants it. How can I be a child of God and still do that?"

"Because you're human. And because you won't give up on this belief that you can earn love. You can't earn love, my dear. I don't love you because of what you've done for me. I just love you. That's it. No strings attached." Willie picked up Blair's hands, touching the diamond as she spoke.

"Listen. When Jesus died, He knew what He was taking on. He saw the sins you would commit, now and in the future. He knew all of that. And He forgave you. He took your place. You're not a prisoner anymore. You can walk away from guilt, stop worrying about being worthwhile. He loves you as you are." Willie squeezed her hand hard. Her voice dropped. "The problem is, you don't want to extend that same grace to Gabe."

The words hit hard, scoring a direct blow on the bubbling cauldron of anger and retaliation that gurgled inside Blair's heart, begging release. She sighed, kicking her toe against the carpet.

"I want to believe that Gabe is sincere, Willie. I want to believe that he thinks more of Daniel and me than his company. I want to believe that I can rely on him. But I just can't. The past *isn't* past! It's right here beside me every day, every time I see him."

"Then let it go. Trust that God is in control and that He will work all things together for good. Give Gabe your trust." Willie's eyes fixed on her steadily, holding her gaze.

"How?" Blair mumbled, trying to look away but not succeeding. "How am I supposed to do that?"

"You know how, Blair. Deep in your heart, you know. Let go of the grudge. It's eating at you, ruining your joy. You can't change the past. You can't make it better. You only have now." Willie's fingers were gentle on her shoulder. "If you can't trust Gabe, you can trust God. Leave Gabe to Him."

It was hard to even think about what Willie, in her own quiet way, was suggesting.

"You want me to offer to sign the prenuptial agreement he had drawn up before, don't you? You think it will prove something to him." Blair crossed her arms and sprawled back on the pew. "You want me to go into this marriage with nothing, no guarantees, no plans to protect my son?"

"Isn't that how you were prepared to go into it before?"

Willie's bright eyes demanded an answer. "You said it was Gabe who wanted the guarantees. That you just wanted to love him. Now you have that chance. Grab it with both hands and stop worrying about what could happen."

Blair reflected on the past weeks, how she'd tried to show Gabe how good she was, good at mothering, good at caring for her grandfather, good at caring for Albert when he needed it; and how bad he was for forcing her into this situation.

"Gabe's just as scared as you, but with more reason. I believe he's never known the love of a family, never been freely given anything. He thinks he has to buy in. That's why the money's so important. It's his ticket to love." Willie rose to her feet and snatched up her purse.

"I promised I'd meet a friend for coffee five minutes ago. I've got to go." She hugged Blair in a tight, throat-clogging hug that told her niece how much she cared. "I want you to be happy, honey. Go into this marriage giving something that costs you dearly. Help Gabe understand that love can't be bought or sold. And remember that, no matter what, Mac and I love you."

"Thank you, Auntie." Blair let her go with a watery smile. "Bye. Have a good visit. I'm going to sit here for a while."

Willie hurried away, and Blair listened to the stairs creak as her aunt bustled downstairs. When all was silent, she let herself dwell on the idea.

Sign the prenuptial when he hadn't even asked? Give up all of her rights, all of Daniel's to help him believe in her love?

"I don't think I can do it, God," she whispered

brokenly. "He owes me that, at least. Is it so wrong to want a little bit of security for my son? Anyway, for all I know, he isn't going to ask me to do that again."

The tears fell unchecked as she wrestled with it. Then her eyes caught sight of the scripture verse sprawled across the front of the church in bold, black letters.

My grace is sufficient for you.

Enough to forgive the times she'd ignored Gabe? Enough to forget the way he'd just let her leave seven years ago? Enough to cover her sarcastic, cutting retorts?

My grace is sufficient.

She could take it or leave it, believe what the Bible said or muddle things up trying to find her own answers. God had done His part. It didn't say His grace *was,* but *is* sufficient. For everything. All the time. If she didn't accept it, was that God's fault?

A line from the pastor's sermon rang around the room as if he'd just spoken it.

"How do you react upon learning that God would rather die than live without you? You can't earn that kind of love."

Blair felt the tears pouring down her face and knew that she'd been trying too hard. She wasn't worthy of love. She never would be. But God loved her anyway. So did Mac and Willie and Daniel. It was time to accept that love and do something with it.

Heavy footsteps made the stairs to the balcony groan. Blair hurriedly dashed away her tears, but stayed where she was.

"Blair? Are you all right? Willie said you were up here thinking. Is it something I've done?" Gabe stood at the end of the pew, his big body partially bent as he tried to stand under the sloping roof. One hand reached out and a finger brushed across her cheek. "You've been crying," he whispered in wonder.

"Just a little." She clasped his hand in hers and tugged. "Can you sit down for a minute, Gabe? I need to say something."

His face tightened, and little worry lines crisscrossed his forehead, but he sat, his fingers still cradled in hers.

"I have to say I'm sorry," she began. It felt good to let go of that tight ball of anger.

"You're sorry? For what?" He stared at her as if he didn't recognize her.

"For nursing a grudge against you all these years. For making things hard for you ever since you've come." She hung her head in shame. "For trying to embarrass you in front of Mac and Willie and Albert so that you'd be uncomfortable. For not telling you about Daniel." The last words oozed out on a whisper of regret. "I stole those years from you, and I had no right to do that."

He reared back, his eyes bubbling with emotion. "No right? You had every right! I'm the one who should be apologizing."

She smiled at his one-upmanship. "Just let me finish."

"Sorry." He stared at their entwined fingers. "Go ahead."

"I want what you do. I want Daniel to have a father and mother who care about him, who do everything they can to make his world happy." *Please, God, help me.*

"What are you really saying, Blair?" Hope glimmered in the depths of his emerald eyes. His fingers tensed on hers.

She couldn't do it—couldn't say the words that would tell him how much she needed him. Something, some tiny reminder of the past, yanked her from the precipice of truth. What if he laughed? What if he left? She temporized.

"I'm saying that I will try as hard as I can to make this marriage work. I don't know how things will work out, how we'll manage everything, but I'll do my best to make sure Daniel sees you in a positive light. I trust you, Gabe."

Sometime during her little speech his eyes had moved to her face. As she spoke they seemed to dim a little, flicker, then cloud over, as if he was disappointed in what she'd said.

"That's all I can hope for," he murmured, dropping her hands. He shoved his into his jacket pockets. "I won't abuse your trust, Blair. I promise I'll do the right thing this time."

He stood, staring at her. One hand reached out to touch her hair in a featherlight caress that sent a tiny shock to her heart. He seemed to want to say more, but couldn't find the words. She thought he would kiss her, but then that fraction of a second was gone. At last he spoke.

"Are you ready to go?"

She nodded, gathered her things and trailed him down the stairs. "I have to stop at the florist's to make sure everything's under control. Could you pick up Daniel, then meet me at the grocery store?"

"Of course." He stood in the foyer, staring at the

sanctuary. "I never went to church regularly, you know. Only with you and because of you. I never thought I was the type who needed it."

Blair waited, breath suspended. He was going to tell her something about himself, something important. She forced herself to stand perfectly still and wait.

"My mother died when I was five. I think my father must have loved her very much. But when God didn't cure her, he sort of turned on the church and everyone in it. Mom made sure I went to Sunday school every week, but my father didn't care if I never went. We started to move around a lot, and I didn't know how to get to the church, so I stopped going. By the time I was old enough to go on my own, I didn't see the need."

He'd said *my father.* Not *dad* or *my dad.* The rock solid steadiness of his voice and the rigid line of his jaw told Blair how much he'd kept to himself.

"I think he was upset that God hadn't taken me and left her."

Blair sucked in a breath of dismay at the horrible words, but she didn't interrupt. He needed to get this out. Somehow she sensed that this festering sore was best treated in the healing light of the present, just as she'd had to face her own hidden anger.

"I was never the kind of son he wanted, you see. I was lousy at his favorite game, basketball. I had no head for baseball statistics, and I was too gawky and introspective to be put on show. I liked books. He hated reading anything but the sports page. I was too curious. I messed things up, and he had to pay to get them fixed." His eyes were almost blank, staring at her as he related his past with detachment.

"What kind of things, Gabe?" She tried to draw him out.

"What? Oh, toasters, his calculator, the radio and television. He sent me to my room for a day for that." Gabe smiled a cold, hard little smile that didn't reach the ice in his eyes. "He did me a favor by doing that. I spent those hours reading up on all kinds of stuff. I guess I was a little too old for my age."

Blair nodded. She knew from their discussions in the past that his IQ was very high. She could imagine how little that endeared him to a man who thought sports was the be-all and end-all.

"He said I needed to learn responsibility, that I'd been babied. I got a paper route and squirreled every dime away. Finally I had enough to get an old, used computer when I was in eighth grade. A teacher at school lent me some parts, and I built Fred."

"I didn't know that." Blair stared at him. "The same Fred you have now?"

He grinned, life surging into his eyes. "Well, not exactly the same Fred. I've changed almost everything inside him about a hundred times, but he's still Fred. He was my playmate, my best friend when we moved too often for me to have friends." He frowned at her. "I don't know how I got started on this. I was talking about Sunday school, wasn't I?"

She nodded, disappointed that he'd closed the door to his past.

"Anyway, last year I got caught behind a car accident. I had to wait until someone could come and tow my car and, since there was a church across the road, I decided to go in and listen to the singing. They had this choir…" He closed his eyes as if remembering that day.

"You always did love music," Blair murmured, loath to break into his happy thoughts.

"Yeah. Well, anyway, they had more than good music there. They had a speaker who made sense of the Bible and God. I finally understood what my mother had taught me all those years before. We got to be friends, Jake Prescott and I. He needed some tech support, and I offered to help."

"He got the president of the company to fix his computer?" Blair blinked. "But you always hated that aspect, the one-on-one."

"This wasn't like that. It was more like two pals. Jake would toss in a comment about a computer being like God with all His intricacies. I guess you had to be there." He shrugged, his cheeks flushing a dark red.

"Anyway, he got me thinking about how I was living my life. He made it sound as if I was as much a pleasure seeker as my dad. I hated that, so I started to rethink things. I came to the decision that I needed to make God the center of my life. I just wanted you to know that we're on the same wavelength. I'm not exactly the same as I was. I'm not pretending Christianity anymore, Blair. It's the real thing now."

She looped her arm through his, giving it a squeeze. "Thank you for telling me that," she whispered as she choked back tears. "It's important to me to know that we're on the same team. I know Mac will be glad when I tell him."

"I've already done that. Your beliefs echo his. I didn't want him to think I'd try to alter that." He looked at her searchingly, his thoughts masked from her. Only the tiny quaver in his voice gave away his uncertainty. "Do you really think we can make this marriage work?"

She wasn't sure at all. But Gabe needed her. She knew it. "If we go in determined to make it work and rely on God's help, I know we can manage." She held her breath when his arm slipped around her waist. "Gabe?"

"I think this is the perfect place to make that pledge," he whispered as his mouth moved nearer. "I promise I won't do anything to make you regret marrying me, Blair. You can trust me."

"I do," she whispered, just before his lips touched hers. Then she gave herself up to the gentle reassurance of his kiss, shoving away the niggling voice that prodded, *Do you?*

Really?

Chapter Six

May seventh, his wedding day. Gabe stared as Jake Prescott, his best man, fraternized with the assembled crowd of townspeople. He shook his head in disbelief.

"I thought Teal's Crossing had a population of five hundred," he whispered to Blair. Her light scent caught on the breeze and carried straight to his nostrils, teasing him with the delicate fragrance of flowers mixed with something spicy. He didn't know what it was, but he liked it.

"It does. But the community is more than the town. Does that bother you?" Blair stood in front of him posing for the picture, her head tilted back. She smiled, and her whole face glowed with the warmth of the sun. And maybe something else. Maybe—happiness?

He thought about it for a moment, then shook his head. "I couldn't care less how many people are here," he told her honestly. "I know they came to see what kind of an outsider you're marrying, what kind of a father Daniel's getting. They're your friends, they naturally want to check me out."

He listened to the photographer's request, then

twisted his arms around her waist, clasping them together under hers, which still held her bouquet. In a bold move, he bent his head and pressed a featherlight kiss to her shoulder. This was the first time he dared such an intimacy, only because he could pretend to her that the photographer was the reason.

"Thank you, Blair," he whispered, resting his chin against the tulle of her wedding veil. He was totally awed by the fact that this gorgeous woman was his wife. Their relationship wasn't exactly the way he wanted it. Underneath her assurances, he knew that she still mistrusted him, still checked to be sure he meant what he said. She still wouldn't let herself need him.

But it was changing. Little by little Blair was getting used to him in her life again.

"For what?" A glossy tendril brushed against his forehead, teasing him.

"For marrying me. For helping me with Daniel. For everything." He felt a surge of something warm and protective well inside. It wasn't love, he knew that. But it was still a good feeling.

"You're welcome." The whisper barely carried on the breeze. "Here he comes again."

Gabe stayed exactly where he was as Daniel raced up to them, jerked to a stop and held out the cushion that had carried their wedding bands earlier that afternoon. He looked so cute in his little black tuxedo, vest and bow tie that Gabe couldn't stop his proud fatherly smile. It widened even more when Daniel spoke to him.

"Hey, Dad, can I get rid of this? I'm tired of hauling it around." He thrust the creamy satin cushion toward them, his dark eyes sparkling. "What do you think, Dad?"

Daniel took every opportunity to use the term *Dad,* often repeating it to himself before he fell asleep. It was as if he couldn't believe God had answered his prayer.

Gabe looked over Blair's shoulder at the little boy, and suddenly he knew exactly how Daniel felt. The truth dawned like a white-hot light searing his brain. This, right here, was everything he'd ever wanted. He was part of it. He felt a tender but fierce protectiveness surge through him. His arms tightened fractionally around Blair's waist.

So he couldn't feel love, so what? He'd give everything he had to make this work. He had to believe that it would be enough for Blair and for Daniel.

"Sure you can, son. Give the cushion to Mac. He'll put it away till your mom has time to look after it." Gabe reached out and tousled the stick-straight hair, then grinned as Daniel jerked away.

"How come you don't have these pretty curls like your mother?" he asked, fingering one delicate strand as it lay against Blair's neck. When she shifted just a bit, he let his arms fall away but kept her hand wrapped in his.

"That's girl hair!" Daniel's voice oozed disgust. "You 'n' me are boys, Dad. We got boy hair."

"You sure are." Blair wiggled her hand out of Gabe's, then reached down and straightened the bow tie. She smiled when it immediately tipped to the right. "Your father has the same problem as you." She turned to face Gabe, her fingers plucking at his tie. "But just the same, you're both very good-looking."

He caught her fingers and held on, the whirring and snap of the camera a faint buzz in the background.

"We're not good-lookin'," Daniel said, obviously disgusted by that assessment. "We're han'some. Aren't we, Dad?"

"You're very handsome, son," Gabe answered, tongue in cheek.

"Girls are good-looking, Mom. Not guys. Right, Dad?"

Daniel's scathing voice drew Gabe's attention from Blair. Which was probably a good thing. He had a feeling he'd been staring at his wife again. Lately he couldn't seem to stop. She fascinated him. Her delicate but strong fingers, her tiny, efficient body, her quick brain.

"Hey, are we gonna get a girl for our family?" Gabe straightened, his attention divided between Daniel and Blair as he considered the request. It was true, Blair didn't immediately tell the boy no, but it was also apparent that she was uncomfortable with the question. He'd have to step in.

Gabe let go of her hand and knelt in front of this precious child, swiping back a hank of Daniel's hair as he did.

"Nobody can know the future, son. We don't know what's going to happen. We just know that today is the first day for us to be a family. Let's enjoy that, okay?"

"Okay." Daniel grinned his half toothless smile and then raced away. He hurried back for just a moment. "I'm going to play with Joey Lancaster." In a whirl of black he was gone, his muddy shoes testament to his lack of concern for the rented suit.

"Joey Lancaster?" Gabe got to his feet, his eyes searching Blair's. "Isn't he the kid Daniel didn't like?"

"Was." She walked beside him over the lush green grass and toward the church. "They're best buds now that Daniel has a father, too." The photographer stopped them beneath a late-blossoming apple tree.

"Oh." Gabe digested that for a moment, amazed at the changes that had come into all their lives. He ignored the camera, though he heard it whirring madly behind them.

"I like your dress. It suits you." He fingered the delicate silk petals sewn over her shoulder, tracing a line to her waist. "It looks simple, but even I can see that it's really quite complex. And very delicate." His fingers traced the ethereal silk chiffon. "It's like you."

"I'm not that complex. Not really." Blair shook her head, curls bouncing. "And I'm not delicate at all. I'm pretty tough. But thank you."

"Are you glad Willie insisted on a traditional wedding?" He grinned at her fingers squeezing the bouquet he'd flown in. "Complete with orange blossoms."

She rolled her eyes. "That was your idea. All I wanted was to be married in a church by a minister with my family nearby." She glanced at the branch hanging over them. "And now it's apple blossoms."

He joined in her laughter, content to share the joy of the moment.

"Everything else about this wedding sort of mushroomed. Mostly because of Willie. She's wanted to do this for ages. I just couldn't stop her."

Gabe glanced to where the older woman stood talking to a group of women, who craned their necks in his direction every so often. Great-Aunt Willie was clearly bragging about her nephew-in-law. He felt a surge of pride suffuse his heart.

"Well, boy. You did it!" Mac bustled toward them, his leathery face wreathed in smiles. "You're glad I sold you that land now, aren't you, son?"

"Yes, sir," Gabe agreed softly, his eyes on his wife. "I'm very glad."

Blair was immediately claimed by Clarissa and Briony, her attendants. They seemed eager to discuss the origins of her dress. Since Gabe knew very few of the locals and even less about wedding dresses, he walked away from the crowd, anxious to snag a few minutes on his own. He shoved his hand into his pocket and felt the sheaf of papers his lawyer had sent for Blair to sign.

Somehow, in all the fuss and confusion, Gabe had forgotten to ask her if she'd sign them.

No, he reminded himself, that wasn't true. He hadn't asked her because he hadn't wanted to remember the past, hadn't wanted to go through it all again. Hadn't wanted to tint this perfect day with the ugly memory of another wedding day.

Gabe let his mind go back to that morning in his penthouse seven long, empty years ago. He remembered the way the incandescent shimmer of joy had drained out of Blair's eyes as she'd read the papers he asked her to sign. He remembered how she'd carefully set down the pen, pressed the thick wad of legal papers on top of it and walked away from him toward the door.

"You don't trust me, Gabe." The hurt on her face still got to him. "You think that by signing that prenuptial agreement I will somehow prove to you that I'm not out to get you, that I won't ever hurt you." She'd shaken her head, that glorious hair tumbling around her shoulders. When she spoke again her husky voice was cracked and broken.

"I can't promise that, my darling. I probably will hurt you. Oh, I won't mean to. But one day I'll do something that will really cut deep and then you'll start to wonder if I'm just pretending, if I'm really after your company or your money. That's what it's all about, Gabriel, isn't it? Your precious money?" One small hand dashed away the tears that dimmed her telltale eyes. "You love your money more than me."

He'd denied it, of course. Tried to reason with her, to tell her that he cared for her. But Blair was adamant, and just as stubborn as he. She would not accept his argument that he was only following legal advice.

"I don't care a fig about your money," she'd insisted. "But nothing I can do is ever going to prove that. You have to trust me, Gabe. You have to take me as I am and believe that I want only the best for you. I won't go into this marriage with a way out already in place, with the steps to divorce already outlined. I won't start off expecting to fail. When I get married, it will be for life, to the one person who feels about me as I do about him."

She'd waited for him to say something then, but Gabe had no words. The fear was like a big cannonball lodged in the depths of his stomach. What if she was like all the others in his life? What if it was all an act, a way to get what she really wanted—not him, but his money? He'd have nothing again. He would have reverted to that sniveling little boy who had always disappointed his father.

"You have to start this marriage with faith, Gabe. That's the only way I'll ever be your wife. Think about it. I'll be waiting. If I don't hear from you, the wedding is off."

Well, he'd started this one with faith, though his lawyer would go crazy when he found out. He was taking a risk, of course. Blair might end up cleaning him out, taking everything he'd worked so hard to achieve.

Gabe shook his head. The idea was preposterous. She hadn't allowed him to pay for any part of the wedding.

"The bride's family pays for the wedding," she'd insisted.

Gabe let a tiny smile curve his mouth. Willie had proven a valuable ally. She'd been his eyes and ears, as well as a worthwhile asset, ensuring Blair wasn't forced to do without anything she wanted. He'd have to remember to thank her. Privately, of course.

Gabe perched on a rock by the creek, his finger rubbing against the band she'd placed there just a half hour before.

"The best man wants to know if the groom finally got cold feet." Jake's laughing voice penetrated his thoughts as his big, beefy arm thunked Gabe on the shoulder. "It's a bit late now."

"No cold feet, buddy. This is the first right thing I've done in a long time." Gabe waited while Jake found a rock to land his bulky body on. "You know I've been praying for an answer, and then God sent me here, thanks to Mac."

"'All things work together,'" Jake reminded him with a grin. "I must say she's a beauty. And that kid of yours is a real heart-tugger. You're going to have to be on your toes to live up to all that admiration."

"Don't I know it." Gabe felt the fear snake up his spine. "I haven't got a clue how to do that."

"Who does?" Jake shrugged. "Most men learn as they go, though they usually start with a baby and work their way up."

Gabe felt the heat singe his face. He grimaced. "Don't remind me," he muttered. "I know all about my sins."

Jake burst out laughing. "If God can forgive, I think you can, don't you?" He waited a moment, then reminded Gabe, "And if He's on your side, the battle's already won."

"It's just that I'm afraid Daniel will wake up one morning and realize that I'm as big a phony as my old man."

Jake frowned. "I don't know what you mean. You're nothing like him. I've seen you with Daniel, don't forget."

Gabe swallowed. "You know my problem, buddy. I'm not the type of guy who needs people. In fact, I function better without them. Nobody gets disappointed that way."

"How do you know? Ever stick around long enough to find out?" Jake shook his head at Gabe. "I know, I know. You think you're not capable of love. That it's not in you. That it got killed or something when you were a kid." He snorted. "That's a bunch of hooey."

"A bunch of what?" Gabe blinked at the vehemence in his friend's voice.

"Hooey. Malarkey. Garbage, pal. Pure and simple. God doesn't make people like robots or computer chips. He makes them with a heart and soul. Your heart isn't dead or frozen or any of those other things you keep thinking." The assurance in Jake's voice rang pure and clear.

"God is your real Father, Gabriel. He's not going to let you miss out on one of the best experiences a human can have. Just relax, enjoy your new family one day at a time. The time will come when you'll wake up and realize that somehow, some way, love got rooted inside of you and it won't let you go. You'll realize that the only person you want by your side for the rest of your life is Blair. Every moment you spend with her will seem like a miracle." He grinned at Gabe's surprise.

"What do you know about it, Jake?" he demanded, pessimism niggling into his brain.

"A pastor learns these things." Jake winked. "Sometimes it pops up in front of you so quick it knocks you off your feet, and sometimes it takes a while to push through the hard rocky soil. It'll come. Just have faith in God's leading."

"Easy for you to say." Gabe eyed him suspiciously. "Anything you want to confess, buddy? Somebody special knocked you off your feet?"

Jake ignored the question. "You can't control love, Gabriel. God's in control, and things work best when you don't apply for His job."

"Who is it?" Gabe leaned forward, intent on guessing. "The pianist? Marion something?" He chuckled at the glimmer of light in the other man's eyes. "I knew you two had something going."

"We do not have something going." Jake glared, his cheeks bright red. "She tolerates me. That's about it. And we're not talking about me, we're talking about you."

"I'm a flop in the people department." Gabe sighed. "Yesterday I made Daniel cry. The day before that Blair nearly decked me. I don't understand what makes them tick. Why didn't God send me a robot? That I could understand, or tear apart until I did?"

Jake burst out laughing. "Life's not nearly as much fun with a robot, Gabe. What did you do, anyway?"

"To Blair?" He shook his head, held his palms up. "I have no clue. I thought I was helping when I told her she should have finished her degree. She's barely scraping by making the candles and honey, and she won't expand because she doesn't want to take on debt. She was holding a pail of honey at the time. I'm lucky I didn't get to wear it, judging by the look on her face." He yanked a despairing hand through his newly short hair. "How am I supposed to help her when I always say the wrong thing?"

"Idiot!" Jake backed off when Gabe glared at him. "Okay, sorry. But think about the past for a minute. She was pregnant—you were no help. What choice did she have but to quit school and go home to have her baby?"

"But after? You have no idea, Jake! She's a fantastic teacher. She made chemistry so much fun when I saw her teach. She's a natural." When he remembered the lights going on in those brains all those years ago, Gabe couldn't believe she'd walked away from it all.

Jake clapped a hand on his shoulder. "You've got

to imagine yourself in her position. Okay, she had the baby. Now she's got to feed him and herself and take care of her kin. She's no doubt still upset, with herself and with you. But worse, she hasn't got any money to go to school, Gabe. She probably even had a few debts, scholarships notwithstanding. You're talking as if she didn't want to go back, when it must have torn her apart to drop out so close to the end."

Gabe shook his head, misery clogging his throat. "Money," he whispered. "It always comes back to money."

"No, it doesn't," Blair interjected as she reappeared. She stood behind Jake, her eyes soft as they met Gabe's. "I wanted to watch Daniel grow, to be there for him. I chose that above college. Someday I'll finish, but it's not a priority."

Jake bounded up from his stone and hugged her, completely disregarding the delicate fabric of her wedding dress. "You're my kind of woman." He chuckled. "Someone who doesn't care about the cash a fellow has. We preachers never seem to have two cents to rub together."

Gabe couldn't say a word. He'd never told Jake about the prenup agreement. He wouldn't now. He only asked himself why Jake was able to so clearly see into Blair's heart when he hadn't.

"Hey, Blair, want to know the most important thing to learn in chemistry?"

She grinned at Jake, her head wagging back and forth in admonishment. "Listen, sonny, I learned that the first day of my first year. *Never lick the spoon.*" She giggled at his downcast look. "Now I've got one for you. How is the world like a beehive?"

Jake frowned. "I don't know anything about bees," he muttered. "It's an unfair question."

"Poor baby! Then I'll give you the answer. We all enter by the same door but live in different cells." She burst into tinkling laughter at his disgruntled look.

"There are some who think that anyone who makes a joke like that should be locked in their cell." Jake's dancing eyes made light of the threat as he hugged her again.

Gabe knew it was time to step in. "May I remind you that this is *my* wife you're hugging? Go after Marion what's-her-name if you need someone to hug." He wrapped his arm possessively around Blair's shoulders. "I can do my own hugging, thank you."

Jake's face grew serious. "I know you can," he murmured softly. "It's nice to see you realize that." Turning to Blair, he bowed gallantly. "I'm leaving you with him, but if you need help, just scream. I'll be glad to dunk him."

"You couldn't," Blair told him, her lips curving in a smile as she glanced at the stream. "It only comes up to his knees."

"Guess I'd have to shorten his legs, then." With that smart rejoinder, Jake ambled across the lawn to talk to Mac.

"I like your friend." Blair turned in the circle of Gabe's arms and met his steady gaze. "He's nice."

"He likes you, too." Gabe studied her beautiful face, accented with just enough makeup to highlight her big brown eyes. Today they seemed even larger and more shimmery. "I'm sorry I said those things about your degree, Blair. Clearly I wasn't thinking straight. It must have been very difficult to manage with a new baby and no income." He felt a stab of regret, but stuffed it away. He couldn't change the past, but he had now. And maybe, God willing, the future.

"It was difficult," she murmured, her hands moving to straighten his cummerbund. "But I'll choose family over anything else every day of the week. That's just the way I am."

"I know." He drew her into his arms and rested his chin on the top of her head. "I thank God for that every time I look at Daniel. You've done a wonderful job with him."

He felt her take a breath.

"Thank you. I had good material."

"I'll try not to mess up, Blair." To his surprise, she pulled back a few inches. Her eyes were darker than ever, her cheeks blazing.

"Will you stop saying that! You're his father, you'll make the decisions you think are proper for him. So will I. I trust you with him, Gabe."

But you don't trust me with you. You think I'll hurt you again.

Gabe brushed his lips against her forehead, then drew her back where she belonged. "Thank you," he whispered, his eyes closed tight as he accepted the tiny crumb of faith she'd just placed in him. It was a start.

They stayed like that for several minutes, the peace of the valley landscape surrounding them, the chattering voices only a few feet away drowned out by the gurgling brook and the babble of birds and squirrels.

"Gabe?" Blair's voice was so soft he almost missed it.

"Yes?"

"Do you think you could kiss me, like a man kisses his new wife, I mean?"

Gabe's eyes flew open in stunned surprise at her hesitant request. At that precise instant he realized their son was about to interrupt. Again.

He tipped her chin up so he could get a good look into her eyes. What he saw there made his stomach quiver.

"I could and I will." He memorized each detail as he spoke, ensuring that she heard what he wasn't saying. "But I'd rather do it when we're alone and can't be interrupted by—"

"Dad! Mom! Come on, Mac says it's time to eat."

Blair shrugged out of the lovely wedding dress and carefully hung it in its protective cover inside the massive cedar-lined closet of her new home. She slipped into her swimsuit, then pulled on her old favorites, a flannel shirt and soft, worn blue jeans. If Gabe wasn't around, she intended to try out that pool.

Seconds later, her sandals clicked against the tile as she slipped out the patio door of the master suite. She paused in the fragrant rose garden and drank in its beauty. Overhead, a blanket of stars twinkled at her in friendly silence.

"How did he do it?" she marveled, walking around the perfectly planned garden.

"Sheer brute force. And threats. Lots of threats," Gabe said, coming up behind her in the garden. "I don't take no for an answer. Plus, most of it has been planned for a while." His hands on her shoulders gently eased her to face him.

"I hope it didn't embarrass you that the men I hired

to transport everything put all your things in there. I thought we'd split the suite. I've been sleeping in the dressing room. I'll stay there."

She nodded, having already suspected this was his plan. Gabe was a proud man. He wouldn't want anyone speculating on his private life. "Is Daniel asleep?"

"Totally conked out. He was in the middle of asking me another question when his mouth drooped and he was out of it." Gabe laughed softly. "He's quite a kid."

"He certainly loves this place." Blair grinned. "And why not? How many kids do you know who have their own private pool, not to mention that playground. He's going to spend tomorrow racing back and forth from one to the other. You'll have to teach him to swim."

Gabe's hands dropped away from her arms. The jerk of his body, the sudden chilly silence made her frown. What was wrong now?

"Gabe? What is it?"

"You'll have to teach him. I can't." Ice shivered through the words.

"But I meant when you learn. I wasn't…all right." Blair wouldn't argue. But something was wrong here. "Is there some reason you don't want to teach him?" she asked carefully.

"A pretty good one, actually." His mocking voice told her how upset he was. "I can't swim."

She vaguely recalled his past words. "Yes, I know. You were going to teach yourself. But, then, why such a big pool? A status symbol?" That explained it. Only the best for Gabe Sloan.

"No!" He exploded, his face contorted into a mask of fury. "I couldn't care less about symbols." He stomped down the path toward the stream that ran behind the garden, his shoulders hunched defensively.

Blair waited a few minutes, then followed him. This wasn't what she'd expected, but she'd promised to be there in good times or bad. Tonight was clearly the latter.

"Gabe?" She found him on the little white bridge that gave a view of the waterfall in the distance. Someone had installed a floodlight, and the sight was breathtaking. Blair decided to check it out another night. She faced him. "Please tell me what's wrong. I'll help if I can."

He snorted, but his voice sounded less harsh. "You can't help. No one can. It's in the past, but I can't let it go." When she didn't say anything, he turned to her, fury darkening his eyes to emerald chips. "I thought I could prove that I was more than what he said, that I didn't botch everything. I thought, Blair swims. She even likes it. I can do that. I'll get a pool and I'll learn to swim. I'll swim in it every day. That'll prove I'm not a wimp, a loser."

Blair almost laughed at his words, then realized he was deathly serious. This was a situation that needed defusing. Now.

"A wimp?" She made herself laugh. "You? How ridiculous! Clearly whoever said that didn't know you at all."

The words seemed to draw him out of his rage, calm him. He turned to her with a question in his eyes.

"Well, think about it. There aren't too many wimps who build a company out of nothing, take on the competitor and buy them out, let their father fleece them out of hundreds of thousands of dollars and still come out on top." She rolled her eyes at his frown. "I read about it. So sue me." She veered back to the subject of this contretemps. "Something is wrong with your picture, Gabe."

She stood beside him in the night, oblivious to the croaking frogs all around them, hearing nothing except the tortured note in his voice.

"How does your not being able to swim fit into this picture, Gabe?" She leaned her elbows on the rail and cupped her chin in her palms while she waited for him to open up. How had she never suspected he had such scars? Why had she never seen them buried under his quiet dignity?

Because you weren't looking for his good side. You only wanted to see his faults.

"I'm not leaving until you tell me," she informed him when long minutes passed without any words.

"Sometimes you are so…bossy. Stay out of it, Blair."

His teeth were clenched. She could see his hand fisting on the wood right next to hers. And suddenly she realized that this wasn't just about the past, it affected the present, too.

"I'm not out of it. I'm married to you. We have a son. This concerns all of us. I want to know why it's so important to be able to swim."

"No." His foot scraped across the wood, signaling that he intended to leave.

"Yes." She stood erect, facing him in the gloomy light. "We're in this together. No secrets, no lies. No pretending. Just honesty. That is what you said today, isn't it?"

He huffed and puffed, but finally sighed his agreement. "Some day you're going to have to learn to back off."

She nodded. "Okay. Some day I will. But not tonight." She took his hand and led him to a patio chair near the pool. "Sit down and tell me what's wrong."

Blair held her breath. Gabe sat, but his mouth tightened to a grim, thin line. His fingers bit deeply into the cushions of the chair. His face grew tortured.

"I'm scared of the water." The words burst out of him like a dam spilling a lake held too long in abeyance. "I'm a chicken, a coward. I can't stand the thought of it closing over my head." His eyes blazed into hers. "So you see, he was right. I am a wimp."

"Wait a minute. Who is *he?*" There was no point in backing off. She knew that instinctively.

"My father." The cold hate in those words cast a chill on the lovely evening.

"And how did he manage to equate being afraid of water with a person's worth? Doesn't that seem a little skewed to you?"

Gabe's head jerked up, his brows joined in a frown. "What?"

"I mean it. The guy obviously has problems or he wouldn't have stolen from you. But since when do you measure yourself against that kind of standard?"

"Since I panic every time I get near the stuff."

Blair tried to pray as she listened, tried to ask for heavenly direction to this very earthly problem. She knew there was something more, something he wasn't saying. Gabe hadn't explained why he was afraid of water. But right now, that didn't matter.

"And you don't want Daniel to see you panicked, is that it?"

His head jerked once in an affirmative.

"Go get your bathing suit on, Gabe."

"What?" He stared at her in worried disbelief. Blair stayed calm. "Look, you've let this rule you for far too long. Fears can be overcome. Everyone has them. It's time to get working on yours." She undid her shirt and slipped off her jeans until she was standing in her swimsuit. "I'll teach you how to swim, Gabe. Go get your suit on."

Some of the tension eased, though his shoulders stayed taut. "You'd do that?"

"Why not? You built this monstrosity. Seems a shame not to get some joy out of it."

His voice barely broke the quiet of the evening. "I was going to force myself, you see. That's why the pool was included in the plans. I was going to acclimatize myself to it, teach myself to take it one step at a time."

"Only you couldn't do it. Of course you couldn't, not by yourself. I'll help you. I love swimming." She sat on the chair. "Go get your suit," she said patiently.

He took his own sweet time, but finally Gabe emerged on the patio in a pair of dark blue swimming trunks.

"I switched on the lights," he told her, his voice losing some of its innate authority as he stared at the glassy-smooth water.

"I saw." Blair got up and walked to the pool's steps. She waited, holding out one hand. "Come on. Let's go in. It's a beautiful night for a swim. Look at those stars."

He didn't look up, he just stared at her. Finally, with effort, he managed to put one foot in front of the other and walk slowly to her side.

"I hate this," he muttered, his eyes blazing as he stepped into the water.

"I love it." She kept walking steadily forward, letting the water slide up her body. "It makes me think of God's love, covering me like a second skin, protecting me."

Gabe searched her eyes, waiting as she walked him deeper into the water. When the water came up to his shoulders, he stopped. "That's enough." His voice was hoarse.

"Okay." She led him back a little way, wincing as she flexed her tightly held fingers. "Gabriel, you are in control here. If you want your head to go under, it will. If you don't want it to, it won't. It's your choice. No one is going to force you."

Blair dipped under the water, then slowly stood, letting it stream down off her head and face. Gabriel stared at her, then, before she could react, dipped himself completely under the water. He came up thrashing wildly, his eyes full of terror, coughing the water from his lungs.

Blair waited until he'd recovered, then smiled. "You have to close your mouth," she whispered tenderly. "You're not going to drown. I won't let you. It's only water. It can't hurt you."

He didn't look convinced.

"Try again," she encouraged. "But this time take a deep breath and don't let it out until your head is out of the water."

"This is stupid." He turned as if to leave.

"What's stupid is letting fear rule your life. It only

makes everything worse." She made no attempt to stop him.

When he got to the steps Gabe halted, then turned back. "It's been there a long time," he told her quietly. "It won't die easily."

"You wouldn't be suffering so much if it were easy." She stood silent, waiting.

Gabe returned, but his mouth was set in a grim line. He gasped a huge breath, ducked his head under and popped up a nanosecond later. "There," he spluttered.

"There what? Are you over the fear? Can you swim here with Daniel now?" She waited.

Gabe muttered something then resolutely forced his head under the water several more times. Each time Blair watched but said nothing.

"When will it be enough for you?" he asked angrily after the last attempt. "I can get my head under. I can stand it. Isn't that enough?"

She shook her head. "While you're under there, your mind screams to get out. You can't swim when you feel like that. You have to relax in the water." Blair took his hand and led him toward the steps. "Sit down here. On this step." When he was up to his neck in water she sat on the step above. "How does it feel?"

"Wet." He let go of the railing long enough to wave a hand through the pattern of light that shone from the bottom. "I should have put in more lights."

"Why? Is there something hiding in the corner? Some monster that will jump out and drown us?" He glared at her in silent anger, but Blair wouldn't give up. "The monsters are here, Gabe." She tapped his head. "It's time to toss them out."

It took a long time, and she was beginning to wish she'd never started this, but finally Gabe sighed.

"All right!" His eyes met hers. "I wasn't much older than Daniel. We'd gone to the lake one weekend. He pushed me out of the boat in the middle of the lake and ordered me to swim to shore. 'Any little wimp can swim, you know.' I had no idea how to stay afloat. I grabbed onto the rope from the anchor but that infuriated him. He grabbed my head and shoved me under. I must have blacked out because the next thing I remember is waking up cold and wet on the shore. He was nowhere around."

The shockingly brutal words stripped away her pretense at nonchalance. Blair could only stare at him in grim commiseration.

"Now you know the truth. Are you happy?"

The biting sarcasm washed off her. He was hurting. And she hurt for him.

"Are you?" she asked softly. "It wasn't the water's fault, Gabe. It was his. Think of it like this—the water is like wings. It buoys us up, lets us travel in ways we never could have without it. It was given to us for our enjoyment. It's one of God's good gifts." She slid one arm along his shoulders. "Lean back against my arm and look up at the sky."

Hesitantly, slowly, Gabe let himself lean back, one hand clinging to the handrail.

"See those stars," she whispered. "They look like thousands of diamonds strewn across God's black velvet cloak. If you keep your eyes on the ground you miss them."

She held him there for a long time, supporting his

head, softly reminding him of all the glories God has provided for his children. When Gabe finally stood, she waited, wondering how far this could go.

Her heart ached for the poor little boy, denied worth by his own father. How could she resent him? How could she add to the misery and suffering he carried still?

"I've had enough. You can swim your lengths if you want. I'll sit here and watch."

Blair nodded and struck out for the deep end, sliding into a smooth, regular front crawl that stretched her muscles and soothed her mind. She'd missed this. The university pool was an extravagance she no longer had when she'd moved home. To be able to swim at night, in the open air, seemed decadent beyond belief.

When at last she could find no more breath, Blair stroked over to the steps and sat beside Gabe, letting the lapping water ease the sting in her chest.

"How did you learn to swim?" Gabe asked.

"Grandpa Mac. My parents died in a boating accident, but he was determined that it wouldn't deprive me of the joy of water. I was about five when he first brought me to the creek. It was freezing cold but he made it all a game. I loved it."

Silence, yawning and cavernous, accentuating the different histories, hung between them. Blair finally got up.

"Good night, Gabe."

His hand on her arm stopped her. He towered over her in the gloom, his eyes glowing. "Thank you," he murmured.

Blair nodded, her smile sincere. "Thank you for the pool. I love it."

She made it to the patio door before his voice stopped her.

"Blair?"

"Yes?" She turned slowly, watched him climb the stairs, pad across the cement.

"I promised you earlier that I'd kiss you when there was plenty of time and no one around to interrupt." He waved a hand. "There's no one else here."

Blair glanced over her shoulder, then nodded. "That's true. They've all gone to bed. First night in their new home. I don't think they'll miss the old place, but we'll leave it there in case one of us needs a hideaway."

"And I've plenty of time."

"So do I." She wouldn't back away, not now. This was not the Gabe she'd known. This man had pushed away her defenses and climbed right into her heart. Whether he knew it or not, he needed her. She wanted him to kiss her.

He stepped forward until there were only millimeters separating them. One hand lifted to cup her chin while the other wrapped itself around her waist. His eyes stared into hers, asking a question. She stared back, hoping he'd understand her answer.

His lips brushed hers in the gentlest of touches before they moved to graze against the tip of her nose and over her eyelashes. They caressed each cheek, then followed the line of her chin to her mouth.

When he finally moved away, he muttered, "It's a good thing nobody saw that. I've been wanting to kiss you for a long time, Blair."

"Me, too," she whispered, before turning tail and dashing into the house to the security of her bathroom where the knowledge glared at her in the mirror, lit by the bright white lights behind her.

She loved Gabriel Sloan, far beyond the silly school-girl infatuation she'd thought was true love back then. The emotion burning deep inside now consumed her. It was pain and pleasure. He didn't love her, but that didn't matter. She wanted only his happiness, his freedom from the fiendish memories that haunted him.

She would help him as much as she could, no matter what it cost her. And maybe someday, Gabe would see that he needed her, too.

Someday.

Blair walked into the massive, empty bedroom and sighed.

What a way to spend your wedding night—alone. Again.

Chapter Seven

"Daddy? Can I help?"

A week after the wedding, Gabe glanced up from the complicated diagram, sparing a glance for the little boy before his attention was lured by the intricate work. "Uh, not right now, okay, Daniel? I've just got a little extra touch-up to do here, and I'll have rebuilt that microprocessor." He studied it more closely, checking and rechecking the alterations he'd made on the diagram.

"What's a micropro—that thing?"

"It sorts through the information. Kind of like the brain." Gabe checked to make sure, but Daniel still stood by his knee, his hands at his side. "Why don't you go play with your blocks for a little while?"

"I want you to come, Daddy. You know how to build it better than me."

"In a minute." Gabe took a second look at his solder. Yes, that would hold. Now if he had thought this through properly… He turned back to the papers.

"I'll hold it, Daddy."

The shrill sound drew Gabe out of his introspection

in time to see one small, chubby hand reaching up to touch the circuit board Gabe had just assembled.

"Don't touch that!" Gabe grabbed for the board, but instead of hanging onto it, his fingers slipped and the assembly crashed to the floor, sending shards of electrical parts all over. Four days of work—gone. "Daniel!"

The boy backed away slowly, his eyes huge in his white face. "I'm sorry. I didn't mean to do it. I just wanted to help. I'm sorry."

"Sorry isn't going to put it back together again, Daniel." Gabe fought to control his frustration. Evidently he took too long because Daniel turned and fled, his little feet pounding up the stairs to the main floor.

Furious at the mess and the time and effort lost, Gabe went looking for the broom and dustpan. He found them and Mac in the kitchen.

"What's biting your ankles? You look like a thundercloud about to dump on someone." Mac sat in his favorite chair, tipping back on it so he could stare at Gabe. "Having some trouble?"

"I wasn't until Daniel knocked an assembly onto the floor." He pinched his lips together, frustration vying with anger, neither of which he intended to let out.

"Was the boy hurt?"

The comment struck Gabe to the quick. The dustpan fell from his suddenly nerveless fingers. "I don't think so," he muttered, feeling the heat of shame burn his face.

"Didn't you check?"

It was a question, that was all. There was no condemnation in Mac's voice. But Gabe felt the guilt all the way to his heart. "He ran away so fast I didn't get a chance." It wasn't an excuse, and Gabe knew it.

He let the broom hit the floor and flopped into the chair opposite Mac's.

"I blew it. Again." He raked a hand through his hair, his shoulders slumping in defeat. "I just got so involved in what I was doing. I forgot he wouldn't understand how delicate everything is. I didn't mean to yell. I just wanted to warn him. Now he'll think I hate him or something." Gabe sighed, then got up to pour himself a cup of coffee.

Mac held out his mug. "He's probably feeling bad, all right," he agreed quietly.

Gabe's stomach plummeted to his shoes. "But that's not necessarily a negative. Next time he might think first and ask permission before he touches something." Mac took his full cup, sipped it and then sighed his satisfaction.

"But I shouldn't have yelled at him. He's just a little kid. He wasn't trying to steal a company secret." Gabe wished he could wipe it out and start again. "Now he'll hate me. I'm doing exactly what my father did."

"Are you?" Mac swiveled his toothpick to the corner of his mouth, his lips smiling. "I don't think so. Parents are people, too, Gabe. They make mistakes. They yell when they shouldn't. Life happens. There's nothing wrong with a child learning that everyone makes mistakes. It's how we handle them that matters."

Gabe stared at him. "I don't think I know what you mean." He managed to squeak the words out, studying the older man's relaxed posture. "You mean you're condoning my mistakes?"

"I mean you walk up those stairs to his room, where the boy is probably sniffing his head off, and you tell him that you're sorry you yelled, that you still love him and that he needs to ask permission to touch your stuff."

A sudden picture floated through Gabe's mind. He'd been, what, six? His father had blown his top when a cup, one of his mother's special ones, slipped from his hand and smashed on the floor. He hadn't meant to drop it. He just wanted to touch it, remind himself of her. Now, years later, he could understand that his father had resented the shattering of her belongings in the same way he'd hated losing the woman he loved so desperately. But at the time, at six years old, Gabe had only understood that he was a clumsy, stupid nuisance.

"I should have known better." He swallowed the strong black coffee without thinking, then winced as the bitterness burned down his throat.

"Do you think you might be expecting too much of yourself? You're not perfect. Apologize and move on." Mac drank the thick black stuff as if it were water. "I've gotta get moving. I'm going fishing."

Gabe watched him amble across the room, the heel of his hand massaging his thigh as he went. "Can it be that easy?" he wondered aloud.

"What?" Blair breezed in through the patio door and poured herself a glass of lemonade from the fridge. "Oh, that's good! I never did say thank-you for the housekeeper. I don't know how we'd manage this place if you hadn't hired her to keep things going." She wiped a hand across her forehead, took another swallow, then flopped on a chair. "Can what be that easy?" she repeated.

Gabe studied her upswept hair, the damp tendrils curling against her neck, her dusty white shirt and worn jeans. She glowed with good health. Did she ever make mistakes?

"Gabe?"

Slowly, he related the incident in his workroom. "I guess I forget he's only five—almost six," he amended with a halfhearted smile.

"And he should know better." She pushed her glass away, plunked her elbows on the table and leaned forward, cupping her chin in her hands. "He wants a father, Gabe. Not an angel."

"I don't think we have to worry there." Gabe pulled his handkerchief out of his pocket and wiped the dirt off her nose. "You're supposed to leave the garden outside."

She grinned. "Dirt's good for the skin. Some people even use mud packs." Her hand closed around his. "He won't hate you, Gabriel. He'll think it through and understand if you explain."

Gabe let her hold onto his hand. It felt good, reassuring. "I'm so lousy at this!" He glared out the window at the burgeoning blooms that seemed to tumble everywhere, out of old pots, a one-handled wheelbarrow, a rusty watering can. "I sounded exactly like my old man."

"He was a father, too," she reminded Gabe softly.

Gabe's head jerked around as he stared at her.

"You can't keep on hating him, Gabe. It'll only eat you alive. You're you. You have your own chance to deal with your child the way you believe is right. Daniel knows you don't hate him. Talk to him. You'll see."

"Will you come?" He held her hand a little tighter, knowing somehow that if Blair was there, everything would be all right.

"I don't think so." She eased her fingers away from his, but one hand lifted to brush his hair off his forehead. "You and Daniel need time together on your own. You're walking on eggshells around him. Therefore he's not sure what to expect. Just be yourself, Gabe. Relax. He's only five."

"That's what scares me," he muttered, knotting his hands together.

Blair leaned over and brushed a kiss against his cheek. "Be strong, big guy," she teased, her voice brimming with something he thought was gentle mockery. Then she got up, bunched her hair under a ratty old sun hat and grinned. "Back to the petunias." She giggled. "I ordered way too many."

"Maybe you should put hives around the yard. With all those flowers, the bees would really work." He was only joking, but Blair didn't know it. Her forehead furrowed as she considered his idea.

"It might work," she muttered to herself, pushing the door open. "And I've got those hives repaired now. I could…" She left talking to herself.

"Daddy?"

Gabe twisted in his seat. Daniel stood in the doorway, tearstains on his cheeks, his feet shuffling nervously.

"I'm sorry. I didn't mean to wreck your microphone thing." A big shiny tear slid down his cheek. "I'm sorry."

Gabe's heart ached for the uncertainty in those eyes.

He'd done that—him, the guy who should know better. "Come here, Daniel."

Daniel took one faltering step forward, but that was enough for Gabe. He scooped him up in his arms and set him on his knee, one arm around his shoulders.

"First of all, it's called a microprocessor. Can you say that?" He waited until Daniel had faithfully repeated the word. "And secondly, you don't have to apologize. I should be doing that. I didn't mean to yell at you. I never wanted to do that. I'm very sorry for it."

"That's okay." Daniel patted his cheek, his eyes bright once more. "I yell when I get mad sometimes. It makes me feel better."

"Well, it doesn't make me feel better. I just feel sad."

He hadn't meant to say it, but with that silky soft hair beneath his chin and the cuddly little body settled on his knee, Gabe was beyond controlling his words. "I don't ever want to scare you or hurt you, Daniel. But I'm not very good at being a daddy and sometimes I might. Will you remind me if I do it again?"

Daniel cocked his head, his eyes searching Gabe's. "I guess." One hand reached up to touch the furrow between his father's eyebrows. "Are you mad now, Daddy? Do you want me to kiss it better?"

All of the angst, the tension, the frustration slipped away as Gabe stared into his son's earnest face. He nodded, his throat too choked to speak. When the pudgy arms slid upward to circle his neck, when the soft little mouth brushed over his cheek, Gabe wanted to cry.

Thank You for this wonderful gift. I don't deserve it.

This special little boy is far more than I ever dreamed of. Please, don't let me mess up.

"Is it all better now?" Daniel's worried voice broke into his thoughts.

Gabe slid his arms around that wriggling little body and hugged for all he was worth. "Thank you, Daniel," he whispered, as he breathed in the half-dust, half-soap scent of his very own child. "Thank you very much."

"Welcome." Daniel hugged him, then giggled. "Your chin scratches me. Can we go help Mommy now? I love planting flowers."

"Sure we can. Then maybe she'd like to go down to the creek and cool off." Gabe let the boy drag him to his feet and lead him to the door. "What do you think?"

"She likes the pool better." Daniel scurried down the path. His voice echoed on the warm spring breeze. "An' I like ice cream. Chocolate ice cream, with marshmallows and nuts."

"Everything okay now?" Mac sat on the patio, whittling something out of a piece of willow. "Got it all straightened out?"

Gabe nodded, unwilling to speak for fear Mac would hear the emotion that still gripped him.

"Thought so. Kids don't hold grudges, Gabe. It's adults that do that. That's why we have the heart attacks and ulcers. The kids have shed all that and moved on. We hang on and let the bitterness fester so bad it affects everything we do. Lesson there somewhere, don't you think?" Mac winked at him, then went on carving and whittling, whistling an old western tune as he worked.

Thus ignored, Gabe set off down the flagstone path

to the gazebo Blair was intent on surrounding with flowers.

Was that what he'd done—let his anger and frustration about the past affect his whole life? Was that why things had looked so bleak after his father had swindled that money? It wasn't because he needed it, Gabe admitted wryly. He could give away three times that much and still fare quite well.

It was the loss of trust that bugged him. His own father had manipulated him into feeling guilty because he'd wanted an ordinary father-son relationship.

Why was that so wrong?

Because you're never going to have it. Face up to the facts, boy. You're not the kind of son he expected or wanted. Now move on.

Gabe wanted to forget it all, he really did. But the hole inside yawned deeper than ever, reminding him that he had no father now. He'd cut him out of his life just like he'd cut out everyone who tried to use him. He was Gabriel Sloan. He didn't *need* anybody.

Up ahead he could see Blair, face glowing with joy as she perched on her hands and knees, digging in the dirt. She didn't have to do it. He'd told her he could hire someone. But she'd insisted. And there beside her, his hands copying his mother's movement, kneeled Gabe's son.

What would happen if he lost them both? Why did even the thought of it fill him with terror?

Chapter Eight

Blair packed the crate with candles and carefully set it on the floor. Automatically her hands reached for another box and she began assembling an order.

Time flew so fast these days. It was hard to believe she'd been married two weeks, that Gabe's castle had been finished well before the deadline and they'd all moved in together.

So little had changed in her life, and yet everything was different. For one thing, she had too much work.

"Can I help?" Gabe stood in the doorway of her workroom, tall and uncompromising.

"If you want. I'm filling orders." She shrugged, unnerved by his sudden appearance. "Aren't you busy with something?"

He and Albert had been closeted for days, building some gizmo that remained top secret to everyone but them. She had to give Gabe credit, however. The moment Daniel came home from school, he put everything on hold to spend time with him.

"Not right now. We've hit a jam." He took the list she

handed him and began selecting items. "Do you have a lot to ship?"

"Quite a few items. Then I've got to get moving on the Christmas stock. That's my biggest season, and everything has to be at the stores by the first of October."

He nodded. "I know. In L.A. last year they hadn't even taken Halloween stuff off the shelves before the Christmas decorations started showing up." He studied her for a minute, as if he was considering his next words. "You look tired."

She rolled her eyes. "Thank you, Gabe. That's nice to hear."

"I meant it more as a question than a complaint," he said mildly. "You're doing too much. Can't you ease off a bit, let someone else do some of these jobs you've taken on?"

Blair felt a little burn start deep inside. "There isn't anyone else. Do you think I'd be doing that fundraising if someone else had volunteered? Besides, I like to be busy."

He shook his head in patent disbelief. "This goes way beyond busy, Blair, and you know it. You used to do this before."

"Before what?" She recounted her order and realized she'd put in too many flared red candles. When Gabe didn't say anything, she stopped what she was doing and looked up. "Before what?" she repeated, annoyed that he was interrupting.

"In L.A., when you were running from one thing to the other. Maybe that's why I never knew much about your family. You were always dashing from one place to the next."

"You weren't exactly sitting still yourself," she reminded him bluntly. "I'm not the one who canceled out every other night because I had to work."

He nodded. "I know. I did a lot of things wrong in those days. But we're talking about you. Who are you racing for now, Blair?"

She sighed, raked a hand through her mussed-up hair and spared a moment to glare at him. "Nobody. Myself. I don't know what you're saying." She threw up her hands in disgust. "There are things to be done, Gabe. I do them. No big deal."

He stared at her for a moment, then walked over, reached out and lifted her hand and, without really trying, slid her rings off her finger and then back on.

"You're losing weight, Blair. You never relax. You're tense all the time. When Willie's up half the night with her nerves, so are you. When the neighbors need a sitter, you rush over. When the school calls about drivers for the field trip, you volunteer, even though it isn't your son's class." He wouldn't let her hand go. "What's wrong?"

"Oh, for goodness' sake!" She yanked her hand away and flounced to the coffeepot. "I like to be busy."

"This is frenetic." His voice held a hint of steel as he lifted the pot out of her hands. "You drink way too much of that stuff." He tossed it down the sink and switched off the machine. "Come on."

Blair was too surprised to stop him until he'd urged her out of her shop and into the yard. "Come where?" she spluttered when she finally found her voice.

"I don't know. For a walk." His hand held hers, not loosening a fraction when she tried to tug away. "It's your day off, Blair. Time to get out of the mad rush and enjoy life."

She marched beside him, her temper rising. "This is rich, coming from the workaholic of the century!"

He ignored her sniping and led her around the side of the house. "I found a wonderful path behind here. There's the loveliest little spot on the top of the hill that overlooks our valley."

Blair sighed. "Gabe, I've lived here for years. I know all the sights."

He stopped and stared at her. "Do you? Really?" She didn't know how to respond to that so she stayed silent. After a moment he resumed walking, tugging her along like a recalcitrant child. Only then did she notice the backpack swinging from his other hand.

"What's in that?"

He glanced over his shoulder, followed her stare to the pack and grinned. "Lunch, al fresco. Sloan style."

"All right, I'm coming. You don't have to drag me, you know." She pulled her hand away and forced herself to walk on, even though his pace made her lungs burn. Why was she so tired?

"Where's your energy now, Blair?"

She looked up. Gabriel stood atop a rolling hill, his hair whipping in the wind, his handsome face perfectly lit by the sun. While she watched he flopped on the ground, stretched out on his back and gazed into the blue sky.

Blair forced herself the last few torturous steps, then collapsed beside him, barely noticing the hardness of the ground as she gasped for breath.

"Remember when we used to go for walks?"

His voice seemed far away, and Blair turned her head to check. Gabe's eyes were closed, his hands crossed behind his head. He looked perfectly content.

"I wondered why you always headed for the beach. I used to think it was the water, but it wasn't, was it? It was the wind." His eyes opened, their clear green startling her with their intensity. "You felt free with it blowing away all the worries."

She shifted so he couldn't see her face.

"You don't have to hide. Willie told me a little."

Blair jerked around. "A little what?"

"A little of your past. That you've always been the responsible one, always protected those you love. It must have been hard to leave them here while you went to school."

"Yes, it was." She wished he'd get off the subject.

"Why didn't you tell me more about them? All I ever knew were their names. 'Grandpa and my great-aunt,' you called them. I can't remember one time when you really talked about them." His hand tilted her chin so she had to look at him. "Why was that, Blair?" He lay on his side, arm tilted so it supported his head.

"I don't know. I guess it just never came up."

"It should have." His fingers played with her hair, twirling the ringlets, then letting them fall against her cheek. "Were you ashamed of them?"

"No!" She jerked upward. "How could I possibly be ashamed of the people who took me in and raised me with nothing but love? No." She shook her head adamantly.

"Then why?" He seemed to ponder the idea for only

a moment before his fingers closed around hers where they lay on the grass, fiddling with a stem.

At his touch, Blair froze.

"It was me, wasn't it? You were ashamed of me. You knew they wouldn't approve of me in your life."

The words pinged softly into her brain, tearing open the truth. "It wasn't shame." He had to know that, to understand. "I loved you then."

"But?" Gabe was sitting beside her. His hand wrapped around hers and squeezed in encouragement. "It's all right, Blair. You can tell the truth."

"I wasn't sure of you. I wasn't sure you knew who I really was." She blurted a stream of hurt. "All you ever saw was this person in glamorous clothes, pretending she fit in with the in crowd. You didn't know the real me, not even when you saw me at school. You thought my degree was just a hobby, didn't you? Something for me to do in the meantime?"

He considered it. "No," he said as he stared out over the valley. "I don't think I ever thought that. You were too good at what you did." His head reared up, his eyes bored into hers. "But you're right, I didn't know you. Not the real you. I thought you liked the fancy clothes, the parties, the glitz. I didn't realize that they meant nothing. I guess I'm only beginning to understand that material things have never really mattered to you."

"I do like the castle, Gabe. You did a wonderful job. I appreciate all the little things you incorporated to make it comfortable for Willie and Mac and Albert." She let the truth ring through her voice. "Not to mention Daniel."

He nodded, his face serious. "That's exactly what

I mean. For *yourself,* you couldn't care less. It's your family you're concerned about. I'm just beginning to understand how much they mean to you."

"My family means everything to me." Suddenly she realized that Gabe was part of her family, too. She could see by the twinkle in his eye that he'd hit on the same idea.

"Even me?"

"Well, of course, you're im-important," she stammered. "I mean, I owe you a great deal."

"You don't owe me anything, Blair. Even in this day and age a man expects to provide a home for his wife and child." He shrugged carelessly.

"And her grandfather, her aunt and a man who's no relation at all?" She kept her gaze steady on him. "That's a great deal for anyone to do, Gabe. Let alone someone who's not…" She let the words die away, unwilling to finish.

"Someone who's not in love?" he asked. He shook her hand off his arm. "I do not want you to feel obligated to me. You do *not* owe me, Blair. Do you hear me? I will not be added to the list of people you have to repay!" He surged to his feet in one lithe move and stood glaring at her. "That's not what I want from you."

Blair sat where she was and studied him. This was the Gabe she remembered, strong, in control. His eyes sparkled, and his hands were planted firmly on his hips, daring her to contradict him.

This was the man she'd fallen in love with. "Well?" He glared at her. "Don't just sit there. I want your word that I'm not going to have to hear you thanking me for every rock and stone of our home. I did it for me, too, you know," he grumbled, his chin thrust out. "I like Mac and Willie. I needed somebody like Albert to keep me on my toes. He's got more ideas than I do."

She burst out laughing, good humor restored. "All right, Gabe. I'll only say it this once. Thank you very much for accepting my family as yours and for giving us such a lovely place to live." She grabbed his hand and pulled herself up, standing on tiptoes to press a kiss against his lips. "Thank you. For the last time."

Before she could move away, his arms came around her waist and his mouth landed on hers. When he finally lifted his head, Blair opened her eyes and blinked twice, only then realizing that her arms were around his neck, her fingers embedded in his hair. She pulled them away and shifted until his arm was loosely around her waist.

"If you say thank-you one more time," he warned, his eyes glinting with suppressed emotion, "I'm going to kiss you again."

"Hmm." She pretended to think about that.

He laughed, hugged her close, then let one arm drop away to snag the backpack. The other he moved to her shoulders, holding her at his side as they walked across the hill.

"Can I ask you something, Blair?"

The uncertainty of the question made her wonder, but she decided to face it head-on and whispered a tiny prayer for help.

"Go for it."

They walked for several minutes before he finally allowed himself to ask, "Why didn't you tell me about

Daniel? Didn't you think about it, wonder if I'd want to know? Were you so afraid I'd take him?"

Blair took a deep breath. "Yes," she whispered, and saw his chest sink as he took the hit. But she had to tell all of the truth. "And no."

"What does that mean?"

"I realized that I didn't want Daniel growing up in your world." She took a deep fortifying breath and let the truth spill out.

"I became someone else there, Gabe. I wasn't me, I was someone who was playing me. You were right. The only time I could really breathe, really feel free, was when I was on the beach. It's hard to pretend on a beach."

"It is?" He frowned, considering.

"It sure is. The wind messes your perfect hair, the sun melts your makeup, the sand gets in your clothes. And the water washes away everything but the basics." She stopped and faced him. "I was living a lie, even though I didn't realize it. By the time Daniel was born, I'd begun to look past the mistakes and see the root problem."

"Which was?" Anger was in his voice.

Blair sighed. "The root problem with me is that I don't fit in in L.A. At first I didn't think I fit in here, either, but it's like buying shoes."

Gabe blinked and knocked his fist against the side of his head as confusion clouded his eyes. "I wonder if I'll ever be able to follow your thinking. What do you mean? Your logic escapes me."

"Just listen. Sometimes I buy shoes that fit like a glove. I hardly notice I'm wearing them. Call them sneakers." She waved a hand. "This place is like my sneakers."

"Okay." He waited patiently, one eyebrow tilted up.

"For me, L.A.—your style—was like a pair of very high heels. Okay for a little while, but eventually you have to take them off or your feet get very sore and messed up."

"Okay to visit but you wouldn't want to live there." He pondered that. "What you mean is that you didn't dare tell me about Daniel because you couldn't imagine me living anywhere else?"

She nodded. "I never dreamed you'd come here. You always seemed intent on frequenting the in places, hobnobbing with the big boys."

He snorted. "Hardly hobnobbing, Blair. I doubt they ever even noticed I was there."

She smiled. "It was the place you wanted to be. I just couldn't see how Daniel would fit into that, even *if* you'd changed your mind."

Sorrow vied with wry reluctance on his face. "That remark will haunt me forever, I'm afraid. I freely admit it, I was a fool. Daniel is a godsend. I'm glad I have a son." He pulled her to a stop. "I'm hungry. Can we eat lunch here? It's so pretty."

Here was a lovely grassy spot beside the creek where it tumbled over rocks. Blair nodded and within minutes Gabe had spread a blanket and laid out some plastic dishes, two napkins and an odd assortment of food.

She watched, mouth pinched in a prim line as Gabe unpacked chips, peanut butter sandwiches, two sugar-free lollipops, a piece of leftover pie, six grapes—rather the worse for wear—and a thermos of—

"Water?" she squeaked.

"Water. You need to lay off that stuff you call coffee. Last night your hand was shaking when you were dipping those candles. It was probably from exhaustion, but all that caffeine doesn't help."

Blair tried to chew her peanut butter sandwich as she considered this. Finally she swallowed. She had to ask. "You're concerned about my health? You, the junk food addict?"

He was affronted. "I'll have you know that I've become very health conscious." He munched on a couple of grapes.

"You?" Blair could hardly imagine it. "The man who loves everything fried and nothing green? Amazing." She glanced at the pie. "Who's that for?"

"Half for you, half for me. I'm not totally reformed." He flashed her a smile that made her tummy clench and her toes tingle. "If you can't stand plain water, I brought along some lemon wedges. Let's see." He rooted through a bag and finally emerged with two plastic-wrapped halves, which he squeezed into her water.

"You've got more on you than in the glass." She sipped it, then forced her pursing lips to unclench. "Lovely." It wasn't easy to suppress the shudder at the sheer sourness of it. "You certainly have changed."

"Well, I'm trying." He took a sip of her water, made a face and handed it back. "That's too sour."

She burst out laughing. "Maybe we could dissolve the lollipops in it. Of course, we'd be putting that fake sugar chemical into our body. That can't be good."

He frowned. "I never thought of that. Hmm. Guess

we'll have to make do with the chips. They're low salt."

"Then why bother?" Blair said grumpily, but she was hungry so she munched on a few of the flat, tasteless chips and the sandwich. Screwing up her courage, she finally asked the one thing that had preyed on her mind for weeks.

"Why did you decide to move, Gabe? Did something happen?"

He was silent a long time. Blair had decided he wasn't going to answer, that it was time to pack up and go home, when he spoke.

"I couldn't go on."

The harsh words hit her hard. "What do you mean?"

"It was gone. All the fun, all the thrill of making things work, the anticipation—it was all gone. I was stuck in a rut making decisions about stuff I didn't care about. I was so bogged down in details there was no time to do what I really liked. I knew if I didn't get out then, I never would. I'd be caught in the cycle of endless meetings."

Blair smiled, remembering his ability to submerge himself in his work without noticing time or people. "You always were a loner. You preferred the solitude of working by yourself. Even I knew that."

He nodded. "So did I." His face tightened. "I knew it but I couldn't accept it. You see, Blair, I figured it was something my father had inflicted on me, that it was antisocial behavior I'd developed from being alone too long." He shoved their lunch remains into the knapsack, shuffled over until he was beside her on the blanket, then picked up her hand.

"I figured I had a flaw, a weakness that needed fixing. The only way I could think of to fix it was to be in a crowd. Do you understand?"

"You mean you were proving something to yourself by hanging around those celebrities?" She couldn't quite see in-control Gabriel as that needy, but then, maybe she hadn't really known him.

"Exactly." He fiddled with her rings. "I hated it. I wished we were somewhere else, just the two of us. Listening to the waves, maybe. Or at the library while you studied." He cleared his voice. "After a while, I thought you were beginning to enjoy it. That really bothered me."

"Enjoy that *circus?*" Blair couldn't help it. She burst into laughter at the mess they'd made of everything. They'd been so stupid, so foolish.

"Do you know how many times I ate snails just because I thought you loved them?" His lips turned down in distaste, and she laughed even harder. "I hate snails—I don't care what they call them or how elite they are."

"I do, too."

"Anchovies?" She waited for his nod. "Caviar?" He shuddered. "Fish eggs? No, thanks!" Suddenly he caught on.

"Screaming over music so loud your ears hurt? Having everyone call you 'darling' because they can't remember your name?"

She giggled at his pronunciation, then laughed even harder when he started on the vernacular she'd never understood. They laughed until their sides ached and they could laugh no longer.

Blair lay on the blanket, peering at the sky as she remembered those days and her fear of doing or saying the wrong thing, of asking to leave early and worrying that Gabe would miss out. After a few moments she turned her head toward him. Gabe was staring at her, his mouth twisted in a lopsided grin.

"You have my permission to shove my head under the water in the pool and hold it there for as long as you want."

She giggled. "You have my permission to demand I wear four-inch heels for the next week without taking them off."

He groaned, closing his eyes. "What a pair of fools! When I think of how many sinus pills I took after breathing that smoke, I could boot myself down the hill."

"When I think of listening to Eunice blabber on about Pippi and Poppi, I could push you down it with no compunction."

He shouted with laughter. "Those ridiculous dogs!" he exclaimed. "How did you stand having them underfoot all the time?"

"Underfoot wasn't bad. It was in my bag that really got me. 'Pippi just adores tuna!'" She repeated the phrase in Eunice's shrill falsetto. "Maybe I owe those dogs. They helped me keep my figure when you kept feeding me those lavish meals."

"Hey, I thought you liked Antonio's!" He held out one hand with a flourish. "We have the chicken cordon bleu that madame loves as the special tonight."

Blair held her aching stomach. "Yuck! I haven't eaten that since I left."

Gabe studied her for a long time, his smile fading. "I'm sorry I put you through all that."

"I'm sorry I pretended to be someone I'm not and made you think it, too."

They looked at each other, awareness tingling between them. Blair was so conscious of Gabe sitting next to her, she could feel the hairs on her arm stand at attention. When he reached out to brush her bangs off her forehead, she leaned toward him, holding her breath as his fingers slid across her brow and over the curve of her cheek. They stopped at her jawbone.

"You're very beautiful," he whispered. "That hasn't changed one bit. I used to be so jealous when you'd get into those discussions with your chemist friends. I had no idea what you were talking about, but I knew they were admiring you."

"I hated the starlets fawning over you." She kept her eyes down. "I couldn't compare and I knew it."

"Blair?" He waited until she looked at him. "I only ever saw you."

Tears pooled in her eyes at the wonderful compliment. "Thank you," she whispered, staring into that dear, solemn face.

A slow, provocative smile took possession of his face until his mouth was a wide white grin in his dark skin. "I told you, I don't want your thanks."

Blair blinked. "What do you want?" she asked warily.

His eyes dared her to listen. "Lots of things."

"Like what?" She couldn't turn away, couldn't get free of his magnetism. He drew her to him with a smile.

"Laughter," he murmured, his hand sliding down her

back. "Lots and lots of laughter." His hand moved up, and moments later her hair tumbled around her shoulders. "Picnics."

"Without lemons." She nodded. "What else?"

His hands cupped her face. "Time," he whispered. "Time to get to know you, to understand why you drive yourself so hard. Time to learn what you really like, what you want from life." He closed his eyes and thought for a moment. "Time to teach Daniel to ride a bike, time to learn how Mac knows so much. Time to help Albert perfect his gizmos. Time to go to church together, to sit all lined up in that pew like a real family."

"Time to let go of the past and build a future." She waited for his response.

His words came on a rush. "Yes. I want that, Blair. I want to start over. I want to build something good, something we can be proud of."

"We've got lots of time," she murmured, her eyes closing as his thumb traced her lips. "All the time in the world."

"I hope so." He kissed her so gently, so tenderly, that the tears fell of their own accord. He wiped them away, helped her up and walked her back without saying a word.

As she stood in her workroom alone, Blair lifted a hand and traced her mouth, remembering. He was so sensitive, so considerate.

But will there ever be enough time for him to learn to love me, God? Will there be time and faith enough for that?

Chapter Nine

"Blair?"

"Yes?" She turned from the delicate task of rolling a sheet of beeswax into an intricate design she'd almost perfected. Gabe stood in the doorway, his face a comical expression of confusion as he studied the mess littering her workroom.

For the past three weeks, ever since the wedding, while busying herself with every job she could find, she'd secretly watched him. The old Gabe seemed to be back, at least the innate curiosity that had drawn her to him in the first place. But a different facet of his personality had also emerged. This Gabe seemed more determined, more purposeful. Which was all right as long as he didn't superimpose his will on hers.

"When is Daniel's birthday?"

Blair clapped a hand over her mouth as reality hit home. "Good grief, I almost forgot! It's Saturday." That glittering stare of his forced her to think a little longer. "Oh, no!" She closed her eyes and groaned. "I promised to help out with the Scouts on that wiener roast."

"I know. Someone named Mona Greeley just phoned

to remind you." Gabe glared at her. "How could you *forget* his birthday?"

"Don't look at me like that!" Anger simmered just beneath the surface. Gabriel Sloan dared to remind her of her own child's birth date? It was laughable. "I've been a little busy, you know."

He nodded. "A little too busy. I told you that a week ago. You can't keep this up, Blair. Daniel doesn't want Willie or Mac reading to him *every* night. Sure, they can pitch in once in a while, but it isn't fair to count on them all the time."

"I don't. It's just been very hectic." She gently squeezed the wax together with the rose imprinter. The simmering inside her inched up a notch to a boil. "They don't mind helping out, and it's good for Daniel, too." She reached for another sheet of wax before glancing at him. "It wouldn't hurt you to read to him. You're his father."

Gabe's jaw tightened. "I know that, thank you. I understand the ramifications of being his father, but I can't do it all. He wants you there, too. He wants you to hear all about his day and listen to his prayers. I've tried, but evidently I don't have the same method as you." Gabe yanked an old rickety chair forward and sank into it. "He keeps asking for you, Blair. Can't you put off your work for just a few minutes to spend time with your son?"

The pot inside her began to boil and bubble, roiling with indignation that edged nearer the top.

"That's rich, coming from you!" She set down the wax in case she damaged it with her taut fingers. "I've spent six years of his life being everything to my son.

I don't neglect him. I don't abuse him. I love him with all my heart. I spend as much quality time with him as I can. I certainly don't need lessons from you!"

His cheeks darkened. "I'm not suggesting you do. I know you love him. But he's confused right now. His whole world has changed, and he just wants his mommy to tuck him in. Is it so much to ask?" His voice rumbled low, condemnation in its depths.

Blair strove to remain calm as she clenched her hands together.

"I do tuck him in, as soon as I get back." She forced her fingers to unbend and started fiddling with the ribbon she wrapped each pair of candles in. She couldn't do anything because she was too angry, but she would put on a brave front.

Silence loomed between them. When Gabe finally spoke there was a hint of reprimand in his tone that scratched against her conscience like a fingernail on a blackboard.

"I thought we were going to make time for each other. To do things together." His hands reached out and stopped hers, holding them still between his palms. His eyes were mossy dark as they met hers. "When, Blair? When do we make time? You're always running."

With a pang, Blair realized she was so tired, she just wanted to cuddle in those arms, close her eyes and let him hold her. She wanted to forget about all the demands on her time, the challenges she'd taken on without thinking them through.

But the table between them was like the gulf that separated them. She loved him. He didn't love her. She had to be strong, reliable, dependable. She couldn't need him. There was no telling where the next test would come from. She had to be ready.

"I'm doing my best, Gabriel." She tugged her hands out of his and moved to the box table, assembling the small white cardboard sets that had her name scripted across the top in gold lettering.

"No, Blair. You're not. You're letting your priorities get skewed." He grimaced, a wry smile on his mouth. "I should recognize the signs. I did it myself for enough years."

The simmering started again.

"Willie has never been better. She doesn't get overwhelmed by things nearly as often, and she hasn't asked me one of her goofy questions in days. Mac is as healthy as he's been in years. He loves working on that fountain you guys started. Albert's knee-deep in his inventions, and Daniel is finishing his first school year." She took a deep breath and glared at him. "Everything seems perfectly fine to me."

"Everyone is adapting to the changes we've made. Everyone except you. You haven't had time to figure out what's changed, what you need to change, because you're too busy running." He stepped around the table and stood beside her. His fingers reached out and plucked the cotton knit away from her rib cage. "This fit you perfectly a month ago. Now it bags and hangs. You've got blue lines under your eyes. Even when Willie sleeps, you don't."

"I'm sorry I woke you. You should close your door," she muttered stiffly, risking a glance in the mirror across the room. He was right, she did look awful. "I have a lot of things on my mind."

"Too many things. You need to get rid of some of them."

She frowned, disbelief fogging her brain. "What did you say?"

"I said it's time to cut down on some of this frenetic busyness. Today. Now." He refused to back down, though she gave him her fiercest glare. "I'll help you, Blair. However you want. But you've got to squelch this inane desire to run yourself ragged."

"I have a business to run!" She shouted it, tiredness and frustration lending an edge to her voice. "You may be able to hire a thousand minions to take over when you disappear for months at a time, but I can't."

He stared at her, his emerald eyes piercing. "Why not?"

She sighed. It wouldn't do any good to argue with him. And she didn't want upsets in the family. She wanted everything to run smoothly. She'd try reason.

"You don't understand."

"Try me."

Peacemaking got shoved to the back burner. "Look, Gabe. It's a complicated process that I developed myself. I take pride in what I sell, and I don't want that compromised."

"So you train someone to do it as well or better. Someone who will do this while you catch up on the important stuff like garnering new accounts, building your business." He waited, one ankle crossed over the other, his perfectly pressed jeans absolutely stain free. "I'll find someone for you if you like. I'll even design a brochure advertising your wares."

"You?" She scoffed at the absurdity of it. "What

do you know about making candles or producing honey?"

"Not a thing. But I do know that you need someone reliable, someone dependable who takes special care in their work." He reached out and pushed a curl off her face.

"I can't afford to hire anyone." She tilted away from his fingers, contrary to the ache in her heart.

"You can't afford not to. If you keep on like this, you'll get sick. The orders will back up, and nothing will sell. It's time for some strategic planning, Blair." He crossed his arms.

For some reason that motion made her burn. "I suppose you think, since you're the big tycoon, that you know all about this."

He chuckled. "I should. I've been through it enough times. Every little bit of growth, I'd have to revamp and revise. I wanted to do it all myself, but I just couldn't handle it. Rich had to practically force me to hire a business manager. He threatened to quit more times than I can count unless I followed the man's advice." He waited a minute, then lifted an eyebrow as if he knew the question that burned on the end of her tongue.

"The answer to your question is yes, I hated every minute of it. It hurt to let go and watch someone else take my ideas and run with them, even though it was my company they were building. I wanted them to be my designs, my work. In short, I wanted to control every minute detail."

"Sounds like you." She sniped at him because he'd just said the exact thoughts that had passed through her head. She hated the thought of relinquishing control. If she did it, she knew exactly what she'd get. Her standards would be met. If she let go…

His hands on her shoulders jerked her attention to him.

"It isn't easy to let someone else in, Blair, but it's the only way to grow."

Was he talking only about business?

"A company that's built on one person is no stronger than a family that is made up of one person. More heads, more shoulders, the idea pot gets richer. Besides…" He grinned and winked. "There are more shoulders to take the stress."

Were they stronger as a family now? Had moving into the castle with Gabe, giving Daniel two parents, had that made them stronger? Or had it weakened her?

"It takes a while, Blair. You have to give it a chance. That's all I'm asking. Let me find someone to help you out here. Someone who won't mind starting off at a lower salary if they can share in the benefits of making the business grow."

"Profit sharing." It was a good idea.

"Exactly." He grinned that big, flashy grin. "If you don't like what I find, we'll keep looking."

She felt foolish for not thinking of it sooner. "I suppose you think this is all rather silly," she muttered, waving a hand around the messy workroom.

He frowned, his head tilted. "Why would I think that?"

"Well, there's you and your company. What do you have now, Gabe, five hundred employees? Annual sales figures that fit right in with the Fortune 500 fellows?" She laughed bitterly. "And you see me struggling with this little company that's liable to get eaten up by the giants. I suppose you think I should dump it all and be content to just be the little wife?" She jerked her head, ready to take it on the chin.

His voice, when he finally spoke, was very quiet. "You already are my wife. I don't see why that makes you any less capable as a businesswoman." His eyes held hers. "I certainly don't blame you for wanting your own successful company. Why shouldn't you want to succeed, just like everyone else?"

A tiny hint of something—what, hurt?—echoed through his words.

"I've never been a snob, Blair. I don't look down on this business or any other. Why should I?" He picked up a bottle of color. "This shade of blue is new, isn't it?"

She nodded, pleased that he'd noticed.

"I imagine it took you hours of mixing and testing to get exactly this shade of greenish blue. You weren't satisfied until it did exactly what you wanted in the wax. I'm guessing that the technical part was fairly easy thanks to your chemistry background, but the trials, the run-throughs, the mistakes and retries, those must have been time-consuming, not to mention frustrating."

She nodded again.

"But you persevered until you had distilled out of that exactly what you wanted. Why wouldn't I admire that?"

"I'm sorry." Shame burned on her cheeks. "I shouldn't have said it."

"I'm glad you did, because it brings home what I've been trying to say." He put the color down and turned to face her fully. "Our marriage is like that color. We need to test things out, make sure we're getting exactly what we want, and if we aren't we need to change the formula, rearrange the sequence, add more of one thing, take away something else."

"And you want me to cut down on work? How is that going to help?" She glanced at her watch, wondering if she'd manage to get anything worthwhile done today. The thought made her flinch.

Wasn't her marriage to Gabe worth some time?

"I don't want you to quit on your company, Blair. I think it's great. I'd like to help you with it, if you want me to. I'd just like to see you cut out some of the other extraneous stuff that takes time away, time that we should be spending with Daniel. And with each other."

The phone rang. Blair let the answering machine take it, her face burning as she listened to the teacher at the day care remind her that they didn't have much time to raise the last bit of money they needed. She glanced away from the machine as the message ended and caught Gabe's look of frustration.

"I'm sorry if you feel I'm neglecting you!" The words spilled out of her with a bitter ring, and she regretted them as soon as she'd said them.

Gabe's lips tightened. His hands balled at his sides. Then he turned and walked to the door, his voice hard and cold. "Forget it, Blair. Just forget it."

Tears welled in her eyes as she heard his truck door slam. She walked to the door and watched him drive away, her heart aching for the stoic look on his handsome face. The quiet, controlled rev of his engine, the steady hum as he drove out of the yard and toward his castle condemned her more clearly than anything else could have.

Why do I do this? Why do I have to prove myself? Is it ever going to be enough?

She flopped down on the doorstep and sighed.

Gabriel Sloan was right. And she knew it. She *had* taken on too much. The worst part was, she didn't know how to get out of all those commitments. Even as she'd thought about it once or twice, more had piled up.

It's just like our marriage. We need time to figure out what works.

Was that what she was afraid of—working out her marriage? Or was she afraid that it would never work out?

Blair closed her eyes and prayed.

Lord, I'm so tired and so confused. I want to do what's best for everyone and I just seem to be making matters worse. Please help me to find a way to reach Gabe.

The relief of admitting she was caught in a situation she couldn't control left her breathless. What to do now?

He wants to help, to be part of your lives. Let him.

Blair shuddered at the idea. Mind Your Own Beeswax was hers and hers alone. She'd started it herself, nurtured it until she had a firm client base with a regular order list. She didn't want to turn it over.

"You want to be in control."

The memory of those words made her blanch. It was true. She didn't want someone to tell her when and how to do things. She wanted to do it on her own. Just as she'd wanted complete control all those years ago.

You've been on your own. Look where you're at now.

Blair couldn't ignore the truth anymore. She sighed and got up. A quick check ensured there was nothing that couldn't wait. She snatched up her keys and locked the door, her mind in turmoil as she tried to think of a way to explain her sudden change of heart to her husband. Nothing but a bald admission of her mistakes came to mind.

She drove home trying to decide how to eat crow.

The perfect sunny afternoon sparkled off the shining windows of Gabe's castle from half a mile down the road. It shimmered in the blooming flowers that snuggled against the sidewalk and sparkled off the brook where it had been diverted to pass through Mac's newly created fountain.

Blair pulled her hair away from the nape of her neck and breathed in the heady fragrance of lilacs that wafted from a bush that had crouched against a huge glacial stone for as long as she could remember.

No one seemed to be around, so she wandered through the house to her room. The patio door stood open to the afternoon breeze. The glittering reflections of the pool beckoned her to dive in. It was an invitation she couldn't resist. Five minutes later she took a header into the water and let it course over her.

She burst to the top, feeling the water stream over her head and down the length of her hair like a cleansing tide.

"I thought you were working." Gabe lay sprawled on a lounger, clad in a white T-shirt and black swimming briefs. His black sunglasses effectively shielded his eyes from her.

"I decided I needed a break." She saw him glance at the phone he held. "Am I bothering you?"

"Of course not." He put the phone on the table. "Feels good, doesn't it?"

She glanced at him in surprise. "You were in?"

"I've been going in two or three times every day."

She waited.

"It's getting easier." He poured himself a glass of iced tea, then held up the pitcher in a question. At her nod, he poured a second glass. "I play silly games that Daniel taught me, like diving for a penny."

"I'm impressed." Blair climbed the stairs, took her glass and sat on the edge of the pool. "I wanted to ask you something, Gabe."

"Ask away." He stayed where he was.

Blair turned so she could see his face. "I wondered if you'd like to donate to the preschool."

He choked on his drink, his head jerking in her direction. Blair didn't like not being able to read his eyes so she got up, walked over and removed his glasses.

"In the amount of two hundred eighty-seven dollars and forty-three cents."

The beginnings of a smile tugged at the corner of his mouth. "You're sure it's not forty-four cents."

"Nope. Forty-three. With your contribution, the preschool will have the requisite one thousand dollars I promised to raise." She dragged a chair around so she was facing him and sitting in the sun. "It's tax deductible," she reminded him when he said nothing.

"Oh, well, if that's the case, sign me up." He studied her.

Blair leaned her head back and closed her eyes,

allowing the penetrating warmth of those rays to pierce right through to her bones. How wonderful to just lie here. "Thank you."

"Can I ask *you* something, Blair?"

She shrugged. "My life is an open book."

"Hardly." He took another drink. "Why the day care? It's not as if Daniel's there."

"It's not really a day care. More a preschool. I was the president the year we founded it. I sort of feel obligated to see it prosper." She remembered the flurry of getting it off the ground and the feeling of overwhelming pride at the looks on the kids' faces that first day.

"How long ago was that?" Gabe's voice rumbled from somewhere deep within his chest.

It sounded like he was laughing at her, but she couldn't be bothered to check. Blair kept her eyes closed and concentrated on absorbing as many rays as she could. "Four years ago."

His chair squeaked a protest. A moment later one big hand covered her arm. "You felt obligated all this time? You didn't think maybe you'd done enough, that it might be time for someone else to pitch in?"

She did open her eyes then, and found his face mere inches from her own. "No," she breathed, almost silently. "I guess I didn't. I just saw a need and decided to do something about it."

"I see." He sat back. "Someone named Marty called about eight cakes you promised for next week."

Blair knew he wanted to say something else, so she forestalled him. "Yes. For the bake sale. It's a missions project that raises funds for Christmas gifts for children in an orphanage in some part of Russia." She opened one eye slowly and winced at the frown on his lips. "I was going to ask some of the other ladies to help me, but most people go on vacation around this time of the year."

"There's a bakery in the next town. Saunder's, I think it's called. I ordered ten cakes. To be delivered the day of the sale." His voice dared her to argue.

She didn't. "Thank you," she murmured. "I was wondering how I was going to manage that."

"Daniel's teacher called to say they have enough money for their field trip, the pastor has found a new recruit to head up the meals on wheels team and Mabel somebody will take your place escorting the Scouts on their trip this Saturday."

Blair sat up, her temper rising as she saw the complacent look on his face. "How dare you!"

"Somebody had to. Willie's driving herself frantic worrying about getting ready for the seniors' retreat. She doesn't want to ask you for help because you're so busy." He tilted his head back and closed his eyes.

"I like being busy." She glared at him, fuming because he couldn't even see the daggers she was tossing his way.

"You're too busy. It's time to let go of some of this. There are other people who'd like to help out, you know. They're just intimidated by you."

It was a horrible thing to say! As if she steamrollered everyone without considering anyone else's feelings. That wasn't her!

"Stop pretending you're asleep and listen to me." She waited until he opened one eye, then launched into her spiel. "I asked for help. No one offered. I've asked for help a number of times. No one ever offers. Somebody's got to do it."

"Maybe they just wanted to be asked. Personally. And left to do the job the way they see fit."

Something in the way he said it made Blair stop. She stared at him for a minute, turning over the words he'd just uttered. Suspicions crept through her brain.

"How did all these things just happen to come together today?" she asked softly as she swung her legs over the side of her chair and moved so she was mere inches from his face. "Exactly what have you done, Gabriel?"

"You always call me by my full name whenever you're ticked." He didn't bother to move back, just sat there studying her with that serious, intent look he gave to some of his biggest projects. "It reminds me of Miss Milton in third grade. She was a termagant."

"What did you do?" She prayed that he hadn't embarrassed her all over town by saying she was tired, haggard, needed help, was unable to cope. She didn't want that kind of attention or pity.

"Me?" He blinked innocently. "I just went for coffee to that little restaurant in town."

"Uh-huh. And my aunt Susan is a truck driver. Spill it."

"I didn't know you had another aunt."

She reached for the pitcher.

Gabe's gaze narrowed as he assessed her seriousness. Apparently he was convinced. "I went for coffee, Blair."

She picked it up and held it above his head.

"Honest!" Gabe held up both hands. "I may have mentioned that I wished my wife had a little more time at home, for me and our son. I can't remember now." He smiled like the wolf enticing Little Red Riding Hood. "It was just guy stuff. You know, newlywed questions and all that."

Blair groaned. She could just imagine it. A bunch of the locals hearing that the groom was being ignored by the bride. Sympathy. Vows to help him out. Calls to their wives.

"My name will be mud." She set the pitcher down, walked to her chair and flopped into it. "I'll be the local laughingstock."

"No, you won't." Gabe moved to the side of her chair and crouched next to it as one hand covered hers. "They genuinely care about you."

"Uh-huh." She closed her eyes and wished she were anywhere but here.

"They do." His hand moved to her chin and tilted it. "Look at me, Blair."

"Yes?" She glared at him angrily.

"Did you ever think that some of those people could do a better job than you? That they were just waiting to be asked to help, to be needed? That they wanted to feel a part of things but were afraid to volunteer for fear they wouldn't measure up to your standard?"

She frowned. "No, I can honestly say I never thought that," she muttered, anger nipping at her tangled emotions. "You make me sound like Attila the Hun."

He shook his head, his eyes dancing as he inspected her body when she lay back on the chair. "I don't think so." He laughed. "More like Mary Poppins. Capable of anything." He stood and pulled her up beside him, hugging her close for just a moment. "I know you can do it all, and you know you can do it all, but let's not tell everyone, okay? It makes them nervous."

After a moment Blair pulled away, chin thrust out as she glared at him. "You're not off the hook that easily," she muttered. "What you're saying is that I tend to take over."

He nodded soberly. "Like a bulldozer. Not that you don't have to sometimes. But not right now."

"And not when there are people, capable people who could do it far better." She sneaked a glance upward and caught an odd look on his face. "Just how did you know about all these things, anyway?" she demanded.

Gabe's arm fell away from her waist. He reached up and took a sheet of silver-gray paper from his shirt pocket—paper that she'd left on her dressing table this morning.

"Ronnie Morris is doing the canvassing. Tina George will take the kids to camp. Maddie and Stu are taking your place as Sunday morning greeters at church. Somebody named Elfie has taken over the Sunday school picnic, and Tatiana—" he glanced up, a frown twitching at the corner of his mouth "—is that right?"

Blair stuffed down the giggle and nodded.

Gabe continued reading from his note. "Tatiana has been conscripted to help out with the Kids' Crusade." He folded the note carefully and handed it to her. "Are you angry?"

"Should I be?" She kept her face solemn, her eyes serious. "You walk in, take over my life and reorganize it all in one half hour. How would you feel?"

"Mad," he confirmed, shoulders slumping as he walked to his chair and sank into it disconsolately. "I'd

say I'm sorry, but I'm not. You were doing too much."
His face hardened. "And you know it."

Blair walked to the edge of the pool and sat near his
chair. She dangled her legs in the water. "Yes, I do know
it," she admitted finally.

"Huh?" He got up from his chair, walked around it and
sank down beside her. "Did I hear that correctly?"

"Don't push it," she warned, but there was a smile in
her voice.

He wrapped his arm around her shoulders and hugged
her. "Thank you for not raking me over the coals," he
whispered against her ear. "I just wanted some time for
us to bond as a family, and I couldn't see how we were
going to do it if you were never here."

"I was here." She looked up and caught the pained
look on his face. "All right! I was gone a lot. I thought
I was helping them."

"You *were* helping them." He hugged her again, and
his mouth brushed against her forehead. There was a
lightness in his voice, a tenderness in his touch that told
her he wanted to do more. "But we need help, too."

She sighed. "I know I'm possessive about my business," she murmured, allowing herself to relax against
him for a moment. "I guess I'm such a control freak
because I'm so scared of messing up."

Gabe pulled away, holding her at arm's length as he
stared at her. "Messing up? You?" He shook his head
in mock reproof, but his voice was confident, brimming
with assurance. "You're not going to fail at anything,
sweetheart. You can do or be whatever you need, if not
with the candles and honey, then with something else.
You don't have to prove to me that you're a success. I

already believe it." He drew her close once more. "I just wish that you did."

Blair closed her eyes and relished being held so tenderly. It had been so long, so very long since she'd felt protected, cared for, *cherished*. She reflected on the word for a moment. Yes, that was it. Cherished. When Gabe held her like this she felt delicate, but oh, so strong. She felt protected, yet ready to defend. She felt—loved.

"What do you mean—you wish I believed it?" She barely whispered the words, hating to break the spell.

"I think you're trying to prove yourself, Blair. Isn't that what all this frenetic activity is about—showing everyone that you can do it, that you can handle whatever you get? Mother, granddaughter, niece, friend, church member, businesswoman." He stopped a moment. "Superwoman," he said, holding her away so he could look into her eyes. "Isn't that it?"

She shrugged, pulling away. He was getting a little too close for comfort.

"I think it is. But don't you see, honey? It doesn't matter to Mac or Willie or Albert, but especially to Daniel, that you've got all these irons in the fire. First and foremost, what Daniel wants is his mommy there when he wants her."

She listened to him without speaking.

"You were wrong, you know." Gabe pressed her head against his chest and swept his hand down the length of her damp hair. "There is no such thing as making quality time. You can't make it. It happens in those moments when you're relaxed and not really thinking about anything. That's when the enlightenment comes, the questions are asked, the biggest decisions are made. You can't schedule that. I should know."

"Why?" she whispered, so afraid to break this sacred time but needing to pull away, to regain her equilibrium. She drew back, but left her arms wrapped around his waist.

"For the first few weeks after my mother died, my father used to make me sit down for a half hour every day after dinner, if he was home. I had to tell him everything I'd done that day. If I missed something, I'd hear about it later." He sighed, fiddling with her curls, wrapping them around his finger and then watching as they sprang away.

"I suppose he thought he was making time for me. What it really felt like was an interrogation. I never did tell him how scared I was of the school bully, or that I hated art class."

He laughed, but to Blair, there was no humor in it.

"I wanted so badly to tell him that Mom usually let me pick out one shirt, a special one. And that I wanted a red shirt, a bright red one. Stupid little things that we might have discussed while we were playing at something or sitting together."

She tilted her head to meet his eyes. "That's what you want with Daniel, isn't it? That time of quiet confidences?"

"I want him to feel that he can trust me with anything. That's the way I want you to feel, too. But we need time together to build that trust."

She sighed, acknowledging the truth of what he'd said. "I know."

"You don't have to prove anything to me, Blair." His

hands held her head so she couldn't look away from that steady regard. "I don't care much what other people think. I *know,* or at least I'm beginning to know who you are deep inside." His voice dropped to a gruff whisper as he set her away and stepped into the pool.

"You don't have to half kill yourself to prove to me that you could get along just fine without my help, Blair. Believe me, I already know that. You've proven it for seven years."

As she watched him submerge himself into the water, eyes squeezed tightly closed, Blair felt her throat tighten up. He thought she only tolerated his presence, that she didn't need him to be in Daniel's life, to be in *her* life.

How had she ever made him believe such a terrible lie?

Chapter Ten

Blair shifted on the tiled edge of the pool, prepared to go to Gabe, to swallow her pride and tell him how wrong he was, to admit she needed him now more than she ever had.

"Mommy! Daddy! Guess what?"

Daniel's excited voice checked the impulse, and Blair stayed put. She would deal with this later, she decided. During some of that time Gabe wanted them to spend together.

"We're out here, son. By the pool."

Gabe emerged from yet another dousing and paddled his way from the deeper water to the shallow.

"Daniel's home," she told him.

In the second that he absorbed her words, Gabriel Sloan transformed right before her eyes. His eyes lit up, and his mouth lost the tense, tight line that held it captive. He climbed the steps eagerly, snatching a towel to dry as Daniel hurled himself through the door that led off the kitchen.

"Are you guys swimming *now?*" he asked, big

eyes round with amazement. "Don't you have to work, Mom?"

Blair cringed inwardly, then forced out a laugh. "Not right now. Right now we're taking a rest." She held out her arms and pulled him close when he ran into them. "Boy, you've grown again. I can feel it." She pushed the hair off his face and smiled. "What's got you grinning?"

"Teacher said to ask if we could look after Babycakes until next fall. She'll take him back when she returns from her summer trip. Can we, Mom? I'd take good care of him. I promise." Daniel crossed his heart, his eyes pleading with her just as his father's had mere moments before.

Blair considered it. "I don't know," she murmured. She tilted her head to stare at Gabe. "Maybe we'd better ask your dad what he thinks."

Daniel raced over to the big man and flung himself into arms he seemed to know would be waiting for him. "Can I, Daddy?"

Gabe snuggled him on his lap in a nearby chair, then frowned. "I don't know," he said.

"I promise I'll take really good care of him. You won't even know he's here. I'll feed him and water him, and take him for walks lots so he doesn't get into any trouble. He can't stay at his own house anymore 'cause they're moving away. And their new place don't allow no dogs. Can I?"

It whooshed out in a jumbled mass of begging and promises that made Blair grin. Especially when she caught sight of Gabe's face.

"What or who is a Babycakes?" he asked, one eyebrow tilted. "A dog, silly." Daniel grinned at his father as if he were teasing. "You know that. I tole you before."

"Oh. Yes. Babycakes, the dog. Right." Gabe blinked, then turned to Blair with a shrug that screamed, "Help!"

"A very large dog. An English sheepdog. A blind English sheepdog." Blair kept her lips pinched together. This organized, helpful man was in for a surprise if he thought Babycakes was a regular dog. "He's sort of the kids' mascot. They all love him. Some folks in town found him early this spring and have let him stay on their farm. But they're moving."

"Oh." Clearly Gabe didn't know whether to say yes or no. His eyes begged her to help out.

"Can we have him here for the summer, Mommy? Ple-e-e-ease." Daniel dragged the plea out to a twelve letter word.

"Babycakes is a boy dog." Blair hid her grin behind her hand. "I don't know, Daniel. I guess it will be up to your father to decide that. I promised him I wouldn't take on any other jobs. He thinks you miss me too much."

Temporarily diverted, Daniel nodded. "I did miss you last night, Mommy. You always come and kiss me good-night."

"I did last night, too," she whispered, her eyes filling with tears. "It's just that you didn't see me because your eyes were closed. All scrunched up. Like this." She made a face and honked a loud snore.

"I was sleeping!" Daniel giggled, wiggling to get a look at his dad. "Wasn't I?"

"If that obnoxious noise can be called sleeping."

Gabe tickled Daniel, then glanced over his head at Blair. "Is this dog thing okay with you?"

She got up, sauntered up the stairs, then paused at the door to the bedroom. She forced her face into a mask of seriousness and turned to face him.

"I'm leaving that up to you." When his eyes widened at her simpering tone, she smiled. "I don't want to volunteer for anything more. My husband might think he was being ignored. I wouldn't want the town gossiping about that. Would you?" She stepped regally into the room and swept the French doors closed behind her, snicking the lock into place.

"Oh, boy, are you in for a surprise, Gabe." She stepped under the shower, her mind busy with a picture of Babycakes loose in the castle. "A really big surprise. If you thought we were busy before, you ain't seen nothing yet."

In the process, Gabe might just discover how very much she needed him right by her side.

He wanted her to trust him? Then that's exactly what she'd do. Blair sincerely hoped her husband knew what he was asking for.

"Would somebody please get this stupid animal off of me?"

Friday morning, Gabe's muffled protests carried through the open kitchen window where Blair was mixing a batch of cookies.

"Please?"

She stifled the burble of laughter that itched to be set free and walked to the patio doors. Gabe lay on the grass, his body swathed by the big woolly body of a wriggling, ecstatically happy dog who busied himself licking his face and anything else within range of his lolling pink tongue. Babycakes. Again.

With a grimace of remorse for the forget-me-nots they'd ruined, Blair shoved open the screen and stepped out.

"What are you doing, Gabe?" she inquired mildly. "I *was* walking. Minding my own business. He got me from behind and knocked me over. Do you mind? I've been lying here begging for help for at least ten minutes." He quickly averted his face as the pink tongue swept across it once more. "Blair, please!"

"I love it when you beg." She put two fingers in her mouth, curled her tongue and whistled for all she was worth.

Babycakes rolled onto his back, legs poking straight up in the air as he froze in position. Gabe scrambled to his feet, rescued his sunglasses from underneath his rear quarters, his cell phone from under his left ear, then marched across the grass to where Blair stood.

"I'm a mess."

"You certainly are." She moved to snap the leash on the dog and led him to the fenced-in area Gabe had constructed two days ago. The dog sat obediently while she unsnapped the leash, then trotted to his water dish. Blair closed the heavy gate with a sigh.

"He hasn't been here a week and we've lost just about every flower. If Mac catches him tiptoeing through the petunias, he'll be sorry." She fixed Gabe with a glare. "So will you. Why did you let him out?"

"I didn't!" His indignant glare convinced her. "That *thing* was lying on the deck sunning. I thought I could sneak past him and I almost made it." He grimaced at the hair covering his elegant black suit pants.

"Why are you all dressed up?" Blair asked, latching the screen.

"I told you, remember? I have to make a quick trip to L.A. Something's happening and they want me back for a couple of hours. I should be home by seven." He made a face at the slobber that covered his sunglasses. "That animal is a menace."

"You told Daniel he could have him here," she reminded him pertly, enjoying this side of the perfectly groomed, always impeccable Gabriel Sloan. "Can't very well change your mind now." She concentrated on forming the little balls of peanut butter dough. "This is the second time this week you've had to go. Is there a problem?"

Gabe shook his head, though his eyes didn't meet hers. "No, just a glitch. Shouldn't take long."

"Now where have I heard that before?" Blair switched the pans in the oven, setting the pan loaded with golden brown discs to cool on the counter. "Last time went considerably longer than you expected. Good thing you picked today. Daniel's still at that sleepover. He'll stay until supper time. By then he should be extra tired."

"Have you got everything you need for his party tomorrow? Anything I can pick up?" He reached out, snagged one of the cookies, blew on it, then popped it into his mouth. "Mmm." He huffed and puffed for a minute, letting the heat dissipate as he chewed, swallowed, then grinned at her. "Very good."

"You're supposed to eat them in bites," Blair scolded,

pushing the pan away so he couldn't reach any more. "You know, actually *taste* them?"

Gabe flicked her ponytail, slipped an arm around her shoulders and tugged her close for a quick kiss. "I did taste them. They taste great," he murmured, his face inches from hers. "So do you."

"Oh, my! I didn't realize I'd be interrupting." Willie stood in the doorway, eyes sparkling. She made no attempt to leave, but stood inspecting Blair's hurried exit from her husband's embrace. "Don't bother on my account. I expected a lot more canoodling from a pair of newlyweds than I've seen from you two."

Blair wanted to groan. She ached to scream a denial, drop her apron on the counter and tear off across the valley to a quiet spot where her emotions didn't do these strange acrobatics, a place where her brain functioned normally instead of sending out little snaps of electricity whenever Gabe came near.

Neither screaming nor leaving was an option with Daniel's cake left to bake. So Blair focused on the job at hand and slid the cookies from the baking sheet to a rack.

"Gabriel, you have white stuff on the seat of those elegant pants." Willie giggled. "Are you going somewhere?" Her voice laughed across the room in a tumbling cadence of genuine pleasure that Blair hadn't heard enough of lately.

"Yes, Willie, I am. I have to make a quick trip to L.A. There's a small problem with my company there, and I need to attend a meeting." He craned his neck and plucked another dog hair off his pants, his mouth stretching in a grimace of displeasure. "If I can get out of here without being attacked again, that is."

"I'm sure Blair didn't mean to attack you," Willie murmured, her back turned as she studied Daniel's elaborate picture of a train cake on licorice tracks. She'd promised to ice the confection if Blair would bake it. "Say you're sorry, dear."

Blair made a face at Gabe. "I'm sorry." She parroted the words without the least bit of sincerity.

"Yes, I can see that." Gabe smirked at her raised eyebrows. "Can I get anything for the party?" he repeated. "I mean, maybe the car isn't enough. It's not…"

Blair set her hands on her hips and glared at him. "A *car* isn't enough for a six-year-old? Enough of this, Gabriel. You can't buy Daniel. As it is you're spoiling him silly. What other six-year-old kid has a toy car to drive around a castle? Hmm?"

She considered the bright red bicycle hidden in Albert's workshop. She'd scrimped and saved to buy it. It had taken months of careful, frugal planning. Without even considering *her* wishes, Gabe had eclipsed that gift a hundred times over.

"I wasn't trying to buy him." The happy banter drained away from Gabe's low voice.

"Well, that's what it looks like from here." Blair stubbornly turned her back on him and rolled out more cookies. Frustration clamored for release as she considered the day to come.

Daniel's sixth birthday. A day she'd planned for ages, long before Gabe had come on the scene. She'd planned to take the kids on a hike up near Lake Timco. They would have a campfire, a wiener roast, sing silly songs, go on a treasure hunt. But Gabriel's arrival had changed all that.

Now Daniel wanted a pool party. The hike and wiener roast had been done before. Steven B.'s party last month was a treasure hunt and *everybody* had wieners. But nobody else had a pool.

Blair sighed. Would Daniel even *want* to ride a bicycle when he could drive a car?

The silence in the room drew her from her reflections. Willie turned from her cake study. A sad look filled her eyes as she studied Blair's rigid backbone. "Excuse me," she whispered after a moment. "My head hurts."

Once she'd left, the tension grew enormously. Blair knew it was her fault. Gabe was doing his best, trying exceptionally hard to be the father he wanted to be. But she couldn't accept that, couldn't just allow him to walk in and take over their lives. Not completely.

She forced herself to keep on working.

"I'm not trying to overshadow you, Blair. Or show off." Defeat edged the solemn words. "I guess we should have talked it over before I ordered the car. I didn't realize you'd have objections, but now that I look at this from your perspective, I'm beginning to understand."

He walked to her, gently turned her so she had to look at him.

"You probably had all kinds of plans for his birthday long before I showed up." He winced, catching sight of the truth she knew was reflected in her woebegone face. "And his gift, too?"

Blair wanted desperately to pretend that it didn't matter. She wanted to be blasé, to pretend an airy non-chalance so he wouldn't see how much it stung. She wanted him to believe it didn't matter that he was usurping her.

But it did matter. It mattered a lot.

She nodded.

He closed his eyes and tilted his head so his chin touched her forehead. "I'm sorry," he muttered, his fingers on her shoulders drawing her closer. "I should have checked with you before I barged full steam ahead."

"It's all right." It cost her dearly to say that. Blair kept her eyes closed so he wouldn't see how much.

"No, it isn't."

She blinked her eyes open and stared as Gabe stepped back, his arms falling to his sides. He shook his head.

"No, it isn't. I keep doing this! Why don't I learn?"

She felt silly and childish as she watched the worry crowd out the joy that had filled his face short moments ago. "You probably put a lot of thought into that car."

"Yes, I did." His troubled eyes studied her. "I wanted to make a big splash, to give him something to remember. The first year his father was there for his birthday." One lip curled. "Go ahead, call me selfish."

"I wasn't going to say that." *Liar.*

"Weren't you?" He raked a hand through his perfectly cropped dark hair. "Then you're more charitable than I. I'll take the car back."

"No!" Blair gaped. He couldn't mean it. Give up the gift every little boy dreamed of? Because of her?

"Yes. We should have decided on something together. Knowing you, you'd have weighed all the pros and cons until you came up with a perfectly planned gift." He shrugged into his jacket. "What did you pick out?"

"A bike." She couldn't believe what she'd done. How had it happened? One moment she was mad because Gabe was trying to usurp her position as Daniel's mother, the next thing she knew, she'd made her son's father rescind his gift.

"That's probably exactly what he needs." Gabe nodded as he considered it. "Yes, it's perfect. That way he can ride down to the neighbors to play for an hour. A boy should have a bike. It can go anywhere. The car would have only worked on the driveway." Gabe tugged out his wallet. "Can I pay for half? That way it would be from both of us."

"Of course, if you want. But what about…" Blair didn't know what to say. She watched as Gabe laid two crisp one-hundred-dollar bills on the counter. "It didn't cost that much."

"Whatever." He shrugged, stuffing his wallet into his pocket and managing to check his watch as he did. "I've got to go. The jet's waiting at the airport. I'll call the delivery people to pick up the car. It was a silly idea, anyway."

"It wasn't silly." *I was.* She felt small, nitpicky. She'd ruined something special, a happy memory. She'd stolen it from him as surely as she'd accused him of trying to do the same to her. Unlike her, Gabe seemed to hold no grudges.

He snatched his briefcase, gave her a quick kiss on the cheek and strode toward the door. "Whatever happens, I'll be back tonight," he told her. "I won't miss tomorrow. Not for anything."

Blair moved to the window and watched him leave. *Selfish,* her conscience chastised. *Have to have*

*everything your own way. Try to shut him out if you will,
but Daniel still needs a father. You're only hurting him,
your own son.*

She squeezed her eyes shut, forced the tears back and
turned to the cookies.

"I can't lose him," she whispered. "I can't let Gabe
buy his love."

"Are you sure that's what he was doing?" Mac leaned
against the door frame, his face reproving. "Are you
certain Gabe wasn't giving Daniel something he wanted,
fulfilling a fantasy of his own?"

"I suppose Willie told you." Blair tugged out the
mixing bowl and began assembling the ingredients for
Daniel's cake.

"He's lonely, Blair. He's been lonely for a very long
time."

"Gabriel Sloan has always had hordes of people at
his beck and call." She cracked the eggs so hard, bits of
eggshell slid into the bowl. She fished desperately for
the elusive pieces.

"Not someone special," Mac reminded her. "Not
someone who cared for him. Not someone of his
own."

Blair dumped the eggs down the drain and started
again. The words stung. *Someone of his own.*

"Daniel isn't just your son. He's Gabe's child as much
as he is yours. You can't deny that, and you can't make
it go away. You've got to accept reality, Blair. You've
got to learn to trust him. Gabe isn't going away."

She dumped in a cup of sugar and started the mixer.
"He just did," she muttered, certain her grandfather
wouldn't hear.

Mac heard. "Not for good." His voice was raised sharply against the noise. Mac frowned. "He'll be back, Busy Bee. He'll always be back. This is his home now."

"Is it?" Blair studied the certainty on her grandfather's face for a moment. "How do you know that?" she demanded, turning away to add vanilla and melted chocolate.

When Mac didn't answer, she stopped what she was doing and turned off the machine. Her grandfather stood by the patio doors, peering over the smooth, clear surface of the pool.

Perhaps he hadn't heard her. "How do you know, Grandpa?"

Mac turned to face her, his mouth stretched in a beatific grin of smug satisfaction.

"Because he said so. And Gabe always keeps his promises."

Would he?

She grabbed the flour canister and measured two and one-half cups. She stirred cocoa into the wet mixture. She heated water to dissolve the baking soda. But still the thoughts pricked at her.

On our wedding day, he promised to love me. Can Gabe keep that promise?

Chapter Eleven

Gabe leaned back in his upholstered first-class seat and closed his eyes. Ten o'clock. L.A. was just coming alive and he was dead tired. No wonder, he was on Mountain Time. As soon as the plane gained cruising altitude and leveled off, he pulled out his cell phone and dialed. He needed a reality check.

"Hi, Jake. It's me. Leaving L.A. Another meeting."

"So how were the meetings?"

"Boring. Deadly dull and boring. Who cares if we gained two more points on the index or if some Korean firm is looking at a major purchase."

Jake chuckled. "I take it there was someplace else you'd rather have been?"

Gabe closed his eyes and thought of Daniel racing in the door from his friend's house. The three of them could have gone for a walk, watched the sun go down, even swam together. Lately Blair had taken to sitting outside in the hot tub long after everyone else had gone to bed. He watched her there, night after night, wondering if she'd welcome his presence. Maybe tonight she'd have told him to stay, to talk for a while. He ached for those words.

"Is this a bad connection or are you daydreaming?"

Gabe winced at Jake's snappy retort. "Daydreaming," he confessed.

"About your gorgeous wife, no doubt? So how is paradise?"

"Messed up." Gabe hated thinking about how stupid he'd been. He'd almost drooled imagining Daniel's expression when he saw that car sitting on the drive with his name on it. Gabe hadn't spared one thought for the way Blair must have felt, the weeks of pinching pennies he knew she must have done so she could get that bike.

"Okay, what did you do this time?" Jake's tone brimmed with long-suffering patience.

Gabe told him the whole story. "I always think about myself first, Jake, about how I'll look. It's the same reason I had to live in L.A. I thought people would take me more seriously if I had just the right address, came from the ritzy part of town, knew the right people." He felt the weight of his stupidity. "I didn't stop to reason out why, or to imagine how it might come across to Blair. I just wanted to show my son that I could get him whatever he wanted."

"And did Daniel want *that* car?"

Gabe swallowed, shifted the phone to his other ear and admitted the truth. "I don't think he even knew it existed until I showed him a picture in a catalogue. After I explained how fast it could go and all the rest, he got excited." Gabe nodded at the copilot and accepted a cup of coffee.

Jake didn't say anything for a long time. Then his quiet voice probed a little deeper. "What's really bothering you, Gabe?"

The window by his elbow gave a view of inky blackness. Gabe could discern nothing, no city lights, no ground cover, nothing. Clouds obliterated the view. It was exactly like his life. No matter how hard he tried, the future he imagined just wouldn't materialize.

"Daniel's a replica of his mother. He isn't impressed much by things," he admitted finally. "He doesn't seem affected by expensive toys or new clothes. Even by the castle. He likes the pool, but I get the feeling the river would work just as well. All he seems to care about is whether or not Blair and I are there."

Jake shouted with laughter. "That's the way it's supposed to be, bud."

"Yeah, I know." Gabe swallowed a mouthful of coffee that he didn't want, brooding on the whole puzzle. "But it's exactly the opposite of who I am. Today Blair accused me of trying to buy Daniel's love with the car."

"Was she right?" Trust Jake to hit where it hurt.

"I don't know. But the more I think about it, the more I'm afraid she was." Gabe thought about her last night, curled up on the cold, dirty ground beside Daniel, trying to coax a squirrel to take some bread from her hand. "I made sure I took care of her family, got her a decent place to live. I bugged her about working so hard, trying to make her see she's killing herself with worry. I thought I was doing all the right things that men are supposed to do when they want to build a family."

"And?"

"None of it matters." Suddenly Gabe didn't want to

pretend anymore. "Willie goes to the old house almost every day. I followed her once. She sits on the porch and stares into space. Then, when she gets too hot or thirsty, she comes back. I didn't tell Blair, but I think her illness is getting worse. She seems to space right out." He took a deep breath. "Mac goes there when he thinks Willie and Blair aren't looking. He pretends it's to help Albert, but it isn't. He sits on a bale of hay by the barn and chews on a piece of straw. In between he whistles."

"Whistles?" Even Jake seemed surprised.

"Uh-huh. That song, 'Beautiful Dreamer,' he whistles it for ages. Over and over and over. He walks to the top of the hill, stares out over the valley for a long time, then goes home. It's weird."

"Why?"

"Because they keep leaving the new home they're in for the old ramshackle one they've left." Gabe shifted as the hurt burned deep inside. What more could he do? Was he losing the only family he'd ever had?

"Perhaps they have some fond memories of the old place. Perhaps they feel more comfortable there."

"But why?" Gabe pushed the cup away. He didn't need more coffee. He needed answers. "I've given them everything they could ask for. Blair will never want for a thing."

"Except maybe love. You've made them beholden, Jake. You haven't loved them."

Gabe closed his eyes as the truth of the words slammed home. "I can't change that, Jake," he whispered. "I'm not that kind of man."

"Aren't you? Then you need to pray for God to change

you. Because the Bible says we're to love our neighbor as ourselves. And that comes right after we love God with all our hearts, all our minds, all our souls, all our strength." He waited a moment, then grumbled his disgust. "Did you hear me, Gabe?"

"Yeah, I heard."

"Then you know the Bible doesn't say we should *try* to love. It doesn't say we should squeeze our eyes closed, take a deep breath and hope we can do it. It says love. It's a command. And if God said it, you can do it."

The fear rose inside him like a mountain of gall, choking him until he could barely say the word. "How?"

"Let go of yourself. Stop thinking about how great you are to do this, how much you can do, how much you've provided, how they should appreciate you. Take you out of the picture. Loving is about the other person. What they want, what they need, what they feel."

"I don't think I can do that, Jake," Gabe said sadly.

Jake laughed. "You've already started. You were concerned at the thought that you were trying to buy Daniel's affection. That's love, Gabe. Call it what you want. You don't want Willie or Mac to suffer alone on the old home place. That's caring, Gabriel." He chuckled, the sound twinkling over the airwaves straight to Gabe's heart. "You want Blair to approve of you, to commend you, to appreciate you. In my book, that's love."

"But—"

"'And He who has begun a good work in you will not stop until it is complete.' That's the Bible, buddy. God's word on the subject. He's working on teaching you love, and He's not going to stop until you learn the whole lesson."

Gabe felt the slight shift in air pressure and knew they were nearing their destination. "Don't you ever get tired of being right?" he complained.

"Nope." Jake laughed at his snarl of disgust. "What you have to do, Gabriel, is put the people first. Forget about everything else. After the people, the rest just doesn't matter. You've married into a family who is smart about these things. They already know what to value. People come first. In thirty years, is Daniel going to remember what he got for his sixth birthday, or is he going to remember that his parents were there, laughing and celebrating with him?"

Prompted by the captain's flashing light, Gabe quickly thanked his friend and said goodbye.

As they descended, then taxied into the airport, he made himself replay Jake's words.

Think about them.

So if he was Blair, in a strange house, married to someone who'd always put his money first, what would he do now?

The answer hit him hard.

Blair was the kind of woman who'd wait and see if the other person was trustworthy. She'd bide her time until she was certain she wouldn't be betrayed again.

It was ironic. If it were him in her position, Gabe knew he'd be long gone. In his books, nobody got a second chance.

You did.

The reminder that God had given him much more than one second chance burned like indigestion. Didn't it behoove him to cut everybody else a little slack? Wasn't it time to stop expecting everyone to applaud him, and start finding out who his family really was?

Gabe let himself into the silent darkened house and set his briefcase near the door.

He moved through the house. The train cake sat proud and colorful in the center of the dining room table, its cars following behind in black- and red-iced abandon. Peanut butter cookies spilled out of the cookie jar and onto a huge tray on the counter.

Gabe tucked three into a napkin, poured himself a glass of milk and headed onto the patio to think over Jake's words. He grinned. It felt good to be back, to be home.

A shadowed figure in the hot tub slowed his steps. "Blair?"

She turned to face him, her features barely discernible in the dim light. "Hi."

"Hi, yourself. How long have you been sitting here?"

She shrugged, waiting until he pulled his chair nearer. "I don't know. A while. I guess I got lost in my thoughts. Couldn't sleep."

"What kind of thoughts?" He couldn't stop the shiver of apprehension that twitched in his brain.

"Actually, I was thinking about what you said the other day." Her head came up, her eyes steady as they met his, dark and glowing in the light from the bottom of the tub. "You said you knew that Daniel and I didn't need you. That's not entirely true."

He took a bite of cookie, more for something to do than because he was hungry. All his nerves stood at attention as he waited for her to continue. *Please, God, don't let her tell me to go. Not now. Not yet!*

"I can imagine how difficult it must have been for you to handle everything, Blair. It's pretty clear that you were doing just fine on your own." He swallowed. "I'm well aware that my presence causes you stress, like impulsively buying that car. That was stupid."

He risked a glance at her and saw she was studying him, a faint smile tugging the corners of her mouth.

"That was brilliant," she muttered. "And if I hadn't been so selfish and petty, I'd have told you that right off. Daniel will love it."

"But, I thought—"

"I couldn't send it back! It's *your* gift to him. Who am I to set up conditions and terms about what you should give your own son? I've always wanted the best for Daniel and now that he's getting it, I'm afraid I have a bad case of sour grapes." She shifted so that the jets pummeled her back. "I'm sorry I did that, Gabe. It was rude."

He stared at her, unable to believe what she was saying. "I shouldn't have presumed to pick out his gift," he mumbled.

"Why not?" Her head tilted, topknot wobbling dangerously as she frowned. "Most fathers pick out a gift for their sons. Why should you be any different?" She laughed, a harsh sound that gave him a clue to the bitterness she felt. "I'm still under construction, Gabe, and God is having a tough time teaching me humility."

"Why should you be humble?" He leaned forward, elbows on his knees. "You haven't done anything to be ashamed of."

"Haven't I?" She gave an odd little laugh that seemed to jerk out of her. "Do you know why I was so mad?"

He shrugged. "I didn't consult you. I ruined your plans. I took over. Take your pick."

Slowly she shook her head. Gabe was fascinated by the movement, fully appreciative of the lovely picture she made, neck rising from the steaming water like a regal swan's. "Believe me, Blair, I know my faults."

"I was mad because you showed me up." Her words hit the night air with a hard, bitter sound. "You went out and bought this shiny car that I knew Daniel would fawn over and all I had was that measly bike to offer."

He gulped, totally fazed by her blunt admittance. "Consciously, I really wasn't trying to buy his love, Blair, though I guess if we look at base motives, that was in there."

Her hands smacked the water, sending a spray of droplets in a wide arc that managed to hit his pants and spatter his shirt.

"Stop being so self-effacing, will you?" Her voice brimmed with frustration. "I'm trying to apologize."

"Oh." He waited until he thought it was safe, then nodded. "Okay, then, I'll accept yours if you'll accept mine. You're the best mother my son could ever have. I wouldn't do anything to jeopardize his happiness." He made sure she was looking at him. "I never meant to show you up, Blair."

"Do you think I don't know that? Well, at least I figured it out once I got over my anger." She shifted to a higher step.

Gabe watched as the steam rose off her shoulders

in a thick white mist, but he held his tongue. She was telling him something. He needed to listen.

"In case you haven't noticed, I'm not very secure in my position as Daniel's mother, not with you around." She didn't look at him.

"Can you tell me why?"

Blair sighed. "It's stupid! I feel as if I've been scrounging just to make ends meet and then in you walk and in one fell swoop, manage to make his dreams come true. All I managed was to put food on the table." She glanced sideways at him, then away.

It wasn't much, but Gabe caught the flash of hurt in her eyes and called himself a fool. He'd stepped all over her pride with his high-handed methods, his determination to make up for the past. He owed her for that.

"Blair?" When she kept her eyes on the wooden bridge over the creek, stubbornly refusing to look at him, Gabe knew what he had to do. He slipped off his shoes and socks, then stepped into the tub to sit beside her, his arm sliding around her shoulders. "Listen to me, Blair."

She stared at him in disbelief, glancing from his sodden clothes to his face with bewilderment clouding her gorgeous eyes. "What are you doing, Gabe? You'll ruin those clothes!"

"This is more important." He grasped her chin in his hand and stared into her eyes. "You gave Daniel everything, Blair. You gave him life, then you loved him enough for both of us. You protected him, you cared for him, you made sure he had everything a little boy could need. Nothing I could buy would ever compare to that, and I know it. So does Daniel."

Shiny silver tears gathered on the tips of her thick brown lashes as she stared at him. Her liquid chocolate eyes filled and overflowed, sending the tears tumbling down her cheeks.

"Thank you," she whispered in a broken sob. Then she threw herself into his arms, her own going around him in a viselike grip that punched Gabe in the stomach.

He brushed a hand over her hair, tugging the comb free so that the glossy strands tumbled down in a riot of bouncy curls. His lips found the velvet cord in her neck and he brushed it tenderly.

"I don't know how you can stand me," she whimpered against his throat. "I've been so mean, so arrogant. All this time I've been trying to make you pay for something that was never your fault."

The truth crystallized in his mind. "It was my fault, Blair. I should never have allowed things to get out of control. I knew it was wrong, but I let passion overrule my conscience." He nuzzled a little closer. "But I've prayed for forgiveness and I believe God's given it. Now I need to ask for yours." He moved her away until he could stare into her eyes.

"Will you forgive me for that night, Blair? And for all the mistakes I've made since?"

She nodded slowly, her words, when they came, whisper soft. "I have to."

He moved her hair so he could see every angle and curve of her beautiful face. "No, you don't have to," he corrected her. "You could go on hating me forever, and I'd deserve it."

As he watched, a light from within began to glow in

the depths of her eyes. They stayed focused steadily on him while her head turned from left to right.

"I don't hate you, Gabriel Sloan."

He whooshed out a sigh of relief and closed his eyes. He leaned until his forehead pressed against hers, searching for some way to tell her what her forgiveness meant.

"I can't hate you. I love you, Gabe. I always have."

His head jerked up as he searched those shiny depths, desperately craving the truth.

"I love you more than life. It just took me a while to realize it." She smiled, one hand lifting to touch his cheek, to brush against the stubble on his chin, smooth the furrow of confusion across his forehead. "I always thought my love for you was a mistake, a childish infatuation. Something I'd grown out of. I was wrong."

"Wh-what are you saying?" He could barely breathe.

"Is it so hard to accept?" she murmured, her innocent eyes laughing into his. "I love you. That's why I wanted to marry you then. That's why I married you now. I tried to hide it, tried to pretend it wasn't real. But I realized today that my pretending only builds walls between us." She leaned forward and kissed him tenderly, her lips featherlight against his. "I want Daniel to know you, to love you the way a child loves and adores his father. I want him to depend on you, to trust you, to run to you when he needs help."

"I'm not a very good father, Blair." It was the only thing that he could say. Fear clutched his throat.

"You're a wonderful father, Gabe. You care about Daniel, you want the best for him. You won't let him down, you'll always do your best to see that he gets what he needs. You're fair and understanding and patient. You love him."

The words pierced his heart like a white-hot arrow, tunneling to the very core of him. Was it true? Was it love, this fierce need to make sure Daniel never wanted for anything, never felt alone or abandoned? Had love made him walk out of that meeting before it was over so he could be here for his son's sixth birthday?

"I know because that's exactly the way I feel about him, too." She smiled at the confusion Gabe knew was written all over his face.

"But that doesn't mean…" He stopped, unwilling to say it aloud, just in case it was true and he'd spoil it all.

"That doesn't mean I love you?" She laughed softly. "I loved you long ago, Gabe. When you were dragging me to all those Hollywood parties, I knew. I only went because I could see that it meant a lot to you, and I didn't want to spoil it for you."

"But how can you forgive me for letting you walk away? For asking you to do something you felt was wrong?" He didn't understand this, didn't want to trust in it, to believe that such forgiveness existed.

"How can I not?" She linked her fingers in his, her forefinger pressing against the wedding band she'd slipped on his hand mere weeks ago. "'By this will all men know that you are My disciples, if you have love one for another.' How can I not love you when God loves and forgives me?"

"It sounds too easy." He frowned, waiting for that steady glow to die in her eyes.

"I know. That's exactly what I said to God. It's too

easy. He should pay for forcing me to leave, to have Daniel alone. It's not fair."

Gabe waited, knowing she wasn't finished. His fingers couldn't help but touch her hair, burying themselves in its glossy fullness. To be near Blair was to touch her.

"I sat here, full of anger and bitterness, pouting. Then the truth hit me. God's son died for me. Was that fair?" She smiled, the tears coursing down her cheeks as she shook her head.

"I'm sorry, Gabe. From here on in, I'm letting go of the grudges, the complaints, the bitterness. It's forgiven. I don't care what you've done or what happened in the past." Her mouth split wide in a smile of pure joy. "I love you."

Gabe couldn't stop himself from basking in that light any more than he could prevent his arms from wrapping themselves around her and pulling her so close he thought he'd never let go.

As her arms fit around his neck and drew his head to hers, a deep sense of peace washed over him. He'd waited for this for so long, wanted to be held like this so many times. How often had he watched her and yearned to hold her in his arms, to immerse himself in a love like this. To feel as if he belonged.

The doubts crept in, clawing their way into the circle that held them together.

"What if I mess up?" he whispered, his hands tight around her. "What if I can't be the husband or father you want?"

Blair's long, elegant fingers slid from his shoulders to cup his face in her hands. She stared into his eyes, her love burning into his like a beacon of hope.

"You already are," she whispered before kissing him.

"I want to be your wife, Gabriel Sloan. Your *real* wife." She slipped from his arms, stepped out of the hot tub and reached out a hand.

As if in a dream, Gabe followed, his fingers threading through hers. She led him through the patio doors and into the room he'd built especially for them.

He stared at her in the darkness, thankful that only the moon cast a glow. Gently, tenderly, he set her away from him.

"This isn't right," he whispered sadly. "It's like before. I'll be taking, and I still can't say what you want to hear. I'm not sure I'll ever be able to do that." He swallowed hard. "I can't love anyone, Blair. That part of me is dead."

She stood there, her swimsuit dark in the moonbeam that flickered through the skylight. Her eyes glistened with unshed tears, unfathomable in the dimness, until she took two steps closer to him.

"It isn't the same, Gabe. Not at all. We're married, and I've committed my life to you. I'm not going to run away, to hide, to wish for more." Her fingers grasped his shirtfront and pulled his face to within inches of hers.

"I love you *exactly* as you are, Gabriel Sloan. Isn't that enough?" She turned away for a moment, and his heart ached as he watched her walk away. When she returned, she held a sheaf of papers in her hand, which she laid on the table in front of him.

"I know you still feel this is necessary. You've kept them hidden, waiting for the right time to ask me to sign them. That's okay. I don't need the security of your money or your company to love you," she whispered, turning pages until she came to the final one. Quickly, with a flourish, the prenuptial papers were signed. She folded them and slid them into the envelope, then held them out. "I love you. I know there are no guarantees with love, but that's okay with me. Love is enough."

Gabe set the envelope on the table as if it burned his fingers, but he couldn't deny the relief he felt. At Blair's questioning touch, he pulled her into the circle of his arms, closing his eyes as the warmth of her love enfolded him once more.

It was enough for her, but was it enough for him? Would she ever really *need* him the way he needed her in his life?

Would he one day regret not being able to say those words, to give her the love she deserved?

Please, God, show me what love is.

Chapter Twelve

Blair whooshed a breath of air in the stillness of her workroom, the sparkle of her rings shafting a glow of happiness straight to her heart.

"My life might be close to paradise in that castle," she grunted as she heaved a pail of honey out of the way. "But it's pure labor on this side of the tracks."

"Hey, Busy Bee, how's it going?" Mac leaned against the doorway, watching from under the brim of his cap.

"It's going." Blair swiped a hand across her forehead and reached for another frame. "It's only mid-July and so far I've got more honey than in any previous year." She struggled to cut the wax free of the frame. "I wish I could afford a machine to do this. It's so time-consuming."

"Ask and ye shall receive." Mac grinned, stepped to the side and waved a hand. "Tada! Enter, gentlemen."

Albert risked one shy smile before turning his attention to the machine he and Gabe carried inside.

"What's this?" She watched as Gabe plugged it in

and Albert demonstrated the machine's ability to uncap the honey in one quick step. "You guys are geniuses!"

Gabe winked at Mac. "I've been telling her that for ages."

"I hope you don't mind that I've been watching you," Albert murmured, his head down. "I had to see exactly what needed doing before I could figure out a design."

Blair laughed in delight as she moved one frame then another through, watching the wax pile neatly. Soon she had enough frames ready to start the extractor.

"Come and watch anytime," she invited. "If this is the result, you guys are welcome at any hour."

"I'd like my thank-you now." Gabe sauntered over and wrapped an arm around her waist, clearly waiting for a kiss of appreciation. She brushed her lips against his cheek. Gradually she was getting used to this new, lighter-hearted Gabe.

"You've got a first-rate crop this year, Busy Bee. And the price is up." Mac grinned, smug delight gleaming in his eyes as he watched Gabe fiddle possessively with her hair. "Looks like I did the right thing when I sold that land, don't you think?"

"Mom!" Daniel raced through the door, his grubby face glowing. He dashed over and wrapped himself around Blair's legs. "Me an' Willie got a surprise for you."

Willie stumbled in the door behind him, gasping for breath, her hand at her throat. "Mercy! I'm about to keel over." Her thin chest heaved. "Haven't run so hard in thirty years."

"I won, though, Willie! I won."

"So you did, boy." Willie collapsed on the chair Mac held out, her narrow face flushed with healthy color.

Blair looked for signs that she was all right, then squatted to smile at Daniel. She shoved the lock of hair from his forehead and brushed at the smudge of dust on his nose. "Willie and I have a surprise," she corrected.

"Do you?" He frowned. "So do we! I'll tell mine first."

"No, I meant it's improper to say me and Willie." Blair sighed at the confusion on his little face. "Go ahead, tell me."

"Can I tell her, Willie? Can I?"

It was clear to Blair that he would tell whether or not he was granted permission, but she kept her lips closed.

"You tell her, Daniel. I have to catch my breath." Willie huffed and puffed in an exaggerated fashion that made Daniel laugh.

"Okay," he agreed. He turned to Blair, hands on his hips, a gleam of barely suppressed joy flickering in his green eyes. "Mr. Bart—" He frowned, glanced at Willie, then started over. "Mr. Bartholemew from the Super Mart said he wants to buy four hundred pounds of honey!" He grinned with delight.

"Four hundred?" Blair looked at Willie for confirmation. "But that's double what he ordered last year!"

Willie nodded, her breathing having slowed fractionally. "He said he's had requests ever since he sold out, and he wants to make sure he doesn't run out this time. He's willing to pay a bit more to guarantee his supply."

When she named how much more, Blair sagged onto

a chair. "Oh, my!" She glanced at the two local women Gabe had hired to help out. They grinned, raised thumbs up and kept right on working. "Four hundred pounds!" She could hardly believe it.

The telephone's urgent peal broke through the rush of excited voices. Blair hurried to the office.

"Yes, this is Mind Your Own Beeswax. I see. Yes, I think so." She listened for a moment, then frowned. "May I ask how you heard of us? Oh, I see." She glanced across the tiny room, searching for and finding Gabe lounging in the doorway. She couldn't help the smile that rose to her lips.

"Yes, that brochure was my husband's creation. If you'll fax me the particulars, I'll get back to you with an estimate. Is that all right?" Assured that it was, she sat holding the receiver until the recorded message asked her to hang up.

"Is everything all right?" Gabe frowned at her lack of response. In two strides he was beside her, his hand gently covering hers. "Blair? What's wrong?"

"Nothing." She blinked, seeing anew his beloved face, closely cropped head, large powerful hands. "I think I've just hit the big time. Some chain of boutiques saw that flyer you helped me design and wants to carry our Christmas candles. They also want me to think about creating a special line just for them."

He grinned. "I knew those colors would go over big if you just spread the word. Good for you! You're going to have to hire some more help, you know."

She gulped. "I know. But there's no room here."

"Then we'll add on." He winked at her. "These are

good problems, Blair. Everyone wants these kinds of problems."

"I guess." She let him hug her while her mind whirled with the potential of it all. "I just thought it would take longer. I'd never have managed it if you hadn't made me see the possibilities."

He brushed a kiss over her forehead, his hand smoothing her hair. "It's the very least I could do," he murmured, arms linked around her waist. He leaned in close and added, "For my wife."

Blair couldn't stop the smile that caught at her lips on hearing those words. They weren't exactly the words she longed to hear, but she wouldn't complain. Gabe had changed so much, a little more wasn't impossible for the Lord, was it?

"Of course your work is selling, dear. I knew it all along. Just took a bit of the right kind of management." Willie moved beside Gabe. She beamed at him proudly. "Didn't take much sense to see that Gabe is the man who helped make those dreams come true. I knew the first time I met him."

So did I. Blair wanted to agree loudly, but not here in front of everyone. She wanted to tell him herself, in private. Later.

"I guess this means your machine will get a real workout, Albert. Thank you so much for thinking of it." She gave him a hug and a kiss on his bald spot. "Now if I could just get the wax purified and treated a little easier. There is a machine, you know. But it's terribly expensive." She fell into thought.

Blair didn't hear anything until Mac's voice cut

through the chatter in the room and flew straight to her ear.

"Maybe you should just buy the wax outright. Spend your time on producing candles, not cleaning beeswax. You could sell your rough stock and buy the finished product. You might even design some colors of your own and commission someone to make them for you."

He scratched his head, his tanned forehead furrowed. "Of course, I don't know much about that sort of thing."

Blair stared at him as the idea took shape. "On the contrary, Grandpa. You are smarter than you give yourself credit for." She raced across the room, flung her arms around his neck and hugged him with delight. "Smarter than anyone I know."

She began dreaming of possibilities right there in the workroom. So immersed was she, Willie, Mac, Albert and Daniel had wandered off to get a cool drink at the castle by the time she blinked at the snapping fingers in front of her and saw Gabe's laughing face.

"And you say I get involved!" He hugged her. "Something's brewing, isn't it?"

"Yes!" She hugged him hard. "I can do this, Gabe! Thanks to you and Albert, Mac, Willie and Daniel, I believe I can really do this." She giggled as he swung her around the room, giddy with joy.

If the inane smirks of her employees hadn't shoved reality into her face, Gabe's cell phone pealing its high-pitched call would have. He made a face but let her go and pulled the tiny phone from his pocket.

"Sloan." His forehead pleated. "Hey, Rich! What's up?" He frowned, his fingers rubbing against Blair's.

Suddenly, all motion stopped. His face grew cold and hard. "He what?"

Blair stood waiting, knowing from the tenseness of his neck, the rigid straightening of his backbone, that something was terribly wrong.

"I'll be there." He clicked the phone closed and shoved it into his pocket. "I have to go to L.A." The clipped, hard tones brooked no discussion.

Blair took his hand and drew him from the room into the freshness of the summer afternoon air. "What's the matter, Gabe? Please tell me."

He lips turned upward in a smile, but no flicker of joy lit his gorgeous eyes. Cold and hard, they stared straight ahead.

"My father's back. He's buying up Polytech shares and offering my employees bigger and better profits if they will sell their stock to him, or at least back him in a takeover."

"A takeover?" She whispered the words, aghast at the man's temerity. How could he do this to his own son? How could he deliberately sabotage the happiness Gabe had found in this one small area of his life?

"I'll have to leave immediately. Rich has already ordered a local chopper to take me to the airfield. That's how badly he wants me there." His jaw clenched and unclenched.

"I know. It's okay. We'll manage, Gabe. We'll be waiting." She stroked his arm, hoping to infuse her words with assurance and calmness. "Do you need me to come with you?"

His head jerked up, his eyes wide. "You'd do that?"

"Of course. I told you, I love you. If you want my help, for whatever it's worth, you've got it."

He stared at her for a long time before his arms reached out and drew her near. He held her against his chest, his head resting on hers. "Thank you, Blair," he murmured at last, the distant purring of the chopper drawing him from his contemplation. "It will be easier to fight knowing that."

She moved slightly to study his face. "Is that what you want to do?" she asked quietly. "You want to fight him over this?"

The air chilled immediately. His arms dropped away. "You don't think I should fight my own father for a company he's only ever tried to destroy?" He shook his head. "No, I suppose you don't. You couldn't possibly understand."

Blair knew she had to force him to look at what was ahead. Part of their problems had stemmed from his inability to get love from his father. He had to come to terms with that.

She gripped his hands, rubbing her thumbs tenderly over the work-roughened knuckles. "I'm not asking about him," she whispered. "I'm asking what *you* want. Truthfully, honestly. Do you want to fight your father on this?"

"Yes!" The affirmative burst from him in heated vehemence. "I want to show him that I will never again be the sissy, the wimp that he terrified all those years. I want him to know that I can take him on, anytime, and win." He paced back and forth.

"You want to punish him."

His head jerked up, his eyes flashed, and his jaw was clenched in a ruthless line. "Yes."

"Where will that leave you, Gabe?" Blair ignored the wild gusting wind from the chopper blades. She knew time was precious, but so was his spirit. "Will you allow yourself to be crushed by unforgiveness? Because, we both know it's only you who will be hurt. A man like that doesn't understand what he's done."

One corner of his mouth tipped in a sneer. "Vengeance is mine, says the Lord. Is that what you mean?" He waited for her nod. "Well, this opportunity is heavensent. I don't intend to throw it away. Then I'm coming back here, Blair. For good."

Blair sighed, her soul troubled but her face smiling. "Then go, do what you must. I love you, Gabe. I'll always love you. No matter what." As the pilot raced across the road, she stood on tiptoes and kissed Gabe, trying to express all that lay in her heart. "We'll be here, waiting, Daniel and I. Hurry home."

He grabbed her and hugged her close, as if afraid he'd never have the chance to do that again. When he set her free, Blair threaded her hand in his and walked with him toward the chopper.

"You'll call me? Every day? Do you need anything?"

He grinned and tapped his forehead. "It's all in here."

"You'll call me if you need me? Promise?" She waited anxiously for his agreement.

When they were less than fifty feet from the helicopter, Gabe's hands on her forearms forced her to stop.

"Thank you for offering," he said directly into her ear.

"But this is something I have to do. I've been waiting for this chance my whole life. I'm going to make him see what he missed." He studied her eyes to be sure she understood. "You need to stay here, take care of our son. Say goodbye to Daniel for me."

Blair held his gaze, imprinting every detail in her memory. Then she nodded solemnly. "Go with God, my love," she murmured as he strode across the grass to the waiting pilot.

Gabe sat tall, silently staring at her, as the craft whirled into the air. She lifted a hand, pressed it to her lips and then held it aloft. Blair told herself he smiled and then mocked her own foolishness as the tears welled and the worry engulfed her.

"Rocks don't smile," her conscience reminded her as she plodded to the work shed. "They don't have feelings."

She bypassed the building and headed up the hill, tracing the steps she and Gabe had taken such a short time ago. When she got to the top, she collapsed on the grass and stared at the shimmering beauty before her.

Why, God? Why did You take him away, just when I was beginning to believe in happily ever after?

Heaven stayed silent.

Chapter Thirteen

"Mommy?"

"Yes, Daniel?"

"Where is my daddy?"

The same words he'd asked months ago, but oh, the wealth of meaning they contained now.

Blair tucked her son into his captain's bed, then brushed a hand over his disheveled hair. "Your daddy loves you very much, Daniel." Of that much, at least, she was certain.

"Why doesn't he come home?" The little eyelids dropped over sad green eyes, reminding Blair of another wounded child and the vengeance he now sought.

"Daddy will come as soon as he can, sweetheart. He just has to finish his work. He doesn't like being away, but it's very important to him. I think we should pray for him."

Daniel nodded and squeezed his eyes closed. His hands folded reverently. "Me first," he insisted, opening one eye to check for her nod. "Dear God, this is Daniel Sloan. That's my name now, remember, 'cause I gots a daddy, just like the other kids. He's a good daddy, and I love him a lot. Did you see the kite he sended me from the big city? I love kites."

Blair smiled, but kept silent. This was Daniel's petition. He should offer it in his own way.

"My daddy's been gone an awful long time." He pried one eye open. "How long?"

."Eight days," Blair told him, suppressing a grin when he shut the eye and continued blithely as if there'd been no pause.

"You prob'ly already know he's been gone that long, and maybe that isn't a long time to you 'cause you made the whole earth and everything in six. But it's a horrible long time to me. I want my daddy back. I want him here, with me. We gotta be a family. My daddy needs a family. He never had none. Amen."

The abrupt ending caught Blair off guard and she hurriedly composed her own prayer. Though it was shorter than Daniel's, it was just as direct and to the point. She wanted her husband, the man she loved, home.

Daniel added another amen after hers, then wiggled under the coverlet. "I know God'll send him pretty soon." He yawned. "I hope I'm not sleeping when Daddy comes home."

"I'm sure Gabe would wake you up if you were." She pressed a kiss to his forehead, her throat tightening as the chubby little arms squeezed her neck in a hug. "Good night, sweetie. Pleasant dreams."

"Night, Mommy."

She snapped off the light, leaving only the sailboat night-light burning. As Daniel's soft snores filled the room, she slipped out, pulling the door closed behind her.

Blair was about to head to the hot tub in hopes of easing the cramps in her neck when the phone pealed its summons.

"Gabe! How are you? Is everything all right?" She sank onto the grass next to the rose garden and listened to the weariness in his beloved voice.

"Couldn't be better. Finally got them with their hands in the cookie jar. Legal proceedings, Rich says. That ought to hold off their bid for a while. Stock's up again. Apparently some people wouldn't mind seeing Farnover's takeover."

"Farnover's? You've been refusing them for a while. Is that who's backing your father?" Though she'd learned a few of the details, Blair could only pretend to understand corporate maneuvering.

"Yeah. They always did operate out of the back door." His voice died away. "How are you, Blair? How's Daniel?"

"He's fine. He prayed for you tonight, Gabe. He wants his daddy home." She said it deliberately, hoping he would understand.

"I'm not abandoning him, Blair. I'll be back as soon as I get that shyster off my case permanently." Bitterness, harsh and painful, laced his tone. "He's determined to cow me. To prove he's a better man. Well, I'm not caving. Not anymore."

Blair sighed. More than ever, Gabe was sounding like the man she'd left in L.A.

"Daniel doesn't know corporate America, Gabe. He just knows his daddy isn't there to tickle him or wrestle with or swim with. He misses you."

The silence stretched unbearably.

"I miss him, too. And you. And Mac and Willie and Albert. I miss the simplicity of it. The relaxed pace. Time here runs from one day into the next, and I forget whether I called you yesterday or not. Is that terrible to say?" He sounded worried.

"Of course not." She waited, but when he didn't volunteer any more information, Blair closed her eyes and pictured him alone, tired, full of bitterness and hatred. "Are you all right, Gabe? Are you eating and sleeping?"

"I'm fine."

"I miss you, Gabe. I love you."

"I know."

Tears squeezed out between her lids. She'd wanted so badly to hear the words. She needed to know he loved her, cared about her, wanted to be there with her. Was that asking so much?

His voice, when it finally came, was thin and sad, making her heart clench with pain. "I wish I could hold you, Blair. I wish I could just hold you, right now, right here."

She swallowed. At least he'd admitted that much.

"Do you want me to come?" she whispered.

"No! I don't want you anywhere near him. He's evil. He ruins everything good in my life."

As she waited, Blair silently prayed, begging for the right words to say to show him her love.

"Are you still there?"

"I'm here," she whispered.

"Why did you call my son Daniel?"

The words shocked her for a moment. Then she

recalled a newspaper clipping Mac had left for her to read. Daniel—his father's name. Oh, no!

Help me, Lord.

"Blair?"

"When I was in labor, the contractions came very hard and very fast. It was a long labor, and believe me, labor is the right word for it. At one point I was so tired and discouraged that I was ready to agree to their suggestion for cesarean delivery."

"But that's so hard on the mother!" His breathing quickened.

"Mac came in to give Willie a breather. She'd stayed with me all through it, and she needed to relax, so when a quiet period came, in he marched." She smiled, remembering his rigid posture that belied the fear lurking in his eyes. "I told him I didn't think I could do it anymore, and he reminded me that my baby was just like Daniel in the lion's den. The contractions were the lions, and he drew this analogy that if I didn't fight to get my baby out, to give him life, the lions would squeeze the life out of him."

Blair grimaced, not totally sure why she'd told him the tale. "It's a weird kind of analogy, I suppose, but I saw exactly what he was driving at. Some things are worth fighting for. My baby was Daniel to me after that, the whole time I fought to get him into this world. And that's what he stayed."

Gabe said nothing for a long time. Then he whispered, "Thank you." Eventually he regained his voice. "That's what I'm doing," he told her. "I'm driving off the lions so my child will have a future."

Blair squeezed the receiver tightly, then asked the question.

"Are you fighting for justice and truth, Gabe? Or are you merely hoping to exact revenge? It's important to know the difference."

"I have to go." The hardness, the edge—suddenly they were back in his voice.

"Okay. I love you, Gabe. So does Daniel, and all the rest of us. We miss you. Please come back soon."

The click of the line told her he was gone.

Alone and unobserved at last, Blair sat in the semi-darkness and let the tears pour down her cheeks. When Willie sank beside her, she didn't bother to hide them.

"He doesn't need us," she sobbed. "He'll never love us now. He's the same old Gabe, Willie. Business first, last and always. He's enmeshed in trying to remake the little boy whose father hurt him. He can't see that he's got a far better future waiting right here."

Willie hugged her close and dabbed at her tears, but she didn't contradict Blair one iota. Instead, in a hushed voice, she began praying for the man who hurt like a child.

Blair pressed the pedal down hard and headed for the work barn she'd called home for the last four nights. The honey crop was heavier than anything she could have imagined.

Daniel, just home from a camping trip with friends, would not be dissuaded from his opinion that his father's return was imminent. If they'd hoped to take the child's mind off his absent father, it wasn't working. Blair wished she had something that would accomplish that for her. She thought about Gabe constantly, wondered how negotiations were going, how he was dealing with it. Gabe had been gone twelve long days. To Blair, they were like years.

She'd worked late the past two nights and hadn't been home in time for his calls. Mac relayed the information, of course, but that wasn't the same as talking to Gabe herself. When she'd tried to call back, his cell phone was off. Though his secretary promised, in a polite, distracted voice, to relay her message and the new phone number of the shop, Blair held out little hope of a return call.

As she steered the truck into the yard, she forced herself to face the fear that had been mounting inside her brain for days. Gabe had been sucked back into his old life. The money, the things, they'd become more important. Keeping them from his father took every moment of time and concentration. Hatred seemed to feed his actions.

She'd lost him.

Blair dashed her tears and climbed out of the cab, determined to go on with a facade of strength and composure. Albert, Willie, Mac, Daniel, they still needed her. Perhaps now more than ever. She had to be strong. She had to manage alone.

"Oh, Blair, I'm so glad you're here. Willie wandered down a few minutes ago, and she's determined to help. I can't seem to stop her." The young assistant Gabe had hired grabbed Blair's arm. "Please make her stop. I'm afraid she's going to hurt herself."

Blair followed her into the shed and saw immediately what she meant. Willie stood by the workbench, lifting cases of candles that had been packed earlier. She teetered her way toward them, straining to hold the stack intact.

Blair was about to lift them out of her arms when Willie tripped. Though she was in obvious pain, she took great care to protect the boxes and landed awkwardly on her left hip. The graying skin tone and grimace of tightened lips told Blair everything she needed to know.

"Where did you hurt yourself, Willie?" She knelt by the older woman's side and swallowed the bitter gall of panic. "Can you get up?"

Willie's tightly clenched lips grew white, and she lay back with a moan. "No. It hurts too much. I'm sorry, Blair. I didn't mean to cause problems for you. I just wanted to help."

"I know." Blair took her hand and felt for her pulse. "Don't worry about that now. I'm going to call an ambulance. I don't want to move you in case it's something serious. Just stay still for a moment."

Oh, Lord, she's so special. Please keep her safe.

Blair directed her helpers to bring an old blanket, the only covering she could think of. They tucked it around the thin, frail woman. Then there was nothing to do but wait.

It seemed eons before the ambulance drivers arrived. It didn't take them long to assess the problem.

"Fractured hip, I'd guess," one of them muttered as they lifted Willie into the ambulance. "Woman her age shouldn't be working in a place like this. It's too heavy."

Blair flushed to the roots of her hair but she didn't

bother to correct his impression. It was more important to get Willie taken care of.

"You go on ahead," she told them, her mind surging. "I'll need a vehicle. My grandfather will want to come, too. I'll follow you."

At home, Mac and Albert sat beside the pool, watching Daniel play halfheartedly in the shallow end.

"Did you see Willie? Silly woman won't give up on this fool idea of doing her share, even if it kills her." Mac crossed his arms. "Did you bring her back?"

There was no way to sugarcoat it. Blair took a deep breath. "She's on her way to the hospital, Grandpa. She fell. The ambulance guys thought she'd probably broken her hip. I'm on my way there now."

"We're coming with you." In a few swift moves, Mac had Daniel out of the pool and was drying him off in a big fluffy towel. "Grab your clothes quickly, son, and let's get going. Willie needs us."

Albert trundled along behind when they finally left the castle. His face was pale, his eyes huge behind the horn-rimmed glasses. "She doesn't like hospitals," he muttered to Blair. "She won't want to stay there."

Blair patted his hand. "I know, Albert. We'll just have to pray." She'd taken Gabe's keys to the Jeep without even thinking, and they piled inside without a word.

Mac gently explained the situation to Daniel as Blair drove.

"Will Willie be okay? I don't want her to hurt."

"I don't either, son. I'm sure God will take good care of her." Mac tried to reassure the six-year-old, but his words didn't quiet Daniel.

"I need to talk to my daddy," he kept repeating. "He'll make it better. He knows what to do."

Gabe! Blair hadn't even thought of him. "We'll phone him as soon as we find out something about Willie. Now just sit quietly and let me drive."

By the time they reached the hospital, they were all tense with worry. The doctor met them inside. "She's fractured her hip. The X rays show a clear break. We're going to have her flown to Denver where a surgeon will insert a sort of screw that holds the bone together. She'll be there for a few days, then they'll bring her back. She should be up and walking by then."

"Thank you, Doctor. Could you let us know when we could see her? It's important for all of us to talk to her before she leaves."

The doctor nodded, then hurried away. Once he'd gone, Blair caught sight of Mac's gray face. His mouth worked impotently for a few moments. His hand gripped her sleeve.

"I want Willie to have the best care, you know that. But he wants to fly her, Busy Bee! We don't have that kind of money. And we don't have insurance to cover that. How will we manage?"

He wobbled, grabbing Albert's arm for support.

"I'll take care of it." Blair led him to a chair in the waiting room and eased him into it. "That's what I do, remember? I take care of things. It will be fine, Grandpa. As long as Willie is all right, we can handle anything." She saw him struggle to take a breath and loosened his collar. "Are you all right?"

"I'm fine. It's my sister I'm worried about. We have

to think about her." He leaned his head against the wall, closed his eyes and began to move his lips.

Blair knew he was praying. She felt the tug on her jeans and squatted in front of Daniel. "What is it, son?"

"Are you gonna call my daddy now?"

She hugged him, then set him free. "Not just yet. I want to see Willie first, talk to her. Then I'll have some news for your dad."

"We should phone him right now. My daddy would come home right now if he knew we needed him." With a frown at his mother, Daniel turned and walked to the chairs. He plunked himself down beside Mac, threaded his fingers in the older man's and closed his eyes, obviously following his grandfather's example.

"I'll stay with them. You go see the nurse. She's been waiting to talk to you." Albert smiled encouragingly, and she hugged him.

"Thank you, Albert. You're a true friend." She dealt with the nurse's questions as efficiently as possible, greatly relieved when the doctor came to tell her Willie could see them for a few minutes.

"She's ready for flight so don't hold her up too long. We like to get these things taken care of as quickly as possible."

Blair nodded, then went to collect the rest of her family. They found Willie comfortably ensconced on a stretcher, though her eyes showed the pain she was in. Still, the same old smile of welcome lifted Blair's weary heart.

"I'm so sorry, Willie. I should never have let you—"

"You couldn't have stopped me. Though I'm sorry to

have caused such a fuss. And so much expense! Dear, dear, how will we pay for this?"

Mac lurched forward, his face gray and haggard. "We have God as our father, sister. He owns the cattle on a thousand hills, remember? He'll supply all our needs. We'll manage just fine. You concentrate on getting well."

Daniel stepped nearer the bed. "I prayed for you, Willie. And my daddy is coming. We'll look after you."

"Thank you, darling." She ruffled his hair tenderly. "Getting Gabe here is exactly what we need. Good thinking."

Albert contented himself with squeezing her hand, and then Willie was gone.

Blair spared a moment to search for her composure. Then she whirled. "All right now, everyone. Let's—" The words jammed in her throat as Mac wavered on his feet, his hand clenching his left arm. "Grandpa, what's wrong?"

His voice emerged raspy and thin, his legs doubling under him as Albert grabbed his shoulders. "Get a doctor, Busy Bee. I think it's a heart attack."

Chapter Fourteen

Blair paced the length of the waiting room for the hundredth time, begging and pleading with God to save her grandfather's life. She was barely aware of Albert and Daniel returning from the cafeteria until Daniel's hand closed around hers.

"Can we call my daddy now, Mommy?" he begged, his green eyes serious. "Daddy loves Mac and Willie. We're his family. He needs to come home."

Blair sat down and hugged him close. "I know he does, honey. And I did call him. But I couldn't reach him. His secretary says he's not there and he doesn't answer his cell phone." She didn't tell Daniel how much that combination of events worried her. Nor did she speculate on where Gabe could be or what he was doing.

Instead she focused her attention on her son and the loyal friend who'd stood by them through an hour of interminable waiting. "I guess the only thing we can do now is wait. And pray."

"Mrs. Sloan?" The doctor stood behind her, his voice solemn.

"How is he?"

"We won't know that for some time. Right now he's in and out of consciousness. He keeps asking for you. I think it might be best if you came with me. Just you."

She nodded, then turned to explain to Daniel.

Albert smiled. "We'll wait here, Blair. You go ahead."

"Thank you." She followed the doctor down the hall and deep into the caverns of the hospital. Finally they came to a room where bleeps and blips of various machines were monitored on the big console at the nursing station.

"We haven't been able to regulate Mr. Rhodes's heartbeat yet," the doctor explained. "He's on oxygen and hooked up to several monitors. Try to get him to relax. That's the best medicine."

Blair nodded, prepared for the worst as she followed the doctor to her grandfather's bed. Mac looked so frail under the white sheet, his fingers thin and gaunt, bluish where the IV dripped into them.

"Grandpa? I'm here. Please try to relax. You need to get your rest. The doctors are trying to help you. Please hold on. Please, Mac?" Blair carefully lifted his unfettered hand and slipped hers into it.

Mac's eyelids fluttered as if he were rousing himself from a deep sleep. Finally they lifted. Blair breathed a prayer of thanks as she saw recognition in his eyes. His fingers tightened around hers for an instant.

"Call Gabe," he rasped, his face contorting with the effort of speaking, his eyes closing.

"I tried." She hurried to reassure him, anxious to keep

him awake and aware. "I couldn't reach him. He's not in the office."

Mac's fingers loosened, and his chest sank as he heaved a weary, painful breath. "Call Gabe. You need him now." The words died away as he sank into some oblivion that Blair couldn't enter.

"I'm sorry, but you'll have to leave now. He needs to rest. We're trying to stabilize him, but it's an uphill battle." The nurse drew her from the room and closed the door.

Blair stood alone in the hallway. Around her, the hospital bustled with medical efficiency, but she paid it no mind. Grandpa might die! He could leave her at any moment, and she'd be all alone.

She walked in a stupor as reality punched her with the utter hopelessness of it all. Somehow she found herself in the waiting room. Daniel lay asleep on his chair, his little body hunched in a defensive curl. Albert rose and helped her into a chair, his face grave.

"Blair, we need to get hold of Gabe."

"Why does everyone keep saying that?" she half-sobbed, her knuckles against her mouth. "Grandpa just said the same thing."

"Then you have to do it. No matter how much it hurts, no matter what it costs you, you have to tell Gabe that you need him here now." Albert's hands cradled hers. "You've been like a daughter to me, Blair. You've nursed me back to health mentally and physically. You've given me so much. Let me give a little back to you."

She blinked away the tears. "Advice?" she asked tremulously.

"I know it seems silly for me to give advice to anyone." He smiled to show he didn't mind her surprise. "But I believe I've learned a lot from your family. And the one thing you do when things get tough is draw together."

She nodded.

"Gabe is part of this family, Blair. He deserves the chance to be here, to be part of this. There may be decisions to be made. He can help you with those, or just support you. You need your husband. Your son needs his father. Isn't it time to admit that this is one thing you can't handle on your own? Call him."

"What if he doesn't come? His business is very important to him, you know." She wiped away the tears and recited all the excuses she'd given herself in the past few hours.

"I believe you're more important to him than anything else in the world. What if you deny him the opportunity to show you that? What if you exclude him from the only family he's ever known, the only love he's ever felt? Mac is as much his as he is yours. Gabe needs to be here."

Having said his piece, Albert walked to his guarding position beside Daniel, bowed his head and closed his eyes.

Blair closed her eyes also, but not in prayer. Her mind replayed the distant past, a time when she'd been so badly hurt. A time when she'd needed Gabe and he hadn't been there for her.

What if he doesn't come now? What if he puts us on hold until his company is straightened out? What if he doesn't want us anymore?

What if he's waiting to be asked? What if he yearns

to be needed, to be wanted? Would you deny him the love you promised him?

The questions raged inside her brain until she could no longer think straight. She glanced at Albert. "I'm going to the chapel," she whispered, and waited for his nod before she left.

As she passed a bank of phones, the pressure inside built to nearly bursting. *Phone Gabe. Tell him you need him.*

With a prayer for help, she lifted the receiver and dialed.

"I'm sorry, Mrs. Sloan, but he hasn't returned. I'll give him your message as soon as he does."

She dialed his cell phone and got no answer.

Blair leaned her head against the cool, solid metal of the phone mechanism and prayed. "I've tried, Lord. I've tried to call him. He's too busy with his old life."

An idea glimmered in her mind. She scrounged through her handbag until she found the decrepit old address book. Gabe's condo number was there. With shaking hands, she dialed again.

The phone rang several times, but no one picked up. Blair moved the receiver from her ear, ready to hang up, then caught the sound of his beloved voice.

"Leave a message. I'll call you back."

Frantically she searched for the words, the right phrase. But the beep signaled her cue, and there was no more time.

"Gabe, this is Blair." She took a deep breath, squeezed her eyes closed and said the words she had never allowed him to hear. "I need you, Gabe. Please come home."

The machine cut her off. Slowly she replaced the

receiver. As she did, Blair felt a deep, cleansing peace surge through her body. She had done the most she could.

"The rest is up to You," she whispered as she pushed open the chapel door and knelt in the back pew. Her eyes caught the tender, loving glance of Jesus as he gazed down at her from a painting.

"Please be with *all* the members of my family and bring us together again. Please bring us home."

Gabe stood on the beach in the twilight, feet bare, jacket tossed carelessly onto the sand.

He'd lost everything.

How could his own father have employed such devious methods? The question drew a bitter smile to his lips. Why was he so surprised?

He stared at the water rushing to shore in big, swelling waves that dashed on the sand in a thousand sparkling droplets. And suddenly he understood Blair's fascination with this place.

The wind spit water on his face, tossed sand against his pants, flipped his perfect tie into wild abandon. For a moment, just one precious moment, he forgot everything but the wonder of the world God had created.

The sky loomed over the sea in an endless swath of darkening blue satin. The beach. He sank to his knees and let a handful of the minuscule grains sift through his fingers. How many grains did it take to make a beach like this? God knew. Jake said He'd even counted the hairs on his head!

Up and down the beach, the stragglers were packing up baskets and chairs and sleepy kids and heading home.

Where was home? Gabe's gut twisted with longing for the home he'd known such a short but wonderful time.

How could he go back now, a failure, stripped of everything he'd once flaunted? Okay, not everything, but enough so that he wasn't king of the mountain anymore. He wouldn't even be a player when his father got through with him.

And yet, compared to Blair and Daniel, compared to Willie's soft, loving touch and Mac's sage advice and generous spirit, what did any of that matter? He ached to be there again, to dunk his head in that stupid pool and watch Blair's face light up with admiration. He wanted to hug Daniel tightly, to keep him close and safe, to protect him from the hurt that chewed at his own heart.

He loved them. The knowledge dawned without warning just as the moon slipped from behind a cloud and moved into the clear sky. Love? Was this love, this fierce need to be wanted, to be needed by the most special people in the world? Was it love that made his throat swell with pride when he remembered Blair carelessly signing those stupid papers just so she could prove she wanted more from him than money?

Was it love when it hurt so bad not to be able to hold her, to breathe her light, spicy perfume, to touch that curling mass of vibrantly alive curls?

Yes. Love.

The wonder of it made him weak. He wasn't a misfit, an oddball. He hadn't been tossed on the scrap heap when emotions were handed out. He felt love! He knew that fierce longing to protect the ones who mattered most, and it had a name. Love.

Compared to that, what did the loss of Polytech matter? He wasn't destitute. They could manage very well. Willie and Mac would be well cared for. Albert would have his supplies. Why was Gabe clinging so tightly to a company that he'd clearly outgrown? Why did he refuse to sell out?

"I want to be a father," he whispered, staring at the sky with its twinkling lights. "I want to be a husband. I want the chance to prove I'm worth her love. Can You show me how?"

As clearly as a bell, the solution pinged his brain. *Let go of the company. Get rid of the deadweight of the past. Move on.*

"Yes!" Gabe surged to his feet, snatched up his jacket, shoes and socks and raced across the sand, the wind tearing at his clothes, sucking the very breath from his lungs as he headed home.

He reached the boardwalk, chest searing but heart soaring. In a few quick moves his feet were clad. He hurried toward his expensive car, then stopped. His eyes saw clearly where Gabe had placed his priorities. This wasn't a car for the father of a six-year-old boy. It was fast, it was expensive, but Blair would hate it.

He climbed inside and mentally ticked off "sell car" as he drove toward the condo he'd never thought of as home. "Sell condo," he muttered to himself with a happy grin. He parked and took the elevator, his mind clicking through all the things he no longer wanted or needed.

Inside the apartment, Gabe looked around. "Sell ugly art sculptures," he told himself, wondering why he'd ever purchased the alabaster. He knew why. Someone had told him it would be valuable one day. "I hope that day is now," Gabe grinned as he inspected the rest of his habitat. "Once I get this junk out of the way, I can go back free and clear."

It was only as he returned to the living room that he caught sight of the flashing light on an answering machine he'd long since forgotten he owned. He punched the play button and waited as the machine rewound. A long silence stretched across the tape and he almost shut it off.

"Gabe, this is Blair." He sucked in his breath, dismay clawing at his brain as he waited for her to blast him.

"I need you. Please come home."

A glow flared inside. It flickered, wavered for an instant and then roared to life.

She *needed* him. *Him!* Nobody had ever needed Gabriel Sloan. He knew right enough that he needed her—he needed her more than life. But organized, self-contained, independent Blair needed him?

Gabe dialed the castle, frowning as the phone rang on and on. No one home. That settled it. He strode into the bedroom. He grabbed a small overnight bag from the closet and tossed in the few clothes he thought he'd need, along with a picture album he'd made all those years ago. Pictures of Blair, the Blair he thought he knew. It was the only thing he wanted from this place. They'd laugh over it years from now. He'd say, "Remember this?" and she'd blush and giggle in that infectious way that drew everyone in on the joke with her.

Gabe shut off the bedroom light, cast one look around the apartment and headed for the door. He didn't care why she needed him. The fact that she did was enough. He intended to be there for her. Always.

A hard, demanding knock on the door erupted a second before he yanked the door open. "Yes?"

Gabe blinked. His father stood in the hallway, his hand still raised.

"Hello, Gabriel."

To his amazement, Gabe felt no flare of anger, no rush of hate, no urge to rant or rave. All he felt was pity. This man knew nothing of what a family should be. For that, Gabe felt only sorrow.

"Hello, Father. I'm sorry, I don't have time to talk. I've got to get home. My wife needs me."

"But the company…the deal?" His father trailed him to the elevator in stunned amazement. "What about that?"

Gabe stepped into the elevator, then motioned his father inside. He punched the floor for the garage, then turned to face his father.

"If the company means so much to you, you can have it. Rich is handling everything from here on in. I built Polytech to prove something."

"To me. I know."

Daniel Sloan nodded. He had that smug, facetious grin that had often made Gabe's fists itch. Now he felt only sadness.

"No, for me. So that I would have something in my life. Something to give me purpose and direction." He stepped out of the elevator when the doors opened, then faced his father as the full import of his decision penetrated. "I don't need the company anymore. I have a gorgeous wife and a life that's more important than anything I ever had here. I'm going back to it, and I'm staying there. You're welcome to take whatever you want. I don't care anymore."

His father grabbed his arm as he unlocked the car. "How can you do this? How can you dump it now, when you've worked for so long? You can't be that much of a…"

"A what? A wimp? A sissy?" Gabe smiled, free at last of the old stigma. "Maybe I am." He tossed his case in the back, then turned to face his father. What he saw was a tired old man who had never figured out what really mattered.

"I have a son, did you know that? He's your grandson. His name is Daniel, too. He's six and he needs me to be with him, to teach him, to raise him with respect and love. You tell me, is Polytech more important than that?"

Daniel Sloan, Sr., stared. "I have a grandson?" he whispered, his face pasty white.

Gabe nodded. "And a daughter-in-law who would make your head spin. As well as some wonderful in-laws who care more about the person than his money or his things. You'd enjoy them. They really live life. They taught me what's important."

He climbed into the car and started the engine. But he couldn't drive away. Not yet. Forgiveness had been offered, regrets tossed away, hatred expunged. But one thing remained.

Love one another.

Gabe rolled down the window. "We live in Colorado, Dad. Not too far away. Ask Rich. He'll tell you how to get there. You're welcome anytime."

His father shook his head but said nothing. He stood,

a solitary figure, lost and alone as he puzzled it out. "Your company, this life you wanted so badly—you'll just let it go without a fight?" he whispered.

Gabe nodded. "In a minute," he agreed. "It's worth nothing compared to loving them. Goodbye, Dad."

Then he headed home.

Chapter Fifteen

Blair glanced at her watch wearily. Seven hours. Surely there must be some news by now. She squeezed her eyes closed and whispered one last prayer as small pudgy fingers curled into hers.

"Daddy will come," Daniel whispered. "He's on his way."

"How do you know that, sweetheart?" Blair couldn't stand to think of the disappointment she'd see contorting those trusting features if her son was wrong.

"I phoned him. He gave me his special number, and I phoned it. Collect. Albert helped me." Daniel glanced proudly at the man by his side before scrounging in his pocket for the business card. Gabe had scribbled his cell phone number on the back.

"Honey, I tried that number a whole bunch of times. Daddy wasn't there." She tried to soften the blow.

"He was when I phoned. And he said not to worry. He was coming home." Daniel's insistent voice rang loud in the chapel.

"Daddy *is* home."

The low, rumbling tones caught Blair by surprise.

She whirled to find herself wrapped in Gabe's strong arms, squeezed against his chest the way she'd only ever dreamed of.

"See! I told you he'd come." Daniel hopped from one foot to the other as he watched them. "I told you."

"You sure did, son. And I'm very proud of you." Gabe reached down and ruffled his son's hair. "Did you and Albert have breakfast yet?"

Daniel shook his head.

Gabe reached into his pocket, then held out a ten-dollar bill. "Well, why don't you treat Albert to a big, hearty breakfast. Then maybe we'll be able to go and see your grandfather. Okay?"

Daniel grinned the widest smile he'd ever managed. "Okay," he agreed. Then his brow furrowed. "Where are you going?"

"I'm going to stay right here and talk to your mom. I've missed her something fierce."

Daniel glanced from his mother to his father, then rolled his eyes. "Prob'ly kissing again," he muttered to Albert.

"Probably." Albert took his hand and led him to the door. Then he stopped, just for a moment, and winked at Blair. "If your mom doesn't mind, why should you?" They disappeared through the doors.

Blair turned to Gabe, anger and frustration vying with tiredness and sheer exhaustion as she glared at him.

"Where have you been, Gabriel? I've been trying to reach you for ages!"

He shrugged, his eyes bright as he slid his arms around her waist and refused to let her go. "I've been correcting a few mistakes," he murmured. "Some old, some new."

"But you took so long!"

He tipped his head and laughed, then glanced around the chapel and winced. "Sorry," he whispered. "But if you'd told me exactly *where* you needed me, it would have been easier."

"Where did you think I'd be?" She stared at him, wondering if he was all right. His eyes were too bright, and he was holding her so tenderly. Not that she minded!

"Denver." He grinned at her uplifted brow. "Daniel," he explained. "He said Willie had broken her *lip* and needed an operation and that the plane took her to Denver. I naturally figured you'd gone along. By the way, she's fine, the operation on her *hip* went well and she's resting very comfortably. I got her some flowers from all of us."

"You saw her?" Blair closed her eyes and breathed a sigh of relief. "Thank you."

"She told me to give you something." Gabe stood silent, his head tilted as he studied her.

"She did? What?" Blair couldn't imagine. Truth to tell, she didn't want to. She was too tired, too glad to see Gabe to even begin puzzling it all out.

"This." He bent and kissed her.

"Oh," she whispered when he finally drew away.

"And one other thing. Her love." He lifted her fingers, tipped her hand and kissed the palm. Then he squeezed her fingers closed around it. His eyes riveted her in their intensity. "Is it all right if I give you my love, too, Blair? Forever. Always."

Blair's mouth dropped open. She couldn't help it.

Shock held her immobilized. But not for long. "You *love* me?" she gasped.

He nodded. "I love you more than I ever knew anyone could love another person. I didn't know anything about love. I was certain I couldn't ever feel that. Today I did. I was standing on the beach and all I could think about was being at home with you. Having all of you near, supporting me, caring for me. And suddenly I understood what love is."

He gripped her shoulders, his stare intense. "I never felt it before, Blair. I should have, but I didn't. I pretended I did, but that's all it was. Pretense. But this time I'm not lying. I know what love is. Will you believe me? Will you trust me with your love?"

"I already did." The tears started then, big fat ones that rolled down her cheeks. "I've always loved you."

He cradled her head against his chest. "I know how hard it was for you, Blair. I know it took a lot of trust to tell me that you needed me. If I'd let you down, if I'd…"

She laid a finger across his lips, her smile tremulous. "God knew," she whispered. "Isn't that enough?"

Then with a boldness born of knowing she was the most precious thing in his world, she wrapped her arms around his neck and snuggled against him. "I'm everlastingly glad you're here," she told him tiredly. "Now we can face Mac's problem together."

He kissed her forehead, delighted to let her rest against him. "Mac's going to be fine," he murmured. "I stopped in there before I came here. He told me where you'd be. He said he knew I'd be back. That I couldn't resist a challenge." Gabe grinned, holding her so he could look into her eyes. "He was right. I couldn't resist the challenge of loving you. Thank God."

They stood for a long time, content to hold each other until someone came into the chapel. Then they wandered outside and sat on a cold, hard cement bench and watched the sun rise.

"What about the company, Gabe? What happened?"

"I left it all with Rich," he told her softly. "By the time my father's finished, I don't think there will be much left of Polytech. But that doesn't matter." He felt immense relief, and nothing more.

Blair poked him in the ribs. "Why doesn't it matter?" she demanded. "What's changed?"

"I have," he told her simply. "I don't care about Polytech. My life is with you and Daniel and the others. I have enough to start something else, if I want to. We'll manage."

"And your father?"

Gabe knew she was worried about that. A little wiggle of joy threaded its way from his heart to his mouth. "I let go of that, too," he told her. "If my father thinks Polytech will make him happy, he can have it. I've forgiven him for the past. I wish him the best. I even invited him out here, if he wanted to come." He frowned. "Was that okay?"

Blair squeezed his hand hard. "That was very okay," she said.

He brushed the gorgeous curls off her face and studied her. "I love you," he murmured, filled with the amazement of those words.

"I know." She grinned in sheer delight. "Isn't it wonderful? I can hardly wait until we're all at home again."

Gabe held her against his heart, his eyes on the peach-tinted horizon. Home. What a wonderful word.

Four months later, in a little restaurant in town, Blair twined her arms around Gabe's neck, her body moving slowly to the music as she danced with him. Gabe couldn't be happier. Polytech had been saved at the last minute and sold to another contender in a secret move arranged by Rich. Gabe was free to live in their castle, free of his obsession. He had everything right here.

Her closed eyes granted him the freedom to study her beautiful face, and he did. When her finger moved to trace his ear, he smiled just the tiniest bit.

"Gabe?"

"Hmm?"

"I need to talk to you about something."

He grinned. He knew what was coming. "Chemistry?" he guessed, kissing the curve of her jaw in a light caress. "Like what puts those little flashes of light into your hair or makes your eyes shine so?"

She blinked her eyes open, their chocolate depths studying him. "No," she said finally, easing away just a fraction. "Actually it's a different science. Biology."

Gabe squinted at her. "Biology?" Would he ever get the hang of this woman's mind? "Uh, okay. Go ahead."

"It's quite a normal event, actually. Happens to a lot of humans." She was teasing him, her face coy. "You'll see the final product in about seven and a half months."

Gabe jerked to a halt, his mind doing a double take as he digested her words. His eyes searched hers, saw her nod, watched her thousand-watt smile reach her eyes. "A baby?" he whispered. "You're going to have a baby?"

"Actually *we* are. Both of us. You'll be the daddy, I'll be the mommy, and Daniel will be the brother. Those are terms for the biological connection between family members." She chuckled at his glare.

"I know that," he told her grumpily. He pulled her close and kissed her so thoroughly they didn't hear when one song ended and another began. Finally he reached down, his left hand enfolding hers. "Come on."

"Where are we going?"

Gabe thought she looked a little confused but very, very happy. Good. That was the way he intended to keep her.

"We're going home. For once in my life I want to be able to surprise *your* family. I can hardly wait to see their faces when we tell them this," Gabe said as they drove home.

When he pulled into the yard, his spirits plummeted as he noticed a car in the driveway. "Company," he muttered. "Why tonight?"

"Come on, you can tell them all. If they don't already know." She grabbed his hand and urged him on.

"Why would they know?" he demanded, unlocking the front door.

"Because they always know," she whispered, standing on tiptoe to kiss him. "That's the way they are."

"Excuse me."

A cleared voice, a faintly familiar voice drew Gabe from his contemplation of Blair's luminous skin. He found his father watching him, an odd kind of smile twisting his lips.

"Gabriel. You said I was welcome anytime. I figured this was as good a time as any."

Gabe swallowed, felt the snug embrace of Blair in his arms and knew he could afford to be generous. He held out a hand.

"You are welcome. Blair and I were just about to share some news with the family. Can you stay for that?"

Daniel Sloan nodded, his eyes widening at the unexpected invitation.

"Dad, this is my wife, Blair. Blair, this is my father."

He watched as Blair engulfed the stiff, formal man in the traditional Rhodes family hug. Not long ago that had been him standing there, getting the same treatment from Willie. Gabe grinned at the memory.

"Welcome to our family. Let's go to the kitchen." She tossed her jacket on a nearby chair and led the way to the spacious, friendly kitchen. "Ah, you're all in here."

"It's too cold to sit outside," Mac joked, his eyes inquiring.

Gabe grinned, introduced his father and had the satisfaction of seeing Mac's head nod in approval. "Blair and I have something we want to share with you," he began, only to stutter to a stop when Willie yanked open the fridge door and pulled out a huge white cake with pink booties drawn on top. "How did you know?" he demanded.

Willie set the cake down, then wrapped her bony arms around him and hugged for all she was worth. "I always know," she whispered. "It's a gift. Just like this baby."

Gabe hugged her back, wallowing in the love. "That's true."

"She didn't know before I did. I told her a week ago that this family would be growing." Mac's smug smile swept around the room. "A patriarch knows things like that."

Gabe ignored the scoffing laughter as he watched Daniel's head peer around the door frame. "Hi, son. Did we wake you?" He scooped the boy into his arms and pressed a kiss against the tousled hair.

Daniel looped an arm around his dad's neck, his eyes riveted to the cake. "Are we having a party?" he demanded. He caught sight of Gabe's father and straightened. "Who is that?" he whispered.

Gabe held him tightly. "That's your grandfather," he whispered back. "He's my father, and he's come for the celebration."

"What celebration?" The big green eyes so like his own sparkled with excitement.

"Mommy's going to have a baby." Gabe waited for the questions.

"Oh, that." Daniel wiggled his way out of Gabe's arms and walked across the room to study the newest family member. "I knew that already. A sister, maybe. Willie told me." He studied his grandfather for a few minutes, then whirled around to grin at his dad.

"Yep, he's ours," the boy proclaimed. "He's got our eyes and hair." He stuck out his hand in manly fashion. "Welcome to our family. What do I call you?"

The older man glanced nervously around the room, then knelt in front of the boy. "My name is Daniel, too," he murmured, tears pooling at the corners of his red-rimmed eyes. "Could I be part of your family, Daniel? You could call me Grandpa Dan."

"Sure," Daniel agreed, shaking his hand. Then he reached out and hugged the old man with all his might. "We got lots of room in our family. It's gonna grow and grow. I prayed about it."

"His answered prayers started this whole thing." Blair's arm crept around Gabe's waist, her fingers warm on his cheek as she caressed his face. "We have a son to be proud of."

He hugged her close. He was truly blessed. He'd gone from no family to all family, from hate to love.

What more could he ask for?

"Thank you," Gabe murmured as Mac proposed an apple cider toast and Willie cut the cake. Albert pulled out a chair for the newest member of the family God had reunited. "Thank You very much, Lord."

* * * * *

Dear Reader,

I hope you enjoyed Daniel and his family. He's like
the child in all of us, constantly hoping. In this day
of the fractured society and problems everywhere,
a family is just about the last stronghold of love we
have. Sometimes even that's missing and we have to
make our own families by loving those God places in
our paths.

As you journey on through life, I wish you a wealth
of love from those nearest and dearest to you. May I
make a request? Will you show some gentle kindness
to someone you meet along the way? Just a smile,
a touch, a caring glance? Who knows, you may
unknowingly be entertaining angels.

God bless.

*Lois
Richer*

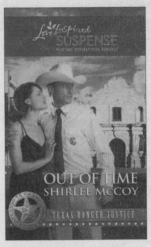

REQUEST YOUR FREE BOOKS!

2 FREE INSPIRATIONAL NOVELS
PLUS 2
FREE
MYSTERY GIFTS

Love Inspired.